LIKE NO ONE ELSE

Tommie continued up the stairs. Just as she reached the landing, the lights blinked again. Ignoring a frisson of unease, she slipped her key out of the pocket of her chiffon skirt and reached for the door. She inserted the key in the lock, then froze.

The door was already unlocked.

A shudder ran through her, a chilly finger from her nape to the base of her spine.

Had she forgotten to lock the door when she left that morning?

Or had an intruder been inside her loft?

Tommie's mouth went dry. She stepped away from the door, her heart thudding against her sternum.

Calm down. There's a perfectly rational explanation for this. You had a lot on your mind this morning. You could have easily forgotten to lock the door on your way out. Or maybe Mrs. Calhoun forgot to do it when she took the peach cobbler up to the loft for you this afternoon. She's sixty-five years old. Maybe her memory is failing her.

Yes, that was it, Tommie decided. Mrs. Calhoun, bless her dear heart, had forgotten to lock the door earlier. No harm, no foul.

But as Tommie stared at the closed door, she felt a whisper of foreboding. As if an evil presence awaited her on the other side.

Like No One Else

MAUREEN SMITH

Dafina
BOOKS

Kensington Publishing Corp.

http://www.kensingtonbooks.com

DAFINA BOOKS are published by

Kensington Publishing Corp.
119 West 40th Street
New York, NY 10018

All Kensington Titles, Imprints, and Distributed Lines are available at special quantity discounts for bulk purchases for sales promotions, premiums, fund-raising, and educational or institutional use. Special book excerpts or customized printings can also be created to fit specific needs. For details, write or phone the office of the Kensington special sales manager: Kensington Publishing Corp., 119 West 40th Street, New York, NY 10018, attn: Special Sales Department, Phone: 1-800-221-2647.

Dafina and the Dafina logo Reg. U.S. Pat. & TM Off.

ISBN-13: 978-0-7582-2741-6
ISBN-10: 0-7582-2741-8

First mass market printing: December 2009

10 9 8 7 6 5 4 3 2 1

Printed in the United States of America

*To every reader who believed Tommie and Paulo
deserved a chance at redemption.*

Acknowledgments

My thanks and heartfelt gratitude to Michael Lopez, Amanda Orozco, and Greta Huddleston, who graciously provided the Spanish translations for this book—no matter how weird the request. *Muchas gracias*!

To my sister and eternal sounding board, Sylvia Hightower, for answering my questions about Houston and lending your medical expertise regarding complications from gunshot wounds. It really pays to have so many registered nurses in the family!

Chapter 1

Fifteen young girls clad in pink leotards and matching tights formed a line at the wooden barre backed by a long wall of mirrors. The dancers' faces were a study of concentration as their ballet instructor walked the length of the studio floor, inspecting postures and manually correcting positions. Her rare nods of approval elicited smiles from the lucky recipients—smiles that evaporated the moment another rapid-fire command was issued.

"Adagio, ladies! Release on one, *demi-plié* on two, pas de bourrée on three, close on four!"

Dressed in a black leotard, a sheer black skirt, and black leggings, with her long dark hair pulled back into a severe ponytail, Tommie Purnell watched as her students executed the steps with fluid, graceful movements.

"Good," she called above the music flowing from a baby grand piano tucked into a corner of the room. The pianist, a stout, elderly black woman with skin the color of almonds and a tight cap of gray curls covering her head, had been hired shortly after Tommie opened her dance studio six months ago.

"And now for the *petit allégro* combination," Tommie announced, facing the class as she prepared to demonstrate. "Stand in first position, *demi-plié*, straighten the knees—" She broke off suddenly, her gaze snared by a darkly handsome Hispanic man who had appeared in the open doorway of the studio. A battered leather jacket clung to his broad shoulders, and black jeans hung low on lean, narrow hips. Dark, penetrating eyes met and held Tommie's in the mirror.

Her pulse thudded.

Abruptly the music stopped, and in the ensuing silence, one last dissonant chord rang out.

Tommie spun around in her pointe shoes to face the newcomer. "What are you doing here?" she demanded.

Paulo Sanchez inclined his dark head. "Hello to you, too, Miss Purnell." Even from across the room, his deep voice made Tommie's stomach clench, a familiar reaction she didn't care to explore.

Seized by a sudden, terrible fear, she stared at him. "Is it my sister? Or Marcos? Did something hap—"

"Francesca and your nephew are fine," Paulo assured her. "And so are your parents and Sebastien."

Tommie inwardly breathed a sigh of relief. She didn't think she could handle another crisis, not after everything she and her family had already been through. Besides, she'd had no reason to panic. If there *had* been a family emergency, someone would have called her immediately, black sheep or not.

Belatedly she remembered her students poised at the barre. They were staring at Paulo, undoubtedly struck by the incongruity of the good-looking, dangerous-edged man who seemed as out of place in that bastion of femininity as a Spanish conquistador at a tea party.

Tommie glanced at her watch and saw that the hour was up. After she issued a stern reminder to her class to practice what they had learned that afternoon, the students, in keeping with ballet tradition, clapped for Tommie and the pianist before they were formally dismissed. Chattering among themselves, the girls stuffed their pointe shoes inside duffel bags, gathered their belongings, and filed out of the room to meet their mothers, who were patiently waiting in a small observation area separated from the main studio by a glass partition. Normally the parents lingered after class to talk to Tommie. Today they departed with raised eyebrows and demure smiles directed at Paulo.

Scowling, Tommie stalked across the room toward him, her ponytail swinging from side to side. "I hope you have a damned good reason for interrupting my class," she groused.

A faintly mocking smile curved firm, sensual lips. "And if I don't?" Paulo challenged.

Tommie's temper flared, even as she silently cursed herself for allowing him to get under her skin. Not that this was anything new. Paulo Sanchez had been getting under her skin ever since she met him four years ago at her sister's wedding rehearsal dinner. From the moment Tommie and Paulo locked gazes, the chemistry between them had been powerful, sizzling with electricity. But Tommie, who had just gotten out of a bad relationship, knew the last thing she needed was a rebound romance. Still, it had taken every ounce of willpower she possessed to resist Paulo, to ignore the way her pulse raced as he'd escorted her down the aisle at the wedding ceremony, to ignore her throbbing breasts and her aching loins as they'd slow-danced together at the reception. By accident or design, Tommie had caught the bride's bouquet while Paulo came away with the garter belt. To this day, she still remembered the wicked gleam in his eyes as his big, cal- lused hands had slowly traveled up her thigh to secure the garter, leaving a trail of scorched nerve endings.

That, finally, had been her undoing.

Right then and there she'd decided to throw caution to the wind and indulge in a one-night stand with Paulo. No strings attached. No empty promises. Just one night of hot, mind-blowing sex between two mature, consenting adults who would go their separate ways in the morning.

After joining the rest of the guests in sending off the happy bride and groom, Tommie had gone in search of Paulo, confident that he would jump at the chance to sleep with her. He'd been seducing her from the moment they met, wearing down her defenses until she'd had no choice but to succumb to him.

But when Tommie discovered Paulo and a leggy bru- nette making out in the bridal suite, she'd been stunned. And crushed. It was abundantly clear that Paulo, having already grown bored with Tommie, had moved on to the next diversion.

Hearing Tommie's shocked gasp, the couple had sprung apart on the chaise longue. To her credit, the brunette had looked suitably embarrassed as she tugged at her tight little dress. Paulo, on the other hand, had met Tommie's outraged glare with a lazy, insolent grin. As if debauching women at weddings was nothing new to him.

Without mincing words, Tommie had ordered the couple out of her sister's bridal suite. The next time she saw them, Paulo was helping the woman into his car. He'd glanced up, and seeing Tommie framed in the doorway of the beautiful waterfront mansion where the wedding had been held, he'd winked and blown her a kiss. She'd felt as humiliated as if he'd jilted her at the altar.

"Why, Tomasina, aren't you going to introduce me to your handsome visitor?"

Pulled out of her reverie, Tommie glanced over to find her pianist, Hazel Calhoun, standing there with an inquisitive smile on her bespectacled face as she eyed Paulo with unabashed curiosity.

Grudgingly Tommie performed the introductions.

"Nice to meet you, Mrs. Calhoun," Paulo said, shaking the woman's hand. "You play beautifully."

Hazel beamed with pleasure. "Why, thank you very much, Mr. Sanchez. I'm so glad you enjoyed the music."

"I did. And please call me Paulo."

Tommie watched in disbelief as her pianist—a sixty-five-year-old grandmother, community activist, and church deaconess—giggled and blushed to the gray roots of her scalp.

"Where have you been hiding this delightful young man?" she said chidingly to Tommie.

"Not far enough, apparently," Tommie grumbled.

"Tomasina!"

Paulo's dark eyes glimmered with amusement. "It's all right, Mrs. Calhoun. Tommie and I haven't seen each other since her sister's wedding in San Antonio four years ago. We've got a lot of, ah, catching up to do."

Hazel smiled warmly at him. "Are you from San Antonio, too?"

"Yes, ma'am. Born and raised."

"Like Tomasina." Hazel seemed inordinately pleased that her employer and Paulo shared a common background. "And now here you both are, in Houston. You must have followed each other," she teased.

Paulo chuckled. "I've been here for two years, so I'll let you decide who followed whom."

Tommie bristled. "I didn't follow you!"

Paulo quirked a brow at her. "No?"

"Of course not! I didn't even know you'd moved here until after I arrived."

"Whatever you say," Paulo drawled.

Tommie scowled. "I didn't—"

"It was awfully nice of you to stop by for a visit this afternoon, Paulo," Hazel smoothly intervened. "I wish I could stay and chat with you longer, but I have to run to a meeting at church." She paused, her dark eyes lighting up as a sudden idea struck her. "Why don't you stay and have dinner with Tomasina? I baked a fresh pan of lasagna for her last night, and there's enough to feed an army."

Stifling a groan at the woman's obvious attempt at matchmaking, Tommie quickly interjected, "That's very generous of you, Mrs. Calhoun. But I'm sure Paulo didn't intend to hang around that long. He's a homicide detective. He's probably needed somewhere this very minute."

"Actually," Paulo countered with a hint of that devilish grin, "I'm off duty. And it just so happens that I skipped lunch this afternoon. A home-cooked meal sounds great."

"Wonderful!" Hazel exclaimed, as if he'd just promised to feed all the starving children in Africa.

When Tommie glowered at Paulo, he chuckled, a low, husky rumble that made her belly quiver.

After Hazel left, Tommie locked up the studio for the evening. As she led Paulo up a flight of stairs to her second-story loft, she could feel the searing intensity of his gaze on her backside.

She unlocked her front door with unsteady fingers

and quickly crossed the threshold, gesturing him inside. *"Bienvenido a mi casa."*

"I didn't know you spoke Spanish," Paulo drawled as he brushed past her.

"There's a lot you don't know about me," Tommie retorted.

He turned to face her, one heavy black brow raised. "Is that a challenge?" he asked softly.

Tommie met his gaze unflinchingly. "Just a statement of fact."

They stared at each other for a long, charged moment.

Paulo seemed to have gotten closer or loomed larger. She could feel the heat from his body, could smell the old leather of his jacket. At least three days' worth of stubble darkened his square jaw, and his thick black hair was longer than she remembered, brushing his collar. His eyes were deep-set and piercing, a shade of brown so intense that at times they appeared to be black. They were accentuated by chiseled cheekbones, a firm, sensual mouth, and a swarthy complexion that attested to his Mexican heritage. He was five foot eleven inches of solid power and muscle. Not as tall as Tommie normally preferred, but tall enough that she'd been able to wear stiletto heels at her sister's wedding without having to worry about towering over him. After the ceremony, in fact, several guests had remarked on what a striking couple she and Paulo made, how perfect they'd looked together—comments Tommie had laughingly dismissed, though deep down inside she'd agreed.

That afternoon, wearing a black leather jacket, black jeans, and scuffed black boots, Paulo looked every bit the tough guy he was. A potent combination of strength, danger, and raw animal magnetism. Tommie told herself to back away from him, but for the first time in her life, her legs wouldn't obey her command.

As she stood there, air trapped in her lungs, Paulo's gaze slid from her face down to the scooped neckline of her leotard, lingering on the swell of her breasts. Her breath quickened, and to her everlasting shame, her nipples hardened under his hot, bold appraisal. His gaze darkened and his nostrils flared slightly, letting her know he'd discerned her body's reaction to him. Tommie had never felt more exposed in her life, and *that* was saying a lot, considering she'd once moonlighted as a stripper.

Slowly, deliberately, Paulo lifted his eyes to her flushed face. She stared at him, acutely conscious of her sensitized nipples rubbing against the fabric of her sports bra, the melting warmth spreading from her stomach to her loins. She couldn't remember the last time, if ever, she'd been so thoroughly aroused by a man merely looking at her. If Paulo chose that moment to kiss her, she honestly didn't know whether she would have the strength to resist him.

And judging by the mischievous gleam in his eyes, he knew it, too.

With one hand he reached up and cradled her face, the pad of his thumb brushing her full lower lip. A shiver rippled down her body. Her heart thundered.

His gaze roamed appreciatively across her face. "You are an incredibly beautiful woman, Señorita Purnell," he murmured huskily.

Tommie said nothing. She didn't trust her voice.

Paulo held her gaze a moment longer, then dropped his hand with obvious reluctance and stepped back. Air rushed into Tommie's lungs as he turned and sauntered away, glancing casually around the loft.

"Nice," he remarked.

Tommie knew *that* was an understatement if she'd ever heard one. She'd purchased the converted warehouse shortly after moving to Houston and had blown all her savings on decorating the spacious second-story loft, with stunning results. The space boasted original hardwood flooring, twenty-foot ceilings, exposed redbrick walls, and a spiral staircase that led to a private rooftop terrace. A collection of stylish, risqué modern art she'd brought from New York complemented furnishings done in bold, dramatic shades of red and black. The open, airy layout featured giant support columns that carved out four large spaces—kitchen, living room, study, and bedroom. A huge expanse of windows stretched the entire length of one wall, keeping the loft perpetually bathed in warm, bright sunlight. Since fall had arrived nearly two months ago, Tommie hadn't needed to turn on the heat once.

She loved her beautiful, trendy loft situated in the shadow of downtown Houston. When she left behind the bright lights of New York City seven months ago, all she'd wanted was a decent one-bedroom apartment and space to hold dance classes a few days a week. She'd found both in a small, converted warehouse owned by a wealthy real estate investor eager to get the property off his hands before he relocated to another area. By the time Tommie had completed her tour of the dusty old building, she knew it was perfect for her. But the sales price had been way out of her price range. As luck would have it, the seller was a huge fan of ballet, and he'd recognized Tommie from a performance he'd attended in New York the previous year. When she told him about her plan to open a dance studio, he'd generously reduced his asking price, enabling Tommie to qualify for a small business loan. She'd used a large portion of the funds to renovate the building, refurbishing the original hardwood floors and installing a barre, floor-to-ceiling mirrors, and a sound system in the studio. Fortunately, the upstairs loft had only needed minor cosmetic work.

Within a month of purchasing the old warehouse, Tommie was comfortably ensconced in her new home and open for business. A glowing feature article in the *Houston Chronicle* had drummed up more clients for her than any amount of advertising she could have done on her own.

She now taught a diverse array of dance techniques including West African, samba, ballet, jazz, tap, modern, and hip-hop. Her clientele included aspiring ballerinas, high school cheerleaders and dance troupes, popular musicians in need of choreography for a new video, as well as local corporations seeking a recreational off-site activity for employees. Tommie knew she'd eventually have to hire additional instructors just to keep up with the increasing demand for her classes. But that was a good problem to have.

Her attraction to Paulo Sanchez, on the other hand, was not.

From the kitchen, Tommie watched as he slowly wandered around the loft before ending up at the wall of windows that offered a scenic view of downtown Houston. Her gaze was drawn to the way his black jeans clung to his powerful thighs and hugged his firm, muscled butt. When her mouth began watering, she knew it had nothing to do with the fragrant aroma of lasagna wafting from the microwave.

Paulo whistled softly through his teeth. "Great view."

You can say that again!

Aloud Tommie said, "I'm certainly enjoying it." As Paulo turned, she quickly schooled her features into a blank mask. "Would you like something to drink?"

"Sure. What're you offering?"

Tommie pulled open the stainless-steel Sub-Zero refrigerator and peered inside. "I have bottled water, mineral water, skim milk, orange juice, pineapple juice, and an unopened bottle of merlot. Sorry—no beer."

Paulo chuckled, starting across the room toward her. "The pineapple stuff sounds good."

Tommie vaguely remembered him having only one or two drinks at the wedding reception, while most of the other single guys had downed beers as if alcohol were going out of style. Throughout the evening several of those men had hit on her, obviously operating under the misguided assumption that her status as a bridesmaid meant she was desperate enough to go home with any half-drunk loser who propositioned her. It was sadly ironic that the only man she'd wanted to sleep with that night had left with someone else.

Shoving aside the memory, Tommie arched a brow at Paulo as she filled two glasses with pineapple juice. "Not much of a drinker, are you?"

"Not anymore."

Something about his cryptic response piqued Tommie's curiosity, but she didn't want to pry by asking him to elaborate. Besides, the less she knew about Paulo Sanchez, the easier it would be to keep him at arm's length.

Or so she told herself.

The microwave beeped, signaling that the lasagna had finished heating. As Tommie fixed their plates, Paulo made his way over to the long breakfast counter that separated the kitchen from the living room. He removed his leather jacket and draped it over the back of a bar stool. He wore a black T-shirt that stretched across his broad shoulders and showcased his muscular forearms. The butt of a gun was visible from his shoulder holster.

"Do you make a habit of skipping lunch, Detective?" Tommie inquired as she set their steaming plates on the countertop, then rounded the corner to claim one of the high-backed bar stools.

"If I'm swamped with cases," Paulo answered as he sat down beside her, "food isn't always a top priority."

"I can understand that," Tommie conceded. "On my busiest days, I don't even think about eating until my last class is over, which isn't until eight on Tuesday and Thursday evenings."

Paulo slanted her a wry smile. "Is that why Mrs. Calhoun prepares meals for you? To make sure you don't starve yourself to death?"

Tommie nodded, chuckling ruefully. "She loves to fuss and fret over me. She can't help herself. She raised four children and has nine grandchildren. Nurturing is second nature to her. But I'm not complaining. I've hardly had to cook since I hired her, and quite frankly, she's much better at it than I've ever been." She watched as Paulo sampled a forkful of lasagna. "How is it?"

"Incredible," he said, sounding mildly surprised. "Probably the best lasagna I've ever had."

"Oh God," Tommie groaned. "Please don't tell Mrs. Calhoun that. You already had her eating out of the palm of your hand after you complimented her piano playing. If you tell her she makes the best lasagna you've ever had, she'll think you walk on water."

Paulo's straight white teeth flashed in a grin. "Now, now. Don't be jealous."

Tommie rolled her eyes. "In your dreams, Sanchez."

He chuckled, taking another bite of lasagna. "So, how are you enjoying Houston so far?"

"I love it," Tommie said sincerely. "I've got this fabulous loft, my own dance studio. I'm close to the downtown theater district, and I've made a lot of friends at the Houston Met."

"The dance company?"

Tommie nodded. "I've already been to several performances there. I never realized Houston had such a thriving arts scene. I feel right at home."

Paulo cocked a brow at her. "You're telling me you don't miss the hustle and bustle of New York, the city that never sleeps?"

"A little," Tommie admitted quietly. "There's no place on earth like New York City. But Texas is, and always will be, my home."

"Is that why you left the Big Apple?" Paulo murmured, studying her with those dark, probing eyes that saw way too much. "Because you were homesick?"

Tommie lifted one shoulder and averted her gaze, becoming absorbed in her meal, even as she felt her appetite waning. She didn't want to think about, let alone discuss, the devastating scandal that had derailed her professional dancing career seven months ago. She'd never told anyone what had happened in New York. As close as she and her older sister had become in recent years, not even Frankie knew Tommie's shameful secret. She certainly wasn't about to bare her soul to Paulo Sanchez, a man who was, for all intents and purposes, a stranger to her.

Deciding to turn the tables on him, Tommie ventured casually, "What about you? What made you decide to leave San Antonio?"

Paulo shrugged, returning his attention to his food. "I wanted a change of scenery."

Tommie's eyes narrowed on his face. Just as before, she sensed that there was a story behind his vague response, and once again, her curiosity was aroused. But the sudden tension in Paulo's broad shoulders and the hardening of his jaw warned her to back off.

So I'm not the only one with secrets.

Oddly comforted by the thought, Tommie said conversationally, "I guess moving to Houston wasn't such a stretch for you. Frankie told me you have family here."

Paulo nodded. "I used to visit them every summer when I was growing up. My cousin Rafe and I were thick as thieves."

Tommie smiled whimsically. "Interesting analogy, considering you both grew up to become law enforcement officers. Guess you both decided it was nobler to play cops than robbers."

Paulo smiled a little. "Never looked at it that way. Rafe always wanted to be an FBI agent. Me? I had a hard enough time just staying out of trouble."

Tommie widened her eyes in exaggerated disbelief. "*You?* Getting into trouble? No way!"

Paulo chuckled. "Good thing I'm a changed man."

Tommie snorted rudely. "Yeah, right."

"What's that supposed to mean?"

She gave him a knowing look. "Need I remind you of the compromising position I caught you in at my sister's *wedding,* of all places?"

"Oh. That." His mouth curved in a wolfish grin. "What can I say? Some people cry at weddings. I prefer to get laid."

Tommie sputtered indignantly, "Sebastien is one of your best friends! You were a groomsman! Couldn't you at least have waited until *after* the reception before you tended to your libido?"

Paulo's grin widened. "Obviously not."

Tommie shook her head in disgust. "Pig."

He threw back his head and laughed, a deep, rumbling sound that did dangerous things to her heart rate. She shifted uncomfortably in her chair, wishing for the umpteenth time that he didn't have such a powerful effect on her. He was sexy as hell with his leather jacket, butt-hugging jeans, cocky swagger, and wickedly irreverent attitude. A man like Paulo Sanchez could only bring Tommie heartache, and that was the last thing she needed or wanted in her life.

Paulo draped his arm over the back of her stool and leaned close, his brown eyes glinting with mischief. "Come now, Tomasina," he murmured, his voice a low, silky caress. "Are you objecting to what you caught me doing at your sister's wedding, or the fact that I wasn't doing it with *you*?"

Tommie stared at him, heat suffusing her cheeks. He knew. The arrogant bastard *knew* that she'd wanted him that day. He knew how humiliated she'd felt when she stumbled upon him with another woman.

Angrily she jerked her gaze away and snapped, "Don't call me Tomasina."

Paulo chuckled, a satisfied gleam in his eyes as he drew back from her. "My apologies," he drawled. "You didn't seem to have a problem with Mrs. Calhoun calling you Tomasina."

She frowned. "That's different."

"How so?"

"Mrs. Calhoun is old school. She doesn't like nicknames, especially masculine-sounding nicknames for females. And she reminds me a lot of my favorite grandmother, who passed away when I was seventeen." Tommie shrugged, idly picking at her lasagna. "As far as I'm concerned, Mrs. Calhoun can call me whatever she wants. You, on the other hand, enjoy no such privilege."

Paulo feigned a wounded look. "That really hurts my feelings."

Tommie couldn't help laughing. "You are so full of it! Which reminds me, you never did answer my question. What are you doing here?"

He shrugged. "I came to see how you were doing. I wanted to see if you were settling in okay."

"Just out of the clear blue?" Tommie's voice was heavy with skepticism. "I've been in Houston for seven months, Paulo. Why did you suddenly decide—" She broke off, her eyes narrowing suspiciously on his face. "Wait a minute. Did my sister ask you to check up on me?"

"No."

"Liar!"

"What?"

"I know the only reason you're here is that Frankie asked—no, begged—you to stop by."

Paulo scowled. "First of all, no one *begged* me to do anything. And even if Frankie did ask me to check up on you, what would be so terrible about that? She's your big sister, she's supposed to worry about you."

Tommie pounced. "I knew it! You *did* talk to her!" Incensed, she shot out of her chair, snatched her plate of half-eaten lasagna off the counter, and stalked over to the kitchen sink.

Behind her, Paulo said evenly, "I don't understand why you're so upset about—"

Tommie whirled around. "Ever since I left New York, Frankie and my parents have been nagging me about moving back home. Every time I talk to one of them on the phone, it's the same thing. 'Why do you want to live in Houston, Tommie?' 'Wouldn't you rather be close to all your family and friends, Tommie?'" She shook her head in angry exasperation. "I know they mean well, but I don't appreciate being treated like some teenage runaway who can't handle the responsibility of being on my own. I'm thirty-three years old, damn it. I think I've already proved that I'm perfectly capable of taking care of myself."

When she'd ended her tirade, Paulo said nothing, staring at her with an unreadable expression. The longer he remained silent, the more Tommie wanted to kick herself for letting her emotions get the better of her. If she *had* been romantically interested in Paulo, bitching about her problems—when they hardly even knew each other—would have been a surefire way to send him running for the hills. Experience had taught her that nothing drove a man away faster than a woman with too much baggage.

Turning away, she busied herself with scraping the remnants of her lasagna off her plate and down the drain. With the faucet running and the garbage disposal grinding noisily, she didn't hear Paulo approaching until he appeared beside her at the counter, placing his empty plate into the sink. Tommie tensed as he reached over, taking her chin between his thumb and forefinger and gently turning her head, forcing her to meet his dark, intent gaze.

"You may be thirty-three years old, *querida*," he murmured, "but you still have a lot of growing up to do." Before Tommie could open her mouth to protest, he laid a finger against her lips and shook his head slowly. "Just hear me out."

Tommie glared mutinously at him.

"I come from a big family," Paulo continued. "I have four siblings and more aunts, uncles, cousins, nieces, and nephews than I can count. One thing I've learned over the years is that no matter what may have happened in the past or what you may accomplish in life, there's nothing more important than family. Nothing. The next time your sister or your parents ask you about moving back home, don't automatically assume they're trying to keep a leash on you. Consider the possibility that *they* need you as much as you need them." He paused, a hint of irony touching his mouth. "And if you think you don't need them, think again."

Tommie gazed at him, his words striking a chord deep within her. Her relationship with her family had been complicated for as long as she could remember, and as much as she liked to believe she'd worked through all her issues during the four years she'd been away from home, she knew she still had a ways to go. Her outburst of a few minutes ago was proof of that.

Suddenly aware of Paulo's finger still resting against her lips, Tommie jerked her head back. "Thanks for the psychoanalysis, Dr. Sanchez," she quipped with an aloofness she didn't feel. "Be sure to send me your bill."

Paulo gave her a small, knowing smile that told her he saw right through her act. As she watched, he reached out and lightly trailed a fingertip down her cheek. Her flesh tingled. Her pulse quickened.

Striving to ignore her body's reaction to his touch, she glared at him. "You really have a problem keeping your hands to yourself, don't you, Detective?" she demanded. But her voice was too breathless, too husky with awareness to convincingly deliver the reprimand.

Paulo's gaze darkened. He shifted closer, subtly trapping her between the counter and his body.

Her heart thudded. She found herself staring at the sensual curve of his lips and wondering, not for the first time, how they would feel against hers, how they would taste.

As Paulo slowly lowered his dark head toward hers, her lips parted.

A cell phone jangled loudly, startling them both.

Frowning at the interruption, Paulo dug the phone out of his back pocket and flipped it open. "Sanchez."

Turning away, Tommie inhaled a shaky breath, thinking of how dangerously close she had come to letting Paulo kiss her.

Letting? her conscience mocked. *You were practically begging him to kiss you!*

Out of the corner of her eye, she saw Paulo's expression turn grim as he listened into the phone. "I'll be right there," he muttered before snapping it shut and shoving it back into his pocket.

Tommie arched a brow. "Duty calls?"

"Yeah." There was a trace of regret in his voice. He held her gaze for a long moment, then turned away.

She watched as he strode around the breakfast counter to retrieve his leather jacket from the back of the bar stool he'd been sitting on. "Well, thanks for stopping by," she said briskly. "As you can see I'm just fine, so you don't have to check up on me anymore."

Paulo sent her a wry look as he shrugged into his jacket. "Is that your not-so-subtle way of telling me never to darken your doorstep again?"

Tommie couldn't help grinning. "You said it, not me." Grabbing her keys off the countertop, she said, "I'll walk you downstairs. I have to lock up the building anyway."

As she followed him down the old stairwell, their footsteps echoed hollowly in the enclosed space, bouncing off the bare brick walls and bounding up to the skylight roof. During the daytime the stairway was flooded with natural light and warmth. At night it seemed cold and cavernous, dimly illuminated with recessed lighting that needed replacing. Getting her dance studio finished had ranked higher on Tommie's list of priorities than having a well-lit stairwell.

As if he'd intercepted her thoughts, Paulo, frowning at the ceiling, advised, "You should probably get those bulbs replaced soon."

"I know. It's a wiring issue, so I have to call an electrician. It's on my to-do list, along with installing a locker room for my students and getting the intercom system fixed."

Paulo nodded. "I'm surprised this entire building wasn't converted into lofts. Those are really popular in this area."

"That's what the previous owner intended to do when he first bought the warehouse. He wanted to divide it into four cozy lofts. He only got as far as completing the first unit before he ran into some zoning issues and abandoned the project altogether. Once the housing market crashed, the building's odd location—not quite in the theater or warehouse district—made it difficult for him to resell without taking a huge profit loss." Which he eventually did anyway when he sold the property to Tommie way below market value.

"I guess you came along at the right time," Paulo observed.

"Most definitely," Tommie agreed. "This building was a steal. I was able to kill two birds with one stone—I found a place to live *and* a place for my business."

"What's the square footage?"

"Five thousand. A bit small by warehouse standards, but more than enough to suit my needs. I would have killed for this kind of space back in New York."

They had reached the landing. To their right, the studio sat dark and empty.

As Tommie followed Paulo to the main door, she said, "Seriously, though. The next time my sister asks you to check up on me, feel free to let her know you're a busy detective with better things to do with your time than babysitting grown women."

Paulo stopped at the door and turned back to her. "The only problem with that," he murmured, his eyes roaming across her face, "is that your sister never asked me to check up on you." He paused for a moment, letting that sink in before adding, "Thanks for dinner. I'll be seeing you around."

Tommie locked the door behind him and leaned against it, her pulse drumming as his parting words echoed through her mind. *I'll be seeing you around.*

Good Lord. The man could make even the most innocuous statement sound like a seductive promise. What had he meant by that? Surely he didn't intend to show up there again, after she'd specifically told him not to?

And what about the other thing he'd said? Did he really expect Tommie to believe that her sister hadn't put him up to visiting her?

She frowned.

Only one way to find out.

Chapter 2

As Paulo emerged from Tommie Purnell's building that evening and climbed into an unmarked police cruiser, his mind wasn't on the crime scene he'd been summoned to a few minutes ago. Instead his thoughts were dominated by the woman he'd just left behind.

Tommie Purnell was as stunningly beautiful as he remembered, with flawless brown skin, long dark hair streaked with honey, sultry dark eyes, high cheekbones, and full, lush lips. She also happened to be sexier than any woman had a right to be—five foot eight inches of voluptuous curves poured into the body of a centerfold. A walking wet dream.

From the moment Paulo met her four years ago, he'd been ensnared by the sensuality she exuded like powerful pheromones. Everything about her, from her smoky voice to the way she moved, was primitively erotic. Dangerous.

Every unmarried man at the wedding, and even some of the hitched ones, had wanted to fuck her. None more so than Paulo. He'd had the privilege of escorting Tommie down the aisle and holding her in his arms as they'd danced together at the reception. And he'd been the envy of every bachelor gathered in the crowd when he'd caught the garter belt, giving him the perfect excuse to run his hands up Tommie's shapely thigh, to feel the hot silk of her skin. When he looked into her glittering eyes, he'd known that beneath her haughty facade, she had wanted him as much as he'd wanted her. But no matter how sexy she was, and no matter how powerful the attraction between them, Paulo's gut instincts had warned him that Tommie Purnell was trouble with a capital *T*. And considering his track record with women, which included a brief, disastrous marriage that had ended in divorce and an affair that had resulted in unspeakable tragedy, the *last* thing Paulo needed in his life was to become involved with a temptress like Tommie.

Since her arrival in town seven months ago, he'd purposely kept his distance. He knew that seeing her again would only remind him of how much he wanted her, and how completely wrong she was for him. Besides, he hadn't come to Houston looking for romance. He'd come here in search of a fresh start, to get his life back on track.

If only he could have stuck to his guns and stayed the hell away from Tommie.

The sight of her in a tight black leotard that outlined her firm, voluptuous breasts, and black leggings that molded those impossibly long legs of hers, had sent his blood pressure skyrocketing through the roof. When their gazes locked in the mirror, Paulo knew that nothing had changed. The chemistry between them was as potent as ever. If his cell phone hadn't rung when it did, there's no telling whether he would have stopped at just kissing her.

Paulo scowled, forcefully shoving all thoughts of Tommie to the back of his mind as he reached his destination, a meticulously landscaped neighborhood located minutes away from Houston's Galleria. Even before Paulo turned onto Woodland Drive, a quaint, tree-lined street flanked by large one- and two-story brick houses, he saw the flashing lights of emergency vehicles. A car from the sheriff's department was already parked at the end of the street, discouraging unauthorized persons from turning into the block. Three vans from local television stations and several other vehicles were staked out along the intersecting road. The reporters and cameramen taped live footage of the scene while the onlookers stood outside their cars gawking at the unfolding drama.

Paulo maneuvered around the police cruiser barricading the lane and nosed into a narrow spot beside the ambulance. He unwrapped a piece of Nicorette gum and stuffed it into his mouth, then reached for the door handle. He climbed out of the car and stepped into the clear, crisp night, grateful for the cold snap that had settled over the city, however temporarily.

As he started toward the single-story redbrick house that was swarming with activity, he saw neighbors hovering in doorways and clustered on front lawns and sidewalks. He felt the weight of their stares as he strode up the front walkway, lined on both sides with carefully tended beds of azaleas and begonias. A white BMW was parked in the driveway, and the house had been roped off with yellow crime-scene tape.

The uniformed officer standing guard at the front door nodded a greeting to Paulo and lifted the tape high enough for him to duck under.

"You the first on the scene?" Paulo asked as he signed the obligatory security logbook.

The officer nodded. "Call came into dispatch about an hour ago. I was the closest, lucky me." He grimaced, shaking his blond head. "It ain't pretty in there."

"It rarely is." Paulo stepped into the spacious foyer and

glanced around the tastefully furnished living room. A cream sofa and love seat, along with a brown leather chaise longue, were arranged around a limestone fireplace that soared to the second-story ceiling. Vibrant watercolors depicting scenes of a bustling Mexican village hung on the walls.

The place was already crawling with crime-scene investigators, detectives from the sheriff's department, and staff members from the coroner's office. Measurements were being taken, the rooms dusted for fingerprints or shoe prints, a vacuum used to suck up any unseen trace evidence. A videographer panned the rooms of the house, throughout which bright lights had been set up.

Another uniformed officer greeted Paulo by name, then ushered him down a long, wide corridor. The air was redolent with the stench of blood and violent death.

At the end of the hallway they reached the master bedroom. A young woman's nude body lay spread-eagled on the floor in a pool of blood. She'd been stabbed multiple times across her throat and chest. Blood from the deep, savage lacerations had leaked onto the oatmeal-colored Berber carpeting beneath her. On the wall above the queen-size bed, the word *LIAR* had been scrawled in blood.

"Jesus," Paulo muttered under his breath.

After fifteen years in homicide, he had acquired enough toughness and objectivity to work even the most gruesome crime scene without an ounce of queasiness. But that didn't mean he'd grown immune to the sight of a dead body, that he didn't feel a twinge of sorrow or anger over the senseless loss of a life. The day he stopped feeling anything was the day he'd quit.

A photographer was busily snapping shot after shot, his flash strobing the grisly scene. Two other technicians were moving carefully around the room, lifting latent prints and searching for trace evidence while the lead forensics investigator, crouching near the victim, took measurements around the body.

Norah O'Connor's bright red hair was pulled back into a severe bun, and her thin, freckled face was set in a grim expression as she concentrated on her task. Hearing Paulo's muttered oath, she glanced over her shoulder at him. "You got here fast. Donovan says he just called you a few minutes ago."

"I was nearby," Paulo said, pulling on a pair of latex gloves. "Where is he?"

"My guess would be the kitchen, interviewing the witness."

"The witness?"

O'Connor nodded. "The victim's coworker. She's the one who discovered the body. She said she came over here after work to check up on the victim, who had called in sick today. She was concerned about her. Apparently they were good friends." O'Connor grimaced. "Needless to say, she's pretty shaken up."

"No wonder." Out of habit Paulo sketched a quick sign of the cross over his heart before entering the room. Watching where he stepped, he approached the body and sank to his haunches on the opposite side of O'Connor.

The victim was moderately tall, at least five-eight, and appeared to be in her late twenties. Her long black hair was in disarray, as if she'd put up a struggle with her assailant. Dark brown eyes stared sightlessly upward. Her dusky skin was now pallid in death. Although her face was bloated, Paulo could tell she'd been beautiful.

As he studied her, he felt a whisper of recognition. He'd met this woman before. *But where? And when?*

"You know the victim?" O'Connor, ever observant, had detected the flash of recognition on his face.

Paulo frowned, shaking his head. "I don't think so."

"You might," a voice spoke from the doorway.

Paulo looked up as his partner, Julius Donovan, stepped into the room. Tall, bald, dark as Jamaican Blue Mountain coffee with the lanky build of a small forward, the detective had been named after his father's favorite basketball player, Julius "Dr. J" Erving. To his father's dismay, Julius had never developed his namesake's aptitude for basketball, preferring activities that appealed more to his cerebral nature, such as solving crossword puzzles and reading science fiction. He'd graduated from college with honors and accepted a lucrative job as a securities analyst for a major brokerage firm. But after just two years, he'd made a drastic career change, deciding to serve his community by becoming a cop. After nearly four years on the force, he'd established himself as a smart, tenacious investigator with good instincts, even if he tended to be a bit overzealous at times. Paulo not only liked the kid; he had a lot of respect for him. Which was something he couldn't say about everyone he worked with.

Paulo warily regarded the younger detective. "What're you talking about?"

Julius Donovan, wearing pleated trousers and a dark sport coat that hung loosely on his narrow frame, advanced farther into the room. "The victim's name is Maribel Cruz. She's twenty-nine years old." He paused, then added pointedly, "She worked as a legal secretary at Santiago and Associates."

Paulo stared at him, his gut clenching. "Shit," he muttered grimly.

Norah O'Connor glanced up from measuring blood

spatter to divide a speculative look between the two men. "Why is that significant?"

Donovan frowned, bemused by the question. "Why? Because Sanchez is re—" He broke off abruptly at the hard look Paulo gave him.

Very few people in the department knew that Paulo was a member of one of Houston's richest, most powerful families. And he preferred to keep it that way. Although he'd been in law enforcement long enough to be considered a seasoned veteran, he was still a relative newcomer to the Houston Police Department. The last thing he needed was to be ostracized or harassed by his peers just because some of his relatives happened to be worth a fortune.

"The victim worked for the largest law firm in Houston," Donovan amended, recovering quickly from his near admission. "Isn't that significant enough?"

O'Connor pursed her thin lips in disapproval. "I hope you're not suggesting, Detective Donovan, that Miss Cruz should receive preferential treatment in this investigation simply because of who her employer was?"

"Of course not. But it doesn't matter. Even if *we* don't make a big deal out of it, the media will."

"Doesn't make it right," O'Connor retorted. "Anyway, why did you say Sanchez might recognize the victim?"

Donovan's mouth curved in a grim smile. "She was a beautiful woman. Sanchez knows a lot of beautiful women."

Paulo smiled briefly, but he was remembering the first time he'd met Maribel Cruz. It was two years ago, shortly after he'd moved to Houston. His cousins, Ignacio and Naomi Santiago, had coerced him into attending a fundraiser dinner hosted by their law firm. The black-tie function had been attended by prominent businessmen, politicians, civic and community leaders, as well as many of the firm's employees, among them Maribel Cruz, who'd flirted shamelessly with Paulo throughout the evening. If he hadn't already promised to be on his best behavior that night, he and the sexy legal secretary probably would have wound up in the sack later.

And now she was dead. Brutally murdered in her own home.

Paulo swore under his breath, lifting his gaze from Maribel Cruz's savaged remains to look at his partner. "Has the ME arrived yet?"

"On his way."

"Has anyone talked to the neighbors?"

"I've got uniforms canvassing the neighborhood. Problem is, most of these folks work during the day. The odds that one of them saw anything are slim to none."

"Has the family been notified?"

Donovan nodded. "Her parents and siblings are flying in from Brownsville. Your fam—er, Maribel's employer was generous enough to pay for their airfare and put them up in a nice hotel downtown. They should arrive later this evening."

Paulo nodded, recalling that it was his cousin Naomi who'd introduced him to Maribel that night. Naomi had spoken very highly of Maribel, which was another reason Paulo had decided she was off-limits. It was one thing to indulge in meaningless one-night stands with women he'd picked up at a bar or a wedding, women he'd never have to see or hear from again. But screwing around with his family's valued employees was just asking for trouble.

Donovan said, "I've asked the coworker, Kathleen Phillips, to hang around a little longer. I figured you'd want to ask her some additional questions."

Paulo nodded distractedly. His gaze had returned to

the bloody word inscribed on the wall above the bed. *Liar.* What the hell did it mean? Was it an indictment of the victim? A message from the killer? A calling card?

Following the direction of his gaze, O'Connor said, "We've already taken a sample of the blood to determine whether it belongs to the victim. But I think we can assume it will be a match."

Paulo nodded in agreement. "Looks like the blood was brushed on the wall. No visible fingerprints."

"None that I can tell," O'Connor said.

"How'd the perp get inside?"

Donovan answered, "Phillips said the front door was unlocked when she arrived. No sign of forced entry. No indication that the lock was jimmied or that any of the windows had been tampered with. But they're still checking around the house, going over the backyard."

"No security alarm?"

"She never had it activated."

Paulo frowned. "How long had she been living here?"

"Phillips said Maribel bought the house three years ago. She remembers because she attended the house-warming party."

Paulo nodded, his gaze shifting back to the body. "She must've put up a fight," he muttered. "Defensive injuries on her hands and wrists."

"I noticed those, too." Donovan hitched his chin toward the dried blood on the wall nearest to where he stood. "I figured the perp made the first cut around this area. After that the blade was bloody, and when he swung again drops flew off and hit the wall."

Nodding, Paulo added, "She turned, trying to run or avoid another blow. He pursues, stabs her from another angle. And that's how the blood spatter ends up on the bedspread."

"Sounds about right to me," O'Connor murmured.

Rising to his feet, Paulo looked around the large room, mentally cataloging every detail. It was clear that Maribel Cruz had spared no expense when it came to decorating her bedroom. The terra-cotta walls were trimmed with fancy crown molding and appeared to have been professionally painted. The polished furnishings were made of carved cherry, the kind that had to be specially ordered and took weeks to be delivered: a huge armoire that looked antique, a dresser, a pair of matching nightstands, and a four-poster bed covered with a cream-and-chocolate satin spread, now bloodstained. Two thick pillows were bunched together against the headboard; the top pillow still bore the indentation made by the victim's head overnight. Other than the bloody, rumpled bed, the room was meticulously neat.

"Anything missing?" Paulo asked, though he already suspected the answer.

"Not that we can tell," Donovan confirmed. "If robbery were the motive, the perp left behind a lot of expensive items. A flat-screen television. A stereo system, computer, laptop, iPod, and some other electronic gadgets. And those paintings in the living room look like originals."

O'Connor shook her head. "Santiago and Associates must pay its secretaries very well. Clearly I'm in the wrong line of work."

Paulo knew for a fact that the employees at his family's law firm were generously compensated, but of course he didn't mention that.

Donovan continued. "Her purse is still here. ID, credit cards, cell phone, seventy dollars in the wallet—everything seems to be accounted for. For now, anyway."

Watching where he walked, Paulo made his way across the room and stepped through an open doorway that led into the master bathroom. The marble countertops were lined with cosmetics and hair and facial products. A pink nightgown lay in a puddle of silk near the shower. Paulo peered inside the glass stall. It was bone dry.

He turned as Donovan appeared in the doorway. "Does the coworker know what time Maribel Cruz called in sick to the office this morning?" he asked.

Donovan flipped through the pages of his notepad. "It was around seven-thirty. Phillips says Maribel called her right after leaving a voice mail message for their supervisor. Maribel told her she was coming down with a bad cold and planned to spend the day in bed resting. Phillips said she sounded terrible, so she decided to check up on her when she got off from work."

"She live nearby?"

"About fifteen minutes away."

"That her Beemer in the driveway?"

"Yeah. Maribel always parked in the garage."

Paulo nodded, glancing inside the bathroom again. After several moments he murmured, almost to himself, "She was about to take a shower. She'd just removed her nightgown when she heard a noise in the other room. She poked her head around the bathroom door, then took a few steps out. And that's when he pounced."

"That would explain why she was nude," Donovan said. "Unless, of course, the killer intended to undress her anyway."

"The ME will determine whether or not she was sexually assaulted," O'Connor said, glancing up from the sketch she was drawing. "If I had to venture a guess, based on lividity and the stage of rigor mortis, I would place the time of death between eight and ten a.m."

Donovan hummed a thoughtful note. "So after calling in sick," he mused, "she decided to take a shower."

"So?" O'Connor prompted.

The detective shrugged. "Just wondering why she'd bother showering first thing in the morning if she were that sick. Who does that? I know *I* wouldn't have. I'd have kept my black ass in bed and watched TV all day."

"Maybe she felt icky," O'Connor suggested. "Maybe she had a fever, and it gave her night sweats. She wanted to wash off the grime."

"Or maybe she had an overnight guest," Donovan countered.

"You think this was a crime of passion?" Paulo asked, his gaze returning to Maribel Cruz's brutalized corpse.

"It would explain why there's no sign of forced entry," Donovan said. "Maybe she played hooky from work to spend the day with her lover. They argued, things got out of hand. He snapped and killed her, then wrote stuff on the wall to make it look like some nut job butchered her."

Paulo lifted his gaze from the dead woman to look at his partner. "Did the coworker tell you that Maribel had a boyfriend?"

"No. To her knowledge, Maribel wasn't seeing anyone. But that doesn't mean she wasn't."

"True." Although Paulo's gut instincts told him that Maribel Cruz had not been killed by an enraged lover, he kept the thought to himself. For now.

Absently he watched as an evidence technician opened one of the nightstand drawers and carefully sifted through the contents. Paulo glimpsed a Bible, a checkbook, and some fashion magazines before the officer opened another drawer and pulled out the only item: a glossy brochure. The man stared at the cover for several moments, then showed it to the officer standing nearest to him. "Hey, didn't I read somewhere that she moved to Houston earlier this year?"

The other man looked at the brochure cover and nodded. "Yeah, the story was in the *Chronicle* a while back. She used to be with some big dance company in New York." He gave a low wolf whistle. "Fine as hell, ain't she? New York's loss is definitely our gain."

"Tell me about it."

By now Paulo had made his way over to the two officers. "Let me see that." He had to practically pry the brochure out of the other man's hand. Once he saw the cover, he understood why. Splashed across the front of the dance program was a photograph that captured Tommie Purnell leaping dramatically through the air, her dark hair flowing behind her, her slender arms raised above her head, her long, glorious legs gracefully extended. She wore a jeweled crown and a red corset with a gauzy, billowing skirt. She looked like a damned goddess.

In late February her dance company had made a stop in Houston as part of its national tour schedule. According to the brochure, Tommie had starred as a lead soloist in that evening's performance.

Touching only the edges of the paper, Paulo flipped through the program until he came to Tommie's biography page. Beneath her smiling photograph she had written: *Great to meet you, Maribel! Don't ever give up on your dreams. Best wishes, Tommie.*

Paulo stared at the inscription, struck by the realization that both he and Tommie had met the murdered woman. Talk about six degrees of separation.

"Damn," Donovan said appreciatively, peering over Paulo's shoulder at Tommie's photo. His eyes narrowed speculatively. "Hey, she wouldn't happen to be the one you told me about a few months ago, would she? You know, the dancer you were trying to stay the hell away from?"

"Yeah," Paulo muttered, regretting the impulse that had led him to confide in his partner.

Donovan grinned, shaking his head. "Lucky bastard."

Before the other two men could ask about Tommie, a uniformed officer stuck his head through the doorway and said to Paulo, "Miss Phillips wants to know if you still need to talk to her."

"Yeah. Why?"

"She's ready to fly the coop. After what happened to her friend here, being in this house is spooking the hell outta her."

Paulo nodded. "Tell her I'll be there in a minute."

After the officer left, Paulo slipped the dance brochure into a plastic evidence bag and passed it to one of the crime-scene technicians, saying, "Run those prints through the system and let me know what you come back with."

The man arched a brow at him, no doubt wondering what Paulo expected to learn from a brochure that might have been handled by any number of people.

Paulo didn't bother explaining himself. He took one last look at the mutilated body on the floor, then walked out of the bedroom and down the hallway to the kitchen.

It was a large room that featured granite countertops, gleaming stainless steel appliances, and ceramic tile floors. No dishes cluttered the sink. Not a fork was out of place. It was as immaculate as the bedroom had been.

A slender, attractive African-American woman sat alone at the round oak table, cradling a glass of water. She was in her late twenties, with skin the color of caramel and shoulder-length dark hair. She wore an emerald silk blouse, gray cashmere slacks, and black snakeskin pumps that looked expensive.

She looked up as Paulo and Donovan entered the room. Her dark eyes were bloodshot and puffy from crying.

"Thanks for your patience, Miss Phillips," Paulo said, briefly clasping her hand. "I know this hasn't been easy for you."

"No, it hasn't." Kathleen Phillips shook her head, her eyes welling with tears. "I just can't believe Maribel's dead. What I saw in there . . ." She paused, shuddering deeply. "Who would do something like that to her? *Who*?"

"That's what we hope to find out," Paulo murmured, pulling out a chair and sitting down at the table. Donovan remained standing in the entryway, keeping an eye out for the medical examiner.

"I know you've already spoken to my partner," Paulo said. "I just wanted to follow up with a few questions. Forgive me if they seem redundant."

Kathleen nodded, blinking back tears. "I want to help any way I can. Maribel was a good friend of mine."

"How long had you worked with her?"

"Three years. We report to the same attorney in the labor and employment law division. His name is Ted Colston. I'm a paralegal. Maribel was Ted's secretary."

"Did she get along with her colleagues? Was she generally well liked? Respected?"

"Absolutely," Kathleen said emphatically. "She was smart and very good at her job, and people liked her because she was friendly and outgoing. You could always count on Maribel to have a positive outlook on things, no matter what."

Paulo nodded, unsurprised by the comments. No one ever spoke ill of the dead, even when it could be justified. "Can you think of anyone who might have had a grudge against Maribel? Personally or professionally?"

Kathleen's eyes widened. "You mean someone who would have hated her enough to do that to her?" she whispered, horrified.

"I'm sure you saw what was written on the wall in her bedroom," Paulo said evenly. "It seemed personal. Can you think of any reason someone would have called Maribel a liar?"

Kathleen shook her head, lifting a trembling hand to the pearl choker at her throat. "I—I don't know why anyone would have written that about her."

"Are you sure?"

"Of course." When Paulo said nothing, she added, "Look, I'm not saying Maribel was perfect, or that she didn't have enemies. I'm sure there were people who didn't like her, for whatever reason. But I just can't imagine anyone *hating* her enough to . . . to—" She broke off, unable to finish the sentence. Her hand shook as she reached for the glass of water on the table and took a long sip.

Paulo waited several moments, giving her time to regain her composure before he continued questioning her. "You told Detective Donovan that Maribel wasn't seeing anyone. Was there an ex-boyfriend in the picture? Or someone she'd recently met at a party or nightclub? A guy she was just getting to know?"

Kathleen frowned, shaking her head. "Not that I know of. She would have told me about him."

"Did she mention anything about someone hitting on her, coming on too strong? Or maybe she noticed a strange man staring at her in the grocery store or while she was out jogging?"

Kathleen smiled wistfully. "Maribel never went jogging. She always said she was too lazy and undisciplined for serious exercise. And it wasn't at all unusual for men to stare at her in public. As you probably noticed, she was a beautiful woman. She was used to guys hitting on her all the time."

Paulo didn't doubt it.

"Garrett's here," Donovan said from the doorway, announcing the deputy chief medical examiner's arrival.

At Paulo's request, Kathleen recounted her discovery of the body, repeating what she had already told the first officer on the scene, as well as Detective Donovan. Afterward Paulo thanked her for her cooperation, gave her his card, and asked her to call him or his partner if she thought of anything else that might help. She gratefully accepted his offer to have an officer follow her home.

As Paulo and Donovan made their way back to Maribel Cruz's bedroom to confer with the ME, Donovan said, "What did you think of Phillips?"

"I think she's hiding something," Paulo said flatly.

The younger detective frowned. "Like what?"

Paulo's mouth curved in a grim smile. "I guess that's for her to know, and us to find out."

Chapter 3

As soon as Tommie returned to her loft after seeing Paulo off, she grabbed her cell phone and dialed her sister's number. After three rings she was about to hang up when a deep, masculine voice answered, "Hello?"

"Hey, Sebastien," Tommie greeted her brother-in-law.

"Hey, girl." His voice was tinged with laughter, as if he'd been enjoying some joke before he picked up the phone. "How you doing?"

"Can't complain. How about you? How's work?"

"Never a dull moment."

"I'll bet," Tommie said wryly.

Sebastien Durand was a homicide detective in the San Antonio Police Department. The first time Tommie met him, he'd been investigating the murder of a dancer who had worked at the same strip club as Tommie. Although Tommie had been instantly attracted to Sebastien, she'd never stood a chance with him. He'd only had eyes for her sister, Frankie. Once Tommie got over her wounded ego—which hadn't been easy—she'd realized just how right Frankie and Sebastien were for each other. *Soul mates* was the term that came to mind every time she saw them together.

"Hey, is Frankie—" The rest of Tommie's question was drowned out by a child's high-pitched squeal in the background. It was followed by the patter of running feet on hardwood and a woman's exasperated voice crying out, "Boy, get your little butt back here!"

Tommie grinned. "Let me guess. Bath time?"

"You guessed it," Sebastien said, laughing. "Marcos just made a jailbreak. Let me go rescue your sister so you can talk to her."

Tommie opened her mouth to tell him she would call back later, but Sebastien had already put down the phone. Tommie heard more laughter in the background as he and Frankie chased their naked two-year-old son around the room. The sound of Marcos Durand's childish giggles melted Tommie's heart, bringing a tender smile to her face. The worst part about living in another city was not being able to see her nephew every day. She adored that little boy. With his father's gray eyes and his mother's thick curly hair, Marcos was already a little heartbreaker.

While Tommie waited for her sister to come to the phone, she slipped off her pointe shoes and padded barefoot into the kitchen. Cradling the phone between her shoulder and ear, she reached into the refrigerator and pulled out the bottle of merlot she'd offered to Paulo earlier.

As she retrieved a wineglass from the cabinet, Frankie came on the line, laughing and sounding out of breath. "I swear that child of mine is going to run track when he grows up. He's so fast! I turn my back *one* second, and he's off like a bolt of lightning!"

Tommie chuckled, rummaging around a drawer for the corkscrew. "Where is he now?"

"Sebastien's getting him ready for bed." Frankie heaved

a gusty sigh. "Who needs membership to a gym? Chasing after Marcos every night gives me more than enough of a workout."

Tommie grinned lasciviously. "I thought that was Sebastien's job."

Frankie laughed.

There was a time that such a joke would have made both women uncomfortable. It would have been laced with bitterness, delivered as a barbed attack. Thankfully, that time had passed. Both Frankie and Sebastien had forgiven Tommie for the abominable way she'd behaved early in their relationship. Her selfish, malicious campaign to sabotage their romance was something she would always regret. She knew their willingness to forgive and forget was more than she deserved.

"I didn't mean to call during bath time," she said apologetically. "Do you want me to call back later, after you've put Marcos to bed?"

"No, that's okay. Sebastien's got it covered. He's reading him a bedtime story. Marcos will be out like a light in five minutes. Anyway, I'm glad you called."

"You are?"

Hearing the wary note in her sister's voice, Frankie laughed. "Of course. You know I'm always glad to hear from you. Mom and Dad are going to be jealous."

Tommie frowned. "Frankie—"

"I know, I know. No lectures this time, I promise." She paused. "But you *could* call them every once—"

"Frankie," Tommie warned.

"All right, all right. I'd better back off before you stop calling me, too."

"You said it, not me," Tommie grumbled, popping the cork on her bottle. She poured the wine, watching as the chilled ruby liquid splashed into the glass.

Contrary to what her sister had said, Tommie hadn't stopped calling their parents. She spoke to them on a regular basis, although, admittedly, they usually initiated the contact. It wasn't that Tommie didn't love her parents; she just didn't have that much in common with them. Unlike Frankie, Tommie didn't share the same interests as their father, a renowned archaeologist who'd been known to spend hours discussing the cultural evolution of ancient civilizations with his elder daughter. And since Tommie didn't have a child, her mother couldn't dispense advice on her favorite topics, which nowadays included ways to tackle potty training, finicky eating habits, and temper tantrums.

"As I was saying," Frankie said, breaking into Tommie's grim musings, "I'm glad you called because I need your advice. I'm giving a big presentation tomorrow, and I can't decide which outfit to wear. I've narrowed it down to two pantsuits and a skirt suit."

"What's the presentation for?" Tommie asked, settling down at the breakfast counter with her glass of wine. Before Frankie could open her mouth, she added dryly, "In layman's terms, please."

Her sister chuckled. A tenured entomology professor at a private university in San Antonio, Frankie had a tendency to lapse into scientific jargon that often went way over Tommie's head.

"My department is seeking a federal grant for a research study on arthropod-borne viruses," Frankie explained. "Tomorrow we're hosting a symposium that will be attended by lots of important people from the National Institutes of Health, the Smithsonian, the National Science Foundation, as well as a number of leading entomologists from around the world. I was asked to make the university's case for funding."

"Wow! That's great, Frankie," Tommie enthused. "Congratulations. What a huge honor."

"Tell me about it. I've got a lot riding on my shoulders, and I really want to make a good impression."

"You will," Tommie assured her. "Hell, you could give that presentation in your sleep."

Frankie laughed. "I don't know about all that, but I certainly appreciate the vote of confidence."

"It's well deserved." Tommie thought of the lecture she'd been invited to give at the University of Houston on Wednesday. Once upon a time she would have bragged about it, trying to one-up her sister because she'd spent years feeling inferior to Frankie and living in the shadow of her brilliance. But those days were behind Tommie. Time had changed her. Life had changed her.

The sound of hangers scraping across a metal rod could be heard in the background. "Okay, I'm standing in my walk-in closet," Frankie announced. "I'm going to send you photos of the three outfits, and you tell me which one I should wear tomorrow."

"Okay." Tommie idly sipped her merlot while Frankie snapped shots using her cell phone camera.

Tommie had always been the clotheshorse of the family, while Frankie had suffered from being severely fashion-challenged, her taste in clothes ranging from conservative to downright god-awful. Four years ago, her wardrobe had consisted of hideous muumuus, shapeless tops, and baggy slacks that did nothing to accentuate her killer body. But all that had changed when she met Sebastien Durand. He'd done for her what no other man ever had. He'd looked beyond Frankie's homely appearance to uncover the beautiful woman hiding beneath. In so doing, he'd given her the confidence—and motivation—to undertake a dramatic wardrobe transformation that would make fashionista Stacy London proud.

Although Frankie still regarded shopping as a mild form of torture, she'd come a long way. So Tommie wasn't too surprised when she saw the stylish selections her sister presented to her for consideration. After deliberating over the photos for a moment, Tommie said decisively, "Wear the red skirt suit. It's sassy and feminine, but still very professional. You look great in red, and the cut of the suit will really flatter your figure. Plus it's not as conservative as the pantsuits."

"Are you sure?" The worried note in Frankie's voice was unmistakable. "Conservative might not be such a bad thing for this audience. These are scientific researchers and scholars, remember?"

Tommie laughed. "So what? They're men, aren't they? Even nerds can appreciate a great pair of legs. You wear that outfit, and by the time you're finished speaking, they'll be lining up in droves to give you the research funds."

"I'd like to think the content of my presentation would be the reason for that," Frankie said wryly.

"Of course. But you know my motto—if you got it, ain't a thing wrong with flaunting it." She grinned, adding impishly, "Too bad you're not breast-feeding anymore. Those milk jugs you had made *me* want to cut you a damned check."

"Tommie!" Frankie gasped.

Tommie laughed. She'd always enjoyed scandalizing her older sister. It was so much fun.

"*Anyway*," Frankie intoned, pointedly changing the subject, "how are your classes going?"

"Great," Tommie replied. "I've got a full plate. I might need to hire another dance instructor sooner than I thought."

"That's wonderful, Tommie," Frankie said warmly. "You know, at the risk of getting all sentimental—"

Tommie groaned.

"—there's nothing nobler than sharing your knowledge and experience with others. Teaching takes an incredible amount of passion, patience, and unselfishness, and not everyone can do it. I'm so proud of you for not only proving that you *can* do it, but for having the courage to try. I hope your students realize just how lucky they are to be learning from such an amazingly gifted and accomplished dancer."

Tommie's throat constricted. "Damn it, Frankie," she grumbled. "Do you always have to be so damned good to me?"

"Yes," Frankie said, a distinct smile in her voice, "because I love you. And no matter what we've been through, I couldn't imagine my life without you."

"Ditto," Tommie murmured, remembering the harrowing ordeal her sister had endured four years ago. Tommie wished it hadn't taken a near tragedy to make her realize how much she'd been taking Frankie, and their relationship, for granted. But then, she'd always been one of those people who had to learn things the hard way.

As Tommie took a swallow of wine and reached for the stack of mail she'd brought in earlier, she asked, "How's Mama August? Still spoiling Marcos rotten?"

Frankie chuckled. "You know it. But you won't hear me complaining. That woman has been an absolute godsend. I honestly don't know what we'd do without her. With my busy schedule and Sebastien's long hours, having his grandmother here during the week to take care of Marcos has been such a blessing. Marcos adores her, and he really enjoys their trips to Rafe and Korrine's ranch up the road. He gets to ride horses and play with Kaia and Ramon all day long. I tell you, between Mama August and Rafe's godmother, all *three* of those rug rats are spoiled rotten."

Tommie smiled, absently sorting through her mail, most of it junk. "How *is* Korrine, by the way? Is she pregnant with her third child yet? Or has Rafe finally changed his mind about wanting six kids?"

Frankie laughed. "If he hasn't, I'm sure Korrine can persuade him to agree to a compromise. She's got that man wrapped around her finger."

"Something else you both have in common. Besotted husbands."

"*Besotted*? Someone's been watching Jane Austen movies again."

Tommie sniffed. "I don't know what you're talking about."

"Right. Of course. What was I thinking, implying that a cool, tough girl like you would actually watch those sappy romantic sagas?"

When Tommie made no reply, Frankie chuckled knowingly. During a previous visit to Tommie's loft, Frankie had been pleasantly surprised to find *Pride and Prejudice* among her sister's DVD collection. She hadn't believed Tommie when she told her that the movie belonged to a friend.

"And speaking of Rafe," Frankie said casually, "have you and his cousin bumped into each other yet?"

"Why?" Tommie asked suspiciously. She'd nearly forgotten that the reason she'd called her sister was to pry the truth out of her concerning Paulo's visit.

"I was just wondering," Frankie answered. "You and Paulo have lived in the same city for seven months now. I just figured you'd eventually run into each other."

Tommie wasn't buying her sister's explanation. "Houston is a big city. The odds of running into anyone you know are slim. Unless you're neighbors or travel in the same social circles. Or unless you go out of your way to see each other." She waited a beat. "Something you wanna tell me?"

"What?" Frankie asked blankly.

Tommie slapped the countertop. "I knew it!"

"Knew what?"

"You *did* tell Paulo to check up on me."

"What? I did no such thing!"

"Frankie," Tommie growled in warning.

Frankie laughed. "I didn't tell him anything, I swear!" She paused as comprehension dawned. "Wait a minute. Are you telling me that Paulo came by to see you?"

"Yes. He just left not too long ago." Tommie frowned. "I thought you'd put him up to it."

"Nope." Frankie hesitated. "Not because I didn't consider it, mind you. I did, to be perfectly honest with you. But I knew you'd be mad if you ever found out, so I kept my mouth shut. Looks like I didn't need to say a word to him anyway. He found his way there all on his own." She sounded inordinately pleased.

"Don't get any crazy ideas," Tommie muttered. "There's nothing going on between me and Paulo. Nothing whatsoever."

"Are you sure?"

Tommie scowled. "What's that supposed to mean?"

Frankie chuckled. "You may think I had my head in the clouds on my wedding day—which is partially true—but I wasn't completely oblivious of everything but Sebastien. I saw the way you and Paulo were looking at each other during the ceremony and at the reception, even during the bridal party's photo session. *A lot* of people noticed.

It was clear that you and Paulo were very attracted to each other."

"So what?" Tommie retorted, tracing the rim of her glass with a manicured fingertip. "That doesn't mean we should start dating. He's not even my type."

Frankie snorted in disbelief. "Since when?"

"Excuse me?"

"Since when is a guy like Paulo Sanchez not your type?" Frankie challenged. "You've always had a thing for bad boys. Paulo's got that whole renegade thing going, right down to the surly grin and cocky swagger. And he's sexy as hell. Seems to me he's *exactly* your type."

"Not anymore."

"Really?" Frankie's voice was heavy with cynicism.

Tommie bristled. "I know this may be hard for you to believe, but I'm not the same person who left home four years ago. I've done a lot of growing up, and my taste in men has evolved. I'm not denying that Paulo's hot. I know he'd make an incredible one-night stand. But that's about all he could do for me, and at this point in my life, I think I deserve more."

"Of course you do," Frankie said softly. "I certainly didn't mean to imply otherwise."

"I know. And I understand where you're coming from. You've found your Mr. Right, and you want me to be as happy as you are. Believe me, I want the same thing, too, if it's in the cards for me. But after all the bad decisions I've made concerning men, the last thing I need is to get involved with a guy who's clearly wrong for me."

"Wow," Frankie murmured.

Tommie couldn't help grinning at her sister's awed tone. "I told you I'm a changed woman." But even as the assertion left her mouth, Paulo's words went through her mind, taunting her. *Good thing I'm a changed man.*

Like hell, Tommie thought.

Frankie said, "I hear what you're saying about Paulo, but I wouldn't be too quick to write him off. I'll admit that my first impression of him wasn't all that great. I thought he was cocky, a little too rough around the edges, a shameless womanizer—"

"I'll stop you when you start lying," Tommie drawled.

Frankie laughed. "The point is, since Paulo and Sebastien are such good friends, I was willing to give him the benefit of the doubt. And I'm glad I did. Because the more I got to know Paulo, the better I liked him. He has a wicked sense of humor, and Sebastien says he's one of the best detectives he's ever worked with. And you should see how good he is with Kaia, Ramon, and Marcos. They positively adore him. I don't know about you, but to me there's nothing sexier than a tough guy with a soft spot for kids."

"Okay, that's the second time you've called Paulo sexy," Tommie said, deliberately ignoring the rest of what her sister had said. "I hope for your sake that Sebastien didn't hear you."

"Oh, hush. Sebastien has no reason to be jealous. He knows how incredible I think he is. And, no, I'm not saying that because he just walked into the room." The low, deep timbre of Sebastien's voice could be heard in the background. Frankie's amused response was muffled, as if she'd covered the mouthpiece with her hand. A moment later, Tommie heard what sounded suspiciously like soft kissing noises.

She rolled her eyes, then cleared her throat loudly.

Frankie came back on the line, mumbling sheepishly, "Sorry about that."

Tommie grinned. "I was going to say you two should get a room, but I guess you're already one step ahead of me."

Frankie chuckled. "Well, let me run. I still need to go over my presentation before bedtime. I'll call you tomorrow to let you know how it went."

"Okay. Knock 'em dead, kiddo. And kiss Marcos for me."

"Will do."

Tommie hung up the phone and took a long sip of merlot, savoring the smooth, rich flavor in her mouth before swallowing.

One of the first good friends she'd made in New York had been a sommelier at an upscale restaurant in midtown Manhattan. Myles Sumter had taught Tommie practically everything he knew about wine, insisting that her preference for margaritas—"party-girl drinks," he'd disdainfully called them—demonstrated an appalling lack of sophistication for one who'd been to Italy and France and should know better. The first time they'd gone out to dinner, Tommie, wanting to impress him, had ordered a glass of pinot grigio. Myles was so mortified she thought he'd swoon to the floor. After lecturing her about the inferiority of pinot grigio while the smirking sommelier looked on, Myles had changed her order to a cabernet sauvignon. After that night, he'd taken it upon himself to give her a crash course in wine appreciation, vowing to convert her into a respectable connoisseur, one who would never, *ever* embarrass herself again by ordering a cheap wine.

At Tommie's going-away party, Myles had surprised her with a gift-wrapped case of his favorite wines, saying sulkily, "Since you insist upon returning to that uncivilized, godforsaken state, this will at least ensure that you don't revert to drinking beer and margaritas."

When Tommie laughingly pointed out to him that

fine wines were also sold in Texas, he'd merely arched a dubious brow at her.

Chuckling at the memory, Tommie raised her glass in a mock toast to Myles before drinking the rest of the merlot. She missed her old friend, as well as the vibrant life she'd carved out for herself in New York City. Her network of friends had included an eclectic cast of dancers and actors, activists and waiters, playwrights and writers—some struggling, others quite successful. When Tommie wasn't touring the country with her dance company, she'd enjoyed shopping with her friends, going to the theater, jogging in Central Park, and attending fabulous dinner parties on the Upper West Side before catching a cab to her favorite nightclub in Harlem. Because she knew the right people, she'd always had a front-row seat at Fashion Week, and stealing kisses with hunky strangers on rooftop terraces had been the highlight of many raucous New Year's Eve parties.

It hadn't taken Tommie long to become acclimated to the frenetic pace of New York City, with its incessant noise and traffic, its crowded streets and pulsing energy. She'd soaked it all up, embracing it so completely that most people she'd met had automatically assumed she was a native. Had her world not been turned upside down seven months ago, she'd still be living there.

But you're not, her conscience mocked. *When the going got tough, you packed up and ran away like a coward. Guess you weren't much of a New Yorker after all.*

Rousing herself from her gloomy thoughts, Tommie rose and carried her empty wineglass over to the kitchen sink. She washed and rinsed the glass, along with the dishes she and Paulo had used. When she'd finished, she switched off the light and headed toward her bedroom. She'd been up since the crack of dawn working on

choreography for a local dance troupe scheduled to perform at the city's Thanksgiving Day Parade later that
month. And tomorrow promised to be an even longer
day, with her last class ending at 8:00 p.m.

The grueling schedule was nothing new to Tommie.
As a professional dancer, she'd begun each day with a
rigorous hour of classroom instruction followed by several hours of rehearsal or a performance in the evening.
The demands of traveling, practicing, and performing
on a nightly basis had been physically exhausting, and
there were many nights, as she'd soaked her aching muscles in a hot bath, that Tommie had questioned her
sanity for wanting to become a dancer. But the doubts
never lasted for very long. Ever since she was a little girl,
twirling around the house in her pink tutu and pink
tights, she'd dreamed of performing on Broadway.
Dancing was in her blood and always would be, though
at thirty-three, even she could admit that the wear and
tear of dancing was beginning to catch up to her. Gone
were the days that she could party all night and still get
up early to exercise without feeling like shit. She needed
her eight hours of sleep as much as she needed a healthy
diet of nutritious, stamina-building foods.

Yawning, Tommie entered her bedroom and flicked
on a Tiffany floor lamp that cast a soft, golden glow over
the room. She crossed to the large window, and with
only a passing glance into the dark night, she drew the
curtains closed. As she started toward the bathroom, she
shook her hair free of its ponytail and peeled off her
skirt, leggings, and leotard, dropping them to the floor
as she went. She'd take a hot shower, then hit the sack.

It wasn't the exciting life she'd led in New York. Not
by any stretch of the imagination.

But for the first time ever, Tommie felt like she was

finally in control of her life. *She* determined the number of clients she took on, *she* dictated the days and times her classes were held, *she* set her own fee schedule.

She answered to no one but herself.

And after everything she'd been through, being able to control her own destiny beat the hell out of *exciting* any day of the week.

Standing in the shadow of a giant oak across the street from the small brick building, the stranger watched Tommie Purnell's silhouette in the bedroom window. He'd timed his arrival to coincide with her nightly ritual of showering before bedtime.

When the light went on in the room, his muscles had tightened. And then she'd appeared in the window, beautiful and alluring, and a hot rush of anticipation slid through his veins. When she glanced briefly outside, he'd huddled closer to the tree, although he knew she wouldn't see him.

Not yet. It wasn't time.

Closing his eyes, he imagined her undressing herself, slowly and seductively because she knew she had a captive audience. He saw the smooth, supple curves of her voluptuous body, her hair tumbling down her back in a rainfall of dark brown. In his mind's eye she looked over her shoulder at him, her pouty lips curving in a sultry smile, her dark eyes beckoning invitingly to him. He imagined joining her in the steamy shower and pinning her against the tiled wall, her nails digging into his shoulders, her long legs wrapped around his waist, her head thrown back to expose her throat and those large, slick breasts as he rammed into her.

He shuddered at the vivid image, his cock stiffening

inside his pants, his blood heating. How he would have loved to cross the narrow street and sneak into the old building, to climb the stairs to the second-story loft and let himself inside. He wanted to roam around her apartment, touching her things, drinking in her scent that lingered in the air. And when she emerged from the shower, he wanted to be there waiting for her. Waiting to strike.

And he would.

But not tonight.

Tonight he would savor the thrill of setting his plan in motion, knowing it was just the beginning. . . .

Chapter 4

It was after ten o'clock by the time Paulo steered his police cruiser through the tall iron gate that guarded the palatial residence of Ignacio and Naomi Santiago. The sprawling Mediterranean-style villa boasted stone columns, second-story balconies, a wraparound veranda, and lush, manicured gardens. The property was situated on five heavily wooded acres in River Oaks, home to Houston's wealthy elite.

Paulo followed the curve of the flagstone driveway and parked in front of the mansion. He took the stone steps three at a time, but just as he reached the massive front door, it swung open to reveal Naomi Santiago peering out anxiously at him.

At age sixty-five Naomi didn't look a day over forty, with her smooth mahogany skin, chic haircut, and trim figure. Whether she was decked out in Chanel or sporting her favorite faded jeans—as she was now—she'd always struck Paulo as having the proud, regal bearing of a queen. And what's more, she had a heart of gold to match.

She took one look at Paulo's grim expression and lifted a trembling hand to her mouth. "Oh my God," she breathed. "I was hoping it was a terrible mistake. So it *is* true. Maribel Cruz is dead."

Paulo hesitated, then nodded. "I'm sorry, Naomi."

As tears flooded her dark eyes, Paulo drew her into his arms. Even as a child he'd hated to see his cousin Naomi cry. Once when he and Rafe were seven, they'd inadvertently gotten separated from the rest of the family at a crowded amusement park. Rafe's parents had been frantic with worry, locating the missing boys after a desperate search that had lasted two hours. The sight of Naomi Santiago's haggard, tearstained face had made Paulo feel worse than any punishment he and Rafe could ever have received. And they'd received plenty.

"I can't believe it," Naomi whispered, her words muffled against Paulo's chest. "How could this have happened? Who'd want to hurt Maribel?"

"That's what I intend to find out," Paulo murmured, though he knew better than to make any promises to her. But it was so damned tempting. After all, this was the woman who'd always been like a second mother to him, bandaging his scraped elbows and knees, nursing him through colds with the same love and affection she'd showered upon her own children. It was no wonder that Paulo's first instinct was to assure her that Maribel Cruz's killer would be caught and brought to justice, even though the cop in him knew it was rarely as simple as that.

After several moments Naomi pulled back and took Paulo's hand, drawing him into the warm house. The entrance hall was massive, with a vaulted ceiling that soared over imported Italian tile floors. The scents from the gardens spilled in to mingle with the perfume of the flowers that had been arranged indoors.

"Where's Ignacio?" Paulo asked.

"On the phone in his study. People have been calling

nonstop ever since we learned what happened. News travels fast." Naomi sniffled, absently reaching up to brush Paulo's hair off his forehead. A soft, tremulous smile touched her mouth. "You need a haircut."

"I know," Paulo murmured, smiling a little. Even now, Naomi couldn't stop herself from mothering him.

"Have you eaten?"

"Yeah." And because he knew she would ask, he added, "I had lasagna. Homemade."

Naomi arched a finely sculpted brow. "Whose?"

Paulo was spared from answering when Ignacio Santiago appeared in the entryway. He was a tall, powerfully built man, well used to taking control, be it in business or family matters. His thick brown hair had turned mostly gray, and his olive complexion came courtesy of his Mexican father, who, like Ignacio, had married a beautiful African-American woman.

Ignacio's piercing whiskey-colored eyes settled unerringly on Paulo. When he spoke, his voice was a deep, rich baritone that resonated with authority. "Good, you're here. Now we can start getting some answers."

Paulo grimaced. "You know I can only tell you guys so much without compromising the investigation."

"We understand," Naomi said, tucking her arm companionably through Paulo's. "Let's talk in the living room. Would you like something to drink? I could ask Lydia to bring you some coffee or sweet tea."

"No, thanks. I'm good."

"Are you sure?"

"Positive. And if I change my mind, I know where the kitchen is."

Naomi returned Paulo's smile as they followed Ignacio from the foyer.

New visitors to the house always remarked on the

sheer elegance of the furnishings. The formal living
room was a decorator's dream, with its coffered ceiling,
beautiful crown molding, priceless antiques, original
artwork, and plush oriental carpeting. A cozy fire crack-
led in the marble fireplace, and on the wall above the
mantel were family photographs framed in gold leaf.

Paulo wandered over, absently studying the familiar
gallery of photos. His lips quirked at a picture of him and
Rafe dressed in their Little League uniforms and sporting wide, gap-toothed grins as they stood with their arms
slung around each other's shoulders. There were the
obligatory portrait-studio photos, Ignacio and Naomi
flanking their four young children against an innocuous
muslin backdrop or an artificial scene from nature. In
the updated versions Angela, Rebecca, and Rafe posed
with their own spouses and adorable offspring. There was
a shot of Daniela, the youngest of the Santiago siblings,
beaming radiantly after being crowned Miss Houston ten
years ago.

It was obvious to anyone looking at the collection of
photographs that Ignacio and Naomi Santiago cherished
their loved ones. Together they'd built a multimillion-
dollar corporation that boasted a family-friendly culture,
a rarity among high-powered law firms. They genuinely
believed in taking care of their employees, treating them
like members of the family. Which was why Maribel Cruz's
death had come as such a devastating shock.

"We couldn't believe it when Ted Colston called to tell
us what had happened," Naomi said, echoing Paulo's
thoughts. "Apparently he was the first person Kathleen
Phillips contacted after calling 911. Ted said she was so
hysterical he could hardly understand what she was
saying. That poor girl."

"Ted Colston was Maribel's supervisor," Ignacio supplied, seated beside his wife on the antique sofa. "He's a partner at the firm."

Paulo nodded. He'd already gleaned as much from Kathleen Phillips. "I'll need to speak to him, as well as Maribel's other coworkers."

"Of course," Ignacio said. "We'll make everyone available for questioning tomorrow. You can come to the office in the morning and use one of the conference rooms for interviews."

"Thanks. That'd be great." Paulo walked over and sat down in an adjacent armchair. "I know you both make a point of getting to know as many of your employees as possible. What can you tell me about Maribel Cruz? How well did you know her?"

"Fairly well," Naomi answered. "As you may remember, I'm very involved in the hiring of professional staff at the firm. Three years ago I had the pleasure of interviewing Maribel as one of three finalists for the secretarial position in our labor and employment law division. I was very impressed with her, which is why we hired her. She was intelligent and dependable, a consummate professional. Ted Colston never had any complaints about her—nor did anyone else, for that matter."

Paulo nodded. "I remember meeting her at the fundraiser dinner two years ago."

"That's right. You *were* there." Naomi smiled sadly. "I was secretly hoping that you and Maribel would hit it off that night. She was such a nice young lady, and I thought you two might make a great couple."

"Really?" Paulo was surprised by the admission. "You made me promise to be on my best behavior."

"Because I didn't want you to be so busy flirting with other women that you'd completely overlook Maribel. She was beautiful, but she didn't advertise her assets the way *some* women do. You know the ones I'm talking about."

Paulo chuckled dryly. "The ones I'm usually attracted to, you mean."

"Well, yes, now that you mention it." Naomi smiled softly. "Maribel wasn't like that. She was modest, and painfully shy when it came to men."

Paulo thought about the way Maribel had flirted boldly with him that evening, and decided not to contradict his cousin's opinion.

"Anyway, I guess Maribel wasn't your type," Naomi continued, a hint of reproach in her voice. "Afterward, when I casually asked her what she'd thought of you, she said you were a hunk, but you didn't seem particularly interested in her." She gave an elegant shrug. "I decided not to push the issue."

Ignacio shook his head, smiling wryly at Paulo. "She's conveniently forgetting the part where I told her not to meddle in your love life."

Naomi snorted. "Since when has that ever stopped me?"

Ignacio and Paulo laughed. The Santiago women had been plotting to find the perfect mate for Paulo for as long as he could remember. In the wake of his bitter divorce they'd intensified their efforts, introducing him to a slew of friends, coworkers, clients' daughters and nieces, even "smart, attractive" women they'd met and chatted up at the hair salon. To date, their matchmaking campaign had been unsuccessful. Paulo wasn't interested in a relationship, and he was perfectly capable of finding his own bedmates.

Unbidden, an image of Tommie Purnell flashed through his mind. He wondered what his family would think of her. Would Naomi regard Tommie as one of those women who shamelessly "advertised" her assets? Would

Angela, Rebecca, and Daniela have anything in common with her?

Paulo scowled at the direction of his thoughts. Why the hell should he care what his family thought of Tommie? It wasn't as if he intended to introduce her to them. Not in this lifetime.

Giving himself a hard mental shake, Paulo returned to the matter at hand. "I understand Maribel was originally from Brownsville."

"That's right," Ignacio confirmed. "She left home to attend college in San Antonio. She—"

"Maribel lived in San Antonio?" Paulo interrupted.

"Yes. She attended St. Mary's University. After graduation she went to work for Crandall Thorne. You've probably heard of him before—"

"Big-time criminal defense attorney? Yeah, I've heard of him. His son, Caleb, is married to a friend of mine's sister."

"What a small world," Naomi remarked.

"You can say that again," Paulo murmured. "So Maribel worked at Thorne's law firm?"

"For two years," Ignacio replied. "She liked it there, but she was unhappy in San Antonio. She said she wanted a change of pace. When she learned about the vacancy at our firm, she immediately applied for the job."

"Although she'd only been out of college for two years," Naomi chimed in, "we were confident that working at a top-tier law firm like Thorne and Associates had given her the skills and experience we were looking for. And we were right."

"You said earlier that no one had ever complained about Maribel," Paulo said.

"Not to our knowledge," Naomi said, glancing at her husband for confirmation. Ignacio shook his head.

"So you didn't know of any conflicts she may have had

with coworkers?" Paulo clarified. "No formal complaints filed against her with human resources?"

Naomi's brows furrowed together. "I don't think so. I believe that's something Ted would have shared with us. You're welcome to double-check with him tomorrow, but I'm fairly certain that the answer to your question is no. I'm not exaggerating when I tell you that Maribel was a model employee."

Ignacio was frowning at Paulo. "Are you suggesting that one of Maribel's colleagues may have killed her to settle a vendetta?"

"I'm not suggesting anything," Paulo said mildly. "But I can't rule out the possibility. You know that."

Ignacio and Naomi exchanged worried glances. The idea that one of their own employees could be a cold-blooded murderer was unthinkable. Paulo didn't want to believe it, either, but it was his job to explore any and all angles, no matter how unsavory.

"Kathleen told Ted that there was writing on the wall," Naomi said faintly. "The word *liar* written in blood. Is that true, Paulo?"

He hesitated, then nodded grimly. "I'm going to ask both of you, as well as Ted Colston and Kathleen Phillips, not to discuss specifics of the case with anyone else. The press is gonna be camped out at your office building all week. Please instruct your employees not to talk to reporters. Ask them to refer all media inquiries to the Houston Police Department."

Ignacio nodded. "Our public relations office will be issuing a statement to that effect tomorrow morning."

"Good." Paulo paused. "I would also recommend sending out a companywide memo to employees urging them to be vigilant at all times."

Naomi's eyes widened fearfully. "Oh my God. You

don't think this was an isolated incident? You think someone may have targeted Maribel because she works at our law firm?"

"I don't know," Paulo admitted. "It's possible. Your firm has represented some controversial clients in the past, and your attorneys have successfully litigated cases that undoubtedly angered the losing side. We have to consider the possibility that Maribel's murder was someone's way of retaliating against the company. Which might explain why *liar* was written on the wall."

"Jesus," Ignacio muttered, scrubbing a hand over his face. "What a damned nightmare."

Naomi gazed imploringly at Paulo. "But it's just a theory, right? You don't have any evidence to support the idea that Maribel was deliberately targeted by a former plaintiff?"

"No, I don't. All I have at this point are a lot of unanswered questions. When I talk to Colston tomorrow, I'll ask him about some of his most recent cases, see if that might provide any potential leads. It's a start."

As Naomi and Ignacio reached for each other's hands, instinctively seeking a physical connection, their wedding rings' light caught the firelight.

"I'm glad you're in charge of the investigation," Naomi said quietly to Paulo. "I wish to God this awful tragedy hadn't happened, but it comforts me to know that you're on the case, doing everything you can to find Maribel's killer."

"I'll do my best," Paulo said grimly, "but I can't make any promises."

"Of course. We don't expect you to." Naomi glanced at her slim gold wristwatch. "It's getting late. Why don't you stay here for the night? Daniela's flying in tonight and would be thrilled to see you when she gets home."

"Where is she?"

"Attending a conference in New Mexico. She switched to an earlier flight after I called to tell her about Maribel. Angela and Rebecca were tied up this evening and couldn't make it over here, but they'll be at the office tomorrow." Naomi paused, lips pursed thoughtfully. "Do you still keep a change of clothes in the trunk of your car for surveillance duty?"

"Yeah," Paulo said, and immediately realized his mistake.

"Great! Then you can just get dressed here in the morning and head out with us to the office. I'm going to help Lydia prepare your room," Naomi announced, and before Paulo could open his mouth to argue, she rose from the sofa and strode purposefully from the room.

Paulo stared after her in amused disbelief for a moment, then looked at Ignacio, who merely lifted one shoulder in a helpless shrug.

"I didn't even say yes," Paulo muttered.

Ignacio grinned. "Since when has that ever stopped her?"

Paulo was running, trying to keep pace with the barking dog streaking through the wooded forest. The night air was thick and suffocating. The moon hung full and bright overhead, threading silver through the dense canopy of trees. Broken branches, exposed roots, and moss-covered rocks littered the ground, slowing his progress. But he kept running, lungs burning, heart thudding in his chest. He was too close to stop now.

The hound's barking had grown louder, more agitated. The animal had found something.

And then Paulo saw it. A woman's nude body.

Swearing under his breath, he knelt beside the crumpled form.

Thick black hair had fallen over the woman's face; even in the darkness, Paulo could see that the hair was matted with blood. He reached out and carefully turned the body over. The tangled hair fell away to reveal Maribel Cruz's face, eyes wide and staring sightlessly, mouth open in a scream no one would have heard out there in the forest. Her throat had been viciously slashed.

As Paulo reached for her, the dog that had led him here gave a low warning growl that brought Paulo's head up. The hound stood rigid as a statue, staring alertly into the shadowy trees. Paulo's skin prickled, the muscles in the back of his neck tightening. He scanned the dark woods. Though he saw nothing, he sensed another presence nearby.

A malevolent presence.

Watching him.

As Paulo's hand eased toward his holstered gun, the woman on the ground suddenly moaned. Startled, Paulo looked down. Instead of Maribel Cruz, he found himself staring into the face of Tommie Purnell.

He recoiled, his gut twisting savagely in protest. No!

Without warning Tommie's dark eyes snapped open. "Help me, Paulo," she whispered. "Please help—"

"Paulo? Are you awake?"

Paulo lurched upright in bed, violently dislodging the hand that had been resting on his shoulder. His heart hammered painfully against his rib cage, choking the air from his lungs. Perspiration dampened his skin.

"Are you okay?"

Shaken and disoriented, Paulo stared at the young woman perched on the edge of his bed, then looked around the semidarkened room, with its gleaming mahogany furniture and thick oriental carpeting. It took several moments for him to realize that he wasn't in a dark, creepy forest kneeling over the body of a dead woman.

Not just any woman. Tommie Purnell.

"Shit," he muttered, scrubbing at his bleary eyes with the heels of his hands. "I need a smoke."

"You quit," Daniela Santiago reminded him.

This time Paulo swore in Spanish.

Daniela laughed, a warm, lilting sound that penetrated the black cloud fogging his brain. "What time is it?" he grumbled.

"Six-thirty. That was some nightmare you were having."

Paulo said nothing, leaning back against the headboard and dragging an unsteady hand through his thick, tousled hair. Naomi was right. He needed a damned haircut.

Daniela was eyeing him worriedly. "Are you sure you're okay, sweetie?"

"Yeah," he said gruffly.

Daniela looked unconvinced. At thirty-four years old she was the youngest of the Santiago siblings. Her silky black hair was cut in a short bob that made her look like an exotic pixie doll. Her skin was golden brown, her oval face characterized by large hazel eyes, high cheekbones, and full, pouty lips. That morning she wore a tailored black designer pantsuit that made her look both businesslike and feminine, attributes she used to her advantage whether she was delivering a closing argument in the courtroom or conducting a meeting at her family's law firm, where she was the youngest partner.

When they were children Paulo had always treated Daniela like a pesky little sister, one who'd thrown temper tantrums when she didn't get her way, followed him and Rafe everywhere they went, and routinely snuck into their room at the crack of dawn to jump up and down on their beds. Now as adults, Paulo and Daniela were closer than anyone could ever have predicted, bonding over their failed relationships—both were divorced—and sharing the unenviable burden of being the only siblings in their families who hadn't yet brought children into the world.

"I was walking by your room when I heard you calling out in your sleep." Daniela hesitated, biting her full lower lip as she studied Paulo. "Who's Tommy?"

"What?"

"Who's Tommy? You were shouting his name when I walked into the room."

"*Her* name," Paulo corrected. "And it's not important."

Daniela frowned at him. "Not important? You sounded terrified, Paulo. Like something had really upset you."

"It was just a bad dream," he muttered. "Don't worry about it."

Before Daniela could argue, Paulo tossed back the covers and swung his long legs over the edge of the bed. After a quick glance down to make sure he hadn't slept in the buff last night, as he often did, he stood and strode across the room to the adjoining bathroom, shutting the door behind him so he could take a leak.

Shit, he wanted a smoke. Just to take the edge off his frayed nerves. The dream had been intense, disturbingly so. The shock and horror he'd felt when the dead woman's face had morphed into Tommie Purnell's had been all too real. His pulse still hadn't returned to normal.

He thought about calling Tommie just to see if she was okay, but what the hell would he say to her? That he'd dreamed about finding her dead, mutilated body in the woods? She'd probably call him a fucking psycho and hang up on him. And he wouldn't blame her. He had no reason to spook her, or to attach any significance to the nightmare he'd just had. Maribel Cruz's brutal murder had been fresh on his mind, considering that he'd left the crime scene just a few hours before he went to bed. It wasn't the first time a victim from one of his homicide cases had worked his or her way into his subconscious, and it wouldn't be the last. It was one of those "occupational hazards" nobody ever mentioned to you when you were thinking about joining the force.

Washing his hands at the sink, Paulo surveyed his reflection in the mirror. He looked like hell, with bloodshot eyes, unruly hair, and nearly a week's worth of dark stubble covering his jaw. He'd have to break down and shave before he left the house that morning. He didn't want to embarrass his family by showing up at the law firm looking like a savage.

Grimacing, Paulo rummaged in the cabinet until he located an electric razor and shaving cream, conveniently supplied by the housekeeper. He wished she'd left a fresh pack of Marlboros for him as well. Hell, he would have loved to draw in a deep lungful of nicotine right about now. Giving up smoking was harder than he'd ever imagined, and he'd kicked the habit more than four years ago. But every so often his body craved what it couldn't have.

Like too much booze.

And Tommie Purnell.

Ruthlessly shoving the thought aside, Paulo opened the bathroom door and called out to Daniela, "When'd you get in last night?"

"Around one." Daniela stood at the French doors, where she'd just opened the drapes to let in the sunlight. "Mom didn't want me taking a cab late at night, so she sent Mr. Mackey to pick me up," she added, referring to the family's longtime driver. "Mom said you offered to do it, but she told you not to because she wanted me to be surprised when I got home and found you here."

"And were you?" Paulo drawled, lathering his face and neck with shaving cream.

"Of course." Daniela grinned. "I know how paranoid you are about keeping your coworkers from finding out we're related. That's the only reason you didn't move into the guest cottage when Mom and Dad offered, even though you wouldn't have had to pay rent and you could have enjoyed Lydia's wonderful home cooking every night. And God knows the guest cottage is a helluva lot nicer than that dump you call an apartment."

"Don't start," Paulo warned, chuckling.

"I know, I know." Daniela heaved a long sigh, stretching out across the foot of the mahogany sleigh bed with her head propped in the crook of her palm. From that angle she could see Paulo through the open bathroom doorway. "Don't mind me. I'm just feeling sorry for myself because I'm a thirty-four-year-old divorcee still living at home with my parents. I guess I just figured if you'd moved into the guest house, you'd always be around to keep me company."

"Not necessarily," Paulo countered, gliding the electric razor along his throat. "Between your long hours and mine, we'd probably see each other about as often as we do now."

"You're probably right." Another deep sigh. "Listen to me, throwing a pity party for myself after the terrible thing that happened to poor Maribel Cruz. I couldn't believe it when Mom called to tell me."

"Did you know Maribel?"

"Not very well. I'd spoken to her a few times around the office, and she seemed really nice." Daniela paused, making a face. "Unlike her boss."

"Ted Colston?"

"Yeah. Him. I never understood how Maribel could put up with him. He's such an asshole."

Paulo raised an amused brow. "He's a lawyer. Isn't that a given?"

"Hey!" Daniela laughingly protested. "*I'm* a lawyer!"

Paulo grinned through the white foam covering his face. "Seriously, though. What's your beef with Ted Colston?"

"God, where do I begin? The first time I met him, he was new to the firm, so he didn't know who I was. When I walked into the conference room for a meeting, he automatically assumed I was a secretary, there to take notes and serve coffee. Before I could even sit down, he proceeded to tell me how he took his coffee—cream with one sugar."

Paulo chuckled. "Uh-oh. What'd you do?"

Daniela's hazel eyes sparkled with mischief. "I got his coffee and served it to him with a smile, sweet as you please. Everyone else was just staring at us, like they couldn't believe what they were seeing. A few people were holding back grins, 'cause they knew Ted was going to feel like a real dumb-ass when he found out who I was. After one of the other attorneys opened the meeting with a few announcements, he turned it over to me, making a point of introducing me as Senior Associate Daniela *Santiago*." She laughed, an infectious, rollicking sound. "You should have seen the look on Ted's face once he made the connection. I thought he was going to shit all over his Armani suit! It was priceless."

Paulo grinned. "What a gringo."

"Tell me about it. Before I got down to business, I looked him in the eye and told him that one day, after my parents retired from practicing law, my sisters and I would be in charge of running the practice, and if he was fortunate enough to still be working for us, he could pour *my* coffee."

Paulo roared with laughter.

Daniela smiled smugly. "He's been kissing my ass ever since that day. But I know deep down inside he believes that the only reason I made partner is that my parents own the firm. But I worked my ass off to get where I am, and I had to pay my dues just like everyone else. If that chauvinistic, self-serving prick wants to believe otherwise, then—"

"Fuck him," Paulo finished calmly.

"That's right!"

The two cousins grinned conspiratorially at each other in the mirror.

Suddenly Daniela's eyes lit up. "Hey, I've got an idea! Let's go to the Breakfast Klub when you finish getting ready."

"This morning?"

"Yeah. We haven't been there in months, and I've been seriously craving some wings and waffles."

"Sounds good, but not today. I need to head to your office this morning and start interviewing Maribel's coworkers, including your friend Colston."

"It's not even seven o'clock yet. We can have breakfast and be at the office by nine. More people will be in by that time anyway. Come on, Paulo," she cajoled, clasping her manicured hands together in a gesture of supplication. "It sounds like you're going to have a pretty full day ahead of you. Might as well start it off right with a lip-smacking, rib-sticking breakfast at our favorite place. Can't you just taste those wings and waffles? The catfish and grits? Mmm-mmm, good."

Paulo grinned. She did have a point. Tasked with a new homicide investigation, he had no doubt that he was in for a very long day; he'd be lucky if he managed to squeeze in a lunch break, today or any other time this week. And the food served at the Breakfast Klub, a popular restaurant near downtown, was second to none.

"Okay," he agreed.

Daniela whooped with delight. "Hurry up and get dressed so we can go," she said eagerly, heading from the bedroom. "I can't wait to tell you about the cute guy I met in New Mexico. I want to get your advice about long-distance relationships."

Paulo chuckled dryly, wondering when she would come to the realization that when it came to relationships, he was the absolute *last* person on earth to be dispensing advice. To her or anyone else.

Chapter 5

"I just don't understand it."

Tommie glanced up from shaking pepper on her grits to smile quizzically at the man seated across the table from her. "What?"

Zhane Jeffers gestured expansively toward the thick Belgian waffle and fried chicken wings piled on her plate, along with a side order of buttery grits. "How do you eat the way you do and still keep that itty-bitty waist?" he said wonderingly.

Tommie laughed. "I'm a dancer."

Zhane snorted. "So am I, honey, and there's no way I could maintain this svelte figure if I pigged out the way you do. As if the waffles and wings weren't fattening enough, you had to order grits, too?" Incredulous, he shook his head, neat black dreadlocks brushing his shoulders. "Your metabolism must be fierce."

Tommie grinned. "At least for now. Knock on wood," she said, rapping her knuckle on the smooth cherry table. She ate a forkful of waffle and let out a deep, appreciative sigh. "Mmm, that is *sooo* good. You don't know what you're missing, Zhany."

"Oh yes, I do," he retorted, lifting a cup of creamy coffee to his mouth. "High cholesterol, high blood pressure, clogged arteries, diabetes, obesity, and heart disease. If you don't believe me, just look at my family. Every last one of them belongs on that reality show for fat-asses who need to lose weight—*The Biggest Loser.*"

"Oh, don't be such a killjoy," Tommie chided, even as she happily went to work on a chicken wing.

Zhane just smiled indulgently and shook his head at her. He was an attractive, dark-skinned man in his early thirties with the trim, lithe physique of a dancer and the moody temperament to match. He and Tommie had crossed paths for the first time shortly after she'd moved to Houston. She'd been at the grocery store, unconsciously doing a series of *pliés* while she waited in a long checkout line, when an amused voice behind her had drawled, "Built like an hourglass, but moves like a prima ballerina."

Tommie had whirled around, hands on hips, a stinging retort on the tip of her tongue for the impertinent stranger. But one look at the dreadlocked black man dressed in drag, and she'd quickly realized she wasn't being hit on. The appreciation glowing in the stranger's dark eyes had been that of one dancer admiring another. They'd quickly struck up a conversation, each delighted to learn that the other had performed on Broadway. Zhane, now a member of the Houston Metropolitan Dance Company, had invited Tommie to a friend's costume party that evening, and they'd been inseparable ever since.

Every Tuesday morning they met at the Breakfast Klub, a hip soul food restaurant best known for its signature dishes—catfish and grits, and wings and waffles.

The surroundings were simple yet stylish, with the works of local artists showcased on the walls and both smooth jazz and gospel drifting from the stereo. Even at that early hour the place was packed, every table and booth occupied. On Saturdays the line went out the door and wrapped around the small building.

"Why don't you blow off your classes today and go to the Galleria with me?" Zhane suggested, spreading raspberry jam on his toast. That was all he'd ordered—coffee and toast. A waste, Tommie thought. "There's a sale at Neiman Marcus."

Tommie groaned. "Why are you torturing me, Zhany? You know I can't go shopping with you. Even if I could cancel the rest of my classes today—which I wouldn't— I'm on a budget."

"A *budget*?" Zhane sounded scandalized, as if she'd just announced she was becoming a Republican.

Tommie laughed. "Yes. A budget. I need to be frugal with my finances. I still want to make a few renovations to my building, and pretty soon I'll be hiring another instructor, who sure as hell ain't gonna work for free."

Zhane sniffed. "Too bad. I saw a pair of Jimmy Choo peep-toe pumps that had your name written all over them, honey."

Tommie whimpered pathetically.

Zhane chuckled. "I know you're enjoying doing your own thing, sugarplum, but in case the teaching gig doesn't work out for you, you know Richard would love to have you on board."

Tommie snorted. "Tell me something I *don't* know," she muttered, thinking of the dance company's artistic director, who made a point of seeking her out every time she attended one of Zhane's performances, smiling and gazing at her in a way that made her skin crawl. Tommie was no fool. She knew Richard Houghton was interested in a helluva lot more than her dancing skills.

"What do you have against Dick?" As soon as the words left his mouth, Zhane grinned at his own double entendre. Several other diners, overhearing the question, glanced over at them and snickered.

When Tommie glared at Zhane, he laughed and waved a dismissive hand. "Girl, don't worry. Nobody's gonna mistake your fine ass for a fishmonger. As I was saying, I can't understand why you don't like Richard. He's smart, talented, reasonably attractive. His family is loaded, and unlike most of the male dancers *I* know, he actually likes women. What more could a straight girl ask for?"

Tommie shrugged, nibbling on the strawberry that had topped her waffle. "I'm sure Richard is a decent guy. But he just doesn't do it for me. To be perfectly honest with you—and I'll *kill* you if you repeat this to anyone—he gives me the creeps."

Zhane's perfectly manicured brows shot up in surprise. "What do you mean he gives you the creeps? In what way?"

"Well, the way he stares at me makes me uncomfortable."

Zhane guffawed. "Honey, please! Have you looked in the mirror lately? Men stare at you all the time. You should be used to it by now."

"I know," Tommie muttered, wishing she'd just kept her big mouth shut. "But it's different with Richard. I don't know how to explain it. The way he looks at me . . . It's like he knows a secret about me, or thinks he does. It's creepy."

Zhane grinned. "Maybe he *does* know a secret about you. I heard you were a naughty little girl up there in New York."

Tommie smiled, but it was forced. Zhane's teasing

remark had hit a little too close to home, reminding her of the reason she'd fled New York in the first place. Although Zhane was the least judgmental person she knew, she couldn't bring herself to tell him about the terrible scandal that had led to her release from the Blane Bailey Dance Company. The one time she'd almost confided in Zhane, she'd quickly talked herself out of it.

Shame was a powerful captor.

Noticing her strained expression, Zhane frowned. "Oh, honey, you're serious about this, aren't you? Richard really *does* make you uncomfortable."

"It's not a big deal. Really. Forget I said anything."

Zhane looked unconvinced. "If he ever says or does anything inappropriate, sugarplum, just say the word and I'll kick his ass for you."

Tommie laughed, though she knew that Zhane could back up his threat. He'd grown up in the Third Ward, one of the poorest, most crime-infested communities in Houston. Throughout his childhood he'd been forced to defend himself against neighborhood bullies who'd routinely picked on him because he was different. It hadn't taken Zhane long to realize that the only way he could survive the bullying was to fight back. So that's what he'd done—and had been doing ever since. Once at a club, Tommie had watched him go off on a big, mean-looking biker who'd made the mistake of calling Zhane a queer behind his back—something the man had undoubtedly regretted by the time Zhane got through with him.

Chuckling at the memory, Tommie drawled, "Thanks for the offer, sweetie, but that won't be necessary. Besides, I wouldn't want to be responsible for getting you kicked out of the dance company for assaulting the director. I'd never forgive myself."

But Zhane was no longer listening to her. He was staring

across the crowded room, an appreciative gleam filling his dark eyes as he announced in a theatrical falsetto, "Hottie alert."

Smiling, Tommie followed the direction of his gaze. And froze.

There, standing near the front of the restaurant, was Paulo Sanchez.

Her heart thumped.

Although he'd obviously shaved, and had traded in yesterday's leather jacket and black jeans for a dark turtleneck and charcoal trousers, Paulo still managed to exude a raw, rugged masculinity that left no doubt that beneath the tamed facade beat the heart of a virile, primitive male.

Not surprisingly, he wasn't alone. Standing beside him, her arm tucked companionably through his, was an exotic young beauty who looked like a haute couture model, with her ultrachic bob and glam Chanel pantsuit. Tommie told herself the dagger of envy she felt had more to do with the woman's killer threads than the way she was latched on to Paulo's arm.

"Mmm, he is *scrumptious*," Zhane purred. "He has that whole rugged thing going on. A dangerous edge. Me likey."

Tommie's mouth curved. "I don't think you're his type, Zhany."

Zhane feigned innocence. "What type? Handsome and fashionably dressed?"

Tommie laughed.

As if he'd picked up on the sound Paulo turned his head, his gaze locking on to hers. Tommie's stomach bottomed out. The laughter died on her lips.

They stared at each other for a long, charged moment.

Without breaking eye contact, Paulo leaned down and

murmured something to his companion, who nodded and glanced across the room. The next thing Tommie knew, the couple began heading toward her table.

"Hell," she muttered under her breath. As if she needed Paulo flaunting yet another one of his playthings in her face.

"Oh my God," Zhane breathed, staring at her. "Do you know him?"

"You could say that. Do I have powdered sugar on my mouth?"

"No. Just a little chicken grease." At Tommie's stricken look, Zhane grinned. "I'm teasing. You're gorgeous. That piece of eye candy on his arm's got nothing on you."

Tommie flashed her friend a grateful smile, though she wished she had time to freshen her lipstick. At least she looked presentable in a pink cashmere sweater, jeans, and thigh-high stiletto boots. She'd never been one of those women who left the house dressed as if she were merely going out to check the mail—even when that was the case.

She summoned a cool, relaxed smile just as Paulo and the couture model reached the table. Deliberately ignoring the woman, Tommie drawled, "If I didn't know better, Detective, I would think you were stalking me."

Paulo's mouth twitched. "Maybe I am."

Tommie stared at him, surprised that he'd made such an admission, even jokingly, in front of his companion. Even more surprising was the woman's reaction, or lack thereof. She smiled at Tommie, an open, friendly smile that lacked even a hint of possessiveness.

Impatient to get the introductions under way, Zhane thrust his hand toward Paulo. "Zhane Jeffers. And you are . . . ?"

"Paulo Sanchez." He shook Zhane's hand before

turning to the woman at his side. "This is my cousin Daniela Santiago."

Tommie's eyes widened. "Your *cousin*?" she blurted without thinking.

"That's right," Paulo murmured, his eyes glinting with amusement because he knew she'd mistaken the woman for his lover. "Daniela, I'd like you to meet Tommie Purnell."

"Tommie?" Daniela Santiago repeated.

Tommie didn't know how to interpret the look that passed between Daniela and Paulo; it was so fleeting she could have imagined it. Only she knew she hadn't. Had Paulo discussed her with his cousin?

"It's a pleasure to meet you," Daniela said, smiling warmly at Tommie.

"Likewise," Tommie murmured.

"How long have you and Paulo known each other?"

"Yes, honey, do tell," Zhane eagerly chimed in. "Inquiring minds wanna know."

Resisting the urge to kick him under the table, Tommie answered, "We met at my sister's wedding four years ago."

"I had the pleasure of escorting Tommie at the ceremony," Paulo added, a lazy smile playing at the corners of his lips. "It was one of the best weddings I've ever been to."

"Oh, I'll bet it was." Unable to resist, Tommie added sweetly, "How *is* she, by the way? You know, the lovely young brunette I caught you molesting in the bridal suite?"

Paulo chuckled softly, shaking his head at her. "Still holding a grudge about that, Tommie? Tell you what. The next wedding we attend together, I'll let *you* molest me during the reception. Afterward, too, if you're really good."

"Paulo!" Daniela gasped, torn between shock and amusement.

With a mischievous grin, Zhane suggested, "Hey, you never know. The next wedding you two attend together might be your own."

This time Tommie *did* kick him under the table. Hard.

"Ouch!" he howled.

Tommie just glared at him, unrepentant.

"Your wings and waffles are making my mouth water, Tommie," Daniela said, her hazel eyes still twinkling with laughter. "I'd better go order my own before I dive face-first into your plate."

"Why don't you and Paulo join us?" Zhane offered, all but daring Tommie to kick him in the shin again. "I know how hard it is to get a table in here. Makes no sense for y'all to wait around when we've got plenty of room to spare."

"That's very sweet of you, Zhane. Do you mind?" Daniela asked, dividing a glance between Tommie and Paulo, who looked distinctly amused as he held Tommie's gaze.

"I don't mind," he drawled. "Miss Purnell?"

"Of course I don't mind. You're both welcome to join us." Really, what else could she say?

Daniela smiled. "Great! I'll go order our food. No, stay," she insisted when Paulo offered to take care of it. "I got it. You always mess up the order, anyway."

"I'll go with you," Zhane said, already on his feet. As he and Daniela started away together, he said to her, "Say, you wouldn't happen to be a member of *the* Santiago family, would you?"

"Guilty as charged."

Zhane let out a delighted squeal. "Go on, girl! You're like Houston royalty!"

Daniela's laughing response was drowned out by the noisy din of the restaurant as they moved off. Tommie and Paulo stared after them for a moment, then looked at each other, chuckling quietly.

"Your friend's quite a character," Paulo commented.

"Yeah. He reminds me of the friends I had back in New York." Tommie sighed contentedly. "It's great to have soul mates."

Paulo cocked an amused brow at her, but said nothing. When he slid into the booth beside her and his knee accidentally brushed hers, heat shot through her veins. She opened her mouth to ask him what the hell he was doing, then changed her mind. She knew he'd sat down next to her, purposely ignoring the other side of the booth, just to unnerve her. She refused to give him the satisfaction of knowing he'd succeeded.

"You come here often?" he asked.

"Every Tuesday. What about you?"

"Haven't been here in months. It's one of Daniela's favorite restaurants."

"Mine, too." Tommie chuckled. "Zhane thinks it's a greasy spoon."

"Yet he comes here every week. Just for you."

"That's what friends are for." Tommie gave him a whimsical smile. "Daniela's beautiful. She looks a lot like her brother, Rafe."

"That's what everyone always says."

"Is she a lawyer like the rest of the family?"

"Yep. Best civil litigation attorney in the state. If you ever need legal representation, she's your woman."

"I probably couldn't afford her," Tommie said wryly.

Paulo chuckled. "That makes two of us."

They grinned at each other.

Without thinking Tommie reached out, touching the smooth, angular curve of his cheek. "You shaved."

"Yeah."

"Nice."

"Thanks," Paulo murmured. "Every now and then I try to look civilized."

Tommie smiled softly.

As they gazed at each other, she was acutely aware of the heat from his body, the teasing scent of his aftershave, the melting intensity of his dark eyes. Light caught in his black hair, which hung over the collar of his turtleneck. Tommie had an overwhelming urge to run her fingers through the soft, thick strands. In her mind's eye she saw herself gently pulling his head toward hers, bringing their hungry mouths together. She saw him touching her, his lips and hands caressing her body.

Paulo's gaze darkened, as if he'd intercepted her thoughts. He shifted closer on the seat, making her breath catch in the back of her throat. Her pulse drummed.

She wanted him. God, she wanted him. If he'd taken her hand at that very moment and led her out of the restaurant, she wouldn't have resisted, as long as their next destination had a bed.

"If you keep looking at me like that, *querida*," Paulo murmured huskily, "we're both gonna be in a world of trouble."

Abruptly Tommie dropped her hand from his face and averted her gaze, her insides quivering. Damn it. What was it about Paulo Sanchez that made her lose her mind every time he was near?

Sex appeal. He's got too damned much for his own good.

Frowning at the thought, Tommie glanced across the room, hoping to see Zhane and Daniela Santiago returning to the table. No such luck. They were still waiting in line to place an order. They seemed to be getting along quite well, their faces animated as they laughed and conversed with each other.

Tommie heaved a long, wistful sigh. "I think your cousin's trying to steal my best friend."

Paulo chuckled, following the direction of her gaze. "Appears that way."

"Oh my God. Did he just compliment her Christian Louboutin shoes?"

Paulo grinned at her outraged tone. "Knowing Daniela, she's probably inviting Zhane to go shopping with her even as we speak."

Tommie gasped. "She wouldn't dare!"

But as she watched in disbelief, Daniela Santiago reached inside her red Hermès handbag and pulled out a BlackBerry.

"Uh-oh," Paulo intoned, his grin widening. "Daniela's checking her calendar. That's never a good sign." After another moment he shook his head, announcing gravely to Tommie, "I'm sorry. It looks like they've set a date."

Tommie scowled in disgust. "Men are so unfaithful. Even the gay ones."

Paulo threw back his head and laughed, drawing several admiring female glances.

Resisting the urge to glare at the other women, Tommie picked up her fork and resumed eating. "So, what's on your agenda today, Detective?" she asked conversationally. "Where are you headed after breakfast?"

"To the office with Daniela," Paulo said.

Tommie arched an amused brow. "Why? Is it Take Your Cousin to Work Day?"

He smiled briefly. "Not quite."

When he didn't elaborate, she prodded, "You're going there on official business?"

He nodded. "I'm investigating a homicide. One of the firm's employees was found murdered yesterday."

"Oh no. That's terrible. Did you know the employee?"

"Not really. I met her once at a function." He paused. "Actually, you met her, too."

"I did?" Tommie asked in surprise.

Paulo nodded. "The crime-scene unit found one of your dance programs in her nightstand. You had autographed it for her when you performed in Houston in February. Actually, I have her photo—" He glanced down at himself, then grimaced. "Never mind. I left my jacket in the car."

"What was her name?"

"Maribel Cruz."

Tommie pursed her lips, searching her memory. After several moments she shook her head, saying apologetically, "The name doesn't ring a bell. I've met hundreds of people after performances, autographed more programs than I can count."

"That's what I figured," Paulo said.

"What did I write?"

"In the program?" At Tommie's nod, he said, "You told her, 'Don't ever give up on your dreams.'"

Tommie ate a forkful of waffle and chewed thoughtfully. "She must have been an aspiring dancer," she mused.

"Why do you say that?" Paulo asked.

"I meet a lot of aspiring dancers, women who approach me after a performance and tell me how much they've always wanted to dance professionally but never had the opportunity. They tell me how much they hate their job because it keeps them from pursuing their dreams. I always encourage them to follow their heart, even though I know better than anyone how hard it is to break into the world of professional dancing."

"Was it hard for you?"

Tommie snorted. "Hell, yeah. I've been dancing and performing ever since I was four years old, but I didn't get my big break until I was almost thirty. Before I moved to New York to tackle Broadway, I worked as a legal secretary. The pay was phenomenal, and the firm I worked for was top-notch. But busting my ass as someone's secretary was *not* what I wanted to be doing for the rest of my life. So I definitely know where these women are coming from when they tell me . . ." She trailed off, staring quizzically at Paulo, who had the oddest expression on his face. "What?"

"I didn't know you were a legal secretary. What was the name of the law firm you worked for?"

"Thorne and Associates. Why?"

He stared at her, his gaze hard and piercing. After a prolonged moment he shook his head, as if to dismiss an absurd thought. "Nothing," he muttered. "Forget it."

But Tommie's curiosity had been piqued, and something in his demeanor had sent a whisper of unease sifting through her. "Come on, Paulo. What gives?"

He hesitated, looking grim. "You may have had more in common with Maribel Cruz than you thought."

Tommie frowned. "What do you mean?"

"She was a legal secretary at my family's law firm." Paulo paused. "Before that, she worked at Thorne and Associates."

Chapter 6

Two hours later, as he waited in Ted Colston's plush, dark-paneled office suite, Paulo was still mulling over the connection between Tommie Purnell and Maribel Cruz. He didn't know what to make of the fact that the two women had worked for the same law firm at the same time, and now one of them was dead. It could mean anything. Or it could be nothing more than a disturbing coincidence.

Except Paulo didn't believe in coincidence.

"I apologize for keeping you waiting, Detective."

Paulo glanced toward the doorway as Ted Colston strode purposefully into the room. He was in his midforties, tall and broad-shouldered with a lean, athletic build that suggested he took full advantage of the firm's state-of-the-art fitness facilities. His dark brown hair was neatly trimmed, not a strand out of place, and he wore an impeccably tailored navy blue suit that reminded Paulo of the story Daniela had shared with him earlier.

"No problem." Paulo rose from the visitor chair and shook the other man's hand, noticing upon closer examination that Colston's face was haggard, the skin around his blue eyes creased with tension and fatigue.

"Thanks for taking time out of your busy schedule to talk to me," Paulo said.

"Of course. Anything I can do to help with the investigation." Releasing Paulo's hand, Colston rounded the large mahogany desk to claim the leather swivel chair behind it. "As you might imagine, it's been a rough morning. Everyone is in shock over what happened to Maribel."

"I'm sure," Paulo said, sitting back down. "I heard that grief counselors are on hand to speak with employees."

"Yes, thank God. I know *I'm* having a helluva time trying to make sense of such a terrible, senseless tragedy." Colston pushed out a ragged breath, passing a trembling hand over his face. His gold wedding band caught and reflected the morning sunlight slanting through the wall of windows. Paulo made a mental note of the fact that the attorney was left-handed.

"I understand Maribel had worked for you for three years," Paulo said.

Colston nodded. "Best secretary I've ever had. Kept things running like a well-oiled machine. It's going to be damn near impossible to replace her." He shook his head, his imploring gaze meeting Paulo's across the desk. "Do you have *any* idea who might have killed her, Detective Sanchez?"

"Not yet," Paulo said evenly. "That's why I'm here. To get as many answers as possible."

Colston held his intent gaze for a moment, then leaned back in his chair and stared vacantly out the window at the downtown skyline, at towering skyscrapers glinting brightly in the sun. "God, I can't believe she's gone," he murmured. "If I had known when she walked out of this office on Friday night that it would be the last time I saw her alive, I wouldn't have been such a jackass to her."

"What do you mean?" Paulo asked, even as Daniela's words echoed in his mind. *I never understood how Maribel could put up with him.*

Colston looked pained. "I was having a bad day on Friday. I got a speeding ticket on my way to the office, I had to deal with a difficult client and put out a fire pertaining to one of my other cases, and then to top it all off, my wife called and we got into a big argument. I was angry and frustrated, and I took it out on Maribel, biting her head off every time she had the misfortune of crossing my path."

"I'm sure she didn't take it personally," Paulo murmured.

"No, she didn't. She never did. Which only makes me feel worse." He grimaced, slowly shaking his head. "Hindsight is a bitch."

Paulo said nothing for a moment. Then, "What did you and your wife argue about?"

Colston turned from the window to meet his probing gaze. "Nothing important. We were supposed to have dinner with friends that evening. When Abby called to remind me, I told her I might be late because I needed to tie up some loose ends at the office. She got angry, and we argued." He smiled ruefully. "We've been married almost fifteen years, but she's never gotten used to my long hours."

Paulo could sympathize. His ex-wife, Jacinta, had complained incessantly about his job and the long hours he'd worked. After two years she'd decided enough was enough, and she'd filed for divorce. There was no doubt in Paulo's mind that if he'd earned the kind of dough Ted Colston was making, Jacinta would have been more forgiving of his busy schedule.

Pushing the cynical thought aside, Paulo asked, "Got any kids?"

A shadow passed over Colston's face. "No. We don't."

Paulo nodded, instinctively sensing that the couple's childlessness was another source of contention in their marriage. He glanced at the five-by-seven photo that sat on a corner of the desk, assuming that the perky blonde with big blue eyes and a bright smile was Abby Colston.

"You mentioned a difficult client," Paulo said, switching gears. "Can you think of anyone who might have wanted to get back at you by harming Maribel? A disgruntled former client? An individual or business you'd successfully litigated against?"

Colston shook his head, frowning. "I've been practicing law for twenty years. In all that time I've never even received so much as a threat."

"Congratulations," Paulo said dryly. "Consider yourself lucky."

"Why? Do you encounter a lot of dead lawyers in your line of work, Detective?"

Paulo smiled faintly. "Ever heard the joke 'The first thing we do, let's kill all the lawyers'?" At Colston's tight nod, he drawled, "Let's just say I've met one or two nut jobs who took the joke literally."

"Christ," Colston muttered under his breath. He raked a hand through his dark hair, unconsciously mussing it. "If Maribel was killed by someone who had a grudge against me, I'll never forgive myself."

"It's just a theory." Paulo paused. "How well did you know Maribel?"

"What do you mean?"

"Did she ever confide in you? Talk to you about personal stuff?"

Colston frowned. "She was my secretary."

"So you took no interest in her personal life? A woman you'd worked with for three years?" There was just enough censure in Paulo's voice to put the other man on the defensive.

"Of course I took an interest in her life. And, yes, she did share some personal things with me."

"Like what?"

"Well, she told me about her family, about growing up dirt poor in Brownsville. I knew she enjoyed dancing as a hobby. One night when we were working late, I caught her doing pirouettes in the copy room. She told me when she was a little girl, she wanted to be a ballerina when she grew up. But her parents talked her out of it, told her she couldn't make a living as a dancer. They wanted her to become a lawyer instead. But Maribel didn't think she could make it through law school, so working as a legal secretary was a good compromise."

"Do you think she was unhappy?" Paulo asked.

Again Colston frowned. "I don't know. I don't think she was. But then again, that's not exactly something you admit to your supervisor when you're working at the top law firm in Houston and making nearly eighty thousand dollars a year."

Paulo whistled softly through his teeth. Damn. Maybe he ought to consider joining the family business after all.

"Do you know if anything unusual had happened to her lately?" he asked. "Strange phone calls or messages, someone she'd noticed turning up wherever she went, things like that?"

"Not that I know of. She didn't seem worried or distracted, and the quality of her work never suffered."

Paulo nodded. "What time did you arrive at the office yesterday morning?"

"Around nine thirty. I had to take my car to the dealership for an oil change. When I got to the office, Kathleen Phillips told me Maribel had called in sick. I listened to the voice mail message she'd left, and sure enough, she sounded awful."

Paulo raised a brow. "Did you have any reason to think she was faking sickness?"

"No, of course not. Maribel was very conscientious. She rarely ever missed work, so I knew she must have been terribly ill." With a flick of his wrist, Colston glanced at the platinum Rolex peeking from beneath the starched white cuff of his shirt. "I don't mean to rush you, Detective, but I have a meeting with a client in an hour, and I still need to figure out Maribel's filing system before we get a temp on board."

"No problem. I understand."

Paulo stood and shook the attorney's hand, giving him his card and the spiel about calling him if he thought of anything else that might help with the investigation.

At the door he deliberately paused and glanced back across the room. "Oh, one more question."

Colston looked wary.

Why? Paulo wondered, intrigued.

"Yes? What is it?"

Paulo hesitated, pretending he'd forgotten what he was going to say. "Never mind. Thanks again for your time."

He left the office and made his way toward the bank of elevators, walking past a labyrinth of mahogany-paneled cubicles occupied by paralegals and secretaries bent over keyboards and talking quietly into phones. More than a few employees were online, catching up on the latest news about Maribel Cruz's brutal murder.

As Paulo reached the elevators he was joined by Julius Donovan. In order to cover more ground that morning, he and his partner had decided to split up to question Maribel's colleagues in the firm's labor and employment law division.

"How'd it go?" Paulo asked as they rode the elevator down to the underground parking garage. "Learn anything interesting?"

"Not really," Donovan said, his gaze trained on the electronic panel above the polished brass doors. "The consensus seems to be that Maribel Cruz was a model employee—smart, dependable, hardworking. A real team player. No one could think of a single person who would have wanted to hurt her. And everyone had an alibi for their whereabouts yesterday morning—they were here, hard at work."

Paulo nodded grimly. "My interviews went pretty much the same way."

"What about Colston?" Donovan asked as they stepped off the elevator and started across the parking garage. "What'd he have to say?"

Paulo gave his partner a quick rundown of his conversation with Ted Colston, concluding, "He seemed pretty shaken up by the whole thing."

"Who can blame him? Based on what one paralegal told me, Maribel was Colston's lifesaver. She did everything for the guy—picked up his dry cleaning, bought his anniversary gifts, scheduled his doctor's appointments, even did his grocery shopping whenever his wife was out of town."

Paulo grunted noncommittally. He couldn't help wondering what else Maribel Cruz had done for Colston while his wife was out of town. It was the oldest of clichés—the handsome, powerful boss having an affair with his hot young secretary, who looked up to him and fulfilled him in ways his wife hadn't done in years. Yeah, it was a cliché. But that didn't make it any less plausible.

When they reached the Crown Vic, Paulo unlocked the doors and climbed behind the wheel. After breakfast he'd swung by Donovan's house to pick him up so they could ride to the law firm together and compare notes afterward.

As Donovan settled into the passenger seat, he said, "I stopped by human resources, asked the manager for a list of all custodial staff and employees that were terminated within the last six months. She said she'd have it for me by tomorrow morning. We can run the names through the system and see if we get any hits."

Paulo nodded, reversing out of the parking space. "As soon as we get back to the station I'm checking in with the cyber guys to see how far they've gotten with Maribel's computer. Who knows? Maybe she sent an e-mail to a friend complaining about some loser following her around."

Donovan snorted. "We should be so lucky."

"Tell me about it."

"Are you gonna keep your family in the loop?"

Paulo shook his head firmly. "I'm doing this by the book. If it turns out that the killer is one of their own employees, I don't want some scumbag defense attorney crying foul because the lead investigator is related to his client's employer."

"Good thinking."

As they emerged from the underground parking garage, Paulo slid on a pair of mirrored sunglasses to shield his eyes from the bright sunlight slanting through the windshield.

Santiago & Associates was housed in an imposing granite and glass high-rise situated in the heart of downtown Houston, one of many skyscrapers that formed the glistening skyline. The suit-wearing, Starbucks-sipping crowd that populated downtown on weekday mornings had thinned after rush hour, replaced by holiday tourists who strolled along Travis Street snapping photos and enjoying the mild November day.

"I met your cousin," Donovan announced, stretching out his long legs in the car.

"Yeah? Which one?"

"Daniela." Donovan let out a long, low whistle. "Damn, why didn't you tell me how fine she is?"

Paulo scowled, charging through a yellow traffic light. "'Cause I didn't want you getting that look in your eyes."

"What look?"

"The one you have right now. The look of a hungry wolf who's just spotted his next meal."

Donovan laughed, his teeth flashing white in his dark face. "Come on, man. You know I'm not like that. I just think Daniela's a beautiful woman, and I wouldn't mind getting to know her a little better. Matter of fact, why don't you put in a good word for me?"

"Hell, no," Paulo said unequivocally.

"Why not? I'd do it for you."

Paulo shot him a dubious look.

Donovan flashed a boyish grin. "Okay, maybe not. But only because you're a notorious womanizer. *I* don't have that rep. So what's the problem?"

"You're too young for Daniela."

"I'm twenty-eight," Donovan protested. "She can't be any more than two or three years older than me."

"Try six."

Donovan did the math. "She's thirty-four?"

"*Sí, señor.*"

"So what? My mom's ten years older than my dad, and they've been happily married for thirty years. What else you got?"

"I'm not hooking you up with Daniela," Paulo growled.

"Why not? Oh, I get it. You think she's too good for me because I'm a lowly cop," he said bitterly.

Paulo scowled. "I don't give a damn about that. Her ex-husband was a rich lawyer, and he was a worthless piece of shit."

"Daniela's divorced?" Donovan asked in surprise.

"Yeah." Paulo cast his partner a sidelong glance. "They met in law school. Their marriage lasted less than half the time it took them to graduate. The guy was a real piece of work. He put her through hell and then some. I don't want to see her hurt again, not if I can help it."

Donovan nodded slowly, thoughtfully. "I understand where you're coming from."

"Good," Paulo grumbled, switching lanes. "So back off."

Donovan chuckled, shaking his head. "I don't know what offends me more, Sanchez. The fact that you don't want me to date your cousin, or the fact that you think I'd actually be stupid enough to hurt her when I know your crazy ass wouldn't hesitate to put a bullet between my eyes."

Paulo grinned narrowly. "If you think *I'm* overprotective, wait till you meet her brother, Rafe—who also happens to be an FBI agent."

Donovan groaned. "On second thought . . ."

Paulo laughed. "Smart man."

As soon as Detective Sanchez left his office, Ted Colston carefully slipped his card into an empty folder, then picked up the phone and dialed Kathleen Phillips's extension. When she answered, he said, "Could you come to my office for a minute?"

There was a pregnant pause. "Be right there."

Ted hung up the phone, his hand trembling slightly.

He blew out a long, deep breath and closed his eyes for a moment, mentally replaying his conversation with Paulo Sanchez. There was something about the homicide detective that had put Ted on edge; something about the way those dark, hawklike eyes had observed Ted's every reaction, as if he were waiting for him to contradict himself.

Ted frowned, his stomach roiling at the thought that he might have given the detective a reason—any reason—to be suspicious of him.

As Kathleen Phillips stepped into his office, he managed a gentle smile for the attractive, well-dressed black woman. "Hello there. How are you holding up?"

Kathleen shrugged, murmuring, "As well as can be expected, I guess."

Ted's smile faltered. Normally when he summoned the paralegal to his office, she strode briskly into the room, notepad in hand, and helped herself to one of the visitor chairs. Now she remained standing by the door, her face impassive, her posture rigid.

Not a good sign.

"I understand how difficult this day has been for you," Ted said kindly. "I know how close you and Maribel were. I should have told you to take the day off."

Kathleen shook her head. "I can't. I have too much work to do."

"One or two days off wouldn't have made a difference."

At Kathleen's surprised look, Ted grimaced. He knew what she was thinking. It was no secret that he was a demanding boss, a relentless taskmaster who'd been known to make his employees work late into the night to complete a project, even on birthdays and holidays. He'd never given a second thought to how they might feel about him, or his management style. Quite frankly he'd never given a rat's ass.

Until now.

Because what Kathleen Phillips thought of him—knew about him—could be his downfall.

"If you wake up tomorrow morning and decide you can't make it in, don't worry," Ted said, his voice full of gentle concern. "If necessary, I'll reassign some of your workload. The others will understand."

"That's very thoughtful of you, Ted. But I'll be fine. It's better for me to be here at work. Helps keep my mind off what happened to Maribel."

"Of course. That's perfectly understandable." Ted paused, then said very casually, "I assume you've already been questioned by Detective Sanchez."

Kathleen nodded. "I spoke to him yesterday. At Maribel's house."

Instead of asking her what she'd revealed to the detective—as he very much wanted to do—Ted said, "I assured him that he has my full cooperation in this investigation. I want the police to find Maribel's killer and bring him to justice."

"So do I," Kathleen said.

Ted wondered if he'd only imagined a note of accusation in her voice. He searched her face for a moment, but her neutral expression gave nothing away.

A knot of apprehension tightened in his stomach.

"Will there be anything else?" she asked civilly.

Ted hesitated, then shook his head. "If you change your mind about coming in tomorrow, just call me."

Kathleen nodded. Without another word, she turned and walked out.

Ted waited several moments, then stood and crossed to the door, closing it quickly. Returning to his desk, he pulled out his cell phone and placed a call to a private investigator he often used for business and personal matters.

"I need a favor," he began without preamble to the gravelly-voiced man who answered the phone.

"I'm listening."

"I need a tail on someone, starting today." Ted paused, glancing toward the closed door before adding, "Her name is Kathleen Phillips. She's one of my employees."

"I see. Care to elaborate?"

"Not at the moment." Ted provided the pertinent information about Kathleen, including her physical description, work schedule, home address, and make and model of her car.

"You have to be absolutely discreet," he said emphatically.

There was a low, mirthless chuckle on the other end. "I've been doing this for twenty damned years. You don't have to tell me how to do my job."

Ted frowned, bristling at the harsh rebuke. "That's not what I meant. The police may have put a tail on Phillips as well, so I just wanted to forewarn you."

"Thanks for looking out," came the droll response. "Will that be all?"

"No." Ted stood and walked to the windows, gazing down at the bustling city street forty stories below. "I also need you to run a background check."

"On who?"

"Detective Paulo Sanchez with the Houston Police Department, Central Patrol. I need to know what kind of skeletons he's got rattling around in his closet."

"Assuming he has any."

"Oh, he does," Ted said with quiet certainty. A cold, narrow smile twisted his mouth. "Everyone has skeletons."

* * *

Paulo and Donovan were nearing the police station on Riesner when the younger detective's cell phone rang. He dug it out of the breast pocket of his sport coat, listened for a few moments, then said briskly, "We'll be right there."

Paulo glanced at his partner as he ended the call. "What's up?"

Donovan's eyes were gleaming with excitement. "One of Maribel Cruz's neighbors just called the station. She says her mother-in-law may have seen someone arriving at Maribel's house early yesterday morning."

Paulo was already making a hard U-turn and heading back toward downtown.

They reached Maribel Cruz's Uptown neighborhood in under ten minutes and parked in front of a two-story redbrick home situated across the street from Maribel's house, still cordoned off with crime-scene tape. The woman who answered the front door was pale and thin, with dirty blond hair that hung limply to her shoulders and gray eyes that regarded them tiredly.

"Thank you for coming so quickly, Detectives," Kristin Ramirez said once they were all settled in the modestly furnished living room. She sat in a leather armchair while Paulo and Donovan claimed opposite ends of an over-stuffed camel sofa. A carved wooden cross was mounted above the fireplace, and several family photographs were neatly arranged upon the mantel. Paulo took note of a good-looking Hispanic man in dress uniform and a small, dark-haired boy with an infectious smile. Kristin Ramirez's husband and child.

"Thanks for calling us," Donovan said, pulling out his

notepad. "Our officers must have missed you last night when they canvassed the neighborhood."

"I wasn't home," Kristin confirmed, tucking her wispy hair behind one ear. Noticing the tiny blue veins that showed through her translucent skin, Paulo wondered, half seriously, how anyone could remain so pale living in a hot, perpetually sunny city like Houston.

"I'm a registered nurse," Kristin continued. "I work nights, from seven to seven, while my mother-in-law stays home with my five-year-old son, Jayden."

"Does she live here with you?" Paulo asked.

Kristin nodded. "She moved in with us a month ago to help me take care of Jayden until my husband returns from Iraq."

"When did he deploy?"

"Just over five weeks ago. His mother has been a godsend. She walks Jayden to and from school every day, helps him with his homework, and makes dinner for us every night. I couldn't have gotten through this time without her, especially since I've been working double shifts for the past week."

"It's nice to have family," Paulo murmured.

Kristin gave him a small, grateful smile.

"How well did you know Maribel Cruz?" Donovan asked her.

"Not very well," Kristin admitted. "We only spoke to each other in passing. By the time she came home from work in the evenings, I was usually leaving for the hospital. But she always seemed like such a nice, outgoing person. I can't believe someone killed her. When my husband's mother came to my room this morning and told me what she saw yesterday, I knew I had to call you guys."

"Was your mother-in-law home last night when we were making our rounds?" Paulo asked.

"Yes. But she never answers the door. Talking to strangers makes her nervous." Kristin hesitated, then added almost apologetically, "She doesn't speak very much English."

"Where's she from?" Donovan asked.

"Mexico." Kristin glanced at Paulo. "I'm hoping you speak Spanish, Detective Sanchez. I'm learning, but I still have a long way to go. Oh, here she is now," she said, rising from her chair as a petite, middle-aged Hispanic woman wearing a floral-print housedress and slippers shuffled quietly into the room.

Paulo and Donovan rose and shook the woman's hand as Kristin performed the introductions. When Paulo addressed Isadora Ramirez in Spanish, her dark eyes lit up with pleasure.

Without releasing his hand, she said warmly, "So handsome! You look like one of my sons. *Te pareces a mi hijo. Está casado?*"

"Mama Ramirez!" Kristin gasped, her cheeks flushing with embarrassment. She smiled ruefully at Paulo. "I'm so sorry about that, Detective. She's not usually so, ah, straightforward."

Paulo chuckled. "It's all right. My grandmother's the same way." To Isadora Ramirez, he replied in Spanish, "I'm not married, señora. But if you're offering your hand . . ."

The woman giggled like a schoolgirl and reached up to pat his cheek. From the corner of his eye, Paulo saw Donovan shake his head and roll his eyes toward the ceiling.

Once they were all seated again, Paulo got right down to business. "Tell me everything you know, Señora Ramirez. *Di me todo lo que sabes.*"

Responding in Spanish, Isadora Ramirez explained, "I was putting the trash outside yesterday morning. It was around five o'clock. As I was walking back to the house, I saw a car pulling into the neighbor's driveway. It was still very dark outside, and the car was black, with black windows."

"The windows were tinted?" Paulo interrupted to clarify.

"Yes. They were tinted. So I couldn't see the driver. I couldn't tell whether it was a man or a woman. The garage door opened, the car went inside, and the door closed behind it."

"Do you know what type of car it was?"

"No. It was too dark for me to see, and I don't know much about cars, anyway."

"You said it was black. Did it have four doors, or two?"

She hesitated, thinking. "Four."

"Did it look expensive?"

"Yes." Mrs. Ramirez smiled wryly. "But then again, where I'm from, most people do not own such vehicles. So all cars look expensive to me."

Paulo smiled a little. "Had you ever seen that car around here before?"

She shook her head. "Never."

"While the garage door was open, did you happen to see Maribel Cruz coming out to greet the driver?"

"No. I didn't see her."

But someone had opened that garage door, Paulo thought. Either Maribel had stepped back inside the house after pressing the keypad on the wall, or the mystery guest had access to the garage door opener. Paulo made a mental note to find out how many of the remote controls Maribel owned.

"Did you see the black car leave?" he asked Mrs. Ramirez.

She shook her head. "After I went back inside, I made

breakfast and got my grandson ready for school. I don't know what time the car left."

Paulo nodded. It had been too much to hope for, anyway. "One more question, Señora Ramirez. Had you ever seen Maribel Cruz with any particular man? Someone who may have visited her more often than others?"

She pursed her lips in thought for a moment, then shook her head. "I've seen different people coming and going. Her friends and coworkers, I think. But I don't know if there was anyone special."

Looking at Kristin, Paulo repeated the same question in English.

"Not that I know of," she replied. "But like I said before, I didn't know her very well. Just because we never saw her boyfriend doesn't mean she didn't have one."

Chapter 7

By 8:15 p.m. the last of Tommie's dance students had departed for the day. After locking the main door, activating the security alarm, and flipping the sign in the window to CLOSED, Tommie returned to the empty studio to clean up. It had been a long, exhausting day with back-to-back classes, including a rigorous two-hour choreography class that had pushed her dancers to the limits of their endurance, and tested her own as well. She looked forward to soaking in a hot bubble bath while sipping from a glass of wine.

As Tommie pushed the dust mop across the hardwood floor, her thoughts strayed to Paulo for the umpteenth time that day. After seven months of living in the same city without so much as a sighting of each other, they had now seen each other two days in a row.

Tommie shook her head, a reluctant smile tugging at the corners of her mouth. Try as she might, she couldn't deny that she'd been secretly thrilled to see Paulo that morning, especially once she'd learned that the gorgeous woman on his arm was his cousin, not his latest conquest. Tommie knew it shouldn't have mattered to her, but it had. Against her better judgment—hell, against her will—

she was irresistibly attracted to Paulo. He did dangerous things to her heart rate, her equilibrium. She had every reason in the world to keep her distance from him. He was completely wrong for her, on every conceivable level. And she was supposed to be focused on running her business and adjusting to life in a new city, not pouring time and effort into a relationship that had no future. Yet the more she told herself that she shouldn't want Paulo, the more she did.

It was downright maddening.

Finished with her task, Tommie put away the dust mop, turned off the lights, and locked up the studio, eager to get upstairs so she could begin unwinding. She could already feel the hot, steamy water seeping into her pores and loosening her muscles, could already taste the chilled wine on her tongue.

Outside, night had wrapped around the old building like a dark, heavy cloak. Wind whistled through the surrounding trees, rustling the dry leaves.

Shaking off a familiar sense of isolation, Tommie made her way down the entrance hall. As she started up the stairwell, the overhead lights flickered. She paused and frowned up at the ceiling. She remembered Paulo warning her yesterday to get the lightbulbs replaced soon. He was right. The last thing she needed was to fall and break her neck because she couldn't see where she was going in the dark stairwell.

But her finances were already stretched pretty thin. She couldn't afford to hire an electrician at this time, unless she could cut corners somewhere in her budget. Making a mental note to balance her checkbook tomorrow, Tommie continued up the stairs. Just as she reached the landing, the lights blinked again. Ignoring a frisson of unease, she slipped her key out of the pocket of her chiffon skirt and reached for the door. She inserted the key in the lock, then froze.

The door was already unlocked.

A shudder ran through her, a chilly finger from her nape to the base of her spine.

Had she forgotten to lock the door when she left that morning?

Or had an intruder been inside her loft?

Tommie's mouth went dry. She stepped away from the door, her heart thudding against her sternum.

Calm down. There's a perfectly rational explanation for this. You had a lot on your mind this morning. You could have easily forgotten to lock the door on your way out. Or maybe Mrs. Calhoun forgot to do it when she took the peach cobbler up to the loft for you this afternoon. She's sixty-five years old. Maybe her memory is failing her.

Yes, that was it, Tommie decided. Mrs. Calhoun, bless her dear heart, had forgotten to lock the door earlier. No harm, no foul.

But as Tommie stared at the closed door, she felt a whisper of foreboding. As if an evil presence awaited her on the other side.

Don't be paranoid. There's no one inside your loft!

Tommie thought of Maribel Cruz, who'd been brutally murdered in her own home. Since learning about her death that morning, Tommie had been trying to convince herself that there was no connection between her and the dead woman, other than the fact that they'd once worked for the same employer and had both relocated to Houston. That certainly didn't mean anything.

Except it wouldn't be the first time one of your coworkers has been murdered.

A rush of wind rattled the glass windowpane in the roof.

The lights flickered.

Tommie swallowed, her nerves stretched taut as wire.

This is ridiculous. You can't stand out here all night. Stop being such a coward!

Tommie drew a deep, steadying breath, then stepped forward.

Suddenly a fist rapped against the main door downstairs.

Tommie nearly jumped out of her skin.

Heart pounding violently, she whirled and raced down the stairwell, nearly tripping over her own two feet. "Who is it?" she called breathlessly through the door.

"It's me. Paulo."

Tommie had never been more relieved in her life to hear another human being's voice. Hurriedly she unlocked the door and swung it open, stopping just short of launching herself into Paulo's arms.

"Hey," she said with as much composure as she could scrape together.

"Hey yourself." As Paulo brushed his windswept black hair off his forehead, his eyes suddenly sharpened on her face. "What's wrong?"

"Nothing," Tommie lied, stepping aside to let him enter, then locking the door behind him. "It's been a long day."

But Paulo wasn't buying it. He reached out and cupped her chin in his big hand, forcing her to meet his dark, penetrating gaze. "You're shaking. What the hell happened?"

Tommie heaved a resigned sigh. Now that he was here, she felt like a fool for letting her fears get the better of her. "It's nothing. My front door was unlocked. I thought maybe someone had broken into my loft, but I don't see how since I've been here all day."

Paulo frowned. He glanced up the stairwell, then back at her. "I'll go check it out. Wait right here."

"But—"

"Don't. Move." His hard tone, as well as his expression, brooked no argument.

Tommie did as she was told, watching as he climbed the stairs to the second landing. When he reached the door, he carefully withdrew his gun from his leather jacket. Leading with the weapon, he disappeared inside the loft.

Tommie waited nervously, her mind racing. What if there really was an intruder in her home? What if Paulo got hurt? Or killed? Maybe she shouldn't have allowed him to go in there by himself. Maybe she should have insisted that he call for backup. If something happened to him, she'd never forgive herself.

Relax! He's a cop, for God's sake. He makes a living chasing and confronting dangerous criminals. He can take care of himself!

After what seemed an eternity Paulo reappeared, holstering his weapon. A wave of relief swept through Tommie even before he announced, "All clear."

"I told you it was nothing," she said, climbing up the stairs to meet him. "Mrs. Calhoun probably forgot to lock the door when she left earlier. I'll ask her about it tomorrow."

"You also might want to check around inside just to make sure nothing's missing." Paulo hitched his chin toward the keypad panel on the wall beside the main door downstairs. "Is your security alarm activated?"

"Yes. It was one of the first things I took care of when I moved into the building."

"Good," Paulo muttered, following her into the loft and

shutting the door behind him. "If I could, I'd pass a law requiring all women who live alone to get an alarm system."

Tommie arched a brow at him. "Isn't that a little sexist?"

Paulo met her gaze directly. "Your equal rights won't mean a damn if you're dead."

"Oh." Tommie swallowed. "I see your point."

"I thought you might." As Paulo removed his jacket, he asked curiously, "What was Mrs. Calhoun doing in your apartment? Does she have her own key?"

"Yes, she does. And she was dropping off a peach cobbler that she baked for me last night."

Paulo shook his head at her. "Man, you *are* spoiled."

"Jealous?"

"A little."

Tommie grinned, reaching for his jacket. "Well, since you were nice enough to check my loft for an intruder, I suppose I could share some of my cobbler with you."

Paulo chuckled dryly. "Your generosity is overwhelming."

Tommie laughed, the tension of the night ebbing from her. She hung his jacket in the hall closet, resisting the urge to burrow her face against the worn leather and inhale his clean, masculine scent.

"Have you had dinner yet?" she asked, slipping off her pointe shoes and padding barefoot into the living room, flipping on lamps as she went. "I was going to heat up some leftover lasagna and toss a salad to go with it. You're more than welcome to join me."

"I don't know," Paulo murmured, coming up behind her as she closed the curtains, shutting out the starry black night. "If you keep feeding me, you might not be able to get rid of me."

Tommie turned from the window, her lips curving in a coy smile. "You make that sound like a bad thing."

Paulo smiled, slow and sexy. "If I didn't know better," he drawled, "I would think you were flirting with me, Miss Purnell."

She laughed softly. "Good thing you know better."

"Hmmm."

"I'm going to take a shower. *Alone,*" she added at the wicked gleam that lit his dark eyes.

"Are you sure you don't need my help? I'm great at washing backs."

"I bet you are," Tommie said, trying not to shiver at the thought of those big, strong hands slathering soap onto her skin and caressing her wet body. *Lord have mercy!*

"Actually," she said, grinning as sudden inspiration struck, "there *is* something you can do for me while I'm in the shower."

Twenty minutes later, Tommie returned wearing a red halter top and dark jeans that sheathed her long, curvy legs like a glove. She'd let her hair down, parting it down the center so that it framed her high cheekbones and those lush, bee-stung lips. Her feet were bare, her toenails painted a deep, racy shade of red.

Paulo, staring at her as she approached, couldn't help wondering if her panties were also red. If she wore any at all.

Dios mio!

As if he hadn't tortured himself enough imagining her in the shower, eyes closed, head flung back, lips parted as water glided over the voluptuous curves of her body. The last thing he needed was to be speculating about the color of her underwear.

When Tommie saw that Paulo had not only fixed the

salad, as she'd asked, but also heated up the lasagna and set the dining room table, her eyes widened with astonished pleasure.

"Wow." She gave him a teasing smile. "So you *do* know your way around a kitchen."

Paulo winked at her. "I know my way around a lot of things."

Tommie laughed, a low, throaty sound that made his stomach clench. "Oh, I don't doubt that."

Paulo pulled out a chair for her, enjoying an eyeful of cleavage as he shamelessly peered down the front of her halter. His hands itched to reach down and cup her plump, luscious breasts, to stroke her dark nipples, to bring them to his hungry, sucking mouth. It took every ounce of self-control he possessed not to act on his urges, to step away from Tommie and take a seat at the small table.

"The salad looks wonderful," Tommie said, reaching for the large ceramic bowl filled with a colorful array of vegetables that Paulo had sliced, diced, and thrown together. "It's not at all what I was expecting."

Paulo chuckled. "Thanks for the vote of confidence."

She laughed, adding a generous helping of salad and lasagna to his plate before serving herself. "Don't worry. I'll never underestimate you again. Wine?" she offered, lifting the bottle of merlot that had been breathing on the table.

Paulo hesitated, then decided one harmless glass of wine wouldn't push him off the wagon. "Sure, why not? I'm off duty."

"Atta boy," Tommie said, filling his glass with a practiced flourish.

As they began eating, Paulo asked conversationally, "So, how was your day?"

"Long. Tiring." She sighed contentedly. "Satisfying."

"Satisfying, huh? In what way?"

"Well, for starters, the students in my beginner ballet class are showing amazing progress. At the start of the semester, one girl in particular was painfully shy and awkward. Her mother enrolled her in the class to help her come out of her shell, but she wasn't terribly optimistic. A few weeks ago she was going to pull Laurie out, but I asked her to be patient and give me more time to work with her daughter. She agreed, and now Laurie is shaping up to be one of my best students. She's poised, confident, and a really quick study. If you saw her, Paulo, you would think she'd been dancing ballet for years instead of just seven weeks."

"Yeah?" Paulo murmured, transfixed by the radiance of her smile, the passion in her voice as she warmed to her subject.

"It's funny," she continued, toying with her salad. "I used to think my sister was crazy for wanting to become a professor, but now I understand what she means when she talks about feeling a sense of accomplishment at the end of the day. When I watch my students overcome their doubts and fears to become good dancers, I feel like I've actually made a difference in their lives. It's an incredible feeling. Powerful." She paused, laughing self-consciously. "Listen to me. I must sound so corny to you."

"Not at all," Paulo said with a quiet smile. "I think you sound like someone who's been lucky enough to find her calling in life. Not everyone can say that."

She beamed at him. "I never thought I'd enjoy teaching as much as I enjoyed performing, but I'm definitely getting there."

"Good. Makes life a helluva lot easier if you love what you do for a living."

"I'll drink to that," Tommie said heartily, raising her wineglass in a toast.

They clinked glasses, their gazes lingering on each other as they sipped the smooth, rich wine.

"So, what about you, Paulo?" Tommie murmured after a moment.

"What about me?" he asked, staring at her plush, dewy lips, knowing they'd feel like heaven beneath his.

"Do you think you've found your calling in law enforcement?"

He smiled grimly. "If I haven't, it's too damned late to do anything about it now."

"That's not true. People your age change careers all the time."

"You calling me old?"

Tommie grinned impishly. "That's payback for telling me yesterday I had a lot of growing up to do."

Paulo chuckled. "You *do* hold grudges, don't you?"

She poked her tongue out at him and he laughed, shaking his head. "And you wonder why I said what I did."

Tommie smiled, idly tracing the rim of her glass with one manicured fingertip. "Just out of curiosity, how old *are* you?"

"Thirty-nine."

"God, you *are* ancient," she teased.

"Keep it up, little girl, and I'll be forced to take you across my knee and spank you."

Her lips curved in a slow, naughty grin. "Promises, promises."

Paulo stared at her for a moment, then shook his head with a low, rough chuckle. "Don't tempt me."

"But it's so much fun," she purred, and damned if his heart didn't knock against his rib cage.

"Jesus," he muttered under his breath, grabbing

his glass and gulping down wine as Tommie laughed, enjoying his reaction.

Setting down his glass, Paulo murmured, "You're a very dangerous woman, Tomasina Purnell."

"*I'm* not the one carrying a gun," she countered smilingly. "And I thought I told you not to call me Tomasina."

He chuckled. "You also told me never to darken your doorstep again. Yet here I am."

"Now that you mention it, what *are* you doing here?"

"I wanted to see you." The words were out before Paulo could stop them.

Tommie looked as surprised as he felt, her dark eyes widening and her lips parting soundlessly. She clearly hadn't expected him to be so candid. Amused, Paulo watched as her sooty lashes lowered and she became absorbed in her meal.

He reached for his own fork, silently counting to ten.

On cue, Tommie said in a carefully measured voice, "I'd be lying if I said I'm not attracted to you, that I haven't wondered what it would be like to make love with you—"

"Incredible."

Her eyes snapped to his face. "What?"

"Our lovemaking. It would be incredible. Like nothing you or I have ever experienced before. Absolutely mind-blowing." He forked up a bite of lasagna. "But please. Continue what you were saying."

Tommie just stared at him. She looked dazed, as if she'd lost her train of thought.

Smothering a grin, Paulo helpfully supplied, "You were about to tell me that no matter how attracted we are to each other, you can't get involved with me. You don't have room in your life for a relationship, and besides, I'm the wrong guy for you." He paused expectantly. "Isn't that what you were about to say?"

"Well, yeah," Tommie muttered, sounding annoyed that he'd beaten her to the punch. "I didn't realize you were a mind reader."

"I don't have to be psychic to know what you were thinking."

"I see." She hesitated. "So you understand where I'm coming from?"

"Of course. You're a beautiful woman who's smart enough to know what is—and isn't—good for you. I commend you for that."

She nodded slowly, searching his face. "And you agree that you're, um, totally wrong for me?"

"Absolutely," Paulo said without hesitation. "Believe me, the best thing you could ever do for yourself is to stay the hell away from me."

Tommie bit her bottom lip, looking intrigued in spite of herself. "Come on. You can't be *that* bad."

Inwardly Paulo grinned. If there was one thing he'd learned about Tommie Purnell, it was that she loved a challenge. The more she was told she couldn't have something, the more she wanted it. And she didn't like having to take no for an answer. Which was why Paulo had to save her from herself.

Or, rather, from *him.*

"Don't worry," he told her with a lazy smile. "As much as it goes against the grain, I won't try to seduce you. I'm going to be a perfect gentleman—even if it kills me."

Tommie stared at him, her eyes narrowed suspiciously. "So you're not going to try to get me into bed?"

"Not even if you begged."

She snorted. "As if *that* would ever happen."

"Maybe not. But if it did—"

"It wouldn't."

A slow, knowing grin spread across Paulo's face. "Never say never."

Tommie lifted her chin, defiance glittering in her eyes. "I've never begged any man for anything, least of all sex. Trust me, I'm not about to start now."

As their gazes held, Paulo couldn't help feeling that a challenge had been issued, the proverbial gauntlet thrown down between them. It certainly wasn't what he'd intended, and God knows he had better things to do with his time, but the idea of putting Tommie's assertion to the test intrigued him. It appealed to his wicked nature, the dominant male in him that enjoyed the thrill of the chase, enjoyed seducing beautiful, unattainable women and coming out the conqueror. And he knew that conquering Tommie Purnell would be the ultimate thrill, like capturing the Holy Grail.

Breaking eye contact with Paulo, Tommie glanced at his empty plate and asked, "Would you like more lasagna?"

"Actually," Paulo said, his mouth curving in a slow, predatory smile, "I'm ready for dessert."

Chapter 8

After dinner, Paulo helped Tommie clear the table and load the dishwasher. As they worked alongside each other, she told him, "By the way, you never did answer my question."

"Which one?"

"I asked you whether you'd found your calling in law enforcement."

"I wouldn't say that," Paulo muttered.

Tommie glanced up from pouring liquid soap into the dishwasher dispenser, one brow arched. "Why not? You don't like being a cop?"

He grimaced. "I don't know if *like* is the word I'd use. I don't like having to inform parents that their son or daughter is never coming home again. I don't like watching murderers walk because of a fucked-up criminal justice system. I don't like having to accept the reality that no matter how hard I work, some crimes will go unsolved." He shrugged, crossing his arms over his broad chest as he leaned back against the counter. "I'm not saying I hate being a cop. But there's definitely a hell of a lot *not* to like about the job."

"Yes, I see what you mean," Tommie murmured,

sobered by his words. "I'm sorry. I guess that was a silly question."

"Not at all." He smiled wryly. "I just wish I had a better answer for you. Something warm and fuzzy."

She made a face. "Good thing I've never been much of a warm and fuzzy person." She hesitated, studying him for a moment. "Any progress on finding Maribel Cruz's killer?"

"No," Paulo said flatly.

"I've been thinking about her ever since you told me what happened. I've had classes all day, so I haven't had a chance to watch the news or look up the story on the Internet. Do you still have her photo on you?"

"Yeah. Where's my jacket?"

"In the hall closet."

As Paulo went to retrieve the photo, Tommie wiped down the granite countertops with a dishcloth soaked in lemon disinfectant. When she'd finished, she turned off the kitchen light and headed into the living room.

Paulo joined her on the sleek red sofa. "Here," he murmured, passing her a five-by-seven photograph.

Tommie took one look at the beautiful, smiling Hispanic woman and let out a surprised gasp. "Oh my God! I remember her!"

"Do you?"

Tommie nodded quickly. "She came backstage after my performance that night. She was really excited to meet me, told me she was a big fan of mine. Her supervisor had given her tickets to the show for her birthday. Front-row seats. I remember telling her how lucky she was to have such a thoughtful, terrific boss, and she agreed. Of course, what else could she do since he was standing right there?"

"Who?"

"Her boss."

Paulo's gaze sharpened on Tommie's face. "Maribel Cruz's supervisor attended the performance with her?"

"Yeah."

"Are you sure?"

"Of course. I thought it was a bit weird at the time, the two of them being there together, but Maribel said that he'd come in place of her friend, who'd canceled at the last minute." Tommie shrugged dismissively. "None of my business."

"Do you remember his name?" Paulo demanded.

Tommie frowned, sorting through her memory bank and coming up blank. "Sorry," she said, shaking her head. "I'm great at remembering faces, but not names."

"So if you saw a photo of the guy you'd recognize him?"

"I might. I recognized Maribel," she pointed out.

Paulo glanced around the room, his gaze landing on the laptop computer Tommie had left on the breakfast counter after checking her e-mail messages that morning. "Do you mind?"

"Go ahead," Tommie said, but Paulo was already up and striding purposefully across the living room to retrieve the laptop.

He brought it back to the sofa and sat down. Tommie scooted closer to him, peering over his shoulder as his fingers flew across the keyboard, quickly pulling up the sleek, modern Web site belonging to his family's law firm. Three clicks later, Tommie found herself staring at a photograph of a handsome, dark-haired man with Nordic-blue eyes and a politician's plastic smile. She recognized him at once.

"That's him," she told Paulo. "That's the man who was with Maribel that night."

"You're positive?"

"Absolutely." She did a quick scan of the bio page, her lips pursed. "Ted Colston. The name doesn't ring a bell, but I definitely remember his face." She chuckled dryly. "I'm not surprised that he's a lawyer. He looks like something out of Central Casting, doesn't he?"

Paulo didn't respond. He was staring intently at the computer screen, his thick black brows furrowed together, a muscle working in his jaw. Tommie could see the wheels turning.

"So what does this mean?" she prodded. "Do you think Maribel was sleeping with her boss?"

Paulo frowned. "I don't know."

"But you suspect she was, don't you? I mean, why else would Ted Colston have agreed to accompany her to the performance if they weren't having an affair?"

"Maybe it started that evening," Paulo muttered, thinking aloud.

"It's possible. I don't remember sensing any sexual tension between them, but then again, that was over nine months ago. It's a miracle I remembered as much as I did about that evening. When you're on the road six months out of the year, performing four or five nights a week, people and places become a blur after a while."

"I can imagine," Paulo said, looking at her. "Yet Maribel Cruz and Ted Colston stood out in your memory."

Tommie shrugged. "They were both attractive. Superficial or not, attractive people are more memorable." She paused, tipping her head thoughtfully to one side. "Haven't there been studies on that?"

Paulo chuckled dryly. "Probably," he said, closing the laptop and gently setting it down on the suede ottoman. As he leaned back against the sofa cushions, Tommie couldn't help noticing the way the stretchy fabric of his turtleneck molded the hard, sculpted muscles of his chest and abdomen. She had a sudden urge to reach beneath the hem of his shirt and run her hands along his warm male flesh. She wondered if his chest was smooth, or covered with a dusting of soft black hair.

"So what're you going to do?" she blurted before her mind began to wander.

"About?"

"About Maribel Cruz and her boss. If they were having an affair, do you think it's possible that he killed her?"

"Anything's possible," Paulo said grimly.

"You have to find out, one way or another."

"I will." And Tommie could tell by the determined glint in his dark eyes that he would.

Tucking her long legs beneath her on the sofa, she began conversationally, "When I first started working at Thorne and Associates, the attorney I reported to couldn't keep his eyes off my ass. Sometimes he'd call me into his office just so he could stare at my butt as I walked out. And he didn't even try to pretend he wasn't doing it! It got so bad that I started buying longer suit jackets just to cover my butt, especially if I was wearing something formfitting like a pencil skirt. But it didn't take him long to catch on. He started turning up the thermostat on our floor, making it so uncomfortable that I'd either have to remove my jacket or go home drenched in sweat every day."

Paulo shook his head in disgust. "Asshole."

Tommie gave a short, humorless laugh. "Tell me about it. And he didn't limit his offensive behavior to just leering at me. He was always complimenting the way I looked and making suggestive comments. After two months of putting up with his crap, I'd had more than enough. But I didn't want him to get just a slap on the wrist. I wanted him gone. So instead of filing a complaint with human resources, I went straight to the top of the food chain."

Paulo arched a surprised brow. "You went to Crandall Thorne?"

"Damn straight. See, Mr. Thorne wasn't your typical CEO. He was very hands-on, involved in the hiring and firing of every employee at his firm. Of course, now that he's remarried and semiretired, I don't know if he's still that active in the business. But he definitely was when I worked there."

"So what'd you tell him?"

"I told him the truth, that I was being sexually harassed by one of his senior attorneys and if he didn't do something about it, I'd have no choice but to file a lawsuit against the firm. Mr. Thorne calmly pointed out to me that my case would be jeopardized by the fact that I hadn't gone through the proper channels for filing a sexual harassment complaint. But it didn't matter. I had proof. The day before I'd used my cell phone to secretly record my boss commenting on my breasts. I played the video for Mr. Thorne, then told him in no uncertain terms that I wouldn't stop at just suing the law firm, I'd go straight to the media with my embarrassing little recording. I think Mr. Thorne was privately impressed with me. He admired my *cojones*, and I knew how much he detested bad publicity. At the end of the meeting he asked me to give him twenty-four hours to handle the matter. When I arrived at work the next morning, Mr. Thorne called me into his office and informed me that my boss had been fired, and I'd been reassigned to another attorney. A woman, this time." Tommie flashed a coolly triumphant smile. "I never had any more problems after that. And to this day, Mr. Thorne and I still keep in touch. He sends me holiday and birthday cards, and he and his lovely wife even flew to New York three years ago to attend one of my performances and take me out to dinner afterward."

Incredulous, Paulo stared at her for a long moment, then threw back his head and roared with laughter. "Damn, woman! Remind me never to piss *you* off."

Tommie grinned. "Too late. You already have."

"Me?"

"Yes, you."

"What'd I do?"

Tommie shrugged. "It's not any one thing in particular," she reluctantly admitted. She shook her head at him. "You just know how to push my buttons."

His mouth curved in a wolfish smile. "You make that sound like a bad thing."

She laughed, recognizing the line she'd used on him earlier. "Good one."

"I thought so." Gazing at her, Paulo said in a low, husky voice, "You have the sexiest laugh I've ever heard. Makes me want to do all sorts of wicked things to you."

Tommie's belly quivered, his words sending a rush of tingling heat through her body. Before she could stop herself, she felt her lips curving in a bold, sultry smile. "Well, what's stopping you?"

His gaze darkened, drifting to her mouth. "I promised to be a gentleman, remember?"

"Some promises were meant to be broken," Tommie murmured.

The words were barely out before Paulo leaned over and crushed his mouth to hers. She lost her breath. Desire tore through her body like the sharp crack of a whip. His lips were even softer than she'd imagined, his kiss hot and demanding. Her lips opened eagerly beneath his, taking his tongue deep. He tasted incredible, like wine and something uniquely male, uniquely him. He explored the inside of her mouth with slow, sensual strokes, licking and tasting her until she moaned with pleasure. He sank one hand into her hair, the other splaying across the curve of her spine to hold her tightly to him. Tommie gasped, the feel of his hard, muscled chest against hers an electric shock to her senses. When Paulo shuddered, she knew she wasn't alone.

With a rough, guttural sound he seized her and lifted her onto his lap to straddle his strong, muscular thighs. She shivered, staring into the molten depths of his eyes, feeling the heat of his thick erection against her crotch. It ignited her blood, made her dizzy with need as her hips moved, writhing against him.

Paulo swore under his breath, his voice harsh and ragged. Cradling her face in his big hands, he kissed her hard and hungrily. She kissed him back with equal fervor, threading her fingers through the thick, silken brush of his hair. As his lips moved across her cheek and down her throat, her head fell back and her eyes drifted closed. He kissed her collarbone and suckled the beating pulse at the hollow of her throat, his hot breath whispering over skin he'd made wet with his tongue.

Tommie felt like she was drowning, drowning in sensation and a dark, savage need that threatened to consume her. She'd been kissed a thousand times, had been intimate with more men than she cared to recall. But she had never experienced anything like this before. It was pure madness. Paulo Sanchez was a rogue, a shameless womanizer. She barely knew him, didn't trust him, wasn't even sure she liked him. But she wanted him. *God*, how she wanted him.

So she didn't protest when his hands scaled her heaving rib cage and cupped her breasts. Her startled gasp turned into a breathless moan as he kneaded and caressed her through the cotton halter, making her nipples tighten until they stung.

"You like that?" he whispered huskily, watching her face.

Tommie nodded helplessly, not trusting her voice.

Paulo leaned forward and kissed her, a deep, carnal kiss that drugged her senses. His tongue slid along her open lips, probing and dancing against hers, drinking in her shallow, panting breaths. Breaking the kiss, he grasped the hem of her halter top and yanked it up over her head, flinging it aside. The cool air on her skin was quickly chased away by the smoldering heat of his gaze, roaming hungrily across her breasts.

"God, you're beautiful," he uttered hoarsely, his voice filled with reverence.

Tommie trembled with arousal, watching as his dark head descended to her naked breasts. He pressed them together with callused hands, drawing both nipples into his hot, silky mouth. She cried out, heat flooding her loins, swelling her clitoris. He used his tongue, lips, and teeth to tease and torment her, causing her spine to arch and her hands to grip the back of his head, holding him tightly against her.

"Oh God . . . Paulo . . ." she whispered, aching for more, desire pounding relentlessly through her body.

The urge to feel his bare skin against hers made her reach down and tug his turtleneck from the waistband of his trousers. She splayed her hands against the broad, muscular expanse of his chest. He shuddered beneath her touch. His pectorals were firm and sinewy. His skin was so hot it scorched her. She ran her fingertips down his flat abdomen, following the arrow of soft black hair that dipped below his waistband. His stomach muscles contracted, and he made a low, growling sound deep in his throat.

In one fluid motion he had Tommie on her back, covering her with the solid weight of his body. His heart thudded against hers, and his breathing was as rapid as her own. She looped her arms around his neck as he seized her mouth in a fierce, ravenous kiss.

Reaching between their bodies, he cupped her sex through her jeans. She moaned, arching against his hand, opening her legs. She wanted him inside her, wanted him to assuage the urgent, pulsing ache between her thighs. When he lowered his head, flicking his tongue over her breast, she whimpered his name.

"What do you want, *querida*?" he murmured, the deep, masculine timbre of his voice vibrating through her. He blew gently on the taut, swollen bud of her nipple, and she shivered uncontrollably. "Do you want me?"

"Yes," Tommie breathed.

"Do you want me to make love to you?"

What the hell kind of question was that? "Yes," she whispered, impatiently this time.

Lifting his head, Paulo smiled, a dark, seductive smile, and slid his tongue slowly across her trembling lower lip. "All you have to do," he murmured silkily, "is say please."

It took several moments for the meaning of his words to sink in. When it did, Tommie stiffened. She stared into his dark eyes glittering with wicked triumph, and her insides turned to ice. Angrily she shoved at his chest, and with a low chuckle Paulo lifted himself off her and sat on the edge of the sofa.

"Tommie—"

"Shut up and hand me my shirt," she snapped.

He hesitated, then reached down and retrieved her discarded halter from the floor. She snatched it out of his hand, seething with fury and humiliation as she yanked on the shirt and pulled it down over her still-tingling breasts.

When she'd finished she sat up, smoothing her disheveled hair away from her burning face. All the while her mind mocked her with the arrogant boast she'd made over dinner: *I've never begged any man for anything, least of all sex.*

Never say never, Paulo had warned, his eyes glinting with challenge.

God, she was such a fool. He'd played her. And she never even saw it coming. She'd been on the verge of doing exactly what she'd sworn she would never do: beg a man to make love to her.

"Look, I didn't mean to upset you," Paulo said, a trace of regret in his voice.

Lifting her chin, Tommie looked him square in the eye. "You've proved your point," she said in a voice chilly enough to freeze water at fifty paces. "Now get out."

Paulo held her gaze a moment longer, then blew out a deep breath and rose to his feet. Tommie was right on his heels as he retrieved his leather jacket from the hall closet and shrugged into it.

At the front door he paused and glanced down at her. "If you think I wasn't right there with you the whole time," he murmured, "think again."

Tommie was unmoved. "Go to hell, Paulo."

He inclined his head, then turned and sauntered out.

When he was halfway down the stairs, Tommie called out, "And, Paulo?"

He glanced back at her.

Standing in the doorway, she said coldly and succinctly, "In case you misunderstood me the first time I said it, let me make myself perfectly clear. I don't want you coming back here again. I mean it. Stay the hell away from me."

Paulo gave her a long look. Then suddenly his mouth curved in a slow, knowing grin.

Tommie gaped at him, shocked and infuriated by his response. "What's so damned funny?"

"I know you *wish* you meant what you just said, but we both know better."

"What the hell are you talking about? I *do* mean what I just said!"

Paulo shook his head slowly, his gaze straying to her breasts, then easing back up to her face like a lazy caress. "Your mouth says one thing, *querida*, but your body doesn't lie."

Tommie opened her mouth to protest, but no words came forth. She made a strangled, ineffectual sound in her throat, then stepped back and slammed the door with shuddering finality.

As she leaned against it, trembling with outrage, Paulo's parting words reverberated through her brain, taunting her. *Your mouth says one thing, but your body doesn't lie.*

What the hell was that supposed to mean? Tommie fumed, glancing down at herself. At the sight of her nipples protruding prominently through her shirt, she closed her eyes and groaned.

Because she knew Paulo had been right.

She could rant and bluster about him staying away from her until she was blue in the face, but nothing would change the fact that she wanted him. Badly. And as long as her body betrayed her, as it had tonight, Paulo would always have the upper hand.

The arrogant bastard knew it, too.

A sudden knock on the door made Tommie jump. Gritting her teeth, she yanked the door open and glared at Paulo. "What?" she snapped.

"I realize you were in a hurry to get rid of me," he

drawled, a smile playing at the edges of his mouth, "but I thought you should know I'm not going anywhere until you come downstairs and lock up behind me."

Tommie stared at him for a moment, then took great satisfaction in slamming the door in his face.

Paulo was still chuckling quietly to himself as he slid behind the wheel of his police cruiser fifteen minutes later, which was how long Tommie had left him cooling his heels in the main foyer before she'd finally emerged from her loft to see him out.

As he cranked the ignition, he didn't bother turning on the heat, though it was cold enough for him to see his breath. He was hoping the frigid night air would cool the fire that had been raging in his blood for the past hour—hell, for the past *twenty-four* hours, ever since he'd laid eyes on Tommie for the first time in four years.

He hadn't intended to kiss her when he showed up at her loft that evening. After being immersed in homicide investigations all day, he'd needed a break. Needed time to be a regular person instead of a cop. He'd sought Tommie out because he enjoyed her company, although he knew he was playing with fire every time he went near her.

Tonight, of course, had been no exception.

Paulo shook his head, shoving away the needle of guilt that pricked at his conscience when he thought of how their latest encounter had ended. So he'd wounded her ego and pissed her off a little—okay, *a lot*. So what? It wasn't as if he'd gotten her all worked up, then rejected her. Hell, he'd wanted nothing more than to peel off her skintight jeans and drive his aching erection into the hot, slick clasp of her body. He'd wanted her sweaty and clinging to him, her thighs clamped around his waist, cries of ecstasy erupting from her throat with each deep, penetrating thrust.

Paulo shifted uncomfortably in the driver's seat and dragged his hand over his face, a grim smile curving his mouth at the irony of his situation. In the process of proving to Tommie that he could make her hot for him, he'd deprived himself of the pleasure of making love to her. Talk about a hollow victory.

With one last look at the old brick building, Paulo backed out of the parking space and swung onto the quiet street lined with giant oaks. As he passed under a streetlamp he glanced out the window, thinking of how remote this corner of town was, with its abandoned warehouses and empty lots. Although Tommie's property boasted easy access to all of the major highways, her closest neighbors were a good ten minutes away. Which made Paulo decidedly uneasy, considering the fact that she was a single woman who lived alone.

Like Maribel Cruz.

Paulo frowned at the thought, his mind flashing on images from last night's dream. Maribel's ghostly face transforming into Tommie's. Tommie's whispered plea for help.

Let it go, man. It was just a dream. It doesn't mean anything. Stop acting like your superstitious eighty-year-old grandmother, who believes every dream is a message from God!

As Paulo slowed to a stoplight, his cell phone rang above the crackling police band radio. He dug the phone out of his jacket pocket and answered, "Sanchez."

"Why didn't you tell me that one of my parents' employees had been murdered?" Rafe Santiago demanded.

Paulo grimaced. "Not my fault. Your mom didn't want you to worry."

"What the hell? I had to learn about the murder on the evening news—a whole day *after* the fact."

"What, you been hiding under a rock or something?"

"No, Korrine and I just got back from a training program in Quantico." Rafe was the assistant special agent in charge at the San Antonio FBI field office, while his wife, Korrine, was quickly establishing herself as one of the Bureau's best and brightest agents.

"What the hell happened to Maribel Cruz?" Rafe asked.

Paulo gave his cousin a quick rundown of the case, describing the grisly crime scene and his subsequent interviews with the victim's coworkers and neighbor. "We've got no suspects or motives so far," he said, "because it doesn't appear that Maribel had any enemies. But the killer obviously had a reason for writing the word *liar* on her bedroom wall. It's some kind of clue or message."

"Any leads on the early-morning visitor?"

"Not yet. While we were at the neighbor's house, we got on the computer and pulled up photos of just about every four-door model you can think of. Mrs. Ramirez—the witness—thought a BMW could be the car she saw, but she wasn't completely sure. And the harder we pushed, the more unsure she became."

"Damn," Rafe muttered. "You think Maribel had a guy over yesterday morning?"

"Probably." Paulo wheeled around a corner and cut across two lanes of downtown traffic, light at this time of night. "My gut tells me the coworker, Kathleen Phillips, knows more than she's letting on."

"What do you mean?"

"When I questioned her yesterday, I got the feeling she was hiding something. If you ask me, I think she's trying to protect someone."

"Like who?"

"Her boss, Ted Colston. I think he and Maribel were sleeping together."

"What? Where'd you get an idea like that?"

Paulo hesitated, knowing he'd open himself up to speculation and innuendo if he revealed that Tommie was his source. "I found out that Colston took Maribel to a dance performance in February."

"Are you kidding me?" Rafe sounded thunderstruck—and disgusted. "What the hell was Colston thinking, taking his secretary out on a date?"

"Good question. Supposedly he bought Maribel two tickets to the show for her birthday. When her date canceled on her, Colston graciously stepped in. Helluva guy, huh?"

"Jesus," Rafe muttered. "My parents aren't gonna be too thrilled to find out one of their partners was having an affair with his secretary. They've both been very vocal in discouraging that type of behavior at the firm."

"Imagine how they're going to feel if it turns out that Colston killed Maribel," Paulo said dryly.

"Aw, *hell*."

Paulo smiled grimly. "If it's any consolation, Colston doesn't own a BMW, or even a black vehicle. Neither does his wife. I checked—just in case he might have been driving her car yesterday."

"That doesn't let him off the hook," Rafe said. "You still think Kathleen Phillips is hiding something. Maybe Colston threatened to fire her if she told anyone about his affair with Maribel."

"I thought about that. If Kathleen and Maribel were as close as she claims, she'd definitely know if Maribel was sleeping with their boss."

"She had to be involved with someone. Who else would've been visiting her that early in the morning?"

"Whoever he was, he had access to her house. I looked through her mortgage papers, and sure enough, she owned two garage door openers. One is missing and unaccounted for."

"And her family doesn't know anything?" Rafe asked.

"Nope. They hadn't seen Maribel since last year when she went home for Christmas. They said she didn't call or visit very often. Seems her job was her life. She only had a couple of friends outside of work. We spoke to both of them this afternoon, but they weren't much help, either."

"When's the autopsy?"

"Tomorrow. The ME promised he'd get it done first thing in the morning."

"Couldn't bully him into doing it today, huh?" Rafe drawled.

Paulo scowled. "Not for lack of trying."

Rafe chuckled dryly, all too familiar with his cousin's reputation for intimidating medical examiners into producing speedier autopsy results. While Paulo was a master at finessing witnesses and outsmarting suspects, he'd never acquired the diplomacy needed for dealing with the officials who were integral to his homicide investigations. As a result, he was always butting heads with them.

"Let me know if you need any help from the Bureau," Rafe offered. "I can run interference with our Houston office."

"Thanks. I'll let you know." Glancing in the rearview mirror, Paulo noticed a black Nissan Altima that was following a little too closely. He frowned, tempted to flip on his siren and lights and pull the idiot over for tailgating. But even as the thought crossed his mind, the other driver slowed down, as if suddenly realizing how close he'd come to getting slapped with a ticket.

"It's too quiet there," Paulo said, shifting his gaze back to the dark stretch of road. "What'd you do with Korrine and the kids?"

"Kaia and Ramon are in bed. Korrine's on a three-way call with her mother and sister, talking about the wedding."

Paulo chuckled. "So Stella's still going through with it?"

"Looks that way."

Rafe's mother-in-law was a two-time widow on the verge of tying the knot with husband number three. After years of stringing along with her lover—a photographer half her age—Stella Beaumont had finally agreed to marry the poor bastard. Paulo hoped to God that Benicio Delgado knew what he was getting himself into. Stella was high-maintenance, an ex-socialite who'd been shunned by all her society friends in the wake of a scandal involving her late husband. The woman's life had been filled with more drama than the television *novelas* watched religiously by Paulo's mother and aunts.

"Just let me know when and where the wedding will be held," Paulo said, grinning, "and I'll be there."

Rafe snorted. "I bet you will. You're the only guy I know who actually looks forward to attending weddings just to get laid."

Paulo's grin widened. "Hey, what can I say? When you're forced to go to as many weddings as I have, you learn to make the most of every opportunity."

Rafe laughed. "Spoken like a true libertine."

"I'll take that as a compliment."

"You would. Anyway, I'm gonna call my parents and offer my condolences."

"I'd appreciate it if you didn't discuss the specifics of

the investigation with them," Paulo said. "One whiff of impropriety or conflict of interest, and my ass will be tossed off the case."

"I know the drill. But at least keep *me* posted, will ya?"

"As if I have any other choice," Paulo retorted before hanging up.

As he shoved the phone back into his pocket, headlights flashed in his rearview mirror. He glanced up, annoyed to see the dark sedan bearing down on his bumper once again. *What the hell?* Paulo thought, scowling. Didn't this asshole know he was tailgating a damned cop? Was he *trying* to get pulled over?

Paulo hit the brakes and watched with perverse satisfaction as the other driver swerved to avoid colliding with him. Just to taunt him, Paulo yanked the steering wheel to the left and veered into the next lane, cutting off the Nissan. The driver slammed on his brakes, his tires screeching loudly in protest. As Paulo continued down the road, the Nissan backed off, slowing to a crawl until it fell several car lengths behind the Crown Vic.

Paulo shook his head in amused disgust. Damned Houston drivers.

Minutes later when he exited onto the I-59 ramp heading south, the Nissan kept going. Good, Paulo thought darkly. He wasn't in the mood for playing traffic cop tonight.

All he wanted was to get home. The sooner he got home, the sooner he could take a cold shower.

An image of Tommie flashed through his mind, her dark hair fanned out across the red sofa, her lips moist and swollen from his kisses, her beautiful, luscious breasts heaving beneath his ravenous gaze.

Paulo groaned, his groin tightening painfully.

Oh yeah. A cold shower was *definitely* in order when he got home.

The colder, the better.

As the stranger watched the dark Crown Victoria accelerate onto the southbound ramp, his blood pounded in his ears, drowning out the noise of the freeway. His fingers gripped the steering wheel so tightly the bones in his knuckles protruded.

How he would have loved to use his car as a battering ram against the police cruiser, forcing it off the ramp and sending Paulo Sanchez plunging to his death. How satisfying it would have been to watch the cop's bloodied, broken body pulled from the wreckage of his vehicle and loaded into the coroner's van.

But, no, he had other plans for the detective.

By the time he was through with him, Sanchez would pray for death.

And I'll be happy to oblige him, the stranger thought with a cold, sinister smile.

Two hours earlier he'd been incapable of smiling.

From his hiding spot behind the tree outside Tommie Purnell's building, he'd watched as the detective arrived in his unmarked cruiser. Sanchez had gotten out and walked to the main door with that trademark cocky swagger, oozing with the confidence of a man who knew he wouldn't be turned away. She'd let him inside, had led him upstairs to her cozy, beautifully decorated loft.

And the stranger had spent the next two hours torturing himself with images of Tommie screwing Sanchez, her voluptuous body glistening with sweat as she writhed beneath him, clawed his back with those long nails, panted, and screamed his name while he drove into her.

Rage burned through his veins, and his stomach twisted violently at the pain of her betrayal. *Lying, cheating whore!*

Her beauty was as treacherous as her faithless heart. She used it as a weapon of seduction, teasing and enticing, luring her unsuspecting victims to their downfall.

But soon she would atone for her transgressions.

Soon she would pay the ultimate price for her seductive promises, her careless whispers.

Your time is coming soon, he thought, staring determinedly through the windshield. *Oh yes, very soon.*

Chapter 9

"My time's almost up—"

A collective groan of protest went up from the faculty, staff, and students who had packed the large campus theater that morning to hear about Tommie's exciting career with a world-renowned dance company, her travels around the country, and the popular artists who now relied on her choreography skills for their music videos.

"Thank you for that," Tommie said, smiling at the audience. "I'm glad you're enjoying our talk, but if I keep you too long, your other instructors will have me permanently banned from the university."

"Most of them are here, too!" someone called out, drawing a round of hearty laughter.

Tommie grinned. "Then allow me to petition on your behalf for extra credit."

More laughter filled the hall.

After another moment Tommie continued. "Before I let you go—and I'm afraid I must—I just wanted to share some final advice for all of you dance majors out there. Aspiring professional dancers need to go above and beyond to gain a cut above the competition. The reality is that dancers today are stronger, more flexible, and more talented than ever. It takes real focus and dedication to get that extra edge you *will* need to get noticed.

"When I auditioned for the Blane Bailey Dance Company, the odds were seriously stacked against me. For starters I was already considered over the hill at twenty-nine—far too old to be trying to break into the world of professional dancing, especially in New York City. I'd never belonged to a professional dance company, and unlike most of the other dancers I was competing against, I hadn't trained at the School of American Ballet, Juilliard, or any other prestigious institution. And, um, in case you haven't noticed, I'm not exactly built like a ballerina."

Someone gave a low, appreciative whistle.

Tommie grinned. "Just for that, *I'll* give you extra credit!"

The audience laughed.

"The point I was making," she continued when the noise died down, "is that even though I faced impossible odds, I understood what I had to do in order to achieve my dream of dancing for the company. I had made the necessary sacrifices and put in the hard work so that when the moment of truth came, I was ready.

"Do you know the major difference between an amateur and a professional? The professional has devoted her life to doing what she loves, while many amateurs just dabble on the side. They're often left wondering why their skill level isn't on par with the masters', and they end up looking for shortcuts that'll make them as good as the pros. Let me just tell you right now, there are no shortcuts. Becoming a skilled dancer takes more than talent. It takes hours of practice a day, study, good teachers, and a good learning environment. You already have excellent teachers and an excellent learning environment here at the university. The rest is up to you.

"I'll leave you with one of my favorite quotes by legendary choreographer George Balanchine. 'I don't want people who want to dance. I want people who have to dance.' If the latter describes you—if you enjoy dancing so much that you've become obsessed, that you absolutely *have* to dance—then don't let anything or anyone stop you. Thank you, and *au revoir*."

The darkened theater erupted into thunderous applause.

As Tommie smiled and bowed gracefully, she was transported back in time, back to when she'd still been a member of the Blane Bailey Dance Company and the audience had been filled with the enraptured faces of people who'd come just to see her. They'd presented her with elaborate bouquets, a profusion of lilies wrapped in tissue and tied with satin ribbons, her due for her featured role in the company's evening performance. After accepting the flowers at center stage, she'd gestured to her fellow cast members, encouraging them to join her in taking another bow because she'd learned the hard way never to hog the limelight.

But those days are behind you, Tommie reminded herself. *You have a great life, inspiring and teaching a future generation of dancers*.

News of her guest lecture to dance students at the University of Houston had generated such a buzz that the faculty coordinator had been forced to open the event to the entire university, which meant moving the venue to the largest theater on campus. To Tommie's surprise, every seat in the house had been filled.

Afterward, a throng of people lined up to speak with her, shake her hand, and tell her how much they had enjoyed her lecture and demonstration. She answered more questions, dispensed more advice, passed out her business card, posed for photos with attendees, and autographed whatever they asked. Some presented her with playbills and programs from her dance performances. One chemistry professor even had a copy of an old catalogue from her brief stint as a lingerie model; the cover featured her in a provocative pose, dressed in skimpy red underwear. The young instructor nearly swallowed his tongue when Tommie, with a naughty grin, scribbled her name in the blank space between her parted legs. He was still blushing and stammering his thanks as she turned away to grant an interview to a local reporter who'd shown up to cover her visit.

Her host didn't come forward until the last attendee had departed the theater. Renee Williams was the university's director of dance. She was an attractive, forty-something woman with skin the color of mocha and the limber, flat-chested physique of a ballerina. She'd danced in New York City and abroad until injury forced her into early retirement. Instead of wallowing in self-pity, she'd founded a contemporary dance company and embarked on a second career in academia. She and Tommie had been introduced to each other by Zhane, who knew "everyone who was anyone" in Houston's happening dance community. The two women had hit it off right away; within a day of meeting each other, Renee had invited Tommie to be a guest lecturer at the university.

"I think that went rather well," she remarked, approaching Tommie.

"I'm so glad they enjoyed the presentation."

"*Enjoyed* it? Honey, they couldn't get enough of you! Or didn't you notice the way they were hanging on to your every word?" She grinned broadly. "I'm going to be the most popular faculty member on campus for bringing you here today."

Tommie laughed. "From what I could tell, you already *are* the most popular professor on campus. Your students cheered when you walked out onto the stage. Thanks for that glowing introduction, by the way."

"I meant every word. I really want you to be our artist in residence this spring, Tommie. Promise me you'll give it some thought."

"If she does, I'll be offended."

Tommie and Renee turned as they were joined by a tall, lean man with dark eyes, an aristocratic nose, prominent cheekbones, and a thin black mustache over a wide, generous mouth. His bronze skin hinted at Native American ancestry, as did the silvery black hair secured in a ponytail at the base of his neck. He was elegantly casual in a gray cashmere sweater and fine wool trousers. He was carrying a bouquet of flowers and smiling warmly at Tommie, whose own smile had slipped a notch. Richard Houghton, the artistic director at the Houston Metropolitan Dance Company, always had that effect on her.

Planting her fists on her nonexistent hips, Renee demanded of him, "And why would *you* be offended if Tommie agreed to do our spring residency?"

"Because I've been trying to convince her to come dance for me," Richard said without breaking eye contact with Tommie, "and she keeps turning me down. If she accepts your invitation, then I'll have no choice but to take her rejection personally."

"You really shouldn't," Tommie said evenly. "As I've told you before, I enjoy running my own dance studio. It's nothing personal."

"Can't blame a guy for trying. These are for you," Richard said, passing her the bouquet. "I ran out to get it while you were tending to your adoring fans. I was fortunate enough to find a florist near campus."

"Thank you, Richard," Tommie murmured, accepting the flowers. "They're lovely."

"Then they're perfect for you." When he smiled, his eyes crinkled charmingly at the corners. "I thoroughly enjoyed your lecture this morning. The stage loves you."

"That's what I've been telling her," Renee chimed in. "She's a natural. I've been inviting guest artists to the university for years. Not only was this the biggest crowd I've ever seen. It was also the first time no one left before the presentation was over."

"Except for Zhane, apparently," Tommie said, smiling wryly as she read the text message Zhane had sent to her cell phone. Had to run, sugarplum. Ma called. More family drama. You were fabulous. Call you later!

"I saw him as I was heading out to the florist," Richard said. "He looked really stressed, said he might have to miss rehearsal tonight."

Tommie frowned. "Did he tell you what was going on?"

"No, but I assumed it had something to do with his family. Which is nothing new."

"I know that's right," Renee muttered, shaking her head in grim disgust. "Between his mother always hitting him up for cash, his sister's baby-daddy drama, and his brothers being in and out of jail, I don't know how Zhane keeps his sanity. Those people are lucky he hasn't cut them off. Do you know they've never been to any of his performances? Not one!"

"Zhane has a very big, forgiving heart," Tommie murmured, typing a response to his message. R U OK? Will check on u later.

"He's very lucky to have such devoted friends." Although Richard's words encompassed both women, he only had eyes for Tommie. "Will you be at Friday night's performance?"

Annoyed by the hopeful look on his face, Tommie replied, "I'll be there. Renee and I are coming together," she added, linking her free arm through the other woman's, half wishing they could pretend to be lovers so that Richard would back off.

"Actually," Renee hedged, looking guilty, "I'm bringing a date that evening."

"*What?*" Tommie exclaimed, staring at her. "You didn't tell me that!"

"I was going to. After your lecture this morning." Renee grinned sheepishly. "Just in case you tried to cancel on me."

Tommie scowled, shaking her head at her. "I can't believe you're dumping me. That's messed up."

Renee laughed, squeezing her arm. "Please don't be mad at me. It couldn't be helped. I met him two weeks ago, and we've yet to go on our first date. We've been trying to coordinate our busy schedules, and Friday night was the only time that worked for both of us." She hesitated, biting her lower lip. "Want me to ask him if he has a friend?"

Before Tommie could respond, Richard interjected dryly, "I'm sure Tommie doesn't need your help finding a date. Besides, she doesn't need to bring a companion to the performance. She's there to support her friend Zhane."

"Of course," Renee agreed, mouth twitching as she met Tommie's gaze. Tommie didn't have to guess what the other woman was thinking. *Could he be more obvious?*

Resisting the urge to roll her eyes, Tommie said to her, "Since you're abandoning me on Friday, you can make it up to me by treating me to lunch. I've got some time before I have to get back to the studio for my next class."

"I'm one step ahead of you," Renee said, grinning as they headed from the theater. "I already made reservations at Sylvia's."

"Mmmm. How'd you know I was in the mood for some enchiladas?"

"Girl, when it comes to food, you're easy to please." Renee hesitated a moment. "Richard, would you like to join us for lunch?"

Tommie's heart sank. She held her breath, hoping he would turn down the invitation.

He divided a glance between her and Renee, clearly tempted to accept the offer. But after an agonizingly prolonged moment he shook his head. "Thanks, but I'd better take a rain check. I have a lot of things to do before rehearsal tonight."

Tommie was so relieved she could have pirouetted across the stage. Instead she smiled and thanked Richard for attending the lecture and buying her a bouquet.

"You're welcome," he said, gazing hungrily at her.

Once they reached the bustling parking lot, Tommie told Renee she'd drive to the restaurant so that Renee wouldn't have to lose her parking space. As soon as they were inside Tommie's sporty red Mazda, Renee burst out laughing.

"Oh my God! What on earth did you do to poor Richard?"

"Hell if I know," Tommie muttered, backing out of the parking space.

As she pulled away, she glanced in the rearview mirror and saw Richard standing by his car, staring after the Mazda with an odd little smile on his face.

A chill went through her.

She thought of what she'd told Zhane yesterday. *It's like he knows a secret about me, or thinks he does. It's creepy.*

Had Richard Houghton learned about her past? Tommie wondered uneasily. Did he know about the scandal that had derailed her professional dancing career?

If so, what did he intend to do about it?

Paulo began his day at the morgue going over Maribel Cruz's autopsy results with the Harris County deputy chief medical examiner. Dr. Wilhelm Garrett was in his late fifties with thinning brown hair, a gray beard, and a ruddy, congenial face that belied his brusque, humorless temperament. He was a busy man who lacked the patience for dealing with the inquisitive detectives who attended the autopsies. The only people Garrett preferred to deal with were the ones who came to him on steel gurneys, the ones who couldn't talk back or ask questions.

Like Maribel Cruz.

Working a tasteless wad of Nicorette gum around his mouth, Paulo surveyed the body that had been pulled from a massive stainless steel refrigerator bearing other corpses. Dark brown eyes stared dully from slitted, bluish lids. Her neck was laid wide open to her spine, the strap muscles severed. Spaced narrowly apart over her left chest and breast were eleven stab wounds that had been inflicted in rapid succession, one right after the other, with a force so brutal that there were hilt marks in her flesh. She'd incurred multiple cuts to her forearms and hands while trying to ward off the slashing motions of a wide, sharp blade.

Paulo listened impassively as Dr. Garrett recited the other injuries Maribel had sustained, injuries not visible to the naked eye. Her left lung had been punctured seven times. Her carotid arteries were almost transected. Her aortic arch, pulmonary artery, heart, and pericardial sac were penetrated.

In short she'd suffered a very violent, painful death.

"No fibers or skin cells were embedded beneath her fingernails," Garrett explained, his voice a flat monotone in the cold, sterile room reeking of antiseptic solution and formaldehyde. "No presence of seminal fluid. However, there *was* vaginal penetration."

"She was raped?"

Garrett shook his head. "Based on my examination, I would say the intercourse was consensual."

"You're telling me the victim had sex on the morning she was killed?" Paulo asked, thinking of the mystery visitor in the unidentified black car.

"That's right. There were traces of latex and a spermicidal lubricant inside her vagina, so it's safe to assume her partner used a condom." Garrett frowned. "Not that the condom would have done her any good."

Paulo looked sharply at the doctor. "What do you mean? Why wouldn't it have done her any good?"

Garrett met his gaze levelly. "Because she was already pregnant."

When Kathleen Phillips found Paulo standing on her doorstep thirty minutes later, not only did she look surprised. She looked petrified.

"Detective Sanchez. W-what are you doing here?"

"You weren't at the office," Paulo said calmly.

"I know. I didn't feel up to going in this morning. Ted told me to take the day off." She swallowed, gathering the edges of her silk robe together as she eyed Paulo warily. "Is something wrong?"

"I need to talk to you. Mind if I come in?"

Kathleen hesitated, looking like she minded very much. But after another moment she stepped aside to let him enter.

Paulo swept a cursory glance around the tiny studio apartment, which was located in the heart of downtown, not five minutes from the law firm. He took in the contemporary furnishings and African art collection before returning his attention to his hostess. She had removed the silk scarf from her head and was self-consciously finger-combing her dark hair, trying to make herself presentable. Nothing could be done for the small bags under her eyes.

"Would you like some coffee?" she offered politely.

"No, thanks."

Once they were seated in the living room, Paulo said bluntly, "You've been holding out on me, Miss Phillips."

She didn't meet his gaze. "I don't know what you're talking about."

"I think you do. And I think you know why I'm here."

Kathleen said nothing.

Undeterred, Paulo said, "You lied when you told me Maribel wasn't seeing anyone. You knew she was, but you didn't want to tell me because you're trying to protect the other person. Why?"

Dark, haunted eyes lifted to his. "Because I promised I wouldn't tell, and I can't go back on my word."

"Even if the person you're protecting is a cold-blooded killer?"

Kathleen flinched as if he'd struck her. "You don't know that," she said faintly. "You don't know that he killed her."

"And you don't know that he *didn't*." Paulo leaned forward intently. "I just came from the morgue. Do you know what I found out? I found out that Maribel was pregnant. So it's highly possible that whoever you're covering for killed not only your friend, but her unborn child as well. Are you telling me you're okay with that?"

Kathleen was staring at him with a stricken expression. "Maribel was . . . pregnant?"

"Yes." Paulo paused, searching her face. "You didn't know?"

She shook her head, tears welling in her eyes. "She didn't tell me. I had no idea."

"She may have just found out herself," Paulo said grimly. "The ME says she was only five weeks pregnant."

"Oh God." Kathleen squeezed her eyes tightly shut, as if to block out the devastating news. "Poor Maribel," she whispered tearfully. "She must have been so scared and confused. I should have been there for her. I should have helped her."

"You still can," Paulo said quietly. "All you have to do is tell me who Maribel was sleeping with."

Kathleen inhaled a deep, shuddering breath. Slowly her eyes opened and settled on Paulo's face. "It was Ted. She was having an affair with Ted."

"How long?"

"Since February." She shook her head ruefully. "And it's all my fault."

Paulo frowned. "What do you mean?"

"It started the night of the ballet."

"Their affair?"

Kathleen nodded stiffly. "Ted knew how much Maribel loved ballet, so when he found out that the Blane Bailey Dance Company was coming to Houston, he bought her tickets to the show for her birthday. I was supposed to go with her that night, but I had to cancel because of a family emergency. Maribel didn't want to go alone, so Ted offered to take her. He said his wife was out of town on a business trip, so he'd just be going home to an empty house. Maribel wasn't entirely comfortable with the idea of being seen in public with her boss, but she felt a little sorry for Ted, and since he'd been nice enough to buy the tickets, she figured what the hell?

"The next morning at work when I asked her how everything went, all she said was that she'd enjoyed the ballet and met one of her favorite dancers. When I asked her if she'd felt awkward being there with Ted, she just laughed it off, wouldn't really give me a straight answer. I should have known then that something was up, but I didn't give it too much thought after that."

"When did you find out about the affair?" Paulo asked.

"About a month later. I'd gone back to the office one night to get a file that I'd forgotten to take home. As I neared my cubicle, I heard voices coming from Ted's office. I figured since Ted was there burning the midnight oil, I could ask him a few questions about a report I was working on. I was about to knock on the closed door when I realized that he was in there with Maribel." Kathleen swallowed, nervously massaging her slender throat. "She and Ted were, ah, making plans for the weekend. His wife was going out of town again, this time to visit her sister. Ted was telling Maribel how they were going to soak in the Jacuzzi together, sip champagne by the fire, and, well, you get the gist of it."

Paulo smiled grimly. "Did you confront them?"

"God, no. I was so shocked and disgusted, I wouldn't have known what to say to them. I got my file and left before they came out of the office and saw me. But I couldn't hold my tongue for very long," she admitted, grimacing. "The next day over lunch, I told Maribel what I'd overheard and asked her what the hell was going on between her and Ted. She told me everything, then swore me to secrecy. She was more worried about Ted getting fired than losing her good reputation at the firm. And she said that Ted could pull some strings for me, get me a promotion."

"So she bought your silence," Paulo said flatly.

"No," Kathleen fired back, bristling. "I told her I didn't want any damned favors from Ted, I was fully capable of moving up in the company on my own merit. I told her she was wrong for sleeping with a married man, and she probably wasn't the first secretary Ted had screwed around with."

"Ouch," Paulo murmured.

Kathleen frowned. "I was very upset. We both were, to the point where we stopped speaking to each other for three whole weeks. I considered asking to be transferred to another division, but I didn't want to raise any red flags. And then Maribel came to me and apologized for the hurtful things she'd said during our argument. She told me she understood why I was so angry and disappointed in her, but she'd never meant to sleep with Ted that night. One minute they were baring their souls to each other, the next minute they were in bed together. Maribel fell in love with Ted, and she didn't know what to do about it."

"Did she ever ask him to leave his wife?" Paulo asked.

Kathleen shook her head. "She wanted to, but she didn't think he would. And she told me she didn't want to be the home-wrecker who destroyed his marriage. Except she didn't use that word," she added wryly. "She used the Spanish word she'd grown up hearing her mother and aunts use to describe women who screwed around with married men. I'm trying to remember what it was. . . ."

"*Puta?*" Paulo offered helpfully. "*Tramposa? Rompe-hogares?*"

Kathleen snapped her fingers. "That's the one! *Rompe-*

hogares." She smiled ruefully. "I'm sorry. I know I'm totally mangling the pronunciation."

Paulo chuckled dryly. "That's okay. It's not a very nice word."

"That's what Maribel said." Kathleen's smile turned mournful. "God, I miss her. I still can't believe she's gone. And now I can't even look at Ted without—" She broke off abruptly, shaking her head.

"Without what?"

Kathleen dropped her gaze to her clasped hands in her lap. She said nothing.

"Do you think Ted could have killed Maribel?" Paulo probed.

"I don't know," Kathleen mumbled miserably. "I don't want to believe he did, but I just don't know. Maribel didn't talk much about their relationship. She knew it was a touchy subject. But based on the things she did tell me, Ted really seemed to care about her. He enjoyed being with her."

"Do you think his wife ever found out?"

Kathleen shook her head vigorously. "Maribel told me that if Abby had known about the affair, she would have confronted Ted immediately. She was just that kind of woman."

"So you don't think it's possible that Abby Colston killed Maribel, or hired someone else to do it?"

Kathleen stared at him, aghast. "I—I don't know. God, I hope not. I've met her before, talked to her at different company functions. She certainly doesn't *seem* capable of murder. But I guess anything's possible. Maribel didn't seem capable of sleeping with another woman's husband, but she did."

Paulo didn't know how to respond to that, so he

didn't. He thanked Kathleen for her time and reminded her to call him if she thought of anything else.

As she walked him to the door, she said, "I guess in a weird way, Detective, we're both partially to blame for Maribel becoming involved with Ted."

Paulo turned, frowning quizzically at her. "How's that?"

"Well, if I hadn't canceled on her that night, Ted wouldn't have gone to the ballet with her, so they wouldn't have slept together. And if *you'd* given her the time of day at the fund-raiser dinner three years ago, who knows? You two might have been happily married by now."

Paulo could only stare at her.

Kathleen laughed softly. "I take it by the stunned look on your face that you didn't think I remembered you, and you obviously had no idea that Maribel was totally into you that night. So much so that she talked about you for an entire week after meeting you. She thought about asking your cousin Naomi to play matchmaker, but she didn't want to seem desperate, especially to her employer."

Paulo remembered what Naomi had told him two days ago about Maribel. *She said you were a hunk, but you didn't seem particularly interested in her.*

His mouth curved in a small, self-deprecating smile. "Maribel was better off not getting involved with me. I make a lousy boyfriend, an even worse husband. If you don't believe me, just ask my ex-wife."

Kathleen smiled sadly at him. "If given the choice between having her heart broken or losing her life, I'm sure we both know which choice Maribel would have made."

Her words struck close to home, stirring painful memories Paulo had spent the past six years trying to outrun. Memories of the woman who'd once made the mistake of trusting him, loving him, only to be brutally murdered.

"Detective Sanchez?" Kathleen's gaze was troubled.

"I'm sorry for saying that. I wasn't trying to make you feel guilty or anything."

"Don't worry," Paulo murmured softly. "Me and guilt, we go way back."

Ted Colston was in the conference room with a client when his cell phone rang. He excused himself and hurried down the corridor to his office to return the important call.

"Just thought you should know that the cop just left Kathleen Phillips's apartment," said the brusque voice on the other end.

Ted felt the blood drain from his head. Detective Sanchez had already interviewed Kathleen the day of Maribel's murder. If he was talking to her again, that could only mean one thing. He thought she knew something.

"Have you made any progress on Sanchez's background check?" Ted demanded.

"Still working on it."

"Damn it, Nolan. I'm running out of time."

"I'll call you when I have something. Sit tight." The line went dead.

Ted swore viciously as he hung up the phone. Damn Hank Nolan! The man behaved as if *he* were the paying client! He'd never made any secret of his dislike for Ted, and the feeling was mutual. If Ted could have found a better private investigator—someone more cooperative, more *pliable*—he would have gotten rid of Nolan a long time ago. But Hank Nolan was the best in the business. If anyone could get the goods on Paulo Sanchez, Nolan could.

Because if the detective had discovered Ted's secret, as he suspected, he would need all the bargaining power he could get.

Chapter 10

Tommie hated hospitals.

She'd learned at an early age to associate them with bad things. When she was five years old, her mother had been taken to the hospital after complaining about severe abdominal cramps; later that day she'd miscarried the baby brother Tommie and her sister, Frankie, had looked forward to welcoming into the family.

At eight years old, Tommie had been rushed to the emergency room after she broke her arm attempting a complicated ballet move. It had been months before she was allowed to dance again.

And when she was a senior in high school, her favorite grandmother had passed away after suffering a massive stroke. She'd died while Tommie and her family were en route to the hospital. To this day, Tommie was haunted by the fact that she'd never had a chance to say good-bye.

As far as she was concerned, hospitals represented nothing but fear and pain, sickness and death. She avoided them at any and all costs. But when Zhane called her just as her last class was ending and told her that his teenage nephew had been shot in an altercation, Tommie didn't think twice about jumping into her car and rushing over to Ben Taub General Hospital. Her best friend needed her, and that was all that mattered.

When she arrived at the hospital, she'd found Zhane and his family gathered in the waiting room in the intensive care unit. Some were huddled together on chairs while others talked on cell phones or paced restlessly. In a corner of the room, Zhane was quietly consoling his distraught sister, whose fourteen-year-old son, Kadeem, had been shot by her boyfriend when he'd intervened in the couple's argument that morning. After gunning down the teenager, Chauncey Booker had panicked and fled. Though the police had issued a BOLO—be on the lookout—for his arrest, he still remained at large.

When Tommie appeared in the doorway of the crowded waiting room, Zhane glanced up and gave her a weary smile. Before he could make his way over to greet her, a heated argument erupted between his two younger brothers and another man Tommie didn't recognize. Someone threw a punch, and before Tommie knew it, fists were flying. More angry shouting ensued. A woman screamed. Zhane's mother, a heavyset dark-skinned woman, swayed precariously on her feet. The small child propped on her hip covered her eyes with her tiny fists and began wailing in earnest.

Without thinking Tommie marched across the room, kissed Zhane's startled mother on the cheek, and swept the crying little girl into her arms.

"We're going for a walk," Tommie informed Vonda Jeffers, who had already turned her attention to the noisy brawl involving her sons. Tommie made it out of the waiting room just as two hospital security guards came running down the hall to investigate the ruckus.

Tommie took Zhane's niece Khadija to the children's playroom on the first floor, where the three-year-old contented herself with stacking multicolored building blocks on top of one another and sliding down the plastic slide with other children. The noise made by the giggling, frolicking preschoolers was an improvement over the screaming and cursing that had peppered the waiting room from which Tommie had just escaped.

After a while Khadija, tired of playing, wandered over to where Tommie sat and climbed into her lap. She was an adorable little girl with skin the color of Hershey's chocolate and a round, cherubic face. It was a face that could bring tears to the eyes of any childless woman past the age of thirty.

Tommie kissed the top of the girl's head and instinctively hugged her closer. "Don't wanna play anymore?" she asked.

Khadija shook her head slowly. "I wanna go home."

"I know, sweetie. And you will soon. Are you hungry?"

Another listless shake of the head.

"Are you sure?"

"Yeah. I already ate."

"You did? What'd you eat?"

The girl mumbled a response that Tommie managed to decipher as macaroni and cheese and applesauce. "Did you eat here at the hospital?" she asked.

Khadija nodded.

Tommie suppressed a mild shudder. Another thing she hated about hospitals. Cafeteria food.

She glanced down to find a pair of big dark eyes regarding her solemnly.

Tommie smiled. "What's up, Kay-Kay?"

"Do you like my uncle Zhane?"

"Sure do. He's my best friend."

"Kadeem says Uncle Zhane only likes boys," Khadija said matter-of-factly.

Tommie made a strangled sound of shocked protest. What on earth was that crazy boy thinking, telling a three-year-old child something like that?

A woman seated nearby, overhearing Khadija's pronouncement, raised a brow at Tommie. Tommie stared the woman down until she looked away, frowning with disapproval.

"Is it true?" Khadija pressed.

Tommie faltered, casting about desperately for a safe, age-appropriate answer. Damn it. This was why she didn't teach children under twelve. They were too inquisitive. Too unpredictable.

Choosing her words carefully, Tommie said, "Your uncle Zhane has a lot of friends who are boys, so yes, technically he does like boys. We both do, actually. Boys are a lot of fun."

She held her breath, silently praying that Khadija wouldn't ask her to elaborate. For several moments the little girl said nothing, her fine brows furrowed together as she mulled over Tommie's words. After an interminable length of time she nodded, seemingly satisfied with the explanation. Tommie inwardly breathed a sigh of relief.

In a small, tremulous voice, Khadija asked, "Is Kadeem gonna die?"

Tommie's heart constricted. "Oh, sweetie," she whispered, her arms tightening protectively around the child's soft, warm body. "The doctors are taking good care of your brother. As soon as they finish patching him up, you'll be able to see him."

Khadija stared up at her, her small chin quivering. "I don't want him to die. Mommy will be sad."

"I know, baby. Everyone will be. And your brother knows that. So he's going to do his very best to get better so he can come home again."

"Do you really think so?"

"Of course," Tommie said pragmatically. "He doesn't really have a choice. Who else is going to tease you and yell at you for playing his Nintendo Wii?"

Khadija grinned, her expression brightening. "Kadeem *does* do that."

"I know. Your uncle Zhane tells me all about it." Smiling, Tommie ran an appraising eye over the child's mussed black hair. "Want me to braid your hair?"

Khadija bobbed her head eagerly.

Tommie dug inside her Louis Vuitton handbag for a comb and went to work on the little girl's hair, parting it evenly down the middle of her scalp and braiding it into two smooth, thick plaits. When she'd finished, she removed a compact mirror from her purse and passed it to Khadija.

"I look like a princess," the girl breathed, admiring her reflection.

Tommie smiled softly. "That's because you are."

Khadija beamed with pleasure.

When Zhane found them fifteen minutes later, Tommie was teaching Khadija how to do a *plié* while several other children looked on in wide-eyed fascination. Khadija ran to her uncle, who scooped her into his arms and planted a loud kiss on both cheeks, making her giggle. With his free arm he drew Tommie into a hug, whispering in her ear, "Thanks for coming, sugarplum."

"You don't have to thank me," Tommie whispered back, smiling.

"I know how much you hate hospitals, so yeah, I do."

She laughed.

As they left the playroom, Khadija wiggled out of her uncle's arms and raced ahead of them to press the elevator button.

"How's Kadeem doing?" Tommie asked Zhane.

He grimaced. "Still in critical condition. They were able to remove the bullet, but Kadeem lost a lot of blood. The doctor says it'll be touch-and-go for a while."

"Oh, Zhany, I'm so sorry."

"Me, too," he said darkly. "I don't know who to be madder at. My sister for having such lousy taste in men, or my hotheaded nephew for getting in the middle of their stupid argument. I know Kadeem was only trying to stick up for his mama, but if I've told that boy once, I've told him a thousand times to stay the hell out of grown folks' business. And don't even get me started on that no-good son of a bitch Chauncey. What kind of man shoots his girlfriend's unarmed son, then doesn't even have the decency to stick around to make sure he didn't kill the poor kid? Fucking coward. He'd better hope I don't find his sorry black ass before the police do."

"Still no word on his whereabouts?"

"Not yet. We've been calling the detective assigned to the case, but he's been giving us the runaround all day. You know how it is," Zhane said, his lips twisting cynically. "The shooting of a young black man in the Third Ward is nothing unusual. The police figure we should be used to this shit by now."

Tommie said nothing. She knew he was right, yet she couldn't help feeling a pang of guilt at the thought of Paulo, who seemed like a genuinely good cop. Not that he deserved her loyalty after what he'd done to her last night.

Don't even go there, she told herself. *You've been doing good all day, keeping yourself too busy to think about Paulo and the way he humiliated you. Don't get sidetracked!*

"Thanks for getting Kay-Kay out of there," Zhane said, lowering his voice as they neared the elevator, where the three-year-old was happily pressing both call buttons.

"It's a damn shame when so-called grown-ups can't control themselves in public. Now you know I'm all for a good knock-down, drag-out, but even I have enough sense to draw the line at fighting in hospital waiting rooms and funeral homes. And before you even ask, yes, my family *has* gotten into fights at funeral homes."

Tommie grinned, thinking of her own sane, boring family and how scandalized they would have been if they'd witnessed the brawl in the waiting room upstairs. "Who was that man your brothers were fighting?"

Zhane made a sour face. "That was Kadeem's father, Lavar. He ain't worth a damn, either, but at least he cared enough to show up after my sister called and told him his son had been shot. Not that he's been any comfort to Zakia since he arrived. All he's been doing is bad-mouthing her and blaming her for what happened to Kadeem. You would think he'd know better than to call her a dumb bitch in front of her brothers, who both have criminal records." Zhane shook his head in angry disgust. "Zakia's feeling guilty enough about what happened this morning. The last thing she needs is deadbeat daddy number one making her feel worse."

"Is he still up there?" Tommie asked.

"Yeah, but he won't be for very long if he utters one more word about Zakia. Anyway, hospital security warned us that if another fight breaks out, we're *all* getting tossed out. You'd be the only one here when Kadeem wakes up from surgery. Which he probably wouldn't mind," Zhane added with a wry smile. "You know that boy's got a big ol' nasty crush on you."

Tommie sighed. "If only he were four years older. Then I could do something about that."

Zhane laughed just as the elevator doors slid open

to reveal his mother. "There you are!" she exclaimed, stepping forward. "I've been looking all over for you."

"Why? Is it Kadeem?" Zhane asked anxiously.

"No, no, everything's fine," Vonda Jeffers assured him, absently lifting Khadija into her arms. "I just wanted to borrow a few dollars to buy a pack of smokes. I left my purse in the car."

Zhane shook his head, muttering under his breath as he reached into his back pocket for his wallet. He pulled out a twenty and handed it to his mother, who smiled sweetly and patted him on the cheek. Her long, lacquered nails were painted a bright shade of red that matched her lipstick, and she wore a tight knit dress with a plunging neckline that barely contained her ample breasts.

"You take such good care of your mama," she cooed to Zhane. "I don't know what I'd do without you."

"God only knows," Zhane grumbled, stabbing the elevator button. "Why don't you take Kay-Kay back upstairs with you? I'm going to grab a cup of coffee with Tommie, and then I'll be right up."

"Okay." Vonda turned, smiling at Tommie. "You're looking good, baby girl. Is that a new Louis Vuitton bag?"

"No, ma'am. I've had this for a while."

"Oh?" A calculating gleam lit the other woman's dark eyes. "Well, if you ever decide to replace it—"

"For God's sake, Ma, she's not giving you her purse," Zhane snapped in exasperation.

"It never hurts to ask," Vonda said, sounding slightly miffed as she boarded the waiting elevator with her granddaughter balanced on her hip. As Tommie blew a kiss at Khadija, Vonda said to her son, "I'll see you upstairs."

The elevator doors had barely closed on her pouting face before Zhane threw up his hands in disgust and huffed, "With a mother like that, is it any wonder I turned out gay?"

Tommie couldn't help laughing. The same thought had occurred to her the very first time she'd met Vonda Jeffers, a greedy, manipulative woman who could drain the life out of anyone faster than a vampire. "Poor Zhany. Come on, let me buy you a cup of coffee."

"I don't want any coffee," he groused. "I just said that to get rid of her."

Tommie grinned. "Then let's just go for a walk," she suggested, tucking her arm through his and steering him down the tiled corridor bustling with hospital staff and visitors bearing flowers and get-well balloons.

When Zhane's temper had cooled, he said, "I'm sorry I had to skip out on you this morning."

Tommie waved off the apology. "Don't be ridiculous. You had a family emergency."

"Too bad Richard wasn't so understanding," Zhane said sourly. "When I called to tell him I'd have to miss rehearsal tonight, he didn't sound too pleased. He made a point of reminding me that we have a performance on Friday—as if I needed a reminder—then he got off the phone without so much as a word about my nephew. No expression of sympathy or support. No offer to say a prayer or light a candle. Nothing."

Tommie scowled. "Asshole. And to think I was starting to feel guilty for disliking him so much."

"You were?" Zhane sounded surprised.

"Well, he took time out of his busy schedule to attend my lecture. He didn't have to do that. And he brought me a beautiful bouquet. After I got home and put the flowers in a vase, I thought to myself, maybe he's not so bad after all." Tommie frowned. "So much for that."

"He's *not* that bad," Zhane countered. "I mean, yeah,

he could have shown a little more compassion when I told him about Kadeem, but I know he has a lot on his mind. The company is very important to him, and he's got a lot riding on his shoulders as our new artistic director."

"Stop making excuses for him," Tommie chided.

Zhane chuckled. "I'm not making excuses. You're just hard on Richard because you don't like him. But I know who you *do* like," he said, sending her a look filled with sly insinuation.

Tommie averted her gaze. "I don't know what you're talking about."

Zhane laughed. "Nice try, sugarplum, but I was there, and I saw the way you were with that hot-tamale detective. I don't think I've ever seen you blush as many times as you did yesterday morning. Look, you're even doing it now!"

"I am *not* blushing," Tommie grumbled. "Black women don't blush."

"*You* sure as hell are." Zhane grinned knowingly. "I don't blame you one bit, honey. Paulo Sanchez is too damned fine for his own good. If I thought there was the slightest chance in hell of drafting him to play for my team, I'd try to steal him from you."

Tommie snorted. "He'd have to belong to me in order to be stolen from me. And he doesn't."

"Doesn't what?"

"Belong to me."

"That can change."

"Who says I want it to?"

Zhane laughed. "Who're you trying to fool, sugarplum? You and I both know you want that man. I wasn't going to mention this, but when Daniela and I were standing in line yesterday, we glanced over and saw you and Paulo gazing into each other's eyes while your hand rested almost lovingly on his cheek. It was as if you'd both forgotten where you were, like you were the only two people in that restaurant. It was obvious to me and Daniela—and anyone else watching—that you and Paulo were totally into each other."

Tommie swallowed, feeling transparent and hating it. "Fine. So we're attracted to each other. That doesn't mean anything."

Zhane arched a dubious brow. "Are you sure about that?"

"Yes." She heaved an impatient sigh. "Look, Zhany, I know you enjoy playing matchmaker, but don't waste your time on me and Paulo. We're completely wrong for each other."

"How do you know that?"

Tommie scowled. "For starters, he's a total man-whore. He uses and discards women like it's nothing more than a game to him," she said bitterly, resentment stirring within her when she remembered the way Paulo had ruthlessly played her last night, kissing and caressing her, teasing and tormenting her until she'd been on fire for him, ready to do whatever he asked of her. She'd come to her senses just in the nick of time, but the damage had already been done, her humiliation complete.

Zhane drawled humorously, "Sounds like what he needs is the right woman to come along and teach him a lesson."

Tommie stopped midstride, staring at her friend.

And just like that, she knew how she would get her revenge against Paulo.

Chapter 11

It was after nine o'clock by the time Paulo decided to call it quits for the day and shut off his computer. As he exited out of the crime-scene files he'd spent the better part of the afternoon reviewing, he knew the gruesome images would remain seared into his brain long after the computer screen had gone black.

On the drive home he ran through a mental checklist of the day's developments. Kathleen Phillips's revelation about an affair between Maribel Cruz and Ted Colston had placed the attorney squarely at the top of the suspect list, which, unfortunately for him, included no other names at the moment. Colston had motive for murdering his secretary. Not only were they sleeping together; he'd gotten her pregnant. Maribel could have made real trouble for him if she'd ever decided to tell his wife or employer about the affair. Maybe she'd even threatened to do so, provoking Colston into killing her.

After leaving Kathleen Phillips's apartment, Paulo had driven straight to the law firm to confront Colston. But when he arrived, he was told that the attorney was out of the office for the rest of the day, supposedly tending to an urgent matter involving one of his clients in Austin.

Incensed, Paulo had instructed the nervous secretary, a temp, to notify her boss that if he left town again without clearing it with Paulo first, there would be hell to pay.

On his way to the elevators he'd run into Daniela, who had just emerged from a meeting in the conference room. She'd grabbed his hand and dragged him into her office, closing the door behind them.

"I know you're not at liberty to discuss the case, so I won't even bother asking you for an update," she said without preamble.

"Thanks," Paulo muttered, still simmering with frustration over Colston's disappearing act.

"Anyway, that's not the reason I pulled you in here." Daniela rested a shapely hip against her large mahogany desk and crossed her arms over the front of her pale silk blouse. "You've been avoiding me."

"No, I haven't."

"Yes, you have. Ever since we left the Breakfast Klub yesterday morning, you haven't returned any of my phone calls. And I think I know why." Her hazel eyes twinkled with mischief. "You don't want me to ask you about Tommie Purnell."

Paulo didn't bother denying it. His cousin knew him too well.

"My God, Paulo, she's fucking gorgeous!"

Amused, he shook his head at her. "Anyone ever tell you that you curse like a sailor?"

Daniela grinned. "Who do you think I learned it from? Anyway, don't try to change the subject. Why didn't you ever tell me about Tommie?"

"There's nothing to tell."

"Like hell. There were enough fireworks between you and that woman to burn down the restaurant! And sitting across the table from you two was like being in the path of a wildfire. Every time your shoulders brushed, or your eyes met, or you reached for the saltshaker at the same time, I thought I'd have to hose you both down." Daniela chuckled, shaking her head in amazement. "No wonder you've been having dreams about her."

Paulo scowled. "It wasn't that kind of dream."

"Whatever you say." She grinned impishly. "I told Mom about her."

Paulo groaned. "Damn it, Daniela—"

"She wants to meet her."

"No."

"Why not?"

"Because it's not like that."

"I beg to differ. I think it's very much *like that*. Mom wants you to invite her over to the house for Sunday dinner."

"Hell, no."

Daniela laughed. "Come on, Paulo. I like Tommie. Oh, she came off a little cool at first, but the more I talked to her over breakfast, the more I warmed up to her. She's really smart and tough, the kind of chick you don't mess with if you know what's good for you. And you might think, based on the way she looks, that she'd be full of herself, but she's surprisingly down-to-earth. I could see the two of us becoming good friends if you and she—"

"We're not," Paulo interrupted flatly.

Lips pursed, Daniela gave him a long, measured look. "Sooner or later," she said quietly, "you're going to have to stop punishing yourself for what happened between you and Jaci."

Paulo's jaw tightened. Without another word he turned and stalked out of the office. Daniela knew better than to go after him.

Work had dominated his thoughts over the next several

hours, keeping him too busy to dwell on the unnerving conversation with Daniela. But as he drove home that night, his police band radio crackling softly in the background, his thoughts strayed once again to his cousin's parting words, bringing a fresh spurt of anger. He knew Daniela loved him and meant well, but he really wished she—as well as her mother and sisters—would butt out of his personal life. He didn't need them psychoanalyzing his reasons for wanting to remain single. And he sure as hell didn't need them interfering in his relationship with Tommie.

Relationship? Is that what you're calling it now?

More like an obsession, Paulo mused, his mouth twisting sardonically. He couldn't think of any other word to describe his preoccupation with Tommie. He thought about her constantly. At odd intervals throughout the day he'd found himself fantasizing about her, wanting her, thinking about wrapping his arms around her and saying to hell with his resolve not to have her. He'd daydreamed about stripping off her clothes, kissing those lush, incredible breasts, tangling his fingers in her long, thick hair as he ran his tongue down her glorious body.

"Shit!" Paulo muttered, so caught up in the fantasy that he nearly missed the turnoff to his street. He gave himself a hard mental shake, forcing thoughts of Tommie out of his mind as he parked in front of his apartment building.

The property featured covered parking, a swimming pool, a newly renovated clubhouse, and a host of other amenities that were wasted on Paulo, for all the time he spent at home. When he first moved to Houston and began apartment-hunting, all he'd required was affordable rent and proximity to the police station. He wasn't looking to buy or put down roots. He still owned a house in San Antonio that he and Jacinta had purchased shortly after getting married, a small starter home with blue shutters and a big backyard that was perfect for the slew of kids they'd planned to have. But the kids never came, and two years later, he and Jacinta went their separate ways. He lamented the absence of children more than the departure of his wife.

Paulo entered his apartment, tossed his keys onto a side table, and hit the light switch. Walking into the living room, he snagged the remote control and turned on the big-screen television, one of the few items Jacinta had let him keep after the divorce.

Seeing the blinking light on his telephone, he checked his voice mail messages. After listening to the soft, purring voices of two women he couldn't readily identify, he muttered a curse on all females who didn't leave their names on answering machines.

Shrugging out of his jacket and shoulder holster, he made his way past the dining room to the small, utilitarian kitchen. He surveyed the meager contents of his refrigerator, grunting in disgust when he found nothing appetizing.

Grabbing a bottled water—though he would have given anything for a cold beer—he twisted off the top and kicked the refrigerator door closed. As he left the kitchen he thought of the delicious home-cooked meal he could be enjoying this very minute if he'd accepted Naomi's invitation to move into the guest cottage at their River Oaks estate. But he'd refused because, as Daniela had noted, it would be pretty damned hard to keep his colleagues from finding out he was related to the powerful Santiago family when he shared the same address.

Paulo knew his modest two-bedroom unit was a far cry from the swanky guest cottage he could have inhabited.

But at least his place was neat, he mused, noting the polished tabletops, gleaming leather furniture, and vacuumed floors. Last year for his birthday, Naomi, after one too many visits to his pigsty of an apartment, had decided what he needed more than anything was a good housekeeper. So she'd bought him a five-year gift certificate to a professional cleaning service. It was the most practical gift Paulo had ever received. It was also one of the best.

He took a long pull from his bottle as he made his way back to the living room, where the evening news was blaring on the television. He flopped down on the chocolate leather sofa and propped one booted foot on the coffee table, knowing this would have earned him a disapproving frown from the cleaning lady.

Paulo chuckled at the thought as he began watching coverage of the day's top stories. The lead segment was about a domestic shooting that had happened that morning in the Third Ward. A man accused of shooting his girlfriend's teenage son was on the run, while the victim remained in critical condition at an area hospital. Paulo had heard about the shooting on his police band as he was driving to Kathleen Phillips's apartment that morning. Although the case was being handled by South Central Patrol, which served the Third Ward, all local law enforcement officers had been advised to be on the lookout for the fugitive.

"In our other top story this evening," the news anchor continued, "police are still searching for a suspect in the brutal slaying of twenty-nine-year-old Maribel Cruz. Cruz, who worked as a legal secretary at the prestigious law firm of Santiago and Associates, was found stabbed to death in her uptown home on Monday night. Police investigators have ruled out robbery as a motive, leaving Cruz's family and friends to wonder who could have killed Maribel—a loving daughter, sister, and friend who will be missed by everyone who knew her."

Paulo grimaced, his gut twisting as Maribel's grief-stricken parents appeared on the television screen to tearfully beseech anyone with information about their daughter's murder to come forward. He sat there watching the couple, battling a sense of frustration and guilt for not doing more to find the monster responsible for putting them through this nightmare. These people deserved justice. Maribel deserved justice.

But if there was one thing Paulo had learned over the course of his career, it was that justice too often eluded the innocent. And there wasn't a damned thing he could do about it.

Brooding, he sat through one more news segment about a fatal car collision on the freeway before he decided he'd had enough. But just as he reached for the remote control to turn the channel, the news anchor, segueing to another story, cheerfully announced, "Aspiring dance students at the University of Houston were treated to a special appearance today by local dancer and choreographer Tommie Purnell."

And there she was.

The woman Paulo had been trying unsuccessfully to put out of his mind for the past twenty-four hours.

Paulo stared at the television, riveted by an image of Tommie addressing a packed theater, followed by footage of her leaping gracefully across the stage as she delighted the audience with a live dance demonstration. His pulse thudded as he watched her being interviewed by the reporter after the lecture. Beneath her serious facade, there was a naughty glimmer in her dark eyes, in the coy smile that curved her full lips. The woman oozed sensuality even when she wasn't trying.

Paulo felt a current of lust in his blood. Before he knew it his mind had wandered, conjuring an image of Tommie lying upon her back, naked and wanting, her lips parted, cheeks flushed, and those sultry eyes glazed with wet, hot desire.

He swore under his breath, cursing his vivid imagination and the damned news broadcast for making it impossible for him to get her off his mind.

Punching off the television in disgust, he downed the rest of his bottled water as if it were tequila and lurched to his feet, intending to do something—anything—that would free his thoughts of the damned woman.

As he started toward the kitchen to make a quick sandwich, the doorbell rang. Paulo frowned, glancing down at his watch. It was ten thirty. Who the hell was visiting him at this time of night?

He strode to the door and checked the peephole. He thought his eyes were deceiving him when he saw Tommie standing on his doorstep, holding a brown paper bag. *You've got to be kidding me,* he mentally groaned. He just couldn't get away from the woman!

Reluctantly he unlocked the door and opened it. "Well, well, well," he drawled, folding his arms across his chest and leaning on the doorjamb with an air of lazy insolence. "I thought you never wanted to see me again."

Those lush lips curved. "That was yesterday. Today's a new day."

"Is that so?" Paulo murmured, deliberately letting his gaze roam the length of her body. Her long, honey-streaked hair was windswept, falling in coquettish disarray about her face and shoulders. She wore black leather boots and a shiny black trench coat that was belted tightly around her waist, making him speculate about what was hidden beneath.

"How did you know where I live?" he asked.

Tommie laughed, low and husky. "Just because I'm not a detective doesn't mean I can't find an address." Without waiting for an invitation she swept past him into the apartment, ushering in the scent of the crisp fall night mingled with the spicy, appetizing aroma of Thai food.

"So this is the proverbial bachelor pad," she teased, taking a slow turn around the foyer before strolling into the living room as if she owned the place. She glanced around at the dark, contemporary furnishings and nodded approvingly. "It's much nicer than I expected. Cleaner, too."

"Gee, thanks," Paulo muttered wryly.

Tommie grinned. "Don't take it the wrong way. You just don't strike me as the type of guy who'd know how to decorate, much less be a neat freak," she said, running a manicured fingertip across the polished surface of a side table.

Paulo considered, then decided against telling her that a professional cleaning service was responsible for the pristine state of his apartment. Let her think she'd been wrong about him.

He followed her as she moved on to the small dining room, setting the takeout bag on the gleaming cherry table, where fresh-cut flowers had been arranged in a crystal vase Paulo had never seen before. Because he tipped generously, the cleaning lady always left nice little surprises for him.

"When I called the station, they told me you'd just left for the day," Tommie said, untying her trench. "I took a chance that you hadn't eaten dinner yet. I hope you're hungry. I ordered a lot of food."

Paulo was hungry all right, but it wasn't the prospect of eating dinner that had him salivating. Tommie had removed her coat, and when he got an eyeful of her in a black shorts jumper that molded the voluptuous curves of her body, he nearly swallowed his damned tongue. The outfit, coupled with a pair of thigh-high stiletto boots, fueled his imagination with erotic fantasies of dominatrix games. Handcuffs, black leather, spanking, and the wicked crack of a whip.

"Where can I hang this up?" Tommie asked.

Paulo blinked at her, feeling dazed. "What?"

Her mouth twitched. "I need to hang my coat in the closet."

"Oh. Here, I'll take it."

She passed it to him, then turned and headed for the kitchen, hips swinging seductively. Paulo stared after her, lust clawing at his insides.

After hanging her coat in the hall closet, he retraced his steps to the kitchen, where he found her leaning over as she surveyed the dismal contents of the refrigerator. Her shorts had ridden up her deliciously round buttocks, and her leather boots molded her long, curvaceous legs like a second skin. Blood rushed straight to Paulo's groin as he imagined those killer legs locked around his waist during hot, no-holds-barred sex.

"What're you looking for?" he asked, his voice so low and rough he hardly recognized it.

Tommie shook her head, chuckling. "Just as I suspected. Bare as a bone. I knew there was a typical bachelor hiding around here somewhere."

"Yeah, well, we can't all have personal chefs who bake lasagna and peach cobblers for us."

She laughed. "Don't be jealous," she teased, grabbing two bottles of Coke from the refrigerator and bumping the door closed with her hip. Paulo dragged his gaze from her luscious butt just as she turned, passing him the drinks.

"Plates?" she asked.

Paulo pointed, then resumed watching her ass while she retrieved two plates from the cabinet.

Once they were seated at the table, he surveyed the fragrant, generous portions of Pad Thai, curry chicken, and pineapple fried rice, and felt his stomach growl softly in anticipation. But as he reached for a fork, he was struck by a sudden thought.

"How do I know you haven't poisoned the food?"

Tommie choked out a laugh. "*Excuse* me?"

"You were pretty pissed off at me last night. And then out of the clear blue you show up at my apartment bearing dinner? How do I know I'm not going to bite into a spring roll and come away with a mouthful of cyanide?"

She chuckled, shaking her head. "What a twisted little mind you have, Detective. But if you knew how much I love eating, you would know I'd never do anything as sacrilegious as wasting perfectly good Thai." She paused, lips pursed thoughtfully. "If I really wanted to kill you, I'm sure I could think of far more creative ways."

Paulo laughed grimly. "I'm sure I'll sleep better tonight knowing that."

Tommie grinned. "And just to prove to you that I haven't tampered with the food—" She picked up his spring roll and bit into it with a low, appreciative moan that made his loins tighten in a hot rush.

"See? No poison. Now your turn." As she held out the spring roll to him, Paulo couldn't help wondering what must have gone through Adam's mind before he'd accepted the forbidden fruit from Eve.

Holding Tommie's gaze, Paulo leaned forward and took a bite of the proffered spring roll. He chewed slowly, watching her eyes turn smoky with desire.

"Good?"

"Very," he murmured.

"I told you," she whispered, biting into the roll after him. Paulo stared at her, wondering how she managed to make the simple act of eating feel like foreplay. Suddenly he wanted to sweep away the food, lift her into his arms, and stretch her out across the table. He wanted to peel that hot little number off her body, drape her legs over his shoulders—leaving the thigh-high boots on—and bury his tongue in the hot, slick folds of her sex.

The urge was so powerful that he had to force himself to look away from her just to break the sensual spell she'd cast over him. Because there was no doubt in his mind that she *had* cast a spell over him.

And something told him she knew it, too.

Paulo frowned, unnerved by the idea of losing the upper hand to her, to *any* woman, after he'd sworn never to let such a thing happen again.

As they ate, he was so preoccupied with his thoughts that he only half listened as Tommie chattered easily about her day, telling him about the lecture she'd given that morning, describing the sense of pride and gratification she'd felt while talking to the dance students afterward. It was only when she mentioned being at the hospital to visit a critically wounded teenager that Paulo snapped to attention.

"Wait a minute," he interrupted, staring at her. "Are you talking about the fourteen-year-old kid who was shot by his mother's boyfriend this morning?"

Tommie nodded. "It's so sad. Zhane and his family are devastated. Kadeem is Zhane's favorite nephew. If he doesn't pull through this—"

"The victim was Zhane's nephew?" Paulo asked in surprise.

"Yes. I said that before." Tommie frowned at him. "Haven't you been listening to me?"

"Off and on," he admitted sheepishly.

She rolled her eyes. "Of course. Hearing about a girly dance lecture doesn't hold your interest, but as soon as I mention a shooting, you're all ears."

"I'm a cop," Paulo said, as if that should explain everything. "Now tell me how it went down."

Tommie blew out a deep breath. "Zhane has a younger sister named Zakia. This morning she—"

"Zhane and Zakia?"

"And two more brothers named Zachary and Zeke." She shrugged, mouth twitching. "What can I say? Their mother had a thing for names starting with the letter z. Anyway, Zakia and her live-in boyfriend were arguing this morning, which, from what I understand, is nothing new. When the argument got a little too heated, Zakia's son, Kadeem, stepped in to defend his mother. I guess Zakia's boyfriend—his name is Chauncey Booker—didn't appreciate Kadeem's interference. He got angry, went for his gun, and shot Kadeem in the chest. While Zakia was kneeling over her son's body and screaming at Chauncey, begging him to call for help, he panicked and took off. No one has seen him since."

"Son of a bitch," Paulo muttered, shaking his head in grim disgust. "How's the kid doing?"

"He's still in critical condition. He lost a lot of blood. The doctor says the bullet just narrowly missed his heart."

Paulo grimaced. "Lucky kid."

"Yeah," Tommie murmured, "but he's got a ways to go before he's out of the woods. I wanted to stay at the hospital with Zhane. I even packed an overnight bag just in case. But Zhane wouldn't hear of it. He told me to go home, said he didn't want his crazy family driving me insane by morning."

"That bad, huh?"

She chuckled softly. "Let's just say they would've made the Osbournes look like the Huxtable family."

Paulo grinned. "That *is* bad."

"Tell me about it." She took a sip of her Coke. "At least Zhane turned out normal."

Paulo burst out laughing.

Tommie lowered her bottle, staring indignantly at him. "What's so funny?" When he just shook his head, her eyes narrowed suspiciously. "Are you saying you don't think Zhane is normal? Because he's gay?"

"I didn't say that."

"But that's what you were thinking," Tommie accused. "I know how guys like you are wired."

"Guys like me?"

"That whole machismo thing. In the Hispanic culture, it's acceptable for men to think they're superior to women, let alone *girly* men. Your manhood is your badge of honor. Your dick is your weapon. The bigger it is, the harder your swagger."

Paulo stared at her, torn between amusement and insult. "First of all," he said succinctly, "don't presume to lecture me about what is, and *isn't*, acceptable in the Hispanic culture. Last I checked, the black community ain't too fond of gay people, either. My reaction to your comment about Zhane being normal had more to do with his wacky personality than his sexual orientation. I don't give a shit who he sleeps with. Matter of fact, if he *weren't* gay, I'd have to worry about him trying to get in your pants. And as for that other matter," he said, leaning forward to bring his lips close to her ear, "if you want to see how big my dick is, I'm sure something can be arranged."

He drew away slowly, watching with satisfaction as Tommie drew a deep, shaky breath and averted her gaze. "Maybe I overreacted a little," she mumbled.

"Just a little," Paulo agreed, his tone mild. "But I get it. You and Zhane are best friends. He probably doesn't get a lot of support from his family, even though he's always there for them. You're protective over him, don't want to see him hurt or wrongly judged."

Tommie stared at him in surprised wonder. "How'd you know all that?"

Paulo shrugged. "I'm a detective. It's my job to be perceptive."

"And you definitely are." Her lips quirked. "It's kind of scary, actually."

He merely smiled.

"Speaking of detectives," Tommie continued, frowning, "Zhane said the one assigned to their case has been giving them the runaround all day. All the family wants is an update on the status of the search for Zakia's boyfriend. Considering what they've been through today, I don't think it's asking too much for someone to return their phone calls."

"I'm sure they'll be notified when more information is available," Paulo said diplomatically.

Tommie gave him a look.

After another moment, he relented with a sigh. "I'll make a few calls after dinner, see what I can find out."

She smiled at him in a way that made him feel absurdly heroic, something he hadn't felt in a very long time. Longer than he cared to remember. Softly she said, "Thank you, Paulo."

"Don't mention it," he said gruffly.

Their gazes held. The moment stretched into two.

"Do you realize this is the third night in a row we've eaten dinner together?" Tommie murmured.

"The thought crossed my mind." Paulo's mouth

twitched with humor. "I'm still trying to get over the fact that you're here."

She shrugged, absently pushing a lone chunk of pineapple around her plate. "I know we departed on bad terms yesterday—"

"You told me to stay the hell away from you."

"That's right, I did. I was angry. And humiliated. But I'm a big girl. After I had a chance to give it some more thought, I realized that the whole thing was actually pretty funny."

"Funny?" Paulo was skeptical.

"Yeah. In a way I brought it upon myself, boasting about how I'd never begged a man for anything. Who could blame you for not resisting such a challenge? If the situation were reversed, I probably would have done the same thing. So no hard feelings."

Paulo wasn't buying it for a second, but he decided to play along. "Thanks for being so understanding," he said humbly.

Tommie smiled. "What's a little forgiveness between friends?"

"Friends?" Paulo repeated, as if he'd never heard the word before. "So now we're friends?"

"Sure, why not? My sister's married to one of your best friends, who also happens to be very close to your cousin Rafe. It makes no sense for the two of us to be constantly at each other's throats when we're going to be seeing each other at birthday parties, graduations, and weddings for the next forty years."

Paulo leaned back in his chair, a slow, lazy smile curving his mouth. "So you want us to be friends?"

"Yes."

"Friends . . . with benefits?"

Tommie laughed, a low, throaty purr that shot straight

to his groin. Eyes glowing with feline seduction, she brought her lips close to his ear and murmured silkily, "If you play your cards right, I'm sure something can be arranged."

Paulo's mouth went dry.

Before he could find his voice, she rose from the table with their empty plates and sashayed from the room, leaving him with the absolute certainty that she'd come to his apartment that night for one purpose and one purpose only: to drive him completely out of his mind.

Oh, she was good. Damned good.

But he was better.

If Tommie Purnell wanted to play games, she'd learn soon enough that she wasn't ready for the majors. Because one way or another, Paulo intended to win.

He would have the last laugh.

Even if it killed him.

While Tommie cleared the table and put away the food, Paulo made the promised phone calls. When he'd finished, he found his guest standing in the living room, her back to him as she studied an oil painting he'd received from Daniela as a housewarming gift.

Paulo walked over to the sofa and sat down. "I spoke to the detective assigned to Kadeem's case," he said.

Tommie turned to look at him expectantly.

"His name's Roberto Mendiola. Turns out we worked vice together several years ago back in San Antonio. He assured me that they're doing everything they can to find Chauncey Booker, and they've got a few solid leads they're following up on. I told him the family would appreciate hearing from him, so he gave me his word he'd call them as soon as he got off the phone with me."

"Thank you so much, Paulo," Tommie said, smiling

warmly as she crossed the living room to join him on the sofa. "Zhane and his family will be very grateful for your help."

Paulo shrugged off her gratitude. "It's no big deal. What good is knowing a cop if you can't call in a favor every now and then?"

"I'll definitely remember that the next time I need to get out of paying a speeding ticket."

They grinned at each other.

Glancing away, Paulo reached for the remote control and turned on the television, though he wasn't particularly interested in watching it. He needed a distraction from Tommie's tantalizing nearness on the sofa, the teasing scent of her perfume, the shapeliness of her thighs as she settled back against the sofa cushions and crossed her long legs.

"There's nothing good on at this time of night," she pointed out, a hint of amusement in her voice as she watched him channel-surfing. As if she knew he was only looking for a diversion.

But she was right, of course. Even with a vast array of cable programming to choose from, there was nothing worth watching at this hour of the night. Paulo finally settled on ESPN, where a sportscaster was rattling off the day's scores while highlights flashed across the screen.

"Do you watch a lot of TV?" Tommie asked conversationally.

"Not really," Paulo answered. "I'm not home very much. Whenever I am here, I mostly use it for background noise."

"Me, too. When I lived in New York, I forgot I even had a television."

He sent her an amused sidelong glance. "Because you were always out partying?"

"Pretty much. Or on the road." She smiled. "There are, however, a couple of shows that I always enjoy watching."

Paulo grinned. "Let me guess. One of them is *Dancing with the Stars*."

Tommie laughed, playfully slapping his shoulder. "Just because I'm a dancer doesn't automatically mean I love *Dancing with the Stars*! That's like me saying you love *Law & Order* just because you're a detective."

"Depends on which series you're talking about. If you mean *SVU*, then yeah, I like the show."

"I bet you only watch it to ogle Mariska Hargitay."

Paulo grinned wolfishly. "I sure as hell wouldn't mind having a partner who looks like her."

Tommie rolled her eyes. "Why am I not surprised?"

"You shouldn't be. So tell the truth," Paulo prodded teasingly. "You love *Dancing with the Stars*, don't you?"

"I still say you're stereotyping—"

"*Ay Dios*, woman! Yes or no?"

She heaved an exasperated breath. "Fine! Yes, I enjoy watching the show. I try not to miss any episodes. There. Are you satisfied?"

Paulo chuckled, resting one booted foot on the coffee table. "I love being right about you."

Tommie snorted. "Oh, please. It wasn't a stretch for you to assume that I'd like *Dancing with the Stars*. If you really want to impress me, tell me something about myself you couldn't possibly have known unless I told you."

Amused, Paulo shook his head at her. "There you go again, issuing another challenge I won't be able to resist."

"Go ahead," she goaded him, her flashing dark eyes daring him to take the bait. "Impress me."

He held her gaze for a long moment, then shook his head with a soft chuckle. "As tempting as the offer sounds, I'm not touching that one with an eighty-foot pole."

"Why not?"

"Because anything I say will backfire on me. It's a lose-lose proposition."

"Chicken," she taunted.

Paulo laughed. "Nice try, but reverse psychology doesn't work on me. Neither does name-calling."

Tommie stuck her tongue out at him.

A wicked grin swept across his face. "Don't poke that thing out at me unless you're prepared to use it in ways you never intended."

As her tongue quickly retreated and a hot flush bloomed on her cheeks, Paulo laughed. It amused and fascinated him to know that he could make her blush, this siren who was at ease with her sensuality as he was with a gun, this temptress who could bring grown men to their knees with just one sultry look.

Still, as dangerous as she was, Paulo enjoyed being with her. He didn't want her to leave, and was glad she seemed in no hurry to.

Laying her head on the back of the sofa, Tommie smiled whimsically at him. "Tell me more about yourself, Paulo."

He instinctively tensed. Enjoying her company was one thing. Baring his soul to her was out of the question. "What do you want to know?" he asked carefully.

"Anything. The usual things."

"Such as?"

"I don't know," she said, sounding mildly exasperated. "What part of San Antonio are you from? Where did you go to school? What do your parents do? What's your family like?"

Paulo felt the tension subside from his body. The questions she'd asked were harmless enough. "I grew up on the south side," he answered. "Working-class neighborhood, taco shack on every corner. My father was an electrician. My mom worked as a seamstress, housekeeper, receptionist—whatever paid the bills. Neither of them went to college, but they were proud, hardworking people who never asked for any handouts, and sometimes refused when help was offered. My siblings and I— I have two brothers and two sisters—never lacked for anything. We wore hand-me-downs and didn't get to eat out much, but everyone we knew was in the same boat, so we never really felt like we were deprived. Well," he amended with a wry chuckle, "except when I used to visit Rafe every summer in Houston. *Then* I'd realize just how much my family didn't have. A big house, closets full of new clothes, two cars, money to spend on nice vacations. And Rafe had something in particular I'd always wanted but could never have—his very own room."

Tommie smiled sympathetically. "Were you ever jealous or resentful of him?"

"Jealous, definitely. Resentful? No way."

"Really? Not even a little?"

Paulo shook his head. "Anyone who knows Rafe Santiago knows it's impossible to resent him. We were like brothers, two peas in a pod. He never made me feel like the poor relation from the barrio. He was generous to a fault, shared everything with me without making a big production out of it."

Tommie smiled softly. "I really admire your relationship with him."

"I'm grateful for it," Paulo admitted.

"Just how are you two related again?"

"Our grandparents were half siblings. Rafe's paternal grandfather was Ramon Santiago. Your father is an archaeologist, so he may have heard of him. Ramon was a famous professor and historian who was always being interviewed for films and documentaries. He also wrote award-winning books about San Antonio's history and culture."

"He sounds like quite an impressive man," Tommie murmured.

"He was. Growing up, I was in awe of him. We all were. Well, except my grandmother Maria," Paulo added, chuckling dryly. "To her, Ramon was just her big brother. And as brilliant as he was, I'm sure even *he* did some things that got on her nerves."

"I'm sure," Tommie agreed, smiling.

"But she adored him, make no mistake about it. He was her favorite brother. When he left home to attend college in Mexico City, she missed him like crazy. She was devastated when the family eventually disowned him for marrying a black woman, even though Abuelita Maria didn't agree with his decision, either. She couldn't understand why he hadn't returned to Oaxaca and married someone from their village, like he was supposed to. So when the rest of the family refused to accept Ramon's bride—Rafe's grandmother—Abuelita Maria went along with them, even though she was dying inside."

"That's a shame," Tommie said, her voice edged with anger and impatience. "Why can't people be free to love whomever they want, regardless of race, income level, or social status?"

"They can," Paulo said with a wry grimace. "They just have to be prepared to deal with the consequences—good or bad. But that was a different time, different culture. What Rafe's grandfather did was practically unheard of."

Tommie's eyes narrowed on his face. "Are you defending your family's decision to disown him?"

"Not at all," Paulo said unequivocally. "I think what they did was terrible. It caused a rift between the families that would be felt for generations, even after Rafe's grandmother was eventually welcomed into the fold."

"How did that come about?"

"They came to their senses after Rafe's father, Ignacio, was born." A sardonic smile tugged at his lips. "In our family, nothing brokers peace faster than the birth of a son. But like I said, by then the damage had already been done. You can't unring a bell. Although Ramon eventually forgave the family for disowning him, he never really got over the way his wife had been treated. It put a strain on his relationship with everyone, including my grandmother. And because he stopped visiting Oaxaca as often as he used to, Ignacio and his siblings grew up feeling somewhat alienated from their father's side of the family."

"So how did you and Rafe ever become so close?" Tommie asked, absorbing every word of his tale with an expression of rapt fascination. Paulo couldn't remember the last time, if ever, a woman had taken such a keen interest in learning about him or his background. He didn't know what to make of it, didn't know whether to be pleased or unnerved.

Remembering that she'd asked him a question, he said, "Despite everything that had happened in the past, Ramon always had a soft spot in his heart for my grandmother. Years later when she followed him to San Antonio—and everyone knows she did—Ramon reached out to her and her husband. He helped them get set up with jobs and a place to live. And when they started having children, he tried to at least bring the two families—his and theirs—together. Growing up, Rafe and I spent almost as many summers at his grandfather's ranch as we did in Houston."

Tommie smiled. "It's a beautiful ranch," she said, adding wryly, "Frankie and Sebastien are over there so much that I've started calling it their second home. And my nephew loves it there, too. He goes horseback riding and swimming every day with Kaia and Little Ramon."

"I have a lot of fond memories of the ranch," Paulo said, idly wondering when his fingers had worked their way into the thick, silken strands of her hair fanned out across the back of the sofa. And was it just his imagination, or were they sitting closer to each other than before?

"Are your grandparents still alive?" Tommie asked.

"My grandmother is. My grandfather passed away a long time ago. But it was only after Ramon died that Abuelita Maria decided to return to Oaxaca."

"So he *was* the reason she came to San Antonio." Tommie sighed deeply. "How touching."

Paulo thought so, too, but he didn't admit it for fear of sounding like a sap. "When Ramon died, he left the ranch to Rafe and divided his fortune evenly among his children, as well as Abuelita Maria."

"He left her money?"

Paulo nodded. "She was too proud and stubborn to take a dime from him when he was alive. This way, she had no choice. She gave some of the money to my parents, then built a nice little home for herself in Oaxaca. For the first time in years, she finally seems to be at peace."

"That's good. Do your parents and siblings still live in San Antonio?"

Again Paulo nodded. "They're not going anywhere."

"How did they feel about you moving away from home? I hope they took it better than my family did."

Paulo chuckled dryly. "Let's just say I've put a lot of miles on my car going back and forth between Houston and San Antonio."

Tommie winced. "Thanks for making me feel guilty."

Paulo laughed. "Hey, you asked."

Her answering smile was distracted as she searched his face, looking as if she had something far weightier than familial duty on her mind.

He waited.

"Have you ever dated a black woman?" she asked bluntly.

Paulo didn't blink, though the question had caught him off guard. "What do you think?"

Her dark brows furrowed. "I don't know. That's why I'm asking you."

"Why do you want to know?"

"I'm just curious. God, why is it like pulling teeth just to get you to answer questions?"

Paulo choked out an incredulous laugh. "What're you talking about? I just spent the past twenty minutes answering your questions!"

"Not without some prodding." She lifted her head from the back of the sofa, forcing him to release her hair, and pinned him with a direct look. "Why are you avoiding my question?"

"Have you ever dated a Hispanic man?" Paulo countered.

Her eyes narrowed. "I asked you first."

"Yes. I've dated black women."

Tommie nodded slowly. "That shouldn't surprise me. You've probably been with women of every race and nationality."

"Just about." He grinned. "What can I say? I had to make up for lost time. Growing up on the south side, most of the girls I knew and went to school with were Hispanic. The only times I encountered black girls were when I visited Rafe in Houston. Which was another reason I enjoyed those summer vacations so much," he added with a devilish wink.

"I'll bet," Tommie muttered.

"Your turn. Have you ever dated a Hispanic man?"

She hesitated, tugging her lush bottom lip between her teeth. "What do you think?"

Paulo held her gaze. "I think you're an incredibly beautiful woman any man would kill to be with," he said huskily.

She blushed, casting her eyes downward. "Thank you, but I wasn't fishing for compliments."

"That wasn't a compliment, *querida*. That was the God's honest truth. Now who's avoiding questions?"

Her eyes lifted to his. "No, I've never been with a Hispanic man."

"Never?"

She shook her head. "Never."

Paulo didn't know whether to be relieved or disappointed. Relieved because he liked being a woman's first, disappointed because her answer suggested he might not even get the chance.

"Any particular reason?" he probed.

She shrugged. "I've always dated only black men," she answered honestly. "It's nothing personal against any other race. It's just a preference." She paused, her lips twisting with bitter irony. "Not that limiting myself to black men has gotten me anywhere. I'm thirty-three years old and nowhere near getting married."

"Is that what you want? To be married?"

"Of course. I mean, don't get me wrong," she hastened to add, "I'm not desperate or anything. I enjoy the freedom of being single and not having to answer to anyone but myself."

"But you get lonely sometimes," Paulo said quietly. "You don't want to have to use the television for background noise. You want someone to be there at the end of a long day, to listen to you vent and make you laugh. You want someone to share your life with."

Tommie gazed at him, her eyes soft with wonder and an unnamed longing that made something tighten in his chest. Something he didn't care to examine too closely.

They stared at each other for a long, breathless moment.

Tommie was the first to look away, clearing her throat and glancing down at her watch. "I should go. It's getting late, and I know we both have a full day tomorrow."

Paulo was surprised by the stab of disappointment he felt at the thought of her leaving. He was even more surprised when he heard himself saying, "Why don't you just crash here for the night?"

Tommie looked equally stunned. "You want me to . . . spend the night?"

"Sure, why not? It's almost midnight. You're already here. Besides, it's not safe for you to be alone on the road this late at night. In case you've forgotten, there's a killer on the loose."

She grimaced. "I definitely haven't forgotten that. But I don't want to put you out, Paulo."

"It's only one night. You can have my bed. The sheets are clean, just changed today."

She wavered. "I don't know. The sofa isn't long enough for you. You won't get a good night's rest."

"Let me worry about that." When she still hesitated, he added, "You said you'd already packed an overnight bag, right?"

"Yes, but that was to stay with Zhane in case he needed me. Not to stay here with you."

Paulo gave her a slow, taunting grin. "What's the matter, Tommie? Afraid you won't be able to resist ravishing me in the middle of the night?"

She snorted out a laugh. "In your dreams, Sanchez. If anything, I should be asking *you* that question."

His grin widened. "You think I won't be able to resist

the temptation of having a sexy, beautiful woman under my roof for one night?"

"Have you ever?"

"Can't say that I have. But there's a first time for everything."

"Yeah, right."

He cocked a brow. "That sounds an awful lot like a challenge, Miss Purnell," he drawled. "Are you sure you're up for it? You're batting oh for one, and I gotta tell you, I don't like your odds on this one. Because as hard as it's been for me to keep my eyes off you in that fuck-me getup, once I hit the sack, I'm pretty much out like a light until morning."

Those dark, magnificent eyes glittered with challenge. "Is that right?"

"Afraid so."

"I see."

Slowly, deliberately, Tommie uncrossed her long, shapely legs sheathed in those fantasy-inducing thigh-high boots. Paulo watched, both amused and wary, as she stood and sauntered over to the table in the foyer where she'd left her purse earlier. When it "accidentally" slipped from her hand and fell to the floor, Paulo wanted to roll his eyes, but he was afraid to miss a second of what came next.

Tommie leaned over to retrieve the fallen handbag, deliberately treating him to a long, mind-blowing look at her round, delectable ass. His body hardened. He swallowed a groan, unable to tear his gaze away.

As if in super-slow motion, she straightened and tossed her long hair backward, combing her fingers through the dark, lustrous strands before reaching inside her purse and removing a set of keys.

She turned and started back toward him, hips undulating, sultry gaze locked on to his, the barest hint of a provocative smile curving her lips. She stopped directly in front of him, keys dangling from her fingertips, legs splayed apart in a centerfold pose.

Good God.

"My bag is in the trunk of my car," she said, her voice like cool silk. "Why don't you run along like a good little boy and get it for me?" If she'd had a whip in hand, she would have cracked it.

Chuckling at the thought, Paulo got slowly to his feet, purposely taking his time. He'd do her bidding, but he wouldn't be rushed.

As he reached for the keys, Tommie held them just out of reach. "Do you know which one is my car?"

His mouth twitched. "I parked beside it two nights in a row. I think I can figure it out."

She smiled lazily. "All right." She placed the keys in his outstretched palm, closed his fingers around them.

As she slowly backed away from him, she reached up and began unbuttoning the jumper, holding his gaze. "I always take a long, hot shower before bed," she purred. "Do you mind?"

Paulo swallowed. "Not at all. Guest towels are in the hall closet."

"Mmm, thanks. You can just put my bag on the bed. I'll leave the bedroom door open for you."

He nodded shortly. "Okay."

As he turned to head for the front door, he caught a glimpse of black lace covering the ripe swell of a breast.

Saliva pooled in his mouth. His erection throbbed.

It was going to be a very long night.

With any luck, he'd make it to morning with his sanity intact.

Chapter 12

When Tommie agreed to spend the night at Paulo's apartment, she'd been so preoccupied with devising ways to torture him that she'd underestimated how *she* would be affected by the overnight arrangement. She'd underestimated the way her fertile imagination would keep her awake with thoughts of him lying just down the hall, his dark hair tousled, his hard, muscular body completely nude beneath a blanket. Because even if Paulo didn't really sleep in the buff, he sure as hell did in her fantasies.

Two hours after she'd turned off the bedside lamp and shut her eyes, sleep eluded her. Unable to resist temptation any longer, she threw back the covers and slipped from the massive sleigh bed. She'd steal a peek at her sleeping host, get a glass of cold water, then come right back to bed.

She started to reach for the silk robe hung across the footboard, then stopped. She glanced down at herself, taking in the slinky pajama tank top and short-short bottoms she'd worn to bed. A slow, naughty grin curved her lips. Why would she cover up with a robe when she was supposed to be giving Paulo a taste of what he was missing?

On the other hand, Tommie thought sourly, if he really

did sleep like the dead, as he'd suggested earlier, then he wouldn't be seeing her anyway. But just in case, she swapped the pajama shorts for a skimpy pair of black lace panties. She'd never believed in doing things halfway.

Chuckling silently to herself, Tommie opened the door and slipped quietly from the room. The hardwood floor was cool and smooth beneath her bare feet as she crept down the hallway.

On the far wall of the living room, moonlight filtered through the sheer draperies, clearly illuminating Paulo's sleeping form on the leather sofa. He was lying on his back, his heavily muscled arms folded behind his head, his breathing deep and slightly uneven, as if he were having fitful dreams. Just as she'd imagined, his black hair was mussed and he wore no shirt, revealing broad shoulders and a wide chest ridged with muscle. Dark hair swirled across his flat abdomen, arrowing into a line that disappeared beneath the covers resting at his waist.

As Tommie stood there gazing at him in the shadowy moonlight, a slow heat spread through her veins and pooled between her legs. She wanted to strip naked, run across the room, and throw herself upon the dark, muscular length of him. She wanted to rub her fevered flesh against his, straddle his powerful thighs, and guide his thick, throbbing shaft into her eager body.

She must have made a sound, because suddenly Paulo stirred and opened his eyes. Moving with lightning-quick reflexes, he reached beneath the pillow and bolted upright on the sofa.

Tommie cried out, shocked to find herself on the business end of his 9 mm Glock. All the air rushed from her lungs. She stood frozen, immobilized with terror.

"Tommie?" His voice was raw, disoriented.

"It's me," she squeaked.

Paulo reached over, flipping on the table lamp. Dark, haunted eyes swept across her face. "Are you okay?"

"I—I don't know," Tommie stammered, taking a step back. "I think I just saw my life flash before my eyes."

Paulo grimaced. He shoved the gun under his pillow, then swung his long legs over the side of the sofa and raked a trembling hand through his hair, mussing it even more. He looked wild, visibly shaken. "I'm sorry," he said, his voice pitched low. "I didn't mean to scare you."

Hand pressed to her racing heart, Tommie drew a deep, steadying breath. "Remind me never to wake you in the middle of the night. My God, Paulo, you nearly shot me! What the hell?"

"I'm sorry," he repeated huskily. He pushed out a ragged breath and closed his eyes, dropping his face into his hands. "I was having a bad dream."

Tommie faltered, studying his bent head and hunched shoulders. "Are you all right?"

"I'm fine."

"Are you sure? Do you want a glass of—"

"I said I'm fine," he snapped.

"Okay, okay," she muttered, holding up her hands as she backed away. "You don't have to bite my head off. It's bad enough you almost *blew* it off."

Slowly Paulo lifted his head and looked at her, noticing for the first time her state of undress. His gaze slid downward, taking in her skimpy tank top, lace panties, and bare feet in one hot, encompassing sweep. As his eyes returned to hers, Tommie was surprised to feel herself blushing.

"What's going on?" he murmured.

"Nothing. I was just on my way to the kitchen to get a glass of water."

A knowing gleam filled his eyes. "You couldn't sleep, huh?"

"I told you, I was thirsty. I'm a dancer—I drink a lot of water."

He grinned. "Liar."

Tommie bristled. "If I had trouble sleeping, it was only because I drank that Coke before going to bed."

"That's funny," Paulo drawled, leaning back against the sofa with his hands clasped behind his head, showing off silky tufts of dark armpit hair. "I drank a Coke, too, and I had no problem whatsoever falling asleep."

Wanting to wipe the cocky grin off his face, Tommie fired back, "Yeah, well, considering the dream you were having, you might want to rethink that whole sleeping thing, Nosferatu."

He blinked at her for a moment, then threw back his head and roared with laughter.

Incensed, Tommie stalked off toward the kitchen. This night was not turning out at all the way she'd envisioned. She was the one who was supposed to be sleeping like a baby while *he* tossed and turned restlessly, unable to stop thinking about her. She was supposed to be getting under *his* skin, not the other way around.

"I've been called many things in my life," Paulo told her, still laughing, "but no woman's ever called me a vampire!"

"Then it was long overdue!" Tommie yelled back.

Marching into the kitchen, she opened the refrigerator and grabbed a bottle of water. She twisted off the cap and took a long swig, wishing it were something stronger. Why on earth had she agreed to spend the night at Paulo's apartment? The man drove her out of her damned mind! It was bad enough that he was sexy as hell and cocky to boot, that he knew just how to push all her buttons. But then to add insult to injury, he'd just pulled a gun on her!

Tommie shook her head, remembering the wild look in his eyes when he'd turned on the light and seen her standing across the room. What kind of nightmare had caused him to react so violently upon waking? More to the point, what kind of demons drove a man to sleep with a loaded gun under his pillow?

Although Tommie had spent the past three nights with him, the reality was that she did not know Paulo Sanchez at all. She knew what he chose to reveal to her, and even that was surrendered grudgingly, as she'd discovered that evening when she'd asked him questions about his background. She didn't know him, but she sensed that he was hiding something beneath his irreverent, devil-may-care facade. She read it in his eyes, heard it in his voice at rare, unguarded moments. An aching loneliness that spoke directly to her own.

Shaking off the maudlin thought, Tommie closed the refrigerator door. As she started from the kitchen Paulo appeared in the entrance, blocking her path.

She stumbled back a step, her pulse drumming as she stared at him. She'd never realized before how broad his shoulders were, the breadth of them seeming to fill the open doorway. His chest was even more magnificent up close, smooth olive skin rippling with taut, sinewy muscle and dusted with black hair. He'd pulled on a pair of dark jeans that rode low on his lean hips. The fly was unsnapped and unzipped.

Intentionally, Tommie suspected.

Swallowing hard, she dragged her gaze back up to his face. He was already watching her, the mischief glinting in his dark eyes confirming her suspicion about the jeans.

"Excuse me," she muttered. When she tried to sidestep him he moved in the same direction, thwarting her escape. She attempted to go the other way, with the same result.

Heaving an exasperated breath, she glared at him. "I'm going back to bed."

Paulo chuckled. "No, you're not," he said mildly. "You woke me up, so now you have to keep me company until I fall asleep again."

"But I have to get up early!" Tommie protested.

He shook his head, unsympathetic. "You should have thought of that before you came out of the room and woke me up."

"I wanted to get some water."

"Which you've hardly touched," he pointed out, nodding toward the bottle in her hand, which was still more than three-quarters full.

Tommie glanced from the water to his head, then smiled narrowly.

Paulo read the intent in her gaze. "Don't even try it," he warned, a split second before she raised the bottle. Quick as a snake striking he caught her wrist in midair, laughing as she squealed in helpless frustration.

"So you want to dump cold water on my head, huh?" he taunted, slowly prying the bottle from her grasp.

Tommie laughed, her fingers tightening as she struggled to hold on to it. But of course Paulo was too strong, and in no time at all he'd wrested it away from her, holding it out of her reach.

"Fine," she huffed, blowing her tousled hair out of her eyes and trying to glare at him. "I hope you enjoy my backwash."

Paulo grinned. "Oh, I don't plan to drink the water," he said, advancing on her slowly and purposefully, a wicked, predatory gleam in his eyes.

Tommie shook her head, eyeing him warily. "Oh no."

"Oh *yes*."

"Don't do it," she pleaded, backing away from him.

"Why shouldn't I? You were gonna do it to me. Turnabout is fair play."

"I wasn't going to dump the water on you! I was only *thinking* about it!"

He grinned. "So it was premeditated. That makes you even guiltier."

"Wait!" Tommie cried, finding herself trapped against the sink.

Paulo stopped, his eyes glimmering with amused mischief as he held the bottle poised in midair. "Yes?"

"Can I cop a plea?"

He paused, his black brows furrowing thoughtfully as he pretended to consider her request. After another moment he shook his head. "Sorry. No deal."

"In that case—" But before Tommie could reach behind her to twist on the faucet, Paulo reacted.

She gasped, choking with laughter and indignation as cold water hit her squarely in the face.

As Paulo stepped back laughing, she managed to turn on the faucet and fling a handful of tap water at him. He ducked out of the way, catching only a few flying drops on his chest. Undeterred, Tommie kept pelting him until he raised the bottle and shook it, letting her see that enough water remained to give her face another good soaking.

"Had enough yet?"

Tommie hesitated a beat, then hurled another handful of water at him, this time getting him right in the face. He yelped in shock, and while he stood there wiping water from his dripping face, she made a run for it.

She didn't get very far before he captured her around the waist and hauled her roughly against him.

Tommie squealed in protest, squirming and thrashing in his arms, trying to escape before he doused her with the remaining bottled water.

It took several moments before she realized that he was no longer laughing.

Another moment passed before she realized that his body had gone completely still against hers.

When she tried to wiggle out of his grasp, he groaned. "Don't move," he whispered raggedly into her hair.

Tommie went still, her mouth running dry.

Paulo tossed the water bottle into the sink, then leaned down and nuzzled her ear, pulling her earlobe between his teeth and sucking it. "God, you're driving me crazy."

Tommie shivered, closing her eyes as the arms banded around her waist loosened, becoming less a hold and more a guide as he gently realigned her hips to his pelvis. When she found her buttocks pressed against the rigid length of his arousal, she gasped sharply. Deep in her belly, a knot of desire unfurled, spreading sensual fingers of heat through her limbs.

Her heart hammered in her chest as strong, callused fingers swept her hair over one shoulder, then cupped her nape and began to stroke her skin in lazy, tantalizing circles. His hands skimmed down her shoulders and arms before sliding upward, cupping her breasts through the damp tank top. "Mmmm, wet T-shirt," he rumbled appreciatively.

Tommie let out a broken moan as his fingers rasped against her jutting nipples, kneading and caressing them until she arched against him like a stretching cat. She reveled in the feel of his bare, muscled chest against her back. His skin was fever hot, scorching her. She could feel the heat of his erection through his jeans, straining against her backside. It inflamed her, deepened the searing ache between her thighs until she thought she might come right then and there.

Paulo buried his face against her neck and bit her, hard, sending waves of carnal pleasure sweeping through her.

"I knew you were a vampire," she purred.

He laughed, a dark, seductive sound, and licked the tender place on her throat that he had just bitten. She turned her face into his and he kissed her, a hot, devouring kiss unlike any she had ever known or imagined before meeting him.

Her head was still reeling when he reached beneath her lace panties and caressed the swell of her butt cheek, a deep, masculine groan of appreciation rumbling up from his chest. "You have the most incredible ass I've ever seen. I've been fantasizing about it ever since I first saw you at the wedding rehearsal dinner, leaning down to tie the ring bearer's shoelaces."

The shaky giggle that escaped Tommie's throat felt alarmingly like a sob. "You have a good memory."

His teeth flashed in a brief, wicked grin. "Your ass is unforgettable," he said, giving it another appreciative squeeze.

Her heart thundered as his other hand slid down over her flat belly, lower and lower, dipping below the waistband of her underwear. She gasped and arched as his fingers cupped her mound, smooth-shaven with just a teasing puff of hair shielding her clitoris.

"Mmmm, very nice," he murmured huskily. "Every damned inch of you is sexy."

Tommie moaned, her legs opening wider, seduced by his words and the velvety, hypnotic timbre of his voice. His teeth sank into her shoulder, biting and licking her while he spread her hot, silky juices over her swollen labia. Sensual tremors swept through her at his skillful touch. Aching with a savage need to have him inside her, she rubbed her bottom against the hot brand of his erection.

He made a harsh animal sound deep in his throat. Seizing the hair at the nape of her neck with his other hand, he pulled her head back until she was forced to turn her head, meeting the feral intensity of his gaze.

"You're a naughty girl, aren't you?" he murmured, his thumb circling her clitoris in a slow, sensual rhythm as he watched her face. "You like torturing me. Strutting around here in those dominatrix boots, teasing me with these see-through panties. You're trying to kill me."

"You know you like it," she taunted. "You—"

Her voice choked off into a keening cry as he thrust a finger deep inside her. She braced herself against the edge of the kitchen counter and widened her stance, opening eagerly for him.

"God, you feel so good," he told her, his voice rough with pleasure. "So tight and slippery."

He slid his finger out of her and thrust again, this time with two fingers, pushing deeper. Tommie let out a sob, her thighs clenching desperately around his hand. A fiery, trembling sensation was spreading throughout her body. An orgasm shimmered on the horizon.

Paulo rocked his hips against hers while his long fingers stroked, caressed, undid her. She came violently in an erotic cascade of hot, bursting pleasure that tore a scream from her throat.

Long moments later when the spasms had ceased, Paulo slowly withdrew his hand from between her shaking thighs. With a deep, purring sigh Tommie turned in the cradle of his embrace and looped her arms around his neck, kissing him softly. She could feel the quivering tension in his muscular body, could feel his heart beating rapidly against her own.

"That was absolutely wonderful," she breathed, nibbling his sensual bottom lip.

His dark, hooded eyes blazed with fierce arousal. "There's plenty more where that came from," he said, low and guttural.

Tommie let out a whispery laugh. "I don't doubt it. But what you just did to me is about all I can handle for now. Can I take a rain check?"

She saw the moment he realized that the tables had turned, that the balance of power had shifted away from him. A dark current of anger and frustration flared in his eyes. His jaw hardened.

He shook his head slowly at her. "No rain checks, *querida*. If you want me, it's now or never."

Tommie held his gaze for a long, charged moment.

She wanted nothing more than to surrender to him, to let him sweep her off her feet and carry her down the hall to his bedroom. She wanted him to make love to her, knew that it would be an electrifying, unforgettable experience. But she'd vowed to make him pay for humiliating her last night, and she wasn't about to pass up what might be her only chance to get revenge.

Hell hath no fury like a woman scorned.

"Not that your offer doesn't sound tempting," Tommie murmured at length, "but I really need to get some sleep if I want to be able to function during my classes today." She reached up, running her fingers through the thick, silky brush of his hair. "God, you have beautiful hair. I've been wanting to do that all night."

A muscle clenched in his jaw. "Tommie—"

She smiled demurely, pulling out of his arms. "If you change your mind about that rain check, come see me sometime."

And with that she turned and strolled out of the kitchen, basking in the sweet glow of victory.

Even if she'd just condemned herself to an eternity of sexual frustration.

She was waiting for him.

Hidden in the shadows of the aging cypress tree in the small backyard, the stranger trained his gaze on the lit bedroom window. At any moment the blonde would emerge from the bathroom, water dripping from her long hair, a towel draped around her pale, supple body.

He waited in the darkness, hearing the sound of his own heartbeat and the soft sigh of the wind rustling the branches of the tree that sheltered him. The night was cool and humid. Rising clouds of mist swirled from the damp ground. Rain had been forecast for tomorrow night, so he'd had to act today.

Because it was late, few lights glowed in the windows of the surrounding shotgun houses. Down the street, a neighbor's dog barked, petitioning to be let inside. But the animal was too far away to pose any threat to him. He'd made sure of that when he chose her.

His next victim.

He checked his digital watch, licked his lips in anticipation.

It was time.

He crept soundlessly across the weed-choked lawn and climbed the old, rickety porch stairs. After days of practice he knew just where to step, knew which floorboards creaked. He'd taken every precaution. Just as always.

At the back door he paused, every muscle tense as he listened for approaching footsteps from within the house.

But he knew she hadn't heard him.

She was waiting for him in the bedroom.

Where she was supposed to be.

He knelt down, reaching inside a potted plant that had shriveled and died a long time ago. His gloved fingers closed around the spare key hidden in the dirt. This, too, was where it was supposed to be.

Barely breathing, he inserted the key. The lock gave way with the barest hint of sound. He opened the door just wide enough to slip through. Once he was safely inside he pocketed the key, to be returned to its hiding place on his way out.

On silent footsteps he walked through the small, darkened kitchen, mentally clucking his tongue at the dirty dishes piled in the sink and the empty beer bottles littering the counter. The blonde was a slob. Unlike the other one, who'd been meticulous to the point of being obsessed.

A brief smile flitted across his face at the thought of Maribel Cruz. Sweet, beautiful, trusting. Too trusting.

Unlike the blonde, who was too jaded to trust anyone.

Except him.

She trusted him.

And it would cost her dearly.

Feeling a hot rush steal through his blood, he crept down the hallway toward his destination, past the cluttered living room and around the first corner.

As he neared the blonde's bedroom he heard her humming cheerfully. He smiled, a cold, narrow smile.

He reached the doorway. She had just stepped from the shower. A cloud of steam floated from the open bathroom door. She was bent over at the waist, towel-drying her long blond hair. A pink towel was wrapped loosely around her body.

At his appearance, she glanced up with a startled gasp. Her blue eyes widened in surprised recognition. "Hey! You're early," she said accusingly.

* * *

If Ted Colston was surprised to find two homicide detectives sitting in his office when he arrived that morning, he didn't show it.

"Gentlemen," he said, striding briskly to his desk and setting down his monogrammed briefcase. Lowering himself into the chair, he divided a speculative glance between Paulo and Donovan, who had made themselves comfortable in the visitor chairs while they waited.

"What can I do for you, Detectives?" Colston politely inquired. "I assume you're here in reference to the investigation?"

Instead of answering him, Paulo said mildly, "I missed you yesterday. I came to pay you a visit and was told you were out of town."

"Yes, my secretary called and informed me. I had an urgent matter to tend to in Austin. It couldn't be helped. Anyway, I'm not sure what else you need from me. I've already told you everything I could about Maribel."

"Not everything," Paulo said, deceptively soft.

The attorney shot a glance at Donovan's impassive face before his gaze returned to Paulo. "Okay. I give up. What did I fail to tell you?"

"That you were sleeping with your secretary, for starters."

Colston, to his credit, didn't so much as blink. He'd obviously prepared himself for the very real possibility that his affair with Maribel Cruz would be brought to light. So he didn't waste time—theirs or his—denying it.

"Sleeping with Maribel isn't something I was proud of," he said in a carefully measured voice.

"Is that why you lied about it?" Donovan asked.

"Of course." Colston grimaced. "I'm a respected partner at this firm, a married man. Obviously I have good

reasons for wanting to conceal the nature of my relationship with Maribel."

"Which makes me wonder," Paulo murmured.

Now Colston looked wary. "Wonder what?"

"Wonder how far you would go to conceal, as you put
it, the nature of your relationship with Maribel."

Colston stared at him, his expression turning from
shock to outrage as Paulo's implication became clear.
"Are you suggesting that *I* killed her?"

Paulo held his gaze unflinchingly. "You just said yourself that you had good reasons for lying about the affair.
My partner and I, we call that motive."

Colston's jaw tightened. "I didn't kill Maribel."

"That remains to be seen."

"You're mistaken, Detective," Colston said succinctly.
"I didn't kill her, and there's not a chance in hell that
you can prove I did."

"Maybe. Maybe not." Paulo shrugged, as if the matter
were of no consequence to him.

Frowning, Colston looked to Donovan, hoping to
plead his case to the more reasonable of the pair. "I
admit I was wrong for withholding information about
the affair, but that doesn't make me a murderer. I never
would have hurt Maribel. I cared about her. She was a
damned good secretary—"

"And a good lay, obviously," Paulo calmly interjected.
"You'd been sleeping with her since February. That must
have been some addictive stuff."

Colston glared at him, anger hardening his features.
"I'm not going to discuss the details of my sexual rela-
tionship with Maribel, if that's what you're expecting,
Detective."

"They're going to come out eventually," Donovan said.
"You can tell us now, or tell a jury later."

Colston flicked him a glance, smiling narrowly. "Nice

try, Detective, but we both know you don't have enough evidence to bring any charges against me. If you did, we'd be having this conversation at the police station, not here in my office."

"True enough," Donovan conceded. "So, do you think Maribel was getting serious about you?"

"No," Colston said quickly. Too quickly.

Donovan arched a brow. "Are you sure? See, it may have been just sex for you, but women are different. From what my partner tells me, Maribel had convinced herself she was in love with you. She wanted you to leave your wife, but she didn't think you would."

"And she was right. I wasn't going to leave my wife. And Maribel never asked me to."

"Even though she knew you were unhappy in your marriage?" Paulo prodded.

Again Colston frowned. "I never said I was unhappy."

"No?"

"No, I didn't. Where did you—" He broke off suddenly as a recent memory surfaced. "Oh, I get it. Just because I told you the other day that Abby complains about my long work hours—"

"And doesn't want kids," Paulo finished.

Colston held his gaze for a long, tense moment, then glanced away. But not before Paulo saw the flash of pain in his eyes. Pain and resentment.

"It's not that she doesn't want kids," he said in a low voice. "It's that she can't have any."

Paulo and Donovan traded meaningful glances. Each understood the significance of Colston's admission, the new questions it raised. Would the attorney have killed Maribel if he'd known she was carrying the only child he might ever have? Or would he have killed her to prevent his wife from learning about the pregnancy? How devastated would Abby Colston have been to discover that while *she* couldn't give her husband any children, another woman had?

"When did you find out about the baby?" Paulo asked quietly.

Colston closed his eyes for a moment, looking as if he were in pain. "She told me a week ago. She came into my office that morning, on the verge of tears. Even before she opened her mouth, I knew what she was going to say."

"How did you feel about it?"

"I was stunned. It was the last thing either of us wanted. We'd taken every precaution."

"Such as?"

Colston grimaced at the intrusive question. "Maribel was on the pill, and I always wore a condom. Like I said, we were careful."

"But Maribel was in love with you," Donovan pointed out. "How do you know she didn't want to get pregnant? How do you know she didn't stop taking the pill without your knowledge?"

"She wouldn't have done that."

"How do you know?"

"Because I know," Colston snapped. "I knew her. She wasn't deceitful like that. She understood that I was never leaving my wife, therefore it would have been irresponsible of her to deliberately get pregnant. She was devastated when she found out. She was ashamed, afraid of what her family and friends would think. Believe me, she wouldn't have put herself through that on purpose."

"Was she going to keep the baby?" Donovan asked.

"No." Colston's expression was grim. "She told me she was getting an abortion. Even if I'd wanted to, I couldn't have talked her out of it. So I gave her some money, told her to let me know if she needed any help making the arrangements."

"How very supportive of you," Paulo drawled, his voice

dripping with sarcasm. "Too bad she never got around to scheduling the appointment."

"Maybe she changed her mind," Donovan suggested.

"She didn't," Colston bit off.

"Then why'd she wait so long to make the appointment?"

"I don't know." A muscle pulsed in Colston's tightly clenched jaw. He reached over, straightened a stack of papers on his desk. "I have a lot of work to do, so if you gentlemen will excuse me—"

"Have you ever been to Maribel's house?" Paulo asked.

"What?"

"Did you ever go to her place, or did you just bang her at your house while your wife was away?"

Colston pressed his lips together until the skin around his mouth showed white. "Yes, I've been to Maribel's house."

"Often?"

"Often enough."

"Often enough to have your own garage door opener?"

Colston stiffened. The tips of his ears reddened. "She gave it to me for safekeeping in case she lost the other one."

Bullshit, thought Paulo.

Seeing the doubt on his face, Colston said defensively, "Just because I had access to Maribel's home doesn't mean I killed her."

"Were you at her house on Monday morning?"

"No. I already told you that I took my car to the dealership for an oil change. I still have the receipt."

"What time does the dealership open?"

"I don't know."

"Think."

Colston frowned. "If I'm not mistaken, it opens at seven thirty. I got there around eight."

"So you could have been at Maribel's house before that."

"I wasn't. I was at home."

"Can your wife vouch for that?"

Colston hesitated, then shook his head reluctantly. "She'd already left for the office. She had to be there early to prepare for a presentation."

"Convenient."

Colston said nothing.

"A neighbor says she saw a car pulling into Maribel's garage around five a.m.," Paulo told him.

"It wasn't me."

"Then I suppose you weren't the one who had sex with Maribel that morning?"

Colston stared at him. Either he was genuinely shocked or a damned good actor. "Was she raped?" he whispered. "Did that animal rape her?"

"The medical examiner says the sex was consensual." Paulo paused. "So the question is, if *you* didn't sleep with her that morning, who did?"

Some unnamed emotion flared in Colston's eyes— hurt? jealousy? anger?—before his face went carefully, deliberately blank. "I can't answer that question, Detective. All I know is that it wasn't me."

Paulo fell silent, his unblinking gaze steady on the attorney's face, on the solitary vein throbbing at his temple.

And for the first time since the interview began, he realized that Ted Colston might actually be telling the truth.

"Sounds like *someone's* in a good mood."

Tommie glanced up from the stack of invoices she'd been poring through to find Hazel Calhoun watching her, a quietly amused smile on her bespectacled face. "Did you say something, Mrs. Calhoun?"

"I said you must be in a good mood. You've been humming to yourself for the past thirty minutes."

"I have?" Tommie asked in surprise.

Hazel nodded, smiling.

"I'm sorry. Did I disturb you?"

"Not at all," Hazel said mildly. "I enjoyed your humming. I prefer it to the muttering and cursing I usually hear when you're doing the bookkeeping."

Tommie grinned sheepishly. "I didn't realize you could hear me doing that."

Hazel chortled. "I'm old, baby, not deaf."

Tommie smiled. "Don't worry. One of these days I'll have to break down and hire an accountant to take care of all this"—she gestured toward the mountain of paperwork in front of her—"so that I can just concentrate on running the studio."

"All in good time," Hazel said soothingly. As her gaze landed on a wilting fern, she rose from the small worktable where she'd been editing her church newsletter and walked across the cramped, windowless room that doubled as an office and supply closet.

That morning, taking advantage of a two-hour break between classes, Tommie had sequestered herself in the office to make a dent in the growing stack of paperwork on her desk. Hazel had arrived shortly afterward.

"Until you can afford to hire an accountant," said the older woman, clucking her tongue at the dying fern, "you just let me know if there's anything I can do to help."

Tommie shook her head. "You do enough already, Mrs. Calhoun. I couldn't possibly ask you to help me with the bookkeeping. You're underpaid as it is," she admitted ruefully.

Hazel guffawed, waving a dismissive hand as she went to retrieve a spray bottle. "You know I didn't take this job for the money. I like keeping myself busy, and I enjoy playing the piano for you and your students. It's one of the highlights of my week."

"Well, I definitely appreciate having you, Mrs. Calhoun. And so do my students."

Hazel beamed. "That's kind of you to say, baby."

"It's the truth." As Tommie watched Hazel spray the drooping plant, an image from last night's water fight with Paulo flashed through her mind, bringing an unconscious grin to her face.

Hazel, ever observant, arched a brow at her over the tops of her bifocals. "Would that look on your face have anything to do with that handsome young man who was here on Monday?"

Tommie's grin disappeared. Clearing her throat, she reached for the pile of invoices on her desk, asking with an air of casual nonchalance, "Do you mean Detective Sanchez?"

Hazel chuckled, not fooled for a minute. "Yes, that's who I was talking about. Such a nice young man. So polite and charming. And did I say handsome?"

"You did," Tommie said dryly.

"Well, he is. Very good looking."

"I suppose." Tommie shrugged. "He's not really my type."

"That's a shame. I thought I sensed something between the two of you. A connection."

Tommie frowned. "With all due respect, Mrs. Calhoun, you only saw us together for all of five minutes."

"I know." Hazel smiled, soft and intuitive. "That was all it took."

Tommie stared at her for a long moment, then dropped her gaze, pretending to become absorbed in her paperwork.

Satisfied that the fern would live to see another day, Hazel walked back to the table and sat down. Instead of returning to editing her newsletter, she reached for a misshapen ceramic mug, a handmade Mother's Day gift from one of her grandchildren, and took a quiet sip of coffee.

Sensing that the woman wanted to say more, Tommie waited, letting the silence stretch between them until her curiosity finally won out. "Is something on your mind, Mrs. Calhoun?"

"Hmm?"

"You look like you're deep in thought."

"Oh, I was just wondering."

"Wondering what?"

Hazel pursed her lips. "I know you come from a good family. Your folks are educated, wealthy. I was just wondering if they would object to you marrying a police officer."

Tommie sputtered out a laugh. "I'm not marrying Detective Sanchez!"

Hazel smiled a little. "I'm not referring to him specifically. I was speaking in general terms."

Likely story. "No, my parents wouldn't object to me marrying a police officer," Tommie drawled wryly. "Given my track record, I think they'd just be happy if the man I brought home didn't have a rap sheet or ten kids."

Hazel gave her a reproving look. "You know they have higher expectations for you than that."

Tommie smiled faintly. "Of course." Though there was a time she hadn't been so certain. "Anyway, I know my parents wouldn't mind me bringing home a cop because my sister married one, and they absolutely adore him."

Which was another reason Paulo was completely wrong for Tommie. After the way she'd made a fool of herself over Sebastien Durand, she had no interest in pursuing another homicide detective. Or so she told herself.

Hazel sipped her coffee, her eyes calculating above

the uneven rim of the cup. "I meant to ask you. Did Detective Sanchez enjoy the lasagna?"

Tommie snorted. "*That's* an understatement. He said it was the best lasagna he'd ever tasted, and he couldn't get enough of your peach cobbler."

A knowing gleam filled Hazel's eyes. "So you've seen him again since Monday night, have you?"

An embarrassed flush heated Tommie's face. Fortunately, she was spared from answering when the bell above the main door tinkled softly, announcing the arrival of a visitor.

Saved by the bell, Tommie thought, lunging from her chair and hurrying from the room. When she heard the soft scrape of boots on hardwood, her heart kicked, and for a moment she wondered—foolishly—if Paulo had stopped by.

But it was another man who stood waiting in the foyer, a man of medium height and build, with skin the color of melted caramel and close-cropped black hair. His hands were thrust casually into the pockets of gray wool trousers as he studied a framed poster of legendary dancer and choreographer Martha Graham.

Tommie froze in her tracks at the sight of him. Her heart slammed against her rib cage.

As he turned slowly to face her, a hot surge of rage swept through her.

Before he could open his mouth, she marched up to him and slapped him across his face, as hard as she could.

"How dare you show your face here!" she spat furiously.

Roland Jackson grimaced, rubbing his reddened cheek. "I suppose I deserved that," he muttered.

"You're damned right you did!" Trembling with fury, Tommie backhanded him across the other cheek, sending him staggering backward with a muffled grunt.

"Tomasina!" came Hazel's shocked exclamation behind her. "What on earth is going on?"

"I'm sorry you had to see that, Mrs. Calhoun," Tommie said through gritted teeth, glaring at Roland through the red haze blurring her vision, "but believe me when I tell you he had it coming, and then some."

"She's right, Sister Calhoun," Roland mumbled against the hand pressed to his split lip.

"*Sister* Calhoun?" Tommie divided an incredulous look between Roland and her pianist. "Do you two know each other?"

"Well, of course," Hazel said impatiently. "Roland is the newest deacon at my church."

"*Deacon*?" Tommie stared at him in stunned disbelief. "*You're* a deacon?"

He nodded, having the grace to look sheepish. "As of last month."

Hazel had reached the foyer, stepping between them as if to prevent further violence. She inspected Roland's bleeding lip, clucked her tongue in dismay. "Lord, child, what have you done?"

Tommie scowled. "Not nearly as much as I should have," she snarled, taking a menacing step forward with her fists balled.

Roland backed away, holding up his hands to ward off another vicious blow.

"Tomasina," Hazel hissed. "Enough!"

Still seething, Tommie shot Roland a look that warned him she wasn't through with him yet.

"I need to put some ice on that before it starts swelling," Hazel muttered, frowning worriedly at Roland's busted lip. "Tomasina, could you run upstairs to your loft and get some ice and paper towels?"

"No."

Hazel stared at her as if she hadn't heard right. "I beg your pardon?"

"With all due respect, Mrs. Calhoun," Tommie ground out tersely, "my answer is no. I won't get some ice and paper towels. Not for *him.*"

Hazel made an exasperated sound. "Fine, then. I'll just get them myself. Behave yourself." She started from the foyer, muttering under her breath, "Don't know what's gotten into the child, attacking people like a wildcat."

When Hazel had disappeared up the stairwell, Tommie rounded furiously on Roland. "You bastard! You've got a lot of nerve showing up here!"

Roland looked pained, though it wasn't clear whether he was reacting to her harsh words or the throbbing in his lip. "I know I'm the last person you want to see—"

"So why the hell are you here?"

"I wanted to see you," he said gently, his gaze imploring. "I wanted to tell you how sorry I am for what I did to you. I'm not the same man I was seven months ago. I've changed."

"Right," Tommie said mockingly. "From UPS driver to church deacon."

"It's true. I found the Lord, Tommie. I got saved."

"How convenient," she said, sneering contemptuously. "Too bad your religious conversion didn't happen *before* you got me drunk and secretly videotaped us having a threesome with your best friend. Too bad you didn't get saved *before* you decided to sabotage my dancing career."

Roland winced as if she'd struck him—again. He sucked his bottom lip into his mouth, licked away blood before saying, "I never meant to get you kicked out of the dance company, Tommie."

"Bullshit! You knew *exactly* what you were doing when you sent that embarrassing videotape to the artistic director. You threatened to circulate it to the media and everyone in the theater and dance community!"

"It was an empty threat," Roland insisted vehemently. "I wanted to humiliate you, that's all. How was I supposed to know the director would actually get rid of you? You were one of the company's best dancers!"

"You're damned right I was!" Tommie roared, the familiar hurt and anger rising up in her throat like bile. "I worked my ass off to earn a spot on that roster. You knew damned well how much it meant to me. But instead of being supportive and happy for me, what did you do? You set out to ruin me. Because you were jealous, because you couldn't handle the thought of me becoming successful and moving on without you!"

Roland swallowed, closing his eyes briefly. "You're right," he said in a low, humbled voice. "I was jealous of you. You left for New York to follow your dreams, while I couldn't even get my act together to move out of my mother's house. After you broke up with me, things really went downhill in my life, and I know it's wrong, but I blamed you."

Appalled, Tommie shook her head at him. "My God, Roland, I'd been gone for nearly four years. That's a long time to hold a grudge against someone for breaking up with you!"

"I know. I was obsessed with you. I see that now, and I'm so ashamed." His face was haggard, filled with anguished contrition.

Tommie wavered, wondering if she could believe him. Wondering if she could trust him. She'd made the mistake of trusting him once before, and he'd repaid her in the worst possible way. Why should she forgive him for what he'd done? Because he claimed to be a changed man? Because he had found God?

"What do you want from me, Roland?" she asked, her

voice brittle. "What did you hope to gain by coming here today?"

"I wanted you to know how sorry I am—"

"Fine," she said curtly. "You've apologized. Your conscience is clear. Now go in peace, do God's work."

Roland frowned. "I wish you wouldn't be so dismissive about me becoming a deacon. I've finally found my calling in life. I would think you'd be happy for me."

"The way you were happy for me?" Tommie jeered, outraged. She couldn't believe the audacity of the man, scolding *her* for not reacting appropriately to *his* good news!

Gesturing toward the open doors of the dance studio, Roland said casually, "You seem to be doing well for yourself. I've read about you in the papers, even saw you on TV last night." He paused. "Maybe what happened to you in New York was a blessing in disguise."

Tommie stared at him, her eyes narrowed in lethal warning. "I hope you're not suggesting that you did me a favor by getting me kicked out of the dance company."

"Of course not," he said quickly. "All I was trying to say is that everything happens for a reason. Being in ministry has taught me that. Our steps are ordained by the Lord, whether we follow Him or not. He knows the beginning and end of all things."

Tommie couldn't resist rolling her eyes. It wasn't that she was a heretic or anything. She'd grown up attending church regularly with her family, and she'd always respected other people's religious beliefs and values. But to hear such sanctimonious talk coming from Roland, of all people, was simply more than she could stomach.

"Mock all you want, Tommie," Roland said with quiet conviction, "but I know what I'm talking about. And one day you will, too."

"Okay. Whatever." She blew out an impatient breath, ready to bring an end to the vexing conversation. "If you don't mind, Roland, I have another class in half an hour, and I'd really like to finish what I was working on before my students arrive."

"Of course. I don't want to take up too much of your time."

"Too late," Tommie snapped.

Gazing earnestly into her eyes, Roland said, "Despite what I did to you, Tommie, I want you to know that I've always loved you. Although you may not remember, we *were* good together once."

"That was a long time ago," Tommie said coldly.

"I know. A lifetime ago." A sad smile touched his mouth. "I hope you can find it in your heart to forgive me. If our heavenly Father can forgive us our sins—"

"I get the point." Tommie crossed to the door, yanked it open. "Good-bye, Roland. Don't ever come back here again."

He hesitated, regret and longing etched into his features as he stared at her. After an endless moment, he left without another word.

Tommie slammed the door behind him, then released a deep, shaky breath and swept back the tendrils of hair that had escaped her ponytail. As she turned, she saw Hazel coming slowly down the stairs. The look on her face told Tommie she'd heard everything.

Tommie managed a rueful smile. "That wasn't exactly the way I wanted you to find out about my fall from grace."

"No, I suppose not." The older woman's eyes were full of gentle concern, not the condemnation Tommie had feared. "Are you all right, baby?"

"I think so." Tommie paused. "That probably needed to happen sooner or later. You know, so I could finally have . . . What's the word I'm looking for?"

"Closure?" Hazel supplied.

"Yeah, that's it. Closure."

Hazel nodded sagely. "I think you may be right."

They fell silent for a moment.

"Where's the ice and paper towels you were bringing him?" Tommie asked, belatedly noticing that her pianist had returned empty-handed.

"Oh, that." Hazel frowned. "I never actually made it into the loft."

Tommie arched a brow. "Were you eavesdropping the whole time, Mrs. Calhoun?"

"Maybe." She sniffed. "Anyway, after overhearing what I did, I figured Deacon Jackson was getting off easy if all he walked away with was a busted lip and a black eye."

Tommie gaped at the older woman, saw the spark of defiant mischief in her eyes, and burst out laughing.

It was only later, in the middle of leading her ballet class through a *grand battement jeté*, that Tommie realized she'd never asked Roland what had brought him to Houston in the first place. She knew for a fact that he'd still been living in San Antonio when he'd mailed the videotape to her artistic director seven months ago.

So when had he moved? she wondered uneasily. And what were the odds that he and Tommie had chosen to relocate to the same city to make a fresh start?

Was it possible that Roland had followed her to Houston?

The answer, she decided, was too disturbing to contemplate.

Chapter 14

Twenty minutes after leaving Santiago & Associates, Paulo and Donovan were back at the police station and wending their way through the homicide division, a wide room filled with cubicles and abuzz with the activity of detectives and uniformed officers walking, talking on phones, reviewing files, or clicking away at computer keyboards.

"I can't believe you don't think Colston is our guy," Donovan said, picking up where he and Paulo had left off in the car. "He was lying through his damned teeth the whole time he was talking to us!"

"I didn't say he isn't our guy," Paulo corrected, winking at an attractive black woman who was sashaying toward them, a cup of coffee in one hand, a computer printout in the other. She smiled flirtatiously at Paulo, mouthing *Call me sometime* as she passed by.

Donovan rolled his eyes, shaking his head at Paulo. "Don't you ever get enough? Oh, that's right," he amended, his face splitting into a wide grin. "Last night you didn't get *any*."

The remark was met with a stony look that promised retribution.

Donovan laughed.

"As I said in the car," Paulo muttered, shoving aside the unwelcome reminder of Tommie and the hellish night she'd put him through, "I don't think Colston slept with Maribel that morning, but that doesn't mean he didn't kill her. If anything, he might have offed her because he found out she was two-timing him."

"The cheating husband gets cheated on," Donovan ruminated. "Talk about poetic justice."

Still relishing the notion, he continued down the hallway while Paulo ducked into his cramped office. His desk was littered with files and crime scene photographs, along with notes and lab reports. After booting up his computer, he checked his e-mail and waded through phone messages that had come in overnight and early that morning. There were messages pertaining to some of his other active cases, and the usual calls from pushy reporters demanding an update on the status of Maribel Cruz's murder investigation. Norah O'Connor from the crime lab had called to confirm that the blood used to inscribe the word *liar* on Maribel's bedroom wall had been her own. Fibers lifted from the blood sample had come from a standard paintbrush, the kind that could be found in nearly every household and purchased at any home improvement store.

Out of habit Paulo called O'Connor back to badger her for more information about trace evidence collected at the crime scene.

"I knew you wouldn't be satisfied with what I gave you," the harried forensics investigator griped at him.

Paulo grinned wickedly. "That's not something I hear very often."

"I bet," O'Connor said with a reluctant chuckle. "Anyway, when I have more results to share, you'll be the first one I call."

"I'll be waiting."

"I bet you say that to all the girls."

Paulo grinned. "But I only mean it when I say it to you."

O'Connor snorted out a laugh. "God, Sanchez, you've got my heart all aflutter." Sobering after a moment, she said quietly, "I heard she was pregnant."

"Yeah," Paulo said grimly.

"Damn shame. I hope you catch the son of a bitch."

"You and me both," Paulo muttered.

He'd just hung up the phone when Donovan strode into the office, his eyes bright with adrenaline and excitement. He kicked out one of the chairs in front of Paulo's desk and quickly sat down.

"What's up?" Paulo asked.

"Seems we've got our own little juicy scandal brewing on Wisteria Lane," Donovan said.

"Wisteria Lane?"

"Yeah, you know. The fictional street on *Desperate Housewives.*" At Paulo's blank look, Donovan shook his head in disbelief. "Man, you really don't watch much TV, do you?"

Paulo snorted. "I sure as hell don't watch *Desperate Housewives.* And if you do, I'm asking for a new partner. Anyway, what scandal are you talking about?"

"I just got off the phone with one of Maribel Cruz's neighbors, a woman named Jayne Walsh. She says she was out of town on a business trip, just got back last night. When she heard on the evening news that Maribel had been killed, she wondered if it had anything to do with the argument she'd overheard between Maribel and Kristin Ramirez."

"The neighbor across the street? The one with the mother-in-law?"

Donovan nodded, leaning forward in the chair. "According to Walsh, about three weeks ago Maribel and

Kristin got into a heated argument during a housewarming party at another neighbor's house. Walsh says she was on her way to the kitchen to get some more wine when she overheard the two women arguing. Get this, man. Kristin called Maribel a disgusting whore, and accused her of sleeping with her husband, Enrique."

Paulo stared at him. "You're kidding."

"Nope. Walsh says Maribel seemed really upset. She kept saying she didn't know what Kristin was talking about. She called her paranoid, a jealous psycho. Walsh couldn't believe what she was hearing. She thought her ears were deceiving her, like maybe she'd had one too many glasses of wine. She peeked into the kitchen just in time to see Kristin shove Maribel against the counter. When Walsh gasped, the two women saw her and stopped fighting. But before Kristin stormed out of the kitchen, she told Maribel to watch her back, told her what goes around comes around."

"Shit," Paulo muttered grimly.

"I know. It's crazy, right? Correct me if I'm wrong, but at no time during our conversation with Kristin Ramirez did she mention threatening the deceased."

"She claimed she'd never seen Maribel with any particular guy," Paulo recalled, frowning. "She said she didn't know her very well."

"Well, it sounds like her husband knew Maribel *very* well."

"Unless she was telling the truth about not sleeping with him."

Donovan looked skeptical. "Considering this is the same woman who had an affair with her boss—another married man—I'm not in any hurry to give her the benefit of the doubt."

Paulo grimaced. "You've got a point." Leaning back in his chair, he scratched at his chin thoughtfully, scraping bristly whiskers as he turned possibilities over in his mind. "So you're thinking that Kristin killed Maribel?"

"She sure as hell had motive. And living right across the street, she definitely had opportunity. She knew Maribel's routine, knew what time she left for the office every morning. Kristin herself worked nights. From seven to seven, she told us. Maribel called in sick at seven-thirty that morning. Kristin could have gotten off from work, parked her car around the corner from their street, then walked to Maribel's house."

"In broad daylight?"

Donovan shrugged. "Suppose she'd changed into a sweatsuit. No one who saw her would think twice about her going for a jog in her own neighborhood. She stops in front of Maribel's house, glances around casually to make sure no one is watching, pulls a letter out of her pocket, then calmly walks up to the front door. If anyone asks later, she can just say she was dropping off misdirected mail."

"How did she get inside the house?"

"There was no sign of forced entry. Maybe she just rang the doorbell and told Maribel she wanted to talk, hash out their differences. Maribel let her inside, asked her to give her a minute to finish getting dressed. She goes back to the bedroom, Kristin makes her move."

Paulo said nothing, running the scenario through his mind. It wasn't beyond the realm of possibility that Kristin Ramirez had killed Maribel Cruz in a jealous fit of rage. After fifteen years in homicide, Paulo had seen enough deadly love triangles to know that anything was possible. But something about the scenario his partner had just described didn't feel right. Something was off.

"Kristin works at Ben Taub," Donovan continued, referring to a large hospital located downtown, "so she could have been home in twenty minutes."

"But she would have had to leave the hospital early in order to get home before Maribel left for work," Paulo reasoned, thinking aloud. "She wouldn't have known that Maribel woke up that morning and decided to call in sick."

"Okay, so we need to find out whether Kristin left work early that day. One phone call takes care of that." Donovan paused. "What about the mother-in-law? Think she knows anything?"

Paulo grimaced. "I don't know. She barely spoke any English. Would she have gone to the trouble of having Kristin call the police if she knew her daughter-in-law had done the deed?"

"She would if she was trying to help Kristin cover her tracks. She could have made up that whole story about the mysterious black car just to throw us off."

"Yeah, but the fact remains that Maribel had consensual sex that morning. *Someone* was there with her."

"Yeah. Ted Colston."

"Not according to him."

"He's lying," Donovan said flatly.

"The jury's still out on that."

"So *you* say," Donovan retorted, his lips twisting cynically.

Paulo chuckled. "Make up your mind about him. This morning you were convinced he was a cold-blooded killer. Now after one phone call from a neighbor, you've got someone else in your crosshairs."

Donovan gave a negligent shrug. "Hey, that's the nature of homicide investigations. They're unpredictable, constantly evolving."

"Yeah, I know," Paulo said dryly. "I've been at this a little longer than you have, junior."

A spark of anger flared in the younger detective's eyes. "Maybe you've been at it a little *too* long," he fired back. "Maybe it's going to take someone with a fresh perspective, someone willing to go out on a limb every once in a while, to solve this case."

Paulo regarded his partner for a long, unblinking moment.

The shift in the tension between them was subtle, but there. A tightening of muscles. A heightened awareness.

"If I didn't know better," Paulo said in a deceptively mild voice, "I would think you were calling me washed up. I would think you were questioning my commitment to the job."

Donovan scowled. "Don't put words in my mouth, Sanchez. I'm not questioning your commitment. If I didn't think you were a good cop, I wouldn't have asked to be your damned partner. All I'm saying is that maybe you've seen too much shit over the years. Maybe it's getting harder and harder for you to work up the same level of enthusiasm for each case. I mean, you're always the last one to arrive at crime scenes."

Paulo's mouth curved in a coolly amused smile. "You think maybe I'm tired of being in the trenches? You think I'm just cooling my heels, counting down the days until I get promoted to some cushy desk job?"

Donovan just stared at him, stone-faced and defiant.

Paulo said softly, "You're a good detective, Jules. Smart as hell, too. Sometimes I look at you and wonder what you're doing here when you could be making a killing at some hotshot brokerage firm. Truth be told, you're probably one of the smartest cops I've ever worked with. But you've got a helluva lot to learn about what it takes to survive in homicide. You haven't been around long enough to understand that it's not about who can make it to a crime scene first, it's about who has the patience and intestinal fortitude to see a tough case through to the end. It's about who can maintain their sanity after years of cramming their mind with images of strangled infants, mutilated little girls, disemboweled corpses, bodies burned beyond recognition. It's about who can ignore the demons, the tiny voices in your head that taunt and torment you until you decide the only way to silence them is to stuff your gun in your mouth and blow your fucking brains out." He smiled narrowly, tapping his temple with his fingertip. "When you've gone to that dark place, Detective Donovan, when you've eaten, slept, and breathed it for a good while, *then* you can come talk to me about working up more 'enthusiasm' for my cases."

Donovan stared at him as if he'd never seen him before.

The silence stretched between them.

Paulo let it hang, waiting.

Finally Donovan shook his head, blinking as if he were emerging from a deep trance. A wobbly grin tugged at his mouth. "Man, I never realized what a crazy motherfucker you are, Sanchez. I mean, I'd heard whispers here and there—"

Paulo grinned. "And you still asked to be my partner? What does that say about you?"

Donovan huffed a laugh. "That's a damned good question."

And just like that, like the snap of a hypnotist's fingers, the tension between them dissolved.

"So here's how I see it going down with Kristin Ramirez," Donovan said, returning to the original subject as if they'd never been interrupted. "After she does the deed, she sneaks back into her house, cleans herself up, and gets rid of the bloody clothes while the mother-in-law is walking the kid to school. The elementary school is a good fifteen minutes away from the house. Mrs. Ramirez is an old lady, walks slow. I figure Kristin had plenty of time to get her shit together before her mother-in-law returned."

Paulo was faintly amused. "You've thought of everything, haven't you?"

Donovan flashed a grin. "If the husband didn't have the perfect alibi—being stationed in Iraq—I'd be looking at him for the murder. You know how crazy those soldiers are. Maybe even crazier than you."

Paulo's answering smile was distracted. He was thinking about the little boy he'd seen in the photograph above the Ramirez family's fireplace. Dark eyes shining with laughter, a happy, infectious grin stretched across his face. Paulo thought of how Jayden Ramirez's life would never be the same again if his mother was convicted of murder and sent to prison for the rest of her life.

And then he thought of the weeping couple he'd watched on the news last night, their faces ravaged with grief, their lives forever shattered by the senseless act of violence that had claimed their daughter's life.

And he remembered why he'd started drinking all those years ago.

"Hell," he muttered, scrubbing a hand over his face and pushing out a deep breath.

Donovan said, "I think we need to pay another visit to Kristin Ramirez, find out why she didn't think it was important to tell us she'd once threatened her now-departed neighbor."

Paulo nodded. "Give me a minute. I need to return some calls."

After Donovan left the office, Paulo reached for the phone on his desk. As he lifted the receiver, his gaze landed on the gruesome crime scene photos scattered across his desk. He paused, realizing that the reason he'd instinctively dismissed the possibility of a female perpetrator was that in his experience women didn't kill in such a manner—with brutality, with cruelty, with a virulent hatred for their own gender.

In his gut he knew that Kristin Ramirez wasn't the monster they were looking for.

But then a chilling memory surfaced. Another time, another place.

And he reminded himself that when it came to finding Maribel Cruz's killer, no one could be overlooked as a suspect.

No one.

The stranger's heart was pounding.

Anticipation snaked through his veins, heating his blood as he crept stealthily through the darkened loft, moving like a shadow from one room to the other. He touched everything he could, letting his hand linger on a pink leotard draped over a wicker hamper. It still held the warmth of her body. And her scent. A heady, alluring scent that went straight to a man's glands. Shamelessly he reached into the hamper and curled his fingers around a pair of black panties. Closing his eyes, he pressed the scrap of silk to his face and inhaled her erotic, feminine scent as greedily as a smoker inhales nicotine. Lust thundered through his body. He lowered the underwear to his crotch and rubbed it against his straining erection, pretending he was thrusting into the real, live woman.

Quivering inside, he slipped the panties into his pocket, the latest souvenir to be added to his collection. He'd been taking little keepsakes from her loft for weeks now, and so far she seemed none the wiser.

The thought brought a sly smile to his face as he continued prowling around the large bedroom that was not as neat as Maribel Cruz's, and was only slightly less cluttered than the blonde's. Tommie Purnell enjoyed nice things. When she saw something she liked, she rarely stopped herself from getting it. Everywhere he looked he saw charming little knickknacks, things she'd purchased from boutiques during her travels abroad. Exotic candles arranged on a stack of wooden chests, a string of pearls spilling from an antique jewelry box, a tasseled footstool beside the bed, a collection of Parisian hat boxes filled with everything from a red beret to vintage linens. A pair of pink threadbare toe shoes, dangling on ribbons hung from a corner of the vanity mirror, had been signed by some Russian ballerina whose name he recognized, but couldn't pronounce.

As he stood at the foot of the four-poster bed, he imagined what it would be like to have her soft, supple body pinned beneath his. He imagined what it would be like to taste her. To feel the heat of her silky skin rubbing eagerly against him. To hear her moan and to see her writhing in ecstasy and opening her legs as he plunged into her, claiming her as his own.

As he reached down to stroke his throbbing cock, his vision cleared, bringing into focus the empty bed with the undisturbed covers. He frowned, his erection subsiding as he remembered that she hadn't slept in her own bed last night. She'd spent the night at the cop's apartment, letting him kiss her, touch her, do unspeakable things to her.

Jezebel, the stranger thought with renewed fury. *Faithless whore!*

He'd followed her last night, had watched as she parked in front of Sanchez's apartment building and climbed out of her car, a rush of wind tossing her dark hair about her face and shoulders. He'd been tempted to take her right then and there. His pulse had quickened at the thought of sneaking up behind her and seeing the abject fear on her face before he snatched her away.

But he'd resisted.

Soon he would make her pay for her sins. For her wanton ways.

Soon, he consoled himself. But not yet.

First things first.

The police had yet to discover the blonde's body. No one loved her the way Maribel Cruz had been loved. It would be another day or two before anyone would even think to come looking for her. But he'd known that when he chose her. He knew he would have to wait a little longer to experience that same thrill rush he'd felt on Monday night as he'd stood watching the police officers and evidence technicians coming and going from Maribel's house, driven by a sense of urgency he'd found almost pitiable.

He knew his gratification would have to be delayed at least another day. But he didn't mind. He was a patient man. He'd had plenty of practice waiting, planning, hiding in the shadows. Biding his—

Suddenly he froze, his pulse pounding in his ears.

He thought he'd heard her voice out in the stairwell.

No! It can't be!

He threw a panicked glance at his digital watch. Seven thirty. He was supposed to have another thirty minutes before her last class ended. Why was she coming upstairs *now?*

And then suddenly he realized that the music had stopped playing on the floor below. He'd been so caught up in his fantasy that he hadn't even noticed. She must have dismissed her students early that night. How could he not have been paying attention? How could he have been so careless?

He gnashed his teeth, angry and disgusted with himself. After all his hard work, the careful planning and preparation he'd done, one stupid mistake on his part could ruin everything. *Everything!*

He listened hard, ears straining over the thundering beat of his heart. And then he heard the soft, distinct click of a lock being turned.

His heart jumped to his throat.

She entered the loft, talking quietly on her cell phone.

His gaze darted across the room to the window. If he tried to climb back down, she would hear him and call the police. He couldn't take that risk. He had to find somewhere to hide until she went into the bathroom to take her nightly shower.

Thinking fast, he slipped quietly into the large closet and took cover behind a row of designer clothes. The minutes ticked past as he huddled in the darkness, sweat beading on his upper lip and forehead, nerves stretched to the breaking point.

If she discovered him hiding there, he'd have to kill her.

He had no other choice.

He waited, breath held in his lungs.

And then he heard her footsteps.

Light and brisk.

Coming straight toward the bedroom.

Chapter 15

"I'm so sorry this happened, Zhany," Tommie said as she walked down the hall to her bedroom. "I can't even imagine how difficult this has been for you and your family. I just wish there was something I could do."

"There is," Zhane murmured. "You can pray for a miracle."

He sounded so weary that Tommie's heart constricted. He'd called her half an hour ago to tell her that his nephew had taken a turn for the worse overnight. Kadeem had needed another blood transfusion and was running a high fever from an infection caused by the bullet shattering part of his intestine. He was hanging on by a thread.

"Are you sure you don't need anything?" Tommie asked gently. "You've been camped out at the hospital since yesterday. I could stop by your apartment and get a change of clothes for you, then bring some food for you and your family."

"That's okay, sugarplum. Visiting hours are over for non-family members, and I already ran home this afternoon and packed an overnight bag. And we had dinner—"

"From the cafeteria?" Tommie asked, wrinkling her nose in distaste.

Zhane chuckled. "No, not the cafeteria, Miss Finicky. Zeke ran out and got pizza for everyone. And I didn't even have to loan him the money."

Tommie smiled. "There's hope after all," she said, stepping through her bedroom doorway and flipping on the light switch. She made her way to the bathroom, and with the phone cradled between her ear and shoulder, she tugged down her leggings and sat on the toilet.

"And speaking of hope," Zhane said, "the detective assigned to our case has been giving us regular updates all day."

"Really?"

"Yeah. He started by calling us last night and apologizing profusely for not returning our calls sooner."

"That's good," Tommie murmured, grateful for Paulo's intervention and pleased that Detective Mendiola had kept his promise to him. "What did he say about the search for Chauncey?"

"He said they have several strong leads that they're pursuing, and he promised us that they were doing everything they could to find Chauncey." Zhane paused. "Are you *tinkling* while I'm on the phone?"

Tommie grinned sheepishly. "I had to go really bad. You know how much water I drink."

"Uncouth," Zhane pronounced, but she could tell he was grinning. It warmed her heart to know that he could still have a sense of humor during such an emotionally trying time.

As she flushed the toilet and washed her hands, Zhane told her, "Richard says I won't be able to perform this Friday since I missed another rehearsal tonight."

"What?" Tommie cried, outraged. "You're going through a family crisis, and *this* is how he shows his compassion and support? How dare he!"

Zhane sighed. "It's all right, sugarplum. It's probably for the best. I wasn't feeling up to performing tomorrow night anyway, what with Kadeem lying in that hospital bed and fighting for his life. I'd never forgive myself if he died and I wasn't here to say good-bye. You felt the same way about your grandmother."

"I know, sweetie," Tommie murmured, still miffed about Richard Houghton's insensitive behavior. "I understand completely where you're coming from. But the decision not to perform should have been yours, not his."

"Now, you know that's not true," Zhane countered mildly. "Richard is the artistic director. *He* has to decide what's best for the company. The show must go on."

"That may be so," Tommie grumbled, too incensed for magnanimity, "but you tell that son of a bitch that if *you* won't be performing tomorrow night, I won't be there, either."

Zhane choked out a laugh. "Now, that's not very nice of you, boycotting the performance when you know how much Richard always looks forward to having you there."

"That's too damned bad," Tommie said mutinously as she stalked out of the bathroom. "He should have thought about that before he decided to behave like an asshole. Please give my apologies to the rest of the company."

Zhane sighed. "All right," he reluctantly conceded, knowing better than to argue with her when she'd made up her mind about something—right or wrong. "Well, I'd better go back upstairs before Ma comes looking for me to bum some money."

A sympathetic grin tugged at Tommie's mouth. "That might be a good idea."

"What're you about to do?"

"Head back down to the studio to work on some choreography for my West African dance class."

"Sounds lovely. I'll be there with you in spirit."

"Back at you, sweetie. Call me if you need anything, and I'll see you tomorrow at the hospital." She made a long, noisy kissing sound that made Zhane laugh before he hung up.

Still smiling to herself, Tommie tossed the phone onto her bed and stepped out of her pointe shoes. As she started to remove her dance skirt, she felt a cold tickle on the back of her neck.

She paused, glancing over her shoulder toward the darkened entrance to the walk-in closet. The fine hairs on her nape lifted. Her skin prickled.

She sensed someone in the room with her, sensed someone breathing nearby.

Don't be ridiculous. There's no one here but you.

Tommie frowned. She'd been edgy and out of sorts all day, ever since Roland Jackson's unexpected visit that morning. After ballet class she'd remembered to ask Mrs. Calhoun if she knew how long he'd been living in Houston. According to Mrs. Calhoun, Roland had joined her church five months ago. A humble, deferential young man with a thirst for knowledge, he'd made such an impression on the church elders that they'd taken him under their collective wing and began grooming him to serve the ministry as a deacon. Mrs. Calhoun couldn't recall when Roland had relocated from San Antonio, or what had prompted the move. But she'd assured Tommie that, in light of what she'd learned about him that morning, she would be keeping a close eye on him from now on.

Smiling at the thought of Mrs. Calhoun's unquestioning loyalty, Tommie padded across the large room to her armoire, where she pulled out a black sports bra and matching spandex shorts. She quickly undressed, trading her sweaty leotard and leggings for the clean bra and shorts.

Once again she sensed a whisper of cold breath against her skin, a hint that something was wrong. Out of place.

She turned, her pulse thrumming in her ears as she scanned the empty room. Nothing looked out of place. Nothing seemed out of place. Yet she couldn't shake the ominous feeling that she was being watched.

Calm down, she ordered herself. *No one's watching you. You're being paranoid!*

Still, she couldn't help thinking about Maribel Cruz, a single woman who had lived alone, who had been found stabbed to death in her own home. Tommie wondered whether Maribel had heard a noise or sensed her attacker's presence before he'd struck.

And then she remembered that it was only two nights ago that she'd found her front door unlocked. Mrs. Calhoun was fairly certain she hadn't forgotten to lock the door. Tommie was certain *she* hadn't, either.

That could leave only one chilling possibility. Someone had broken into her loft.

And the intruder, whoever he was, had returned.

Tommie swallowed hard, fear splintering through her body.

Don't panic! You don't even know if someone's really here!

She strained to listen, not moving a muscle, hardly daring to breathe.

Outside, she heard the sigh of the wind rustling the leaves of the giant oaks in the front yard.

Inside the loft, she heard nothing but silence.

But she glanced quickly around the bedroom, searching for something she could use as a weapon. If only she'd followed through on purchasing a gun and taking shooting lessons, as she'd planned to do after her sister was terrorized and assaulted four years ago. But after moving to New York, Tommie had gotten sidetracked with pursuing her ambition of becoming a professional dancer, and eventually she'd just convinced herself that violent crime couldn't strike twice in the same family.

She frowned, silently cursing her own willful naiveté.

If she were confronted by an intruder this very minute, she had nothing to defend herself with.

The thought sent another tremor of fear slicing through her.

Heart hammering in her chest, she peered into the gaping darkness of her closet, imagining she could sense a malevolent presence within, could feel a pair of reptilian eyes watching her, waiting to pounce.

Slowly she began edging toward the door. If she could just make it out of the loft, she could race down the stairs, run outside to her car, lock the doors, and call the police. She'd worry about what to say once she—

Riiing!

Tommie jumped, letting out a startled cry.

Her cell phone had rung. Heart in her throat, she hurried to her bed and snatched it up with trembling hands.

"Hello?" she croaked.

"Girl, what's this I hear about you skipping out on Friday's performance?"

Relief swept through Tommie at the sound of Renee Williams's indignant, yet wonderfully reassuring voice. She let out a deep, shuddering breath and sank weakly onto the bed. "You talked to Zhane, I see."

"I just got off the phone with him. I called to see how his nephew was doing, and before our conversation ended, he told me he wouldn't be dancing tomorrow. He also mentioned that you wouldn't be there, either. What gives?"

"I'm boycotting in protest of Richard's decision not to let Zhane perform. You and I both know Zhane is the most dedicated and most experienced dancer in the company. If anyone can afford to miss a rehearsal or two, it's him."

"I know that's right. Hey, listen, I'm right around the corner from you. Do you want to grab a cup of coffee? Or were you in the middle of—"

"No!" Tommie all but shouted into the phone. At Renee's soft chuckle, she said in a calmer voice, "I mean, I'd love to get some coffee."

"Sounds like someone needs a caffeine fix. Meet me outside in five minutes."

"I'll be ready," Tommie promised, already shoving her feet into a pair of sneakers and grabbing a sweatshirt draped across a chaise longue. She'd probably freeze her ass off once she got outside, but she didn't have time—or the inclination—to change into something warmer.

At the bedroom door she paused and glanced over her shoulder, surveying the silent, empty room. She felt no whisper of movement, saw no evil eyes glowing at her from the darkened closet.

It was all in your mind, she told herself.

With one last lingering look, she turned off the light and hurried from the room, trying to shake the eerie feeling that she hadn't been alone.

Paulo was dead tired.

He'd spent the day catching up on paperwork, going over autopsy reports, and interviewing witnesses, all the while waiting for some lead that would break the Cruz case wide open.

The interview with Kristin Ramirez had not gone the way Donovan had hoped or planned. When he and Paulo arrived unannounced at her house, she hadn't looked surprised or terrified to see them; instead she'd looked resigned, as if she'd been expecting them at any time. With Isadora Ramirez hovering worriedly in the living room doorway, Kristin had admitted to accusing Maribel Cruz of sleeping with her husband and threatening her at the neighbor's housewarming party. She admitted she was wrong for not telling Paulo and Donovan about the incident the first time they'd interviewed her, but she hadn't wanted to upset her mother-in-law with the news that her favorite son had cheated on his wife.

When Paulo asked Kristin if she had proof of the affair, she'd closed her eyes, tears leaking out of the corners, and quietly explained how she'd come home early from taking her son to a birthday party to find her husband, Enrique, returning from Maribel's house. His clothes had been rumpled, Kristin recalled, and he'd smelled so strongly of sex there could be no mistaking what he and Maribel had been doing that afternoon. Not wanting to cause a scene in front of their son—who'd gotten sick at the birthday party, prompting their early departure— Kristin had waited until Jayden was safely napping before she'd confronted her husband. Enrique had denied any wrongdoing, telling Kristin that he'd promised to fix Maribel's leaky faucet before he deployed to Iraq. Kristin hadn't believed him, not for a second, but she'd decided to drop the matter for the sake of peace.

"He was leaving for Iraq in two days," she'd whispered tearfully. "If something happens to him over there, I didn't want our last words to each other to be angry, hurtful words."

But while she'd been willing to forgive her wayward husband, her generosity had not extended to the other woman. Kristin acknowledged that she'd wanted to hurt Maribel—had wanted to "yank every last strand of hair from her scalp and scratch her eyes out"—but she insisted that she hadn't killed her. And she had an alibi. On Monday morning she'd been trapped at the hospital until ten thirty covering for another nurse who'd gotten stuck in a major traffic accident on I-45. One call to Kristin's supervisor had confirmed her story.

By the time Paulo and Donovan left the house, the younger detective had formulated another theory. "I say they're all in it together—Colston, Kristin, and the mother-in-law. They were all betrayed by Maribel in one way or another. Therefore they all had a motive for revenge. And are you thinking what I'm thinking about the baby Maribel was carrying?"

"That it might have been Enrique Ramirez's instead of Ted Colston's?" Paulo nodded. "The thought crossed my mind."

Donovan shook his head, muttering, "What a damned mess."

For the first time that day, Paulo agreed with his partner. For all the good it did either of them.

At the end of another long, frustrating day, Paulo found himself glaring at the grisly crime-scene photos on his computer monitor, his brain hurting from the effort to make sense of what he was viewing, to connect the missing pieces that eluded him.

That afternoon Maribel's body had been released to her family so they could return home to Brownsville and begin the difficult process of making funeral arrangements. The DA wanted answers, Paulo's family wanted answers, his captain was breathing down his neck, and he was no closer to knowing who had committed the heinous murder than the day he'd walked into Maribel's house.

He craved a smoke so bad he'd been tempted to bum a cigarette from one of the other officers. The Cruz case was getting under his skin in a way that only nicotine could salve.

Of course, the murder investigation wasn't the only thing getting under his skin.

A pair of dark eyes, sensual and inviting, flashed through his mind.

Paulo swore savagely under his breath, scrubbing a hand over his face as if to erase the tormenting image.

His preoccupation with Tommie Purnell had all the earmarks of a full-fledged obsession. He thought about her constantly. The more time he spent with her, the more he wanted her. And though he knew she was bad for him, he couldn't get enough of her.

So it came as no surprise to him when he found himself driving to her loft that evening after leaving the police station. He could no more stop himself from going to her than he could change his blood type.

He was relieved to see her red Mazda parked outside the small building, even as he silently marveled that a woman who looked like her didn't lead a more active social life. Not that he was complaining.

As he climbed out of his police cruiser and walked to the main door, he could hear music coming from the building. Something with a heavy, pounding rhythm. So she was definitely home.

He knocked on the door and pressed the doorbell, figuring she might have a hard time hearing him over the loud music. And her intercom system was broken, so he couldn't even buzz her.

After a full minute passed he tried the doorknob, frowning when it turned in his hand. Damn it! Didn't she know better than to leave her door unlocked with a killer on the loose?

He stepped inside, closing and locking the door

behind him. The foyer was in darkness, but lights glowed at the end of the hallway and music spilled from the open doors of the dance studio. Paulo followed the pounding beat of the drums, the pulsing rhythm of the percussions.

By the time he reached the doorway, he was all set to lecture her about not locking her front door and foolishly endangering her life.

The words dried in his throat at the sight that greeted him.

Tommie was alone on the floor, dancing to a drum solo that reverberated from Paulo's ears to his toes. The haughty, austere ballet instructor he'd encountered a few days ago had been replaced by this wild, uninhibited creature twisting and contorting her body in a series of primal, undulating movements that stole his breath. He watched her, pulse pounding in his ears, heart knocking against his ribs.

She wore a black sports bra and matching spandex shorts that rode the flare of her hips and molded her firm, lushly rounded buttocks. Her stomach muscles, emphasized by a slick gleam of sweat, shimmered and contracted in a fierce, provocative tempo. Her feet were bare, her hair flying about her face in tangled disarray. The way she moved her body was unlike anything Paulo had ever seen in his life. He stared, riveted by the fluid grace of her arms, the flexing of her torso, the frenzied, undulating rhythm of her hips. She was powerful, ruthlessly seductive, primitively erotic.

He couldn't take his eyes off her.

He was mesmerized and seduced, the tribal music beating in time to the heavy throbbing in his groin. When she rolled to the floor and struck a pose with her body arched like a bow, her head flung back and her eyes closed, he lost it.

As she glided to her feet he strode toward her, impatiently peeling off his leather jacket and flinging it aside.

Tommie spun at the sound of his footsteps, her breasts bouncing softly with the movement, her eyes widening at the sight of him. With her tousled hair framing her flushed face and her brown skin glistening with perspiration, she looked like some lush, primeval creature. An ancient goddess of sex.

Her lips parted in surprise. "Paulo—"

He reached her in three long strides, crushing his mouth to hers, swallowing her startled gasp. He lifted her into his arms, and she wrapped her legs tightly around his waist. He groaned deep in his throat, cupping the ripe swell of her buttocks and grinding his aching erection against her. She moaned, sinking her fingers into his hair, twining her tongue sensually around his. Lust roared through his blood. His heart thudded in sync with the pulsing drums.

He backed her against the long, mirrored wall as their kiss grew hotter, wilder, more intense. Using the wall to brace her, he dragged the sports bra over her head, swore as he watched those voluptuous, incredible breasts spring free. He tossed the bra aside, took a moist, beaded nipple into his mouth, and sucked greedily. She sobbed with pleasure, her hands fisting in his hair.

A moment later those hands were pulling frantically at him. He heard something rip, dazedly realized it was his shirt. She clawed it off his shoulders, ran greedy hands over his heaving bare chest. He lowered her feet to the floor long enough to kneel and yank her shorts off her legs. And then she was back in his arms, her thighs locked around his hips, their mouths tearing voraciously at each other. He reached between their bodies, found her hot and drenched. Later, he would bury his face in the luscious banquet of her sex, lap it up like the starving man he was. But not now. Right now all he wanted was to be buried deep inside her. He'd been tortured long enough.

He pressed her back against the wall and reached down to fish a condom out of his wallet and unzip his trousers. He tossed the wallet aside, his hands trembling with anticipation as he quickly covered himself. Heart hammering, he deliberately rubbed the tip of his throbbing penis against the slick, swollen folds of her labia.

Tommie shuddered in response, bit his lower lip hard. "Don't you dare tease—"

He drove into her, and she let out a primal scream that ignited his blood. Their gazes locked, speechless. He began thrusting into her, driven by the sheer pleasure of her tight, wet heat stretching around him, sheathing him so perfectly it was as if their bodies had been created for each other.

The room was like a sauna, hot and steamy. Droplets of sweat drizzled from their joined bodies and splashed onto the floor. Paulo thrust hard and deep, taking her roughly and possessively. She matched him stroke for stroke, her hips pistoning furiously against his, her long nails digging into the slippery slope of his shoulders. He cupped her bouncing breasts, one in each hand, and sucked both nipples in turn, licking and caressing the plump curves.

Over the pounding drumbeat he could hear her desperate pleas and demands, mingling with his own guttural moans. He lifted his head from her breasts and fused his mouth to hers, swallowing her cries, feeding on them as he rammed in and out of her. Harder and faster as the music swelled to an aching crescendo.

She came in a violent rush, screaming his name and clawing at his back as her body convulsed in the intense grip of an orgasm. He shouted hoarsely as he began coming, spurting into the condom, milked dry by the feminine muscles clenching and pulsing around him. The pleasure of it tore through him, leaving him shattered and shaking uncontrollably as he and Tommie clutched each other, gasping for air.

Somehow he managed to hold on to her as they slid to the floor in a boneless heap. For several minutes neither could move or speak. They lay limply together on the smooth hardwood floor, Tommie gloriously naked, Paulo with his trousers bunched around his ankles. Dimly he realized that the music had stopped playing. Their ragged, panting breaths were amplified in the sudden silence of the room.

After another moment Paulo groaned, the sound of an unconscious man struggling toward awareness. Tommie laughed, low and husky, and nestled against him.

As his lazy gaze roamed the length of her body, he noticed that she had a pretty little mole on the curve of her hip. Before the night was over, he intended to learn and explore every exquisite inch of her.

"Well," she murmured. "That was a first."

"What?"

"I've never done it in a dance studio before."

Paulo chuckled. "Neither have I."

She propped herself onto one elbow, brushing his sweat-dampened hair off his forehead as she smiled down at him. "So you *haven't* experienced every delight known to man."

He shook his head slowly. "After tonight, I realize I hadn't even scratched the surface."

She blushed demurely, her smile softening with pleasure. "It *was* pretty incredible."

"I told you it would be," he murmured, stroking her smooth back. Her body was a banquet, a feast for the eyes.

Sleek and sublimely curvy with those generous breasts and endless legs. Just like that, he wanted her again.

Her gaze drifted downward to where his penis lay against his belly, stiff and engorged. She licked her lips, her eyes darkening with hunger. Heat flared inside him, like a flame ignited by gasoline.

He was already reaching for her as she sat up and straddled him. Her hot, womanly scent wafted up to his nostrils, making him salivate. She braced her hands on either side of his head and leaned down, the ends of her hair tickling his chest as she kissed him, slow and sensual.

"We should probably go upstairs," she whispered against his mouth. "I have a bed, you know."

Paulo lifted her by the waist, felt her sharp intake of breath as he impaled her. "Maybe next time."

Chapter 16

Sometime after midnight, Tommie found herself lying facedown and sideways across her bed, her bones limp as water, her body spent and satiated. The sheets were hot and tangled, damp and musky with the scent of sex. In the warm glow of the bedside lamp she could see Paulo lying on his back, his eyes closed, his chest rising and falling rapidly.

After leaving the studio they'd headed for the loft, making it halfway up the stairs before a fresh wave of passion overtook them. One moment they were kissing feverishly; the next moment Paulo had Tommie pinned against the wall and clinging to him for dear life as he pounded furiously into her. He didn't stop until she was gasping and crying, her throat raw from screaming, every nerve in her body strained to fever pitch. They made love so many times she lost count of the number of orgasms he brought her to, lost track of everything but the mind-blowing pleasure he was giving her.

"I can't move," she croaked now, blowing her hair out of her eyes.

Paulo chuckled, a low, husky rumble. "I'm not even going to try."

She grinned weakly. "I suppose this *has* been a bit much for you, being an old guy and all."

He reached out, slapping her on the butt.

She jumped, laughing. "Ouch! I thought you weren't going to move!"

"I made an exception. Come here." He dragged her into his arms, kissed her forehead as she snuggled against him and tucked her head beneath his chin.

Tommie couldn't remember the last time, if ever, she'd felt so warm and contented. As experienced as she was—and there was no use denying it—no man had ever made love to her as passionately and intensely as Paulo had. And for as long as she lived, she would never forget the fierce, determined expression on his face as he'd strode toward her at the end of her dance. She shivered just thinking about it.

"Cold?" Paulo murmured.

She shook her head, smiling as she ran her hand over the hard, sculpted planes of his chest, enjoying the flex and play of his muscles. "I was just wondering what about my dancing brought out the animal in you tonight."

He chuckled low and deep in his throat, the vibration of it making her belly quiver. "You don't have to be dancing to do that to me. But yeah, that dance was something else. You were hypnotizing, erotic as hell."

Tommie warmed with pleasure at his husky words. "I'm glad you enjoyed it. It was inspired by a West African mating dance."

He laughed. "No wonder. And now you know it works."

"Oh yeah. Beyond my wildest dreams." She smiled against his chest, sighed languorously. "We should go salsa dancing sometime."

"What makes you think I know how to salsa?" he challenged. "Because I'm Hispanic?"

"No," she laughed protestingly, slapping his muscled shoulder. "It was just a suggestion."

"Uh-huh. Likely story."

"It's the truth. Anyway, do you?"

"Do I what?"

"Know how to salsa?"

He hesitated for so long she thought he wouldn't answer her. Curious, she lifted her head to search his face in the soft lamplight. "Well?"

His lips quirked. "Yes," he admitted sheepishly.

"I knew it!" she said with a triumphant laugh.

He chuckled. "My aunt taught me when I was a kid. I had no choice."

Tommie grinned, shaking her head at him. "You've got some nerve, Paulo Sanchez, trying to make me feel guilty for stereotyping you," she chided, poking him playfully in the ribs. "Just for that, you're going salsa dancing with me. I want to see what kind of moves you've got."

He flashed a wicked pirate's grin. "I thought I just showed you what kind of moves I've got."

Indeed he had, she mused. Against the wall. On the floor. In the stairwell with the flickering lights. All over the bed. "I'm talking about on the *dance* floor," she clarified.

Paulo arched a brow. "Didn't we start off on the dance floor?"

A helpless laugh escaped. "You know very well what I mean." Suddenly embarrassed, Tommie buried her hot face against his chest and groaned. "God, I'll never look at my studio the same way again. Every time I step through the doors, I'll remember the things we did in there."

Paulo chuckled, lazily caressing the swell of her backside. "You make that sound like a bad thing," he drawled.

Tommie lifted her head to glare reproachfully at him. "Considering that I'm running a dance school, and a majority of my students are minors, you can see how me fantasizing about sex during class might not be so good for business."

Again he flashed that devilish, irreverent grin. "I still don't see what the problem is."

"Oh, you don't, do you?" Slowly, deliberately, Tommie slid down his body and insinuated herself between his strong, muscular thighs. Holding his dark gaze, she ran her fingers through the silky black hair that arrowed down to where his thick penis lay against his abdomen, swelling and stiffening before her very eyes.

"Mmmm," she purred in throaty appreciation. "Maybe I should come to *your* job and seduce you, Detective. See how *you'd* like having flashbacks of me doing this—" She flicked her tongue out, snakelike, catching a pearly drop of precome from the tip of his shaft.

Paulo jerked, swearing hoarsely under his breath.

"Or this—" She wrapped her fingers around him, dragging a groan of pleasure out of him. His penis was hot and hard, the soft skin gliding beneath her hand as smooth as marble. She gave him a bold, stroking caress. Long, firm pulls milking him all the way to the tip.

He sucked in a harsh breath, closing his eyes as if he were in agony. *"Dios mio."*

"Or how about this—" She took him deep into her mouth, reveling in the violent tremor that shook his body. She licked around and over the head of his shaft, then up and down the throbbing length until it was slippery from her saliva and his own juice. With one hand she grasped the thick base, while with the other she cupped his engorged testicles and massaged them slowly and sensually. She could feel the tension building inside him, like a deadly storm gathering force.

Fighting her own burgeoning arousal, she purred seductively, "How would you like *this* going through your mind every time you're interrogating a suspect or—"

With a guttural oath Paulo reared up, rolling her over and pinning her beneath him. Tommie's triumphant laughter dissolved into a shuddering sob as he thrust into her, filling her with one long, brutally erotic stroke.

Gazing into his dark, smoldering eyes, she wrapped her legs around his hips and grabbed his buttocks, pulling him into her body as far as she could take him. He lowered his head, sucked a taut, swollen nipple into his mouth. She cried out, jolts of sensation rushing to her loins. Her hips bucked beneath him as he pumped harder, deeper, faster, driving her toward another soul-shattering, mind-blowing orgasm.

They rocked together, moaning and shouting encouragements to each other with each deep, penetrating thrust. Tommie pulled his hair, felt tears burning the backs of her eyelids. And when the end came for both of them in an explosive climax that left them gasping and trembling, Paulo seized her mouth in a hot, ravenous kiss and whispered huskily, "Turnabout is fair play."

Friday, November 13

The call came at 5:00 a.m.

Paulo, in a deep, sated slumber, almost didn't hear it. When the ringing phone finally registered, he opened a bleary eye, groaned, and reluctantly rolled over, away from the silky warmth of Tommie's naked body. Reaching across the bedside table, he snatched up his cell phone, half wondering at what point during the night he'd had the foresight to place it within easy reach.

"Sanchez," he mumbled, his voice a low, nearly unintelligible growl.

"We've got another body." It was Donovan, sounding grim.

Paulo sat upright in bed, rubbing his eyes. "What?"

"Same MO as the Cruz homicide. Only this time the victim is a stripper."

"Shit," Paulo muttered, throwing his legs over the side of the bed and going in search of his discarded shirt and trousers.

Groaning softly, Tommie rolled over and switched on the bedside lamp. Pushing her dark hair out of her face, she squinted groggily at him. *What's going on?* she mouthed.

Paulo held up one finger, signaling that he'd respond to her in a minute.

Donovan continued. "The officer who responded said she'd been stabbed multiple times in the throat and chest. And there was a word written in blood on the bedroom wall. *Whore.*"

A dagger of foreboding sliced through Paulo's heart. "Whore?"

"That's what the officer told me. Maybe because the vic was a stripper?"

"Shit," Paulo muttered again. He found his dark briefs, tugged them on before continuing the search for his shirt and pants, wondering why the hell they weren't in the vicinity of his underwear. Tommie pointed, leading him in the right direction. *Your shirt's still in the studio,* she mouthed the reminder to him.

Right. The shirt that she'd torn last night.

"We'd better go check out the scene," Donovan was saying.

Paulo dragged on his trousers. "I'll meet you there."

"You sure? I can be at your place in five minutes."

"I'm not home."

"Ohhh." A sly, knowing grin crept into the younger detective's voice. "Did you and the lovely Miss Purnell kiss and make up, by any chance?"

"None of your damned business. What's the address?"

After Donovan provided the location of the crime scene, Paulo hung up and shoved the phone into his back pocket.

"What happened?" Tommie had slipped out of bed and donned a black silk robe that caught her at midthigh. She looked tousled, sleepy, and sexy as hell. Paulo wished he had time for a quickie, though he knew that wouldn't be nearly enough to satisfy his appetite.

Dragging his gaze away from the enticing vision she made, he said brusquely, "There's been another murder."

"By the same person who killed Maribel Cruz?" Tommie asked faintly.

Paulo frowned. "We don't know yet," he muttered, striding to the dresser and grabbing his badge, wallet, weapon, and keys.

Tommie followed him down the hallway and past the living room, where the first light of dawn was streaking the sky beyond the windows. She walked him downstairs to the studio, watched from the doorway as he shoved his arms into his torn shirt and shrugged into his jacket, which had also been left behind in his haste to get her into bed.

At the main door, he cupped her face in his hands and pressed a hard kiss to her mouth. "Go back to bed. I'll call you later."

"Okay." She bit her lip almost shyly. "Dinner at nine?"

Paulo hesitated, then smiled softly. "Sounds good. I'll bring something this time."

She grinned. "Sounds good."

Unable to resist, he kissed her again before stepping out into the chilly November morning. As he strode down the sidewalk to his cruiser, he tossed over his shoulder, "Lock the damned door this time. It's not safe to be leaving it unlocked with a psycho on the loose."

"What're you talking about?" Tommie called after him.

Her words stopped him cold in his tracks. He turned around, staring at her. "Yesterday when I arrived, the main door was unlocked. How do you think I got inside?"

"I don't know."

He took a step toward her. "What do you mean you don't know?"

"I locked the door last night. I always do." She frowned, folding her arms across her chest in an almost protective gesture. "Before we got, ah, sidetracked last night, I was going to ask you how you got into the building."

Paulo frowned, the muscles in the back of his neck tightening. "Are you sure you didn't forget to lock it?"

"Positive. I'm very mindful of that, living out here"— she gestured to encompass her remote surroundings— "all by myself. That's why I was so freaked out about finding the door to my loft unlocked on Tuesday night."

"Did you ask Mrs. Calhoun about that?"

"Yes. She's pretty sure she remembered to lock it. And I believe her. She's not forgetful like that. In fact, she's one of the sharpest people I know."

Paulo didn't like the dark suspicion that was taking root in his mind. Haunting images from the nightmare he'd had about Tommie—twice now—had nagged at his conscience all week. Two nights ago he'd pulled a gun on her, nearly mistaking her for the faceless menace in his dream who had erupted from the dark forest wielding a bloody knife. Every time Paulo remembered the look of horror on Tommie's face, the terror in her eyes as she'd stared at the gun in his hand, he got a sick feeling in the pit of his stomach. And no matter how many times he told himself he wouldn't—*couldn't*—have shot her, nothing eased the guilt he felt.

It was better to just pretend the whole incident had never happened.

As if he could pull that off.

"Did you go out any time last night?" he asked her.

Tommie nodded. "I ended my last class a little early to take a call from Zhane. I was worried about his nephew and wanted to get an update, and we'd been playing phone tag all day. After I talked to him, I went out for coffee with a friend. I got back around nine, shortly before you showed up."

Paulo could tell by her troubled gaze that there was something else, something she wasn't telling him. "Did anything happen yesterday that I should know about?" he gently prodded.

She hesitated for a long moment, pulling her bottom lip between her teeth. "It's nothing," she said at length, looking embarrassed. "An old boyfriend stopped by un-expectedly. It threw me off for the rest of the day. I told my friend about it over coffee, and still had it on my mind when I got back home." She shrugged. "Maybe I was so distracted I *did* forget to lock the door."

Paulo was surprised by the stab of jealousy that went through him at the idea of Tommie being so preoccu-pied with thoughts of another man—not just any man, but an old boyfriend—that she'd forget something as routine as locking her door.

Before he could respond, his cell phone rang. He dug it out of his pocket, glanced at the caller ID, and grimaced. It was Donovan, probably calling to make sure he was on his way. Pushy bastard.

"I gotta run," Paulo said to Tommie.

"I know. I didn't mean to hold you up."

"You didn't." He searched her face. "Are you sure you're okay?"

"Positive. Now go," she said, shooing him away.

"I'll check up on you later."

"No need. I'll be fine."

But as Paulo drove away, he couldn't shake the feeling that Tommie had been hiding something from him. He hoped it was nothing more serious than her rekindled romance with an old flame.

That he could learn to live with.

Her life being in danger?

Not so much.

Ten minutes later, Paulo turned down a street flanked by shotgun houses that became smaller and more decrepit as he approached his destination. Overgrown lawns, sagging porches, chipped paint, and an overall look of decay characterized the neighborhood where the latest victim had been found.

He parked as close as he could get to the white ramshackle house, shoved a tasteless piece of Nicorette gum into his mouth, and climbed out of the car. The crime scene was roped off and already being processed.

A grim-faced Donovan met Paulo at the front door and walked him down a short hallway to the bedroom, where Norah O'Connor and her team were hard at work collecting evidence.

"Looks like your guy has struck again," she said to Paulo without glancing up from her task. "Same MO as before. Only this time we have a pretty good idea how the perp got inside."

"How?"

"He used a spare key hidden in a potted plant on the back porch. It's the same way the neighbor got into the house this morning when she came over to ask for a jump. She got worried when no one came to the door, so she went around to the back and used the key to get in. That's when she discovered the body and called 911."

Donovan added, "Apparently it wasn't unusual for her to let herself into the house. She and the victim were always borrowing stuff from each other and keeping an eye on each other's homes whenever the other was on vacation."

"Where's the neighbor now?" Paulo asked.

"Went to drop her kids off at day care after one of the officers jump-started her car. She said she'd be back shortly to answer any more questions we might have."

Nodding, Paulo absently sketched the sign of the cross over his heart before stepping into the room. As he worked his way carefully toward the eviscerated corpse lying in the middle of the floor, he glanced around the small room, taking in the cheap wood furnishings, the clothes spilling from open drawers, and the trio of empty beer bottles on the cluttered nightstand before his gaze landed on the word WHORE scrawled in blood on the wall above the unmade bed.

Save for the untidiness of the room, which was the complete opposite of Maribel Cruz's immaculate bedroom, the scene was exactly what Paulo had expected.

But as he knelt and got his first good look at the victim, he felt a jolt of recognition that rocked him back on his heels and sent a chill of foreboding lancing down his spine.

Noting his reaction, O'Connor stared sharply at him. "What's wrong?"

Without lifting his stunned gaze from the body, Paulo whispered hoarsely, "I know her."

Paulo had met Ashton Dupree for the first time when they were ten years old. He and Rafe had been sent away to a summer camp located an hour's drive from Houston. Despite Naomi's best efforts, Paulo had not been looking forward to a whole week of roughing it in the woods, fending off bloodthirsty mosquitoes, and sitting around a campfire every night singing lame songs with a bunch of kids he'd probably never see again. For the life of him he couldn't comprehend why Naomi—or his parents, for that matter—would subject him to such torture. He'd been homesick before he even stepped foot on the grounds of Camp Cullen.

All that changed when he met Ashton Dupree, a cute, tough-talking blonde who, like him, thought camp was the worst form of torture ever inflicted upon unsuspecting children, a racket supported by cruel parents who shipped their kids off to camp under the guise of exposing them to "new and enriching experiences."

Proving true the adage that misery loves company, Paulo and Ashton had bonded immediately, a pair of misfits who'd grudgingly participated in the camp's daily activities, but had refused to admit, even to each other, that they were actually having fun. At night Ashton had given her counselor the slip and snuck into the boys' cabin, crawling into Paulo's bed and convulsing with giggles until he'd had to clamp his hand over her mouth to shush her. They'd shared a few quick, sloppy kisses and had groped each other under the covers, but that was the extent of their experimentation. Ashton had once confided to Paulo that she was adopted because her real father had liked touching her too much, and even at ten years old Paulo had understood that she was damaged goods, that the emotional scars she bore would probably haunt her for the rest of her life.

He'd seen her at camp over the following two summers, and then not again for twenty-seven years, when she'd gotten arrested for soliciting an undercover cop four months ago. The moment she was hauled into the station, kicking and screaming and shrilly demanding her rights, Paulo had recognized her. He'd taken over for the arresting officer, who'd already sustained several cuts and bruises in the skirmish and was on the verge of snapping. Overjoyed to see her old friend, Ashton had thrown her arms around Paulo and showered his face with kisses, raising more than a few eyebrows around the busy police station. While Paulo processed her, she'd filled him in on everything that had happened in her life since the last time they saw each other. She told him about dropping out of high school, getting kicked out of her adoptive mother's home, going through a string of abusive boyfriends that led her to abort three babies. She confided that she worked as a stripper and did "odd jobs" on the side to supplement her income. When Paulo arched a brow at the notion of a thirty-nine-year-old stripper, she'd smiled coyly and offered to give him a private show so he could see for himself that Father Time had been very good to her. Paulo had taken her word for it.

"What's really hard to believe is *you* being a cop!" she'd said laughingly. "My God, Paulo, there's a reason I used to call you *El Diablo*. You were the wickedest kid in camp! Remember the time you stole the pack of cigarettes from the camp counselor, then started smoking right in front of him while we were all sitting around the campfire? And you were so cool about it, too. You just leaned into the fire, lit your cigarette like it was a joint, then laid back on your elbows and blew a curl of smoke into the sky. When the counselor started yelling at you, you just told him, as calm as can be, that if *you* weren't allowed to smoke, *he* shouldn't be, either." She let out a peal of laughter at the memory. "God, you were my idol! How could you sell out like this?"

Paulo had chuckled softly. "I guess we all have to grow up sometime."

Ashton had sobered, and for the first time since that long-ago night she'd told him about her father, Paulo had noticed a hint of vulnerability in her eyes. The vulnerability of a woman who'd been betrayed by everyone she knew, who'd learned at an early age that trust was a commodity that should never be surrendered too easily.

Paulo had pulled a few strings to get the charges against her reduced to a lesser fine. When she'd offered to repay him with sex, he'd turned her down, telling her that the only way she could repay him was to get her life together. She'd been offended, had accused him of thinking he was too good for her. And then she'd stormed out of his office, snarling bitterly, "Thanks for the memories. Have a nice fucking life!"

Paulo had tried calling her, but after several unsuccessful attempts to reach her, he'd given up in angry frustration.

He couldn't have known that the next time he and Ashton Dupree were reunited, one of them would be dead.

Dr. Garrett, who'd looked none too pleased about being summoned to the scene of another gruesome homicide less than a week after Maribel Cruz's murder, estimated that Ashton had been dead at least twenty-four hours. He wouldn't commit to a date and time for the autopsy, saying only that based on his preliminary visual examination, he fully expected Ashton's injuries to be similar to Maribel's. After getting as much information out of him as they could, Paulo and Donovan left the bedroom to allow O'Connor and her crime lab team to continue vacuuming, photographing, videotaping, measuring blood spatter, and dusting the scene.

They stepped outside to wait for the neighbor's return so they could ask her a few more questions. As they stood on the rickety porch, Paulo took inventory of their surroundings. Uniformed officers were making their way up and down the dilapidated street, knocking on doors and talking to neighbors in the hopes that someone had seen something, anything, that might lead to a crucial break in the case.

Paulo frowned at a group of reporters, cameramen, and curious bystanders gawking at them from behind the police barricade erected at the end of the street. Two sheriff's deputies were filming the crowd, their cameras clipping off pictures of anyone who seemed out of place or exhibited suspicious behavior. Later, when Paulo and Donovan returned to the station, they would review the tape and compare it to the one from the previous crime scene to see if they noticed any repeat visitors. In cases like these, it wasn't uncommon for a killer to return to the crime scene to revel in the havoc wrought by his handiwork.

"The house is mortgaged to a Dorothy Dupree," Donovan said, breaking into Paulo's thoughts.

He nodded. "Dorothy Dupree was the woman who adopted Ashton when she was eight years old. She was a foster parent to several children over the years, but Ashton was the only one she ever adopted. She left the house to her when she died a few years ago."

"Maybe some of the other foster kids weren't too happy about that," Donovan speculated. "Maybe we need to track them down and check out their stories."

"It wouldn't hurt. I can only recall Ashton mentioning one foster sibling all those years ago, but for the life of me I can't remember his name."

"His?"

"Yeah. A brother. The last time I saw her, I think she said something about him living in Sugarland."

"Sugarland?" Donovan whistled through his teeth. "That's some pricey real estate."

"I know. So it's not likely he would have killed her over this house. But we still need to find him and notify him. And we should talk to her boss and coworkers at the strip club."

Donovan was nodding vigorously in agreement. "As soon as I heard she was a stripper, the first thing I wondered is whether one of the club's customers had become obsessed with her and started stalking her. Whoever killed her knew about that spare key on the back porch. He must have been watching her for some time, learning her habits and routine."

Paulo grimaced. "The other possibility is that she was killed by someone she was sleeping with for money. She once told me she was doing odd jobs on the side to earn some extra cash."

Donovan gave a derisive snort. "'Odd jobs.' Is that what they're calling it now?"

Something inside Paulo snapped. He shoved his face into Donovan's and snarled, "She had a hard life, okay? She was molested by her damned father and got bounced around from one foster home to another until Dorothy Dupree decided to take her in, and even *she* wasn't exactly Mother Teresa. I'm not making excuses for the choices Ashton made in life, but until you've walked a mile in someone else's shoes, don't fucking judge them. Got that, wiseass?"

Donovan jerked back, looking shocked, offended, hurt even. "Whoa! Chill out, Sanchez! It was just a little joke. No harm intended, man. We're on the same side, remember?"

Paulo drew away, his jaw tightly clenched as he dragged an unsteady hand through his hair. His nerves were stretched taut, guilt over the way he'd left things with Ashton was tearing at his conscience, and he wished like hell he could take a long, deep drag on a cigarette.

Concerned, Donovan stared at him. "This case is really starting to get to you, isn't it?"

"You could say that." Paulo resisted the urge to pace the length of the porch, not wanting to give the reporters a show, and not entirely sure the decaying floorboards could support his weight.

Questions were racing through his mind at warp speed. What was the connection between Maribel Cruz and Ashton Dupree? The two women were as opposite as black and white, night and day. One came from a good family, the other had been orphaned from childhood. One had held a respectable job, the other had dabbled in the oldest profession known to man. One had boasted a tony uptown address, the other had lived in a shantytown. Maribel and Ashton had come from two different worlds, had probably never caught a whiff of each other's paths. What had put them on the killer's radar?

"I guess if I were in your shoes I'd be coming a little unglued, too," Donovan said grimly. "Man, what are the odds of you knowing *both* of the victims?"

"I don't know," Paulo muttered darkly, "but I don't like it. Not one damned bit."

"Me, neither. Something's off about this whole thing.

Seriously off." Donovan paused, frowning. "I didn't expect him to kill again so soon. Maribel's body was still lying on a slab in the morgue as of yesterday. At this rate we could be looking at another dead body by Monday."

Paulo's gut twisted at the thought of who the killer's next target might be. An image from the nightmare flashed through his mind.

Maribel Cruz's ghostlike face morphing into Tommie's.

Tommie's whispered plea, *Help me, Paulo. Please help—*

"I'm going back inside to see if they're done with the room," he said abruptly, stalking past the officer guarding the front door.

He strode into the house, by now accustomed to the rancid scent of death that assailed his nostrils upon reentry. Instead of returning to the bedroom, he continued to the kitchen and stepped out the back door. Standing on the decrepit porch with his arms folded across his chest and his heart still thudding, he watched as the crime scene techs searched the grounds for trace evidence.

They'd already concluded that the perp had gained access to the house using a spare key hidden in a potted plant. But it remained to be seen whether the small backyard would yield any clues about his identity or the path he'd taken. The grass was badly overgrown, rotting, and choked with tall weeds that swayed in the cool morning breeze. The odds of finding a shoe imprint, impressions in the dirt, or any other type of physical evidence were slim to none. Especially when they were dealing with a cunning, methodical killer who'd thus far made no mistakes.

"But sooner or later you will, you son of a bitch," Paulo growled under his breath. "It's just a matter of time."

He only hoped it happened before another innocent person was slaughtered.

Chapter 17

After wrapping up her last class of the day, Tommie drove to Ben Taub General Hospital to visit Zhane's nephew and keep her friend company. When she stepped through the door of the ICU room, she found Zhane sitting in a chair at his nephew's bedside. He was holding Kadeem's hand and staring intently at his sleeping face, as if he were afraid the boy's soul would quietly depart if he looked away or let go.

A lump of sorrow rose in Tommie's throat. Tears misted her eyes.

As if sensing her presence, Zhane glanced up and smiled wanly at her. "Hey, beautiful."

"Hey yourself," Tommie murmured. Blinking back tears, she walked over to him and kissed the top of his head. His soft dreadlocks tickled her lips.

"Are those for me?" he asked, indicating the floral arrangement she'd set on the bedside table.

"No, this is," she said, passing him a cup bearing the Breakfast Klub's logo.

"Mmmm. It smells divine."

"It should. It's a karmel macchiato." Before he could open his mouth, she warned, "And I don't want to hear a word about how fattening it is. You've probably lost about ten pounds since you've been here. I think you can afford to indulge in one measly macchiato. Now shut up and drink."

"So bossy," Zhane complained. But he dutifully complied, taking a long, grateful sip and sighing with pleasure. "That's yummy."

Tommie smiled, tugging on one of his dreadlocks. "See what you've been missing?"

As she turned her attention to the hospital bed, her heart constricted at the sight of fourteen-year-old Kadeem Masters lying beneath the stiff white sheets, looking much too fragile for a boy who possessed boundless energy and laughter, who enjoyed playing basketball and wolfing down pizzas. Tubes fed into and out of him, sustaining his vital organs. Beside the bed, monitors and machines blinked and beeped intermittently, their display screens filled with glowing medical hieroglyphics.

"How's he doing?" Tommie asked in a hushed voice.

Zhane sighed. "No changes, really. He's been in and out of consciousness, said a few words. The doctors are doing everything they can to keep the fever down and stabilize his blood pressure. But it's still touch-and-go."

Tommie nodded, brushing a gentle hand over the boy's warm forehead. "Where's the rest of your family? I didn't see any of them in the waiting room."

"My other nieces and nephews went to school, my brothers are at work, and Zakia and Lavar are downstairs having lunch. Yes, girl, Lavar is still here," he added at Tommie's raised brow. "This is the longest he's ever stuck around for his son. Maybe there's hope for him yet, though I'm not holding my breath. Anyway, Mom took Kay-Kay home with her. Being here at the hospital with all these crazy, stressed-out grown-ups was starting to wear on her nerves."

"I can imagine," Tommie murmured. "Poor baby."

"I was talking about Mom."

Tommie stared at him for a moment, then burst out laughing.

Zhane smiled at her. "Lord, that's music to my ears."

"What is?"

"The sound of your laughter. It's like a ray of sunshine from heaven, breaking through the clouds of my stormy day."

Tommie eyed him curiously. "Is that Langston Hughes?"

"No, sugarplum, that was all me."

She sighed dreamily, laying a hand over her heart. "Careful, Zhany. With beautiful poetry like that, you're going to make me fall in love with you."

He laughed, taking a sip of his macchiato. "You keep bringing me these drinks, honey, and I just might have to reconsider being gay."

Tommie grinned. "Don't get my hopes up."

He chuckled, rising gracefully from the chair. "Come on, sugarplum, let's go for a walk. I need to stretch my legs and do a few pirouettes to remember what it feels like."

"As if you could ever forget." Tommie leaned down and pressed a gentle kiss to Kadeem's forehead.

A camera bulb flashed. She glanced up and saw Zhane holding up his cell phone, a wide grin on his face.

"I had to capture the moment. Without proof, Kadeem would never believe me if I told him you kissed him while he was sleeping."

Tommie smiled. "If he pulls through this, I'm giving him a big, fat kiss right on the lips."

Zhane laughed. "You'd better hope he can't hear you, 'cause he would definitely hold you to that!"

Walking arm in arm, they left the room and started down the tiled corridor toward the elevator. The ICU was quiet except for the sound of beeping machines. A middle-aged black woman with braided hair sat behind the nurses' station, watching the monitors and talking on the phone. She glanced up at them as they passed, smiling and nodding when Zhane told her, "If my sister gets back before me, tell her I went for a short walk with Tommie."

When they reached the elevator, Zhane turned and gave Tommie a long, appraising look.

"What?" she asked curiously.

"There's something different about you. I've been trying to figure it out ever since you—" Suddenly his eyes widened in disbelief. "Oh my God! You got laid!"

"Shhh, not so loud!" Tommie hissed, clapping a hand over his mouth and glancing around quickly to make sure no one had overheard him. Other than the nurse at the desk, who looked like she was trying very hard not to laugh, there were no other visitors or staff around.

Tommie blew out an exasperated breath, shaking her head at Zhane. "If I didn't love you so much, I'd kill you."

He laughed, prying her hand away from his mouth. "I can't believe you got laid and didn't tell me!" he said in an exaggerated whisper.

"I would've gotten around to it eventually," Tommie muttered, an embarrassed flush heating her face. "I had other things on my mind when I got here. Like finding out how your nephew was doing, for starters."

Zhane's eyes glittered with wicked amusement. "I'm going to assume the man you got it on with is that scrumptious Detective Sanchez."

Tommie grinned. "That's a safe assumption."

This time Zhane covered his own mouth to muffle a delighted squeal. "Girl, *what* in the world happened? When you left here the other night you were talking like you wanted nothing to do with him!"

"Things change," Tommie said with an enigmatic little smile.

"Don't go getting all mysterious on me!" Zhane cried as the elevator arrived on the fourth floor. "I want details!"

Tommie shook her head, wagging a finger at him. "A real lady doesn't kiss and tell."

Zhane snorted, following her onto the elevator. "A real lady also doesn't pee while she's on the phone with friends, but that's never stopped you before."

Tommie laughed, unfazed. "Becoming abusive is no way to make me give up my secrets."

Once the elevator doors closed behind them, Zhane gave her an amused sidelong glance. "You can at least tell me if it was any good."

A slow, naughty grin spread across Tommie's face as she stared up at the electronic panel above the doors. "Let's just say it was so good, he had my pussy doing pirouettes."

Zhane was still howling with laughter when they stepped into the hospital lobby minutes later, colliding with a man who'd been waiting to board the elevator.

"No problem," he said, acknowledging their apologies with a polite nod.

As he made to move past them, Tommie got a good look at his face and realized that she knew him. "Arthur?"

When he glanced back at her, his eyes widened in surprised recognition. A broad smile swept across his face as he reached out, warmly clasping her hand. "Hello there, Tommie. How are you?"

"I'm doing well," she said, smiling easily. "It's great to see you again. What brings you back to Houston?"

"Actually, I never left," he said ruefully. "My mother got sick, so being her only child, I didn't feel right about leaving her behind. I was just on my way up to her room to visit her. She just completed another round of chemotherapy. Ovarian cancer," he explained.

"I'm so sorry to hear that," Tommie murmured.

"Thanks, I appreciate that. She's a tough cookie, and her doctors are optimistic about her chances. So I'm very grateful."

"That's good." Turning to Zhane at her side, Tommie quickly performed the introductions. "This is my best friend, Zhane Jeffers. Zhane, I'd like you to meet Arthur Lambert, who made it possible for me to open my dance studio and have a place to live when he sold his building to me."

As the two men shook hands and exchanged pleasant greetings, Zhane gave the newcomer a slow, assessing once-over.

Arthur Lambert was a tall, rugged-looking man in his late forties. His eyes were a silvery shade of green, and his hair was light brown with a sprinkling of gray at the temple that made him look slightly older, but no less attractive.

Zhane drawled, "Tommie has had nothing but wonderful things to say about you, Arthur. It's nice to put a face with the name of her hero."

Arthur laughed good-naturedly. "That's very kind of you, but I'm afraid there was nothing heroic about what I did. The warehouse had been sitting vacant for a long time. I'm just glad Tommie came along when she did and took it off my hands."

"For virtually pennies," she reminded him sheepishly.

He smiled. "That's all right. Knowing that the property has been put to such good use is all the compensation I need."

"It's a great place. I'm thoroughly enjoying it."

"Good, good. Have you had any problems?"

"Just some faulty wiring in the stairwell. I haven't gotten around to calling an electrician yet."

"I'm really sorry to hear that," Arthur said, his brows creasing in a frown. "I thought we resolved all those electrical issues before we went to closing."

Tommie bit her lip. "Not quite."

Because the property had been such a steal, and she knew Arthur had taken a huge profit loss, she'd been reluctant to make too many demands when it came to negotiating the sales contract. The building inspector she'd hired had assured her that the faulty wiring could be easily repaired at a later date and shouldn't be a deal breaker for her.

"Tell you what," Arthur said. "Are you going out of town next week for Thanksgiving?"

She nodded. "I'm leaving on Wednesday."

"Why don't I stop by before then and have a look at the problem? Then I'll send someone back to take care of it for you."

"Oh no, I couldn't ask you to do that, Arthur. You've been generous enough."

"It's no big deal," he said, waving off her gratitude. "The wiring should have been fixed before you bought the building, and quite frankly I'm annoyed with myself for letting that slip through the cracks."

"Well, it's my problem now, not yours. So please don't worry about it, Arthur. God knows you've got enough on your mind with your mother being in the hospital."

"One thing's got nothing to do with the other," he told her. "I'll give you a call on Monday and set up a good time to send the electrician over. And don't you worry about the cost," he added when Tommie opened her mouth to protest. "As much business as I give these contractors, they're always more than willing to do a favor for me."

"Well . . ." Tommie couldn't deny that his offer was tempting. She was on a very tight budget, and after crunching the numbers yesterday, she knew she didn't have the funds to pay an electrician. But the lights in the stairwell needed replacing, and that couldn't be done unless she first resolved the wiring issue. She'd never been too proud to accept help from others when it was absolutely necessary. And her grandmother had taught her never to look a gift horse in the mouth.

Seeing the capitulation on her face, Arthur smiled broadly. "I'll call you next week and set up the appointment."

"All right," Tommie said meekly. "Thank you, Arthur."

"You're very welcome. I'm glad to help. Anyway, I'd better head upstairs."

"Give your mother my best," Tommie said.

"Thanks, I will. Pleasure to meet you," he said, shaking Zhane's hand.

"Likewise," Zhane murmured.

Arthur boarded the elevator and waved to them as the doors slid closed on his smiling face.

"Well," Zhane said, drawing out the word as he raised his eyebrows at Tommie. "*That* was interesting."

Tommie bit her lip, feeling guilty. "You don't think I should have accepted his offer, do you?"

Zhane snorted. "Sugarplum, he didn't give you much of a choice. And I think you did the right thing by accepting his help. We both know you're flat broke, and ain't a damned thing wrong with letting a handsome man take care of your needs if he's willing and able." He sighed, tucking his arm through hers as they started down the corridor. "Must be nice."

"What?"

"Knowing that every man you meet wants to fuck your brains out."

Tommie laughed. "Not *every* man," she said pointedly, elbowing him in the ribs.

Zhane grinned. "Honey, when you've got someone like that hot-tamale detective giving you pirouette-inducing orgasms, why look any further?"

Laverne Witten, a single mother of three with over-processed hair and a smoker's rasp, had lived next door to Ashton Dupree for the past three years. After dropping off her children at day care, she returned to the crime scene, as promised, to answer more questions by Paulo and Donovan. She recounted her discovery of the body early that morning, confirming that she'd entered the house using the spare key Ashton had previously provided for her. She explained, once again, that she and Ashton had often borrowed household items from each other and watched each other's homes while the other was on vacation. Because of the late hours Ashton normally kept, Laverne had thought nothing of ringing her doorbell at 4:00 a.m. to ask for a jump, especially since Ashton had already mentioned to her that she'd taken a few days off from work. When Laverne noticed at the end of Thursday that Ashton's car had not moved from the driveway all day, she just assumed Ashton was catching up on some sleep. She hadn't noticed any strangers loitering in the neighborhood, so she had no reason to suspect that a violent psychopath had let himself into Ashton's house and butchered her.

When Paulo and Donovan tried to press her for more information, Laverne confided that while she and Ashton had been on friendly terms and had always helped each other out in a pinch, she didn't know enough about Ashton's personal life to be able to tell them whether she'd had a steady boyfriend or had been expecting company on the night she was killed. She couldn't tell them whether Ashton still kept in touch with her foster brother or had any friends who frequently visited. She couldn't tell them much of anything.

They thanked Laverne for her time, gave her their cards, and told her to call if she thought of anything else. After letting them know how sorry she was about Ashton, how sick to her stomach she'd be for the rest of the day, she then asked them what would happen to Ashton's house now that she was gone.

"I have family who've been looking to move closer to me," Laverne explained. "They might be a little queasy at first about buying a house where someone got killed, but I know they'd get over it eventually."

Paulo didn't even know how to respond. So he didn't bother. Turning away in disgust, he let Donovan handle it.

After the woman left, Donovan wandered over to where Paulo stood in the living room studying a framed photograph of Ashton. In it she was smiling coquettishly into the camera, her wavy blond hair swept over one shoulder, her blue eyes sparkling with that irrepressible mischief Paulo remembered so well.

Shaking his head in grim disgust, Donovan muttered, "I've heard of greedy relatives swooping in like vultures to fight over property after the death of a family member, but *neighbors*? That's got to be an all-time low. Man, did Ashton Dupree have *any* true friends?"

"No," Paulo said in a low, flat voice. "She didn't."

Not even me, he added silently.

"Detective Sanchez?"

Paulo glanced over his shoulder to see one of

the evidence technicians standing behind him. Paulo recognized the man from Maribel Cruz's crime scene, but drew a blank on his name. Something like Scott. Or Skip.

"Yeah?" he said, turning around.

The man passed him a plastic evidence bag. "I just found this in the victim's top nightstand drawer. After the last time, I thought you'd be interested in seeing it."

Even before Paulo looked down and saw what was inside the bag, he knew.

His heart knocked against his rib cage. Icy fingers of dread ran down his throat.

Gingerly he reached inside the bag and withdrew the glossy dance brochure featuring Tommie on the cover.

"Holy shit," Donovan breathed, staring over his shoulder. "Is that what I think it is?"

Paulo nodded mutely.

Earlier he'd wondered what had put Maribel Cruz and Ashton Dupree on the killer's radar.

Now he knew.

The connection between the two dead women was none other than Tommie Purnell.

Chapter 18

"Ashton Dupree doesn't work here anymore," the owner and proprietor of Slicksters Gentlemen's Club announced without preamble when Paulo was shown into his office later that day.

"That's actually why I'm here. To talk to you about Ashton." Without waiting for an invitation, Paulo sat in one of the leather visitor chairs opposite the large desk.

Woody Digger, an ironically befitting name for a man who ran a strip joint, bore a striking resemblance to the actor Michael Chiklis, with his gleaming bald head, burly frame, piercing blue eyes, and tough-guy demeanor.

"Look, I don't want any trouble, Detective," Digger said through gritted teeth. "I run a good, clean establishment here. I don't tolerate no funny business."

Paulo cocked a brow. "Who said you did?"

Digger scowled. "You think I don't know about those undercover cops who've been crawling around here for the past two weeks, trying to catch my girls doing something they're not supposed to be doing?"

"I wasn't aware that your club was the target of an undercover operation," Paulo said blandly. "I don't work in vice."

Digger's blue eyes narrowed suspiciously on his face. "You said you were here to ask about Ashton."

"That's right." Paulo paused. "Is that why she was fired? Because she was doing something she wasn't supposed to?"

Digger clenched his jaw. "I didn't say she was fired."

"So she quit?"

Digger's mouth curved in a mirthless smile. "Let's just say she was encouraged to resign."

"Why?" Paulo's tone was mild, but the steely glint in his eyes let the other man know he wouldn't accept another evasive, bullshit answer.

Digger heaved an impatient breath. "She was bad for business."

"In what way?"

"Well, for starters she had a mouth on her. She was combative, always talking back. To her manager, to the other dancers and waitresses. It didn't matter who it was, she always had to have the last word."

"Was she ever reprimanded? Written up?"

"All the damned time. Made no difference. She was a hellcat through and through." His lips compressed in an expression of disgust. "We called her Ash because when she got through lighting you up, that's all that was left of you—ashes."

"I guess it's safe to assume she wasn't very popular with the other dancers," Paulo dryly surmised.

Digger snorted. "That's putting it mildly. They hated her guts."

Hated her enough to kill her? Paulo wondered.

As if he'd read his mind, Digger said, "But they were terrified of her, every last one of 'em. They thought she was bat-shit-crazy. Avoided her like the plague whenever it was possible. Plus she was much older than most of them, so they didn't have a lot in common with her anyway."

"What about the customers? How'd they feel about Ashton?"

"Well, that's the thing," Digger grumbled, scratching his chin that bore a faint cleft. "They loved her. She was one of our best dancers. She put on a helluva good show."

"But she was bad for business," Paulo reminded him.

Digger frowned, his jaw hardening. "Like I said before, I don't want any trouble. Seems like every time I turn around I'm hearing about another strip club being raided by the police, dancers getting arrested for prostitution in sting operations. This year alone there've been at least five major busts. I don't want no part of that. My girls know the three-foot rule. They know they're not allowed to get any closer than that to customers. And they sure as hell know they're not supposed to offer them sex for cash."

"But Ashton did it anyway," Paulo concluded.

Digger hesitated, then nodded shortly. "She was using the club as her own personal referral service," he growled, nostrils flaring in anger. "Giving out her business card, setting up appointments right under my damned nose."

"When did you find out?"

"A week ago. One of the other girls came and told me, thought I should know since the undercover cops were crawling all over the place." He shook his bald head. "Ashton's damned lucky she didn't approach the wrong guy."

"Maybe she did," Paulo murmured.

Digger's gaze sharpened on his face. "What do you mean?" His eyes narrowed. "Wait a minute. If you're not here as part of a sting operation, then what—?"

"I'm a homicide detective." Paulo paused, letting that sink in before adding, "Ashton Dupree was found dead in her home this morning. She was murdered."

The other man's eyes widened in horror. The color leached out of his face, leaving him ashen. "Jesus!" he whispered, staring incredulously at Paulo. "Is this some kind of a joke?"

"No, unfortunately."

Digger leaned back in his chair, passed a trembling hand over his face. His shock seemed real, Paulo thought, but that didn't mean squat. After seventeen years on the force, fifteen in homicide, he'd encountered more than his fair share of accomplished liars and actors. Sometimes the higher the stakes, the more convincing the performance.

"When was the last time you saw or spoke to Ashton?" Paulo asked.

"A w-week ago," Digger stammered, still looking stunned. "I called her in here and told her what I'd just found out about her. She didn't even bother denying it. She said she needed to earn some extra cash, and since I wasn't paying her enough, she'd decided to take matters into her own hands. Pun intended, she joked." He shook his head. "I warned her about the vice cops, told her I wasn't about to get put out of business or thrown into jail just because *she* was being a greedy, opportunistic bitch." He grimaced at the memory.

"And how did she respond?"

"She said it was none of my damned business how she chose to supplement her income. And I told her that if she couldn't abide by the house rules, she'd better find someplace else to work. She said that's exactly what she would do. She claimed she could get hired by another club in a heartbeat, and I said something about her being over the hill," he admitted guiltily. "She told me to fuck off, then slammed out of the office. That was the last time I saw or heard from her."

"Do you know who any of her customers were?" Paulo asked.

"You mean the ones she was screwing?" He shook his head. "She wouldn't tell me their names, and I couldn't even try to guess for you. She was friendly with all the customers, always more than happy to give a lap dance. Truth be told, I could see any of those guys going home with her."

"Would any of the other girls know?"

Digger hesitated. "Casey might."

"Casey?"

"Yeah. She's the one who came to me in the first place."

"Is she working today?"

"No. Not till Saturday evening. If you come back then, you can talk to her."

Paulo nodded. "Where were you on Wednesday night between the hours of ten p.m. and five a.m.?"

"I was here until midnight. Went home after that."

"Alone?"

Digger frowned. "Did I leave here alone, or do I live alone?"

"Both."

"Yes to both. I left here alone that night, but I had someone waiting for me at home."

"Girlfriend?"

A hint of a suggestive grin touched Digger's mouth. "I guess you could call her that. When it's convenient."

Paulo pretended to misunderstand. "Convenient for an alibi?"

"No." The grin stretched meaningfully. *"Convenient."*

"Ah." A look of amused understanding passed between the two men. "I'll need her name and a number where I can contact her. To verify your alibi, of course."

"Of course." Digger reached for one of his business cards, neatly displayed in a glass holder. He jotted down the information on the back and passed the card across the desk.

"Thanks," Paulo said, sliding it into his jacket pocket. "I know you said Ashton didn't get along with her coworkers. Can you think of anyone who might have wanted to hurt her?"

Digger frowned. "No one here hated her enough to kill her, if that's what you're getting at."

"How do you know that?"

"I make it my business to know what kind of people work for me. They're not cold-blooded killers, I can tell you that."

"What about the customers?" Paulo prodded. "Do you remember any altercations she may have had with a rude customer? Maybe someone who'd had one too many beers? Or a guy who came on to her and refused to take no for an answer?"

Digger shook his head. "Like I said, she was friendly with all the customers, and even if one had come on a little too strong, she knew how to take care of herself."

Apparently not, Paulo thought grimly, his mind flashing on an image of Ashton's brutalized remains.

Giving himself a mental shake, he asked, "Do you know if she was seeing anyone?"

"Someone other than her johns, you mean?" Digger drawled, his lips twisting sardonically.

Paulo just looked at him.

"No, I don't think she was seeing anyone. Not that I know of, anyway."

"How well did you know her?"

"She worked here for over seven years. I think I knew her well enough." He frowned. "Like I said before, she had a serious mouth on her. I always told her that mouth would

one day get her into trouble with the wrong person. I hope
to God I wasn't right about that."

You and me both, Paulo thought.

"One more question. If Ashton was such a problem
employee, why didn't you fire her seven years ago?
Why'd you keep her around for so long?"

Something like resentment flickered in Digger's eyes.
"Believe me, if it were left up to me, she would have been
canned a long time ago."

Paulo frowned. "Why wasn't it left up to you? I thought
you were the owner."

"I am. But I've got a partner. A silent partner who
wasn't so silent when it came to Ashton. Keeping her was
nonnegotiable."

Intrigued, Paulo asked, "Who's this partner?"

Digger looked uncomfortable. "He's a silent
partner—"

"I need a name."

"I'd rather not say."

Paulo's muscles tightened. He leaned forward, a cold,
feral smile curving his lips. "Just because I don't work
in vice doesn't mean I don't know people," he said, dangerously soft. "One phone call is all it would take to clear
you—or bury you."

Digger stared at him, his mouth tightening. "My partner
is Ashton's foster brother. A lawyer named Ted Colston."

That evening, Ted Colston was striding toward a sleek
silver Jaguar in the law firm's underground parking garage
when his cell phone rang. He groaned inwardly, praying to
God it wasn't a client calling with an emergency or some
other issue that would detain him at the office for the rest
of the evening. He'd already stayed longer than he should
have, and tonight of all nights—his fifteenth wedding

anniversary—he couldn't afford to be late for dinner with his wife. Not after everything he had done to her.

The phone trilled again.

Heaving a resigned breath, Ted dug the phone out of the breast pocket of his suit jacket and checked the caller ID. When he saw the number displayed, his pulse quickened. He pressed the Talk button.

"I sure as hell hope you have more information for me than you did the last time we spoke," he bit out tersely.

There was a low, grating chuckle on the other end. "Good evening to you, too. Did I catch you at a bad time?"

"I'm on my way home," Ted said impatiently, throwing his briefcase into the car and sliding behind the wheel.

"Ah yes. Today's the big day, isn't it? Can't have you working late on your fifteenth anniversary, now, can we?"

Ted said nothing, unnerved that the private investigator knew so much about his personal life. About him, period.

"Got any special plans with the missus?"

"We're going away for the weekend."

"How romantic. Someplace nice and secluded, I hope?"

Ted didn't answer.

Hank Nolan chuckled dryly. "Not in a very talkative mood today, are you?"

Ted clenched his jaw. "Stop wasting my time. Do you have information for me or not?"

"As a matter of fact, I do." He paused, and Ted knew it was purely for dramatic effect. "I completed the background check on the cop."

"It's about time. You've had me waiting for days." *While Sanchez has been circling me like a damned shark in blood-infested waters,* Ted added silently. When the detective called the office an hour ago, Ted had instructed his secretary to tell Sanchez that he'd already left for his weekend getaway with Abby. When he emerged from the building that evening, he'd half expected to find the detective leaning insolently against his Jaguar, waiting for him.

"Well, you know what they say," Nolan murmured. "Good things come to those who wait."

Anticipation tightened in Ted's belly like a knot. Gripping the phone tighter, he demanded, "Well? Don't keep me in suspense, damn it. What did you find out?"

"Enough."

"Enough? What the hell's that supposed to mean?"

Again that soft, creepy chuckle filled the phone line. "Let's just say that if you play your cards right, Detective Sanchez will never become a problem for you."

"Never?"

"*Ever.*"

"Royal flush!" Tommie declared, grinning triumphantly as she displayed her cards on the table. "Read 'em and weep, baby."

Zhane groaned, throwing down his losing hand in disgust. "If this is your idea of keeping my spirits up so I won't be depressed about missing tonight's performance, it's not working."

Tommie bit her lower lip. "I'm sorry, Zhany. You're right. Beating you at poker all night is no way to cheer you up. Tell you what. I'll let you win the next hand."

"Hell, no! I don't want your damned charity. I'm beating you fair and square!"

Tommie laughed. "It's on like Donkey Kong, baby," she said, rising from the chair and scooping up her Gucci handbag. "Just as soon as I get back from taking a leak."

Zhane made a face. "See, I didn't need to know all that," he complained as she strolled from the waiting room. "All you had to do was excuse yourself to use the bathroom."

Tommie blew a kiss at him and was still chuckling

when she reached the restroom around the corner. After relieving herself, she flushed the toilet and walked to the row of sinks to wash her hands.

As children, she and her sister had always hated to use public bathrooms. While Frankie had been worried about catching germs, Tommie had imagined bogeymen and child molesters hiding in the stalls, waiting to pounce on unsuspecting little girls who were not accompanied by an adult. So she'd never gone to the restroom without dragging along her sister or mother.

As Tommie checked her reflection in the mirror, she felt a cold draft, a whisper across her skin, as if someone had just walked past. She turned around, eyes narrowed as she quickly scanned the room, checking for feet under the stalls. But the room was empty. And silent.

Unnaturally silent.

Get a grip, Tommie told herself, turning back to the mirror. *There's no bogeyman lurking in the stall any more than there was someone hiding in your closet last night!*

Yet she couldn't help remembering what Paulo had told her that morning about finding the main door to her building unlocked. That, coupled with the sinister presence she'd sensed in her bedroom, made her skin crawl.

Had an intruder been inside her loft yesterday?

Again she thought of Maribel Cruz. And now, apparently, another woman had been found dead in her home, according to what little Paulo had shared with her. Two brutal murders in less than one week. Was a serial killer on the loose? Would she have anything in common with the second victim, as she had with Maribel?

Tommie stared at her reflection in the mirror. She looked like she'd seen a ghost, eyes wide as saucers in her face.

Good Lord. She couldn't go back out there looking like

this. Zhane would take one look at her and think something terrible had happened, and she couldn't have him worrying about her when he had enough to worry about with his poor nephew lying at death's door.

Get yourself together, girlfriend.

Taking a deep, calming breath, Tommie reached inside her purse for a tube of lipstick. As she rummaged around, her cell phone rang. She grabbed it and brought it to her ear.

"Hello?"

There was no answer.

"Hello?" she repeated.

Dead silence.

The hairs on the back of her neck rose. A cold shiver trickled down her spine.

Calm down. It must be a wrong number. Or someone's playing a dumb joke on you. Today's Friday the thirteenth, remember?

But as she started to hang up, she heard the soft, haunting strains of classical music. It took a moment before she recognized the song. A song she had danced to countless times in her starring role as Eurydice in *Black Orpheus.*

Which the caller must have known.

"Who is this?" she whispered, fear knotting her stomach.

The phone went dead.

Her heart pounded.

Suddenly the bathroom door burst open.

Tommie let out a startled shriek.

A young woman entered the room, herding a small, dark-haired girl who was pulling up her corduroy dress and whining, "I have to go, Mommy! *Hurry!*"

The woman gave Tommie a brief, embarrassed smile before following her daughter into a stall and shutting the door.

Hand pressed to her galloping heart, Tommie closed her eyes and blew out a deep, shaky breath. She'd never been more relieved in her life to see another person in the restroom! She'd been so terrified a moment ago that if she hadn't already emptied her bladder, she would have peed her pants when the door suddenly burst open.

When she heard a plaintive "Uh-oh, Mommy, I didn't make it" from inside the stall, a helpless giggle bubbled up in her throat. Afraid the poor woman would think she was laughing at her daughter's misfortune, Tommie stuffed her phone back into her purse and hustled out of the bathroom.

Once she reached the waiting room, she received another shock that brought her up short.

Paulo was standing across the room talking to Zhane.

When he glanced up and saw her frozen in the doorway, his dark eyes softened in a way that melted her insides.

Oh, God. Please help me.

"Hey," she murmured, stepping into the room. "What're you doing here?"

"I got your message," Paulo said simply.

Tommie just stared at him.

Zakia Jeffers and Lavar Masters had gone home shortly after Tommie arrived that afternoon, promising to return early in the morning to continue their son's bedside vigil. Not wanting to leave Zhane alone at the hospital, especially on the night of his dance company's performance, Tommie had called Paulo to let him know she wouldn't be able to have dinner with him that evening. She'd left the message on his voice mail, figuring he'd be so busy with the new murder investigation that she wouldn't hear from him for days.

She certainly hadn't expected him to show up at the hospital.

Zhane planted his hands on his narrow hips, looking indignant. "Sugarplum, why didn't you tell me you had plans with Paulo this evening?"

Tommie grinned sheepishly. "Because I knew you wouldn't let me stay if I told you."

Zhane sputtered. "You're damned right I wouldn't have. This man works his ass off all day trying to keep the streets of Houston safe. And *this* is how you repay him? By skipping out on dinner with him?"

Tommie gaped at Paulo, whose eyes were glimmering with amusement. "*What* did you say to him?" she demanded accusingly.

Paulo blinked innocently. "Nothing."

"He didn't have to say anything!" Zhane interjected. In a gentler tone, he said, "Now, you know I always enjoy your company, sugarplum, but it's time for you to go."

"But—"

"No buts. I insist." Before she could protest again, he grabbed her jacket off the back of a chair, draped it around her shoulders, then gently but firmly steered her from the room.

At the doorway Tommie paused, laying a hand against his face as she searched his eyes. "You sure you'll be okay?"

He smiled. "I'll be just fine."

She kissed his cheek. "I'll call you tomorrow, okay?"

"Okay."

As Paulo snagged Tommie's hand, leading her away, Zhane called after them, "You kids have fun. And don't hurt yourself doing too many pirouettes, sugarplum!"

Tommie laughed. "I'll try not to!"

Paulo gave her a puzzled look. "Pirouettes?"

"Mmm. I'll tell you later." She reached up, nibbled his earlobe. "Much later."

Chapter 19

An hour later, Tommie polished off her fifth slice of pepperoni pizza and pushed her plate away with a deep sigh of satisfaction. "That was absolutely wonderful."

Lying beside her on the living room floor with an empty pizza box wedged between them and a drowsy fire crackling in the fireplace, Paulo gave her a soft, indulgent smile. "You're not very hard to please, are you?"

Tommie laughed. "Not when it comes to food. Especially if I'm starving. Which I was."

"I noticed. Why didn't you get something to eat from the cafeteria?"

She gave a mild shudder. "I may be greedy, but I draw the line at eating hospital food. Yuck."

Paulo chuckled, shaking his head at her. "What if you ever need to be hospitalized?"

"Not gonna happen."

He arched a brow. "Really? What about when you're in the hospital for three days after giving birth? What're you gonna do then? Starve yourself?"

Tommie sniffed. "Assuming that ever happens, my loving, doting husband—or whoever is responsible for knocking me up—will have to bring me food from outside everyday. Breakfast, lunch, dinner, and a light evening snack." She shrugged. "I figure that's the least he can do for putting me through nine months of hell."

Paulo grinned, giving his head another shake. "Damn, you're spoiled."

She sighed. "But I'm *so* worth it."

"If you say so."

She kicked him on the leg and he laughed. Grinning, she plucked up her glass of cabernet sauvignon and took a long, appreciative sip. "Mmm, that is so good."

"It is," Paulo agreed. "You've got quite a wine selection."

"It was a going-away present from a friend. He works as a sommelier in New York, took it upon himself to teach me everything he knew about wine." She smiled. "He was appalled by my preference for margaritas, didn't want me embarrassing him every time we dined at a fine restaurant."

Paulo chuckled dryly. "You've got some very interesting friends, *querida.*"

"Aren't they great? I miss that Myles." She ran her tongue over her lips to savor the taste of the wine. "I think I'll introduce him to Zhane at some point. They'd probably hit it off right away."

"Or so you hope."

"I know. Playing matchmaker for friends is always a risk." She sighed wistfully. "But Zhany's lonely. He needs someone."

"He has someone—you."

Hearing the jealous edge to his voice, Tommie laughed. "Why, Paulo, if I didn't know better, I would think you felt threatened by Zhane."

Paulo shrugged, a surly grin tugging at his mouth. "He's the other man in your life. Why wouldn't I feel a little threatened?"

Tommie stared at him, afraid to believe her ears weren't deceiving her. Afraid to realize how much she wanted what he seemed to be offering. "What are we doing here, Paulo?" she whispered.

He met her gaze. "Right now? We're having a pleasant conversation that we probably shouldn't ruin with things neither of us is ready to discuss."

Tommie went still. She'd received the message loud and clear, and was surprised by how hurt she felt. And disappointed.

What did you expect? her conscience mocked. *A declaration of undying love and devotion after just one night of incredible lovemaking? This is Paulo Sanchez we're talking about, the man who flirted shamelessly with you at your sister's wedding, then went home with another woman. The man who thought nothing of using your words against you and humiliating you just to score a point. He's made it clear he's not interested in having a serious relationship, and you shouldn't be, either!*

Wordlessly she got up and gathered their empty plates and trash and carried them into the kitchen. She stiffened as Paulo came up behind her, placed his hands on her tense shoulders, and turned her gently around. When she refused to lift her eyes, he put his finger beneath her chin, forcing her to meet his dark, penetrating gaze.

"I owe you an apology," he said quietly. "That comment I made about feeling threatened by Zhane. I meant it. But I didn't mean to say it, not yet, and it scares the hell out of me to realize just how easy it's becoming to let down my guard with you."

Tommie swallowed, her heart thudding. "I'm scared, too."

"You are?"

She nodded. "I've had rotten luck with relationships."

He smiled faintly. "Then we should probably run as far away from each other as possible."

She let out a whispery laugh. "Probably."

Sobering, Paulo searched her eyes with his own. "I was married once before."

Tommie stared at him, surprised.

"Her name was Jacinta. We met eight years ago, thought we wanted the same things out of life. Turns out we didn't. I wanted kids, she didn't. I wanted to remain a cop, she wanted me to take a six-figure job as head of security at my family's law firm. She couldn't understand why I had turned down the offer, and she let her feelings be known every chance she got. The marriage was a disaster, doomed from the start, and two years later she did us both a favor by asking for a divorce. I can't even say it was entirely her fault we didn't work out. I made a real mess of things, made a lot of mistakes I can never undo." His voice softened. "I want to take my time with you, Tommie. I want to see where this road is going to lead us. Can we do that together?"

"I suppose." She shrugged, smiling. "I'm not doing anything else at the moment."

Paulo smiled, gently brushing his knuckles over her cheek. The gesture was so tender it made her throat ache.

After another moment Tommie turned away, busying herself with straightening up the kitchen. "I was surprised when you showed up at the hospital tonight. I thought you'd be tied up with that new murder investigation all weekend."

"I wanted to see you." He corked the bottle of wine, returned it to the refrigerator. "I'm worried about you."

Tommie stared at him. "Why?"

She could tell by the grim set of his mouth that she

wasn't going to like what she heard. "You may have met the second victim as well."

She felt a tremor of foreboding. "What do you mean? Where?"

"At the same performance attended by Maribel Cruz in February."

"You found another autographed dance program?" At his tight nod, Tommie whispered, "Oh my God."

Paulo walked to the hall closet to retrieve the latest victim's photo from his jacket. When he returned and showed it to Tommie, she didn't know whether to be relieved or disappointed that she didn't recognize the smiling, beautiful blonde in the snapshot.

"I don't remember her," she murmured.

"Are you sure?"

"I'm positive. That doesn't mean I didn't meet her, I just don't remember her." She passed the photo back to him, then rubbed the goose bumps prickling her bare arms. "You think the killer was at the performance?"

"It's highly possible," Paulo muttered.

Tommie shivered. Had she come within striking distance of pure evil and not even known it?

Paulo said briskly, "I've contacted someone at Jones Hall and asked for a complete list of attendees to that evening's performance based on ticket sales. I also requested a copy of the video. With any luck there's some footage of the audience."

"You've got your work cut out for you," Tommie told him. "It was a packed house that night. Close to three thousand people, we were told. Might be like trying to find a needle in a haystack."

"I know. But it's worth a shot."

Tommie nodded. "What are the odds of two women who attended the same ballet performance months ago being killed within days of each other? Is it just a horrible, tragic coincidence?"

Paulo's gaze was steady, unblinking. "I don't believe in coincidence."

She swallowed, raked a trembling hand through her hair. "I need a drink," she muttered, returning to the living room where she'd left her glass of wine on the table. She gulped down the rest of the cabernet sauvignon, then, still feeling chilled, sat cross-legged in front of the fireplace.

Paulo walked over and stretched out beside her on the floor. Gazing into the leaping flames, he murmured, "There's something you're not telling me. Something that's been bothering you. What is it?"

Closing her eyes, Tommie blew out a deep, shaky breath. "Last night after class, when I was getting dressed in my bedroom, I thought . . . I sensed that someone was in there with me."

"In your bedroom?"

She nodded. "I didn't see or hear anything. It was just an eerie feeling I had, like I was being watched. I half convinced myself I was just being paranoid, but then when you told me this morning that you'd found the main door unlocked when you came over last night . . ."

"You knew someone else had been inside the building," Paulo finished.

Tommie opened her eyes and looked at him. His face was taut, tense with worry. "After what happened tonight at the hospital," she whispered, "I'm almost convinced someone else was here yesterday."

"What the hell happened at the hospital?"

"When I was in the restroom, I got a call on my cell phone. The caller never said a word. But there was music playing softly in the background."

"Music?"

"Yes." She drew a shallow breath, felt her skin prickle at the memory. "It was a song from *Black Orpheus*, which I danced to at the concert in February."

"Ay Dios mio!" Paulo exploded, lunging to his feet with the agility of a panther. An enraged panther. "Goddamn it, Tommie! Why didn't you tell me this sooner?"

"I—I don't know," she stammered. "I was just so surprised to see you at the hospital. I guess I forgot—"

"You *forgot?* Some lunatic called you and played music from one of your performances—a performance attended by two women who are now dead—and you *forgot* to mention it?"

"I didn't want you to worry," Tommie said feebly.

His black brows slammed together in a ferocious scowl. He jabbed a finger at her, opened his mouth as if to let her have it again, then seemed to reconsider. As if he'd realized he might say something he would later regret.

She watched in wary silence as he began pacing up and down the floor, muttering profanities in Spanish and English that singed her ears. "That's it," he growled, reaching a decision. "You're coming home with me. No way in hell are you staying here alone."

"But—"

"But nothing! It's too damned dangerous for you to stay here!"

"Listen to me," she tried again, striving for a calm, reasonable tone. "I need to be here. I have morning classes on Monday and Tuesday before the Thanksgiving break. Traffic in this city is horrendous. I was almost late to class yesterday when I spent the night at your apartment."

"Then I'm staying here," Paulo said flatly. Daring her to defy him.

She had no intention of doing so. "Okay."

He glowered at her, a muscle working in his jaw.

"Okay," she repeated, in case he hadn't heard her over the red haze of fury fogging his brain.

He nodded curtly.

"Now will you do me a favor?" she asked.

"What?"

She patted the floor beside her. "Come sit back down."

He hesitated, then slowly walked over and lowered himself to the floor.

"Thank you," she murmured, stifling a smile. "You were making me a little nervous, prowling back and forth like a caged lion."

"Your life is in danger, Tommie," he bit out. "I don't think that's a laughing matter."

"I'm not laughing, believe me. The idea of being stalked by some homicidal maniac scares the crap out of me. I have a security system that I always remember to activate. If someone got inside the building without my knowledge, then it can only mean one thing. He has a key."

Paulo's expression hardened, became more grim. "You have to change the locks. ASAP."

"I know. I'm calling a locksmith first thing on Monday morning. And I'm getting my cell number changed, too." The thought of receiving another creepy phone call sent a chill down her spine.

"Did a number come up on caller ID?"

She shook her head. "It was unavailable."

"Figures. Have you noticed anything missing from the loft?"

"No. But then again, I haven't been looking."

"Start looking," Paulo said tersely. "Tomorrow."

"Okay." She hesitated. "What was the victim's name?"

"Ashton. Ashton Dupree."

Something in his low voice prompted Tommie to ask, "Did you know her?"

A pause. "Yes."

"I'm sorry, Paulo."

He said nothing. But his silence spoke volumes. Ashton Dupree had meant something to him.

Telling herself she was crazy for envying a dead woman, Tommie murmured, "Would you mind telling me what she did for a living?"

Paulo frowned. "She worked at a strip club."

Tommie felt the blood drain from her head. "What did you say?"

"She was a stripper."

"Oh my God."

He stared sharply at her. "What?"

"I don't believe this," Tommie whispered. "*I* used to be a stripper."

Paulo's eyes widened. "You're kidding me."

She shook her head, dread coiling in her stomach. "Four years ago, I moonlighted as an exotic dancer at a strip club in San Antonio. I'd been working there for three months when one of the other girls got killed and—"

"I remember. Sebastien was the primary on the investigation. The press called it the case of the Spider Tattoo Killer." Paulo stared at her, incredulous. "I never knew *you* worked at the Sirens and Spurs."

"It wasn't for very long," Tommie explained. "I was desperate, at a low point in my life. I took the job naively hoping to get discovered by a talent agent. It had happened to one of the other dancers who worked there, so I figured it could happen to me. But it didn't work out that way. I became good friends with the girl who was murdered. It was only by the grace of God that the killer didn't set his sights on me instead." She shivered, chilled by the realization that she hadn't been so lucky this time. The eerie phone call she'd received at the hospital was proof that she'd come into a madman's crosshairs.

And she could tell by the look on Paulo's face that the same thought had occurred to him.

"My God," Tommie whispered as another idea struck her. "It's like this killer is recreating my life. First with Maribel, who was a legal secretary like I was, right down to working at the same law firm. And now with Ashton, a stripper. It can't be a coincidence."

Paulo was silent, his jaw tightly clenched, his eyes glittering like obsidian. She could see the synapses in his brain firing rapidly as he turned possibilities over in his mind.

Sounding as if he were thinking aloud, he said, "If what you're suggesting is true—if you're the ultimate target—then we have to consider the possibility that the killer is someone *you* know, not the other victims."

Tommie suppressed a horrified shudder. She couldn't imagine anyone she knew being capable of brutally murdering innocent people.

"Have you ever had a stalker?" Paulo asked.

She shook her head quickly. "No."

"Are you sure?"

She gave him a look. "I think I'd remember something as terrifying as being stalked."

"What about an obsessed fan? Someone who sent you disturbing letters and e-mails?"

She frowned. "I'm not a movie star. My fans were people who have a genuine appreciation for the arts, for ballet—"

Paulo cut to the chase. "You're an amazingly gifted dancer, Tommie, but with all due respect, not everyone who came to watch you perform limited themselves to admiring how well you do pirouettes and pliés and evoke emotion. You have to know that there were men in the audience—and more than a few women, I'd bet—who were only interested in getting an eyeful of your big tits and your juicy ass in those tight leotards and revealing costumes you wear."

Tommie gasped, torn between laughter and affront at his crass language. "Paulo!"

He shook his head at her. "I'm not into theater or dance, but I'd sure as hell fork over my last dime to watch you perform any day of the week. Obviously I'm not alone. You sold out theaters and concert halls—"

"As part of an ensemble," Tommie interjected.

Paulo gave her a knowing look. "I appreciate your modesty, *querida*, but I hope you don't expect me to believe there weren't people who came just to see you."

"I was part of a dance company," she reiterated emphatically.

"Your dance company wasn't with you on Wednesday morning when you packed out that campus theater. Don't forget I saw the news coverage that evening. Those people came to see *you* and you alone, Tommie. So again I ask, do you remember receiving any fan mail that made you uncomfortable? Ever meet or correspond with any fans who seemed obsessed with your work or tried to get a little too close to you?"

Tommie frowned. "I don't know—"

"*Think.*"

She flinched at his brusque tone. "Do you have to be so pushy and mean?" she groused.

He didn't crack a smile. "I'm not your friend or lover right now, Tommie. I'm a homicide detective who's trying to stop a sadistic monster from killing again. If your hunch is right, then we're running out of time."

She stared at him, chilled to the bone. "What do you mean?"

Paulo's expression was grim, as if he'd rather not say what he knew he had to. "This predator isn't wasting too much time between killings. Three, four days seems to be the pattern, although it's true that we only have two murders to go on. My partner and I are worried that he might strike again soon. If your theory is correct—that he's trying to recreate your life, as you put it—then he's working forward, not backward."

"I don't understand."

"What was the first job you ever had?"

"Out of college?"

"No, when you were a teenager."

"Oh." She smiled. "I worked at Sonic."

"Okay. The killer didn't start off by targeting some hapless teenager serving chili cheese coneys and cherry limeades at Sonic. He started in your adulthood, when you worked as a legal secretary. After that you got the side gig as a stripper. What came next?"

Tommie sighed. "When I moved to New York, I did what any self-respecting starving artist did—I waited tables." She paused. "Are you telling me that the next victim could be a waitress?"

"I don't know. It's entirely possible that he might target a waitress aspiring to become a dancer. That's the common denominator here—dancing. According to her supervisor, Maribel Cruz enjoyed dancing as a hobby and had always dreamed of becoming a ballerina. Ashton Dupree was an exotic dancer. See the pattern?"

Tommie nodded mutely.

"That's why I think you got on the killer's radar through your dancing. That's why I'm leaning toward the possibility of him being an obsessed fan, someone who attended all of your performances, collected all of the memorabilia—brochures, playbills, ticket receipts, anything with your name or face on it. Someone who was there that night in February, who watched you smile and autograph programs for Maribel and Ashton and maybe even for him. That's why it's so important for you to remember any strange letters or e-mails you may have received over the years."

"I'm trying," Tommie muttered, rubbing her temple as she felt the onset of a headache. "My days with the dance company are somewhat of a blur now. We were on the road most of the time, living out of suitcases and maintaining long, grueling schedules. Most of our fan mail was routed through the public affairs coordinator. Sometimes people wouldn't know a dancer's name, so they'd just write to our artistic director and say how much they'd enjoyed so and so's translation of a piece, or thought so and so didn't give a strong enough performance. Many people didn't write directly to us because they knew, with our demanding tour schedule, that it could be months before they received a response.

"But, yes," she continued with a wry chuckle, "I do remember getting the occasional oddball fan letter. A couple years ago, after attending our debut production of *Black Orpheus*—in which I danced in the lead role as Eurydice—one guy wrote to let me know that he'd dreamed about sharing the stage with me as Orpheus. He said the dream was so vivid that he woke up weeping and reaching toward his bedroom floor, as if he were Orpheus rescuing me, Eurydice, from the underworld. In case you're not familiar with the story, it's about—"

"Two lovers who are reunited after death," Paulo finished impatiently. "I know the story. I took Greek mythology in high school. What I *don't* know is why you weren't freaked out by some nutcase telling you he dreamed that you were his long-lost lover."

Tommie shrugged. "I figured the guy was harmless. A bit of a screwball, but harmless. He didn't make any lewd sexual overtures or say something off the wall about the two of us being destined for each other. I didn't feel in the least bit threatened by the letter. In a nutshell, he just wanted to tell me how moving he thought my performance was."

"Did he ever write to you again?"

"Not that I know of."

Paulo frowned. "Do you still have the letter?"

"No, I didn't keep it." She grimaced. "My studio apartment in New York was so ridiculously tiny, I tried not to accumulate too much stuff. Which was hard, because I like buying and collecting things."

"Do you remember receiving any other strange letters?"

"Nothing that alarmed me enough to tell my director or call the police."

"Are you sure?"

"Positive."

"What about the lecture you recently gave at the university? Afterward, when people came up to meet you and get your autograph, did anyone strike you as odd?"

Tommie pursed her lips, deep in thought for a moment. "There was a young professor. A chemistry instructor, if I recall. He had a copy of an old catalogue with me posing on the cover. *That* was a little odd."

"Why?"

"Well, it wasn't a dance catalogue. It was from my brief stint as a lingerie model."

Paulo looked intrigued. "You were a lingerie model?"

"For about a month."

"How'd that come about?"

Tommie arched an amused brow. "Are you asking as a homicide detective, or as a curious male?"

He blinked innocently. "A detective, of course."

"Of course." But she gave him a look that told him she knew better. "Anyway, when I first got to New York, I knew I really wanted to break into professional dancing, but I went on auditions for just about everything, just to see what doors might open for me. I had casting directors offering me roles in their porn flicks and music videos, telling me that with a body like mine, I could make a killing as a porn star or a video vixen. I had no interest in becoming either. But a girl's gotta eat, so I chose the lesser of the evils and signed on as a lingerie model with a fledgling modeling agency. I'd already worked as a stripper, so I had no qualms about going from one photo shoot to another dressed in nothing more than skimpy lingerie beneath my trench coat."

She let out a small sigh and lifted a shoulder. "Anyway, it was a short-lived gig. A month after I'd signed the contract, the modeling agency went bust. Even though I received some interest from other small agencies, I decided it was time to get serious about my dancing aspirations. Not many people even know about me working as a lingerie model, and the catalogue I was featured in didn't have a wide circulation. So I was surprised that the chemistry professor had a copy of it."

Paulo frowned. "Do you remember his name?"

"No. I'd have to ask my friend Renee Williams. She's the director of dance, and the one who invited me to lecture at the university."

"Then do it," Paulo said shortly. "Get the guy's name from her. I'll check him out."

"Yes, sir."

Paulo scowled at the mock salute she gave him, but let it pass. "Did anyone else rub you the wrong way after the lecture?"

"Other than Richard?" Tommie said sourly.

"Who's Richard?"

She immediately felt contrite for bringing up his name. "Richard Houghton is the artistic director at the Met. But I didn't mean to imply that he might be the killer," she added hastily.

"Why does he rub you the wrong way?"

She shrugged. "The way he stares at me makes me uncomfortable. And he's not a very nice guy, contrary to what Zhane thinks. I don't trust him."

"But you think he might be interested in you."

"I think that's a safe assumption. He brought me flowers after the lecture," she said, hitching her chin toward the elaborate floral arrangement on the dining room table.

Paulo followed the direction of her gaze. "Nice. Looks expensive."

"I suppose."

"So if you dislike the guy so much, why'd you accept flowers from him?"

"Because it would've been rude not to. Besides, every ballerina loves to receive bouquets after a performance," she grumbled sheepishly. "It's in our DNA."

"Ah." Paulo nodded, lips quirking. "So other than accepting his flowers, have you ever given Richard any reason to think he might have a chance with you? Have you ever gone out with him?"

"No way. And he's never asked, thank God."

"So his only crime is giving you expensive flowers, staring at you, and possibly being an asshole?"

Tommie glared at him. "Are you making fun of me, Detective?"

"Absolutely not," he said with a straight face. When her eyes narrowed, he added, "Richard Houghton is going on my list of people to check out."

"Fine. But just for the record, I don't think he's our guy. An asshole, maybe. But not a killer."

"I'll keep that in mind," Paulo said dryly. "Do you have any enemies?"

She snorted. "Doesn't everyone?"

"Some more than others. What about you?"

She shrugged. "I've always had people who didn't like me. Sometimes it was justified, other times not." She hesitated, then added, "I don't make friends very easily." The minute the words were out of her mouth, she was embarrassed.

Paulo said quietly, "That's not the impression I get from watching you and Zhane together. You two seem like you've known each other a lot longer than seven months. And you told me before that you had a lot of friends back in New York."

"I did. But they were rare, a special breed of people. They didn't judge me." She shook her head, feeling like she was digging herself deeper into a hole the more she talked. The more she revealed. "It's hard to explain."

"I think I understand," Paulo murmured.

Tommie met his gaze. And, somehow, she knew he did understand. And that scared the living daylight out of her.

Glancing away, she cleared her throat. "You asked me about enemies. I wasn't very popular with the other dancers in my company. I'm sure more than a few of them were happy to see me go. But I certainly wouldn't suspect any of them of being a ruthless killer. Ruthlessly competitive, yes. But not ruthlessly homicidal."

"What about ex-lovers?" Paulo prodded. "You said an old boyfriend stopped by unexpectedly yesterday."

Tommie nodded tightly, anger flaring in her chest at the reminder of Roland Jackson's visit.

"You said it threw you off for the rest of the day. Why?"

She shook her head slowly. "If it's all the same to you, Paulo, I'd rather not discuss it."

He stared at her for a long, tense moment, then nodded wordlessly.

Rising from the floor, Tommie grabbed her empty glass from the table and headed toward the kitchen. "I need more wine. Want some?"

"No, thanks." He sounded surly.

Was he jealous of Roland? Tommie wondered. Did he think she and Roland were getting back together? If only he knew!

"What was the name of the attorney you reported to at Thorne and Associates?" Paulo asked her.

She glanced over her shoulder at him, frowning. "You mean the one who sexually harassed me?"

"Yeah."

"His name was Harold Van Gundy. Why? Is he going on your list, too?"

"Of course. He has motive for wanting to hurt you— you got him fired."

"He got himself fired," Tommie muttered, opening the refrigerator. As she poured wine into her glass, she was struck by a chilling new thought.

Leaving her drink on the counter, she walked to the doorway and stared across the living room at Paulo, who was still sitting and brooding by the fire.

He glanced up at her, frowned at the troubled look on her face. "What is it?"

"I just thought of something. We've been spending all this time trying to figure out if the killer is someone I know. But I'm not the only one who came into contact with both of the victims. You did, too." She paused. "So what if the killer is actually someone *you* know?"

Chapter 20

"The thought crossed my mind," Paulo said in a low, flat voice.

Tommie nodded. "Of course. You're the detective here, not me."

He held her gaze another moment, then rose to his feet and walked over to the sofa. He sat down heavily, closing his eyes as he shoved stiff fingers through his black hair. He looked like he had the weight of the world on his shoulders.

Tommie joined him a moment later, silently passing him a glass of wine.

He arched a brow at her. "I thought I said I didn't want any more."

"What you want and what you need are two different things."

"True enough." He raised the glass to his lips and took a long drink.

Setting her own wineglass on the table, Tommie said, "Now it's my turn to interrogate you."

Paulo let out a short, humorless laugh. "It doesn't work that way."

"Why not? Because you have the badge and the gun?"

"Basically."

"I don't think so."

"Too bad."

"Look, two women that we both knew or encountered were brutally murdered this week. You said yourself that you don't believe in coincidence. Neither do I. So like it or not, Paulo, we're in this together."

He shook his head, bristling with impatience. "Okay. Whatever." He downed the rest of his wine, set his glass down with a thud.

Undaunted, Tommie asked, "Do you have any enemies?"

"I'm a cop," he said, as if the answer should be obvious.

"Right. You've put away a lot of dangerous criminals who'd like nothing more than to get even with you."

"Your powers of observation are amazing," Paulo said sarcastically.

Ignoring the barb, Tommie forged ahead. "What about people in your personal life? Maybe you've unknowingly gotten on the wrong person's bad side and—"

"Tell you what," Paulo cut her off, coldly mocking. "Why don't you just leave the police work to the paid professionals?"

Her temper flared. "Damn it, Paulo, I'm trying to help here! Why are you shutting me out?"

"I'm not shut—"

"Yes, you are!"

"Yeah? Well, that communication thing works both ways!" he fired back.

Tommie stared at him, comprehension dawning. "Oh, I get it. You're throwing a tantrum because I didn't want to talk about my old boyfriend."

Paulo scowled. "I'm not throwing a damned tantrum. I'm trying to get to the bottom of who's behind these murders. If you really wanted to help as much as you claim you do, then you wouldn't refuse to answer any of my damned questions."

Fury swelled in Tommie's chest. "You want to know about my old boyfriend? Fine! I'll tell you! Roland Jackson is the son of a bitch responsible for getting me kicked out of the Blane Bailey Dance Company. That's right." She sneered at the surprised look that crossed Paulo's face. "I didn't walk away of my own accord. I was given the boot. Why? Because my malicious ex-boyfriend sent an embarrassing videotape of me to the artistic director and threatened to circulate it to the media and everyone in the theater and dance community."

Paulo stared at her. "What was on the videotape?"

"Me," Tommie spat furiously. "Having sex with Roland and his best friend."

She watched Paulo's face, waiting to see contempt, anger, disgust, disappointment—all the emotions she knew he must be feeling.

But his expression remained neutral. He regarded her calmly, silently, waiting for her to continue.

So she did. "The Blane Bailey Dance Company has a proud, rich tradition of performance excellence and achievement, of being a cultural icon and ambassador to the world. The artistic director didn't want to risk tarnishing the company's reputation with a tawdry sex scandal, so he had no choice but to let me go." She shook her head, her mouth twisting bitterly at the painful memory. "He wasn't too happy about it. He said he'd always hoped to have me dancing for him until I was too old and decrepit to lift a toe. But his hands were tied. He had to take Roland at his word that he'd make good on his threat to distribute the videotape. And that's why I didn't even bother auditioning for another dance company. I didn't know what Roland was capable of, didn't want to take any chances."

"So you left New York and came here," Paulo murmured.

Tommie nodded, her throat raw from the effort of holding back tears. "I couldn't return to San Antonio. I was too humiliated. When I left home four years ago, I felt like a failure. But at least there was hope, a light at the end of the tunnel if I could just will myself to keep moving toward it. But to leave home *feeling* like a failure was one thing. To come back *as* a failure was more than I could handle."

"You're not a failure," Paulo said gently. "You went to New York and did what you set out to do. You joined an elite dance company, traveled around the country, and saw the world. How many people can say that?"

"Don't," Tommie said, holding up a hand, steeling herself against the power of his kind words, his compassion. "I don't want or deserve your pity. I made my own bed, so to speak, when I put myself in that compromising situation with Roland. No one held a gun to my head. No one's ever made me do what I don't want to."

"Tell me what happened, Tommie."

She shook her head. "I don't—"

"Tell me." The steely glint in his eyes, and the tone of his voice, let her know it was no longer a request.

Closing her eyes, she rested her head against the back of the sofa and drew a deep, fortifying breath, gathering courage to tell him things she'd never shared with anyone else. "It happened four years ago," she began in a low monotone. "A few months before I left home for New York. I was depressed at the time. About everything, really. My dead-end job as a secretary, my mounting credit card debt, my strained relationship with my father, who rightly thought I lacked direction and focus. Even my relationship with Frankie depressed me. I was insanely jealous of her. Jealous of her genius IQ, jealous of her great career, jealous of her wonderful relationship with our father.

"The one constant in my life, the one thing I could rely on, was my boyfriend, Roland, who I'd been dating for two years. He was a UPS driver who'd flirted shamelessly with me every time he brought a delivery to the law firm, until one day I agreed to go out with him. He wasn't my ideal guy. He lacked ambition, didn't seem terribly bright, and he still lived at home with his mother. But we had fun together, and at the time I believed he genuinely cared about me. He treated me well and seemed to accept me for who I am. And unlike my father, Roland supported my dream of becoming a dancer. Frankie did, too, but at the time I was so consumed by jealousy and bitterness that I questioned every kind word she ever spoke to me." Tommie shook her head, feeling the familiar pang of guilt over the way she'd treated her sister, one of many mistakes from her past she wished she could undo.

"Anyway," she continued after a moment, "one night after work I went over to Roland's house. I was upset and feeling sorry for myself because I'd auditioned for a local production, and had just found out that I didn't make the final cut. I wanted to get drunk, smashed out of my mind. Whatever it took to make me forget my pain, my anger, my disappointment with life. Roland was only too willing to oblige me. His mother was out of town, so we had the place to ourselves. He made me a margarita, just the way I liked it. One turned into two, then three, and before I knew it I'd drunk every last drop in the blender and was asking for more. I'd always been able to hold my liquor, so I thought I'd be able to handle whatever else Roland gave me. He handed me the Courvoisier he'd been nursing. After taking a few sips, I started feeling a little fuzzy, disoriented. So out of it that I didn't even realize when Roland's best friend, Simeon, came over. I'd always thought Simeon was kinda cute and smart, so I started flirting with him. Not enough to make Roland mad, but enough to make myself feel better. See," she said, her lips twisting with bitter irony, "one thing I've always known I could count on is my looks. When all else fails, I've always been able to look in the mirror and be proud of what I saw on the outside, even if I hated what was on the inside."

"Baby—"

"I'm not finished," she said sharply, lifting her head from the sofa and glaring at him. "You wanted to hear what happened that night, and now I'm telling you."

Paulo clenched his jaw, but said nothing more.

"It was late. I had to get up early for work, but I knew I was in no condition to drive myself home. Roland put on some music, and we started dancing. All three of us. And then Roland started kissing me, fondling me, and I was too drunk to care that Simeon was watching. And then the next thing I knew, he and I were dancing together while Roland watched. When Simeon kissed me, I jumped back in shock. I couldn't believe he'd had the nerve to kiss me in front of Roland. But Roland didn't seem to mind. *That* pissed me off, so I told him I was ready to leave. I asked him to drive me home since he hadn't had as much to drink. He said he'd take me home after I calmed down, and he made Simeon apologize for kissing me. I should have called the cab my damned self. But I didn't. I sat back down, let Roland pour me another drink, and listened to some more music." She closed her eyes, drew a shuddering breath before whispering, "The last thing I remember about that night was Roland removing my shirt, looking into my eyes, and telling me he was going to make me feel better."

"But he didn't." Paulo's tone was hard, flat.

Slowly Tommie shook her head. "I tried, but for the life of me I couldn't remember what had happened that night. And whenever I asked Roland about it, he just told me that we'd had a good time together, that he'd done what was necessary to take my mind off my problems. He even assured me that Simeon had gone home before he and I made love. I didn't find out the truth until four years later when I saw the videotape. My director didn't want to give it to me. He could tell by the horrified look on my face that I hadn't known a thing about it. But I insisted that he let me have it. And then I went home and forced myself to watch it, to sit through every lurid, degrading minute of it. When it was over, I screamed at the top of my lungs, railed at the injustice of what had been done to me. And then I burned the videotape and vowed that nothing like that would ever, *ever* happen to me again."

When she'd finished speaking, a heavy silence fell over the room. Paulo didn't say a word, and Tommie didn't look at him, afraid to let him see the shame and humiliation she felt, afraid of what she might see reflected on *his* face. Mrs. Calhoun had not judged or rejected her, but even if she had, Tommie, though hurt, could have handled it.

She couldn't handle being judged or rejected by Paulo.

It would kill her.

But after several long, agonizing moments of silence, she couldn't take the suspense anymore. She had to know, one way or another.

When she hazarded a glance at Paulo, she nearly recoiled from the leashed fury blazing in his eyes, turning them black, hardening his features. But underneath the fury was another emotion she hadn't expected: ten-derness. Raw, naked tenderness.

Oh God, she thought as hot tears rushed to her eyes. She didn't want his tenderness. Anything else she could have fought off. But God help her, she had no defense against tenderness. She couldn't defend against some-thing she'd spent all her life seeking and craving.

"No," she whispered, shaking her head at him. "I can't—"

Paulo pulled her close in a fierce, protective grip. With a strangled sob Tommie dissolved in his arms, burying her face in his neck and surrendering to the anguished tears she'd never allowed herself before. She wept with anger at the cruel violation she'd suffered, wept with frustration at her own stupidity and helplessness, and wept with sorrow for everything she had lost and could never regain. And through it all Paulo held her tightly, brushing his lips across her forehead, whispering tender endearments.

Even after she'd stopped crying, and lay still against him, he wouldn't let her go. Thankfully, she didn't want him to.

Long minutes passed before she could find the strength to speak again. "I've never told anyone else," she confided in a low, husky whisper.

"Thank you for telling me," Paulo murmured, gently stroking her hair.

She smiled against his chest, feeling his strong, steady heartbeat. "You didn't give me much of a choice."

"I'm sorry for pushing you," he said humbly. "If I'd known how painful—"

She shook her head, forestalling the rest of his apol-ogy. "It's okay. Really. I'm glad you know. I don't think I like having secrets between us."

He kissed the top of her head, murmured something soft and endearing in Spanish.

Tommie closed her eyes, felt her heart expand in her chest. She'd never felt more cherished, more protected in all her life. "Mrs. Calhoun knows, too," she said softly. "She overheard me and Roland arguing when he showed up here yesterday morning."

"What the hell did he want?" Paulo said in a low, controlled voice. As if he were trying very hard not to upset her again.

"He claims he wanted to apologize," Tommie said sarcastically. "He wanted me to know he was a changed man. He'd found God, joined a church. Became a deacon."

Paulo muttered a vicious oath under his breath that made her smile, even as she said, "It's not for me to judge whether he's truly had a change of heart. That's between him and God, and I've always believed that everyone deserves a second chance. But the sight of him standing there, with that hangdog look on his face, made me see red. Just thinking about it makes my blood boil. If Mrs. Calhoun hadn't intervened when she did, I think I might have killed him!"

"You would have been justified," Paulo growled.

That startled a laugh out of Tommie. "Thanks. That really means a lot to me, coming from a homicide detective. I guess you could have testified in my defense at the murder trial," she said wryly.

"And speaking of murders," Paulo muttered, "I don't like the fact that he just showed up one day out of the clear blue. How long has he been living in Houston?"

"I don't know. Mrs. Calhoun says he joined her church five months ago. But I know he was still living in San Antonio when he sent the videotape. I saw the postmarked envelope and called his mother's house when I couldn't remember his old cell phone number. She didn't say he no longer lived with her or had moved to Houston, she just told me he wasn't home. So he can't have been living here for very long."

"It wouldn't surprise me one damned bit to find out he followed you here," Paulo said through gritted teeth.

"The thought crossed my mind," Tommie admitted. "After his mother gave me his new cell phone number, I left him several scathing messages. But he never returned any of my calls."

"Fucking coward," Paulo snarled.

Tommie smiled. "I believe that was just one of the things I called him, among others. Anyway, shortly after I moved here, the *Houston Chronicle* did a feature story on me to help me drum up business for my studio. It's possible that Roland read the article online or heard about me moving to Houston through the grapevine." She frowned. "But why would he follow me here? He had to know I'd want absolutely nothing to do with him."

"Since when has that ever mattered to a stalker?"

Her frown deepened. "Good point."

"I think I'll pay Mr. Jackson a visit tomorrow, ask him a few questions."

Tommie wasn't fooled by his deceptively mild tone. She lifted her head from his chest, searched his impassive face. "Please don't do anything stupid," she warned.

"Like what?"

"Paulo."

"Relax. I'm just going to ask him a few routine questions, see if he has an alibi for the dates and times of the murders."

Tommie studied him a moment longer, eyes narrowed. Satisfied that he was telling the truth, she resettled her head on his chest and nestled against him. "As much as

I loathe and despise Roland, I just can't imagine him being a murderer. I dated him for two years. Isn't that something I would have picked up on?"

"Not necessarily," Paulo murmured, stroking her hair. "The most ruthless serial killers in history mastered the art of hiding in plain sight and disguising their true selves from the people closest to them. And with all due respect, *querida*, you never would have imagined Roland was capable of hurting and betraying you, but he did, didn't he?"

Tommie nodded, closing her eyes against a fresh wave of anger and pain.

In a very gentle voice, Paulo asked, "Have you considered the possibility that you were drugged that night?"

A cold fist clamped around Tommie's stomach. "Are you asking me if I think Roland slipped a roofie into my drink?"

Paulo nodded. "It would explain the memory loss you experienced."

She swallowed. "I wondered about that. But I was also very drunk that night."

"Have you ever gotten so drunk that you couldn't remember a thing the next day?"

She hesitated, then shook her head. "No."

"I didn't think so." He picked up her hand and threaded his fingers through hers, soothing her even as he gently navigated her through painful, turbulent waters. She silently marveled at it, his ability to be a concerned, protective lover and a justice-seeking cop at the same time.

"Did you ever think about pressing charges?" he asked.

"Yes," Tommie murmured. "But then I thought about how difficult it would be to prove my case. Four years had passed. Even if Roland did slip a roofie into my drink, it's not as if my blood could be tested for the drug years after the fact. The only other evidence was the videotape, which I'd already burned. You can best believe Roland would have destroyed any copies he made. And even if he didn't, I'm not so sure a jury would have convicted him and Simeon based on the video alone. I looked out of it, definitely, but I'm sure any capable lawyer could have convinced a jury that I was a willing participant. A little drunk, but willing." She drew a deep breath that burned in her lungs. "It would have come down to my word against theirs, and quite honestly I don't know if my credibility would have withstood a defense attorney dredging up my sexual history and the fact that I'd been a stripper."

"But you started working at the Sirens and Spurs *after* that night, not before," Paulo pointed out.

"I don't think that would have mattered," Tommie said in bitter resignation. "You and I both know they would have found a way to use it against me. Remember, we're talking about a trial that would have occurred four years after the fact. They would have cited my employment as a stripper as yet another example of my sexual promiscuity and voyeuristic tendencies. They would have claimed that I enjoyed being videotaped that night, that I secretly fantasized about having threesomes while I was performing onstage and taking my clothes off for strange men." She shuddered at the thought of being dismantled on the witness stand, of being forced to relive the entire humiliating, traumatic incident. "I couldn't put myself or my family through that. I just couldn't."

Paulo angled his head to stare into her face. "And you don't think there's a correlation between what happened that night and you getting a job at the strip club shortly afterward?"

"No. I don't. I didn't remember what happened that night."

"Maybe not," Paulo countered stubbornly, "but deep in your subconscious you must have sensed that something was wrong, otherwise you wouldn't have kept asking Roland about it."

"Maybe you're right," she conceded, holding his intent gaze. "But that's not the reason I started working at the strip club. I told you my reason. I was hoping to get discovered. It was an immature, shallow, calculated decision on my part, but that's all there was to it." *I'm sorry,* she almost added, because she sensed that he wanted to believe what he was telling her. But she couldn't lie to him, or to herself.

She reached up, gently touching his face. "I know you think I was a victim—"

"You were, damn it," Paulo growled.

His fierce protectiveness made her heart ache. If she hadn't already cried her tear ducts dry, she might have wept again.

"Listen to me," she murmured, cupping his face in both hands as she gazed into his dark, troubled eyes. "Are you listening?"

He hesitated, a muscle clenching in his rigid jaw.

"Paulo?"

He gave a short nod.

"I was victimized, but I'm not a victim. No, hear me out," Tommie said when he opened his mouth to protest. "Roland and Simeon violated me that night. There's no getting around that. They took advantage of me in a way that I wouldn't wish upon my worst enemy. But as horrible as the experience was, I'm relieved that I don't remember what actually happened. Maybe Roland did me a favor by drugging me that night. Watching the videotape was traumatic enough. I can't even imagine how much worse it would have been if they'd forced themselves upon me and I had to relive that every time I closed my eyes and went to sleep, every time I looked in the mirror, every time I even *thought* about being intimate with another man. At the Sirens and Spurs I worked alongside women who had been molested and raped, and I can tell you right now I didn't envy their ability to recall, in sickening detail, what their attacker had done to them. I pitied them. My heart broke for them.

"Seven months ago, when I watched Roland's video-tape and saw what had been done to me, I thought of those girls at the strip club, and I realized, even then, how lucky I was. Because I had four years of blissful ignorance. I'm not saying that I don't have flashbacks to that night, that disturbing images from the video don't pop into my mind when I least expect it. It happens. But I'm not con-trolled by those memories, and I thank God for that."

She smiled softly, combing her fingers through the thick, silky brush of Paulo's hair. "I've always had a healthy sexual appetite, and I make no apologies for that. Part of the reason I enjoy dancing so much is the sense of liberation it gives me. The permission to be a passion-ate, powerful, sensual being. I love our lovemaking, Paulo. I wanted you the moment I met you at the wed-ding rehearsal dinner four years ago, and that wanting has only gotten stronger over time. Even tonight, sitting here with you, I've found myself thinking of how soon I can get you into my bed. Now that I've told you about my past, I hope you're not going to run for the hills or—God forbid—start handling me with kid gloves. That's the last thing I want. In case you didn't hear me the first time, let me repeat myself. I *love* our lovemaking. They didn't take that away from me. I hope you won't, either."

Paulo said nothing as she rose from the sofa, gathered their wineglasses, and walked to the kitchen, where she set his empty glass on the counter. She carried her own untouched drink into the bedroom and placed it on the bedside table, then proceeded to undress and take her nightly shower. She took longer than usual, hoping Paulo would join her. But as the minutes wore on and he didn't appear, her hope dwindled. Fear and a growing sense of desperation began to overtake her.

By the time she climbed into bed, alone, she was downright dejected. It was clear that Paulo would not be coming to her. He'd decided that she was damaged goods, and his conscience simply wouldn't allow him to continue sleeping with her when he knew they could have no future together.

So much for seeing where that *road is going to lead us,* Tommie thought bitterly, blinking back tears as she remembered his earlier words to her. She gulped down her glass of wine, hoping it would dull the sharp edges of her pain and help her fall asleep faster.

When she finally heard Paulo coming down the hallway, she assumed he was going to ask her where she kept the spare blankets so he could camp out on the sofa.

As he stepped through the doorway, she barely lifted her head from her pillow, saying tonelessly, "They're in the hall closet."

"That's nice," Paulo muttered, peeling off his shirt, kicking off his jeans, and striding purposefully toward the bed, powerful and gloriously naked, "but you already cost me one sleepless night on a damned sofa. No way in hell am I going through that again."

Tommie nearly wept with joyous relief as he pulled back the covers and slid into bed with her, seizing her mouth in a fierce, plundering kiss that stole her breath. His hot, sweet tongue delved inside her mouth while his callused hands gripped the hem of her nightshirt, yanked it up

over her head, and flung it aside. She trembled with pleasure as he pressed her breasts together and licked the
deep valley between them, his breath a warm, silky caress
against her skin.

She clutched his hair and moaned as he slid down the
length of her body. He drew her legs up and rubbed his
stubble-roughened cheek against the smooth, sensitized
flesh of her inner thighs, making her shiver.

Inhaling her scent into his lungs, he groaned thickly.
"God, you smell so good."

Tommie let out a shocked cry of pleasure as he drew the
tender bud of her clitoris into his mouth. She writhed
under the slow, erotic lash of his tongue, her hips buck-
ing in his strong grip. He held her ruthlessly still, licking
and lapping at her, his tongue swirling in sensual circles
against her swollen labia. He licked her as if she were an
exotic fruit dripping with sweet, succulent nectar. As if he
could never get enough of her. He feasted until she
was sobbing and pleading, her hands tangled in his hair,
her thighs quaking uncontrollably. Just as she began to
wonder if it was possible to die from sexual torment, he
pushed her over the top and sent her flying apart with a
loud, keening wail.

As her body convulsed, he lifted his head and watched
her face with a look of dark, masculine satisfaction.
"More?"

"*More*," she whimpered.

He gently unwound her hands from his hair and
kissed each of her fingers, his molten eyes blazing down
at her with fierce, unmistakable purpose as he rose up
over her. He folded her legs back against her chest so
that when he drove inside her, his thrust had his whole
weight behind him.

She cried out at the sheer force of it, feeling him deep

in her womb, where she was still throbbing from the first mind-shattering orgasm.

He cupped her face in his hands, leaned close. "Don't ever question how much I want you," he said huskily. "Do you understand?"

She jerked her head in a tight nod, unable to speak.

Slowly he withdrew from her, almost to the tip, then plunged back inside with a hoarse groan of pleasure that joined her own. She twined her arms around his neck, her nails digging into his back as he began thrusting into her, deep, slamming thrusts that rocked the bed, rocked her to the core of her being. She sank deeper into the pillows, arching herself, offering him everything.

"I can't get enough of you," Paulo whispered raggedly, kissing her with passionate yearning. "Tell me what you want, *querida*, and I'll give it to you."

Tears stung her eyes at the desperate longing in his voice. She clasped her legs tightly around his hips. "I want everything you've got," she urged breathlessly. "Give me everything. Don't hold back."

He shuddered, and taking her at her word, he thrust harder, faster, reaching deeper with every urgent stroke.

Tommie gave herself completely over to their savage lovemaking, the primal joining of body and soul. Time ceased to have meaning. All she knew was the pleasure of his solid weight upon her, the plunge and glide of his hot, thick shaft inside her, the wet, slapping sounds of their bodies filling the room. She wanted their lovemaking to last forever, but they were already hurtling toward the cliff together, free-falling over the edge.

She stared into his face and cried out with a wild, exultant joy as he exploded inside her, filling her with his scalding heat, calling her name hoarsely and reverently as his rapid thrusts triggered her own sweet, shimmering explosion. She buried her face against his chest and melted into tears, both frightened and exhilarated by the feeling of euphoria sweeping through her, a feeling unlike anything she had ever known before. She wanted to freeze this moment in time, a moment of profound intimacy and complete perfection.

They clutched each other for a long time, panting and trembling. At length Paulo lifted his head and gazed deep into her eyes. "Are you okay?"

Tommie smiled, soft and dreamy. "Better than okay."

He kissed the tears from her cheeks, brushed his mouth across hers with exquisite tenderness. She breathed a sigh of contentment as he gathered her protectively against him, nestling her bottom against his lap and drawing the covers over their damp, cooling bodies.

"I must be losing my damned mind," he murmured, his warm breath caressing the back of her neck. "I haven't had unprotected sex since I was fourteen, and twice in two days I've forgotten to use a condom with you. I'm sorry."

"It's all right," Tommie mumbled with another sleepy, satiated smile. "I have an IUD. One of those long-term ones. Besides, I love feeling you inside me. All of you."

He kissed her nape, tightened his arms around her waist.

As she yawned and closed her eyes, she drowsily reflected on what a roller-coaster day it had been. Another innocent woman had been found dead, and after receiving an eerie phone call that evening, Tommie had to face the chilling reality that she, too, was in danger. But as she drifted off to sleep, her last thought was of the man who held her securely in his arms. She had confided her darkest, most painful secrets to Paulo, and he hadn't run away. He'd stayed and comforted her, nurtured her, made sweet, passionate love to her. Proving just why she'd fallen hopelessly, irrevocably, in love with him.

Chapter 21

When Paulo awakened the next morning, the sun was shining brightly through the windows, the bed was empty beside him, and the fragrant aroma of coffee and bacon wafted from the kitchen. Smiling to himself, he rolled out of bed and padded into the adjoining bathroom to relieve himself. When he'd finished he grabbed the spare toothbrush Tommie had provided—the woman had a spare of everything—and quickly brushed his teeth. Returning to the bedroom, he tugged on his jeans, which he'd found with relative ease this time.

He shuffled down the hallway, dragging a hand through his unruly hair and yawning. As he neared the kitchen, he could hear Tommie humming softly to herself. That brought another smile to his face.

He found her standing at the stove flipping pancakes on a griddle while bacon sizzled in a frying pan. Her dark hair was tousled, her feet were bare, and she wore the same black silk robe she'd had on yesterday morning, the one that made him wish he'd had time for a quickie. When she reached up to remove two plates from the cabinet, the hem of the short robe climbed up her shapely thighs. His mouth went dry, and he marveled that even after a night of intense lovemaking, he still couldn't get enough of her.

She glanced up at his entrance and gave him a smile of such radiant warmth his heart slammed against his rib cage. "Good morning."

He stared at her for a moment, riveted by that smile, by her fresh morning beauty.

She eyed him quizzically. "Is something wrong?"

"Not at all," he said, advancing into the kitchen.

She let out a startled squeal as he spun her away from the stove and opened her robe, cupping her warm breasts and slanting his mouth hungrily over hers.

"Oh my," she whispered breathlessly when they at last drew apart. "Someone woke up on the right side of the bed this morning."

"Mmmm," Paulo murmured, nibbling her lush bottom lip. "If you come back to bed with me, we can christen the *left* side, too."

"Very tempting offer," she purred, dark eyes glittering with laughter, "but first we eat. Oh! The pancakes!" She turned away and flipped them, sighing in relief when she saw that they hadn't burned. "Whew. That was close."

When Paulo reached for an exposed breast, she swatted at his hand with the spatula and tugged the lapels of her robe together. "Go away. I'm trying to make breakfast here."

Paulo chuckled softly, reaching inside the cabinet for a mug. He bypassed a bright pink mug emblazoned with the words DANCERS DO IT PRETTIER, and grabbed a plain white one that wouldn't call his manhood into question.

"Your cell phone rang while you were in the bathroom," Tommie told him as he helped himself to coffee.

"I didn't think I should answer it. In case it was official police business—or one of your other women."

Paulo grinned, swatting her on the backside as he walked over to the breakfast counter, where he'd left his phone last night after making a few calls. *Please, God,* he mentally prayed as he reached for it. *Not another body. No more bad news.*

When he checked caller ID and saw that it was only Rafe's call he'd missed, relief swept through him. He dreaded the idea of being summoned to another crime scene. He needed more time to work the puzzle, to try to piece together the missing clues of who was behind the gruesome murders.

And selfishly, he wanted more time to spend with Tommie.

As he watched her moving around the kitchen, humming cheerfully as she put the finishing touches on breakfast, he realized that he could get very used to waking up to the sight of her every morning. He could get used to the warm domesticity of sharing a bathroom with her, sitting down to breakfast with her, returning home to her at the end of a long, tiring day.

He could get used to having her in his life, period.

It was a scary, jarring thought, but one he couldn't deny.

He sent up another prayer. *If we can just make it through breakfast without interruption, I'd be ever so grateful.*

"Who called?" Tommie asked curiously.

"Rafe." Calling, no doubt, to ask about Ashton Dupree's murder. Although Rafe hadn't bonded with her the way his cousin had at summer camp, her untimely death would still come as a shock to him. As it had to Paulo.

"Are you going home for Thanksgiving?" Tommie asked, removing the bacon from the burner.

Paulo grimaced. "I had planned to, but I don't think it's gonna happen. Not with the way this case is going. I'll probably just stay in town and have dinner with the family. Rafe and Korrine and the kids will be here, too. What about you?"

"I'm going home. Frankie and Mama August are cooking, so the rest of us are just bringing our appetites. Which I always do, anyway," she added, grinning.

Paulo smiled. "When are you leaving for San Antonio?"

"On Wednesday. I don't have any classes, so I can leave early enough to beat the holiday traffic."

"Good," Paulo said. The best thing for her was to get out of town for a while, get out of the killer's crosshairs. But he kept the grim thought to himself, not wanting to spoil her good mood. She looked so cheerful, so happy, that one would never suspect her life was in grave danger.

Was it possible that being with *him* made her happy? Paulo wondered, shaken and humbled by the thought. After his disastrous marriage to Jacinta, he'd all but given up hope on the idea of being able to make any woman happy. Until now. . . .

"Breakfast is ready," Tommie announced in a singsong voice. "Let's eat upstairs on the terrace. It's supposed to be a gorgeous day—the first warm day we've had in over a week!"

The rooftop terrace was decorated with a vibrant profusion of plants and boasted a panoramic view of the cool, glistening facade of downtown Houston, with its towering glass skyscrapers and lush green parks. But as Paulo and Tommie sat down to eat, they were oblivious of the stunning vista stretched before them. With their chairs pulled together at the glass-topped wicker table, their eyes kept straying to each other, and their hands and mouths soon followed. They fed each other pancake and slices of fresh cantaloupe, licked the juice from each other's fingers, and traded soft, intimate smiles.

By the time the meal ended, they were both so hot

and aroused that they didn't bother clearing the table. With only a look passing between them, Paulo grabbed Tommie's hand and led her back downstairs to the loft.

Inside her bedroom they hurriedly undressed each other before Paulo lifted her into his arms and strode purposefully into the bathroom. He twisted on the water faucet and carried her inside the steamy shower stall. As he pinned her against the marble wall, she wrapped her legs tightly around his hips, gasping and throwing back her head as he thrust into her. She caught his rhythm and began moving with him. Faster and faster. His blood pounded against his eardrums as hard as the hot needles of water pounding against their bodies, heightening the sensuality of their coupling. He slicked back her hair and ground his mouth against hers, greedily devouring her. Her lips were wet, her tongue soft, her mouth unbearably sweet.

Enveloped in a private, sensual cocoon of heat and steam, Paulo let himself pretend that they were the only two people in the world, that there were no sadistic killers lurking in the shadows, waiting for the opportunity to strike.

He let everything else drift out of his consciousness so he could savor being inside her.

He let himself go with a triumphant shout, his hips pulsing rhythmically against her as he emptied himself into her throbbing womb.

And moments later, as they lay shuddering in each other's arms beneath the bedcovers, he let himself hold her, stroke her, whisper tender, nonsensical words to her.

Because he knew it was only a matter of time before reality would come crashing down on both of them.

And what happened after that would be beyond their control.

* * *

Two hours later, Paulo swung into the parking lot of a small brick Baptist church with stained-glass windows and a prominent sign in the yard announcing the Sunday worship times and the theme of tomorrow's sermon: "Giving Thanks in the Season of Thanksgiving."

An attractive, thirty-something man was stepping out of the only car in the deserted parking lot. Paulo parked beside the shiny black Nissan Altima and climbed out of his cruiser. As he sauntered toward the other man, he noted his split lip and the bruised skin around his left eye, and smiled inwardly at Tommie's handiwork.

"Roland Jackson?"

The man nodded, eyeing him suspiciously. "Who's asking?"

Paulo flashed his badge. "Detective Sanchez. I'd like to ask you some questions."

Jackson frowned. "About what?"

"Tommie Purnell."

Jackson didn't blink. "What about her?"

"I understand you paid her a visit on Thursday."

"Yes, I did." An incredulous look swept across Jackson's face. "Wait a minute. Don't tell me she called the cops just because I went to see her?"

"No," Paulo said evenly, "but maybe she should have."

Jackson scowled. "What are you talking about? She had no reason to call the police. I didn't do anything to her."

"No?"

Jackson glared at him. "I don't know what she told you, but all I did was talk to her. If anything, *I* should be filing assault charges against *her*."

"For that?" Paulo said, hitching his chin toward the man's split lip. He snorted derisively, shaking his head. "You'd get laughed out of the police station."

Jackson's face reddened. "I don't have time for this," he snapped. "I have a ministry meeting to prepare for—"

"How long have you been living in Houston?" Paulo asked abruptly.

"*Excuse* me?"

"I didn't stutter." Paulo's voice was remarkably calm, considering that he wanted to smash his fist into Jackson's face. He'd been trying to keep a tight rein on his temper since last night, when Tommie told him what her old boyfriend and his buddy had done to her four years ago. Paulo had been furious, devastated that she'd had to go through such a painful ordeal at the hands of someone she'd trusted. He'd wanted blood. Although he'd had an entire night to cool off, the rage, along with the frustration and injustice he'd felt, had not abated. They were like fire under his skin, ready to ignite at any moment.

He'd promised Tommie he wouldn't do anything stupid. He intended to keep that promise—or so he'd told himself as he set out for Roland Jackson's apartment that morning. Jackson was just leaving when he arrived, so Paulo had followed him across town to the small Baptist church. As he did, he'd been struck by a memory of being tailgated one night by a black Nissan Altima—just like the one he was following.

When they reached the church and Paulo saw the empty parking lot, he'd felt a dark glimmer of satisfaction. Like a feral animal who knows it has successfully cornered its prey.

"I don't see how it's any of your business how long I've been living in Houston," Jackson said hotly. "I haven't broken any laws."

"Did you follow Tommie here?"

"*What?*"

"You heard me." Paulo's voice was menacingly soft as he took a step forward. "Did you move here to harass her?"

"No!"

"I don't believe you."

"You can believe whatever you want, Detective," Jackson said archly. "I'm a deacon at this church, a respected member of the community, a God-fearing man."

"Is that right?" Paulo mocked, advancing another step. "Then you won't lie to me when I ask you whether you moved to Houston after Tommie did."

"I didn't."

"Wrong answer, preacher. According to your apartment lease, you moved here exactly *one* week after Tommie did. Are you telling me that's just a coincidence?"

"It must be," Jackson insisted, stepping backward. "I didn't even know Tommie lived here until recently, when one of the other deacons happened to mention during a meeting that she worked part-time at a local dance studio. When I asked her the name of the studio, that's when I found out it belonged to Tommie."

Paulo smirked. "How convenient."

"The Lord works in mysterious ways. At least to those who don't know Him." A superior smile curved Jackson's mouth. "If you're not walking in God's perfect will, Detective, then you can't begin to know or understand why things happen the way they do. God led me to Houston for a reason. For all you know, He may have preordained Tommie to be my wife."

Paulo's eyes narrowed. "Like hell."

"So says the unbeliever."

Paulo got in his face, snarling contemptuously, "Do you really think she would take you back after what you did to her, you disgusting piece of shit? Are you that delusional?"

Jackson's face flushed with anger. He staggered back a step, glaring reproachfully at Paulo. "You're way out of line here, Detective," he warned. "You didn't come here in an official capacity. This is harassment, bordering on police brutality. If you don't leave the premises right now I'll—"

"You'll do what?" Paulo taunted, sneering. "Call the cops? Be my fucking guest."

Jackson stared at him in stunned disbelief. And then suddenly, without warning, a wide, knowing grin swept across his face. "She's still got it," he marveled, shaking his head. "After all these years, she's still got the magic touch. The Tommie-mojo."

"What the hell are you talking about?" Paulo said through gritted teeth.

Jackson laughed, giving him an almost pitying look. "I don't know you from Adam, but I'm sure you're a decent man. A good cop. Yet here you are, about to throw away your career over some woman you hardly even know. But it's not your fault, man. You've been put under a spell. You've fallen victim to the Tommie-mojo. The way she walks, the way she talks, the way she smiles. She could step into a room, and a blind man would sit up and take notice. When we were dating I couldn't keep any friends because they all wanted to sleep with her. Even my seventy-five-year-old grandfather couldn't keep his eyes off her at summer cookouts. I've known some beautiful women in my life, but none of them had the Tommie-mojo. So believe me, Detective, I sympathize with what you're going through. But take heart. You weren't the first casualty, and you definitely won't be the last."

When he'd finished speaking, Paulo raked him with a look of scathing contempt. "You're full of shit, Jackson. I've seen your type before, and it's always the same garbage. Blame the victim. It's the child's fault for being so irresistible her father couldn't keep his filthy hands to himself. It's the high school cheerleader's fault for being at the wrong place at the wrong time when some pervert snatched her off the street in broad daylight. It's the beautiful woman's fault her pathetic loser of a boyfriend couldn't accept the fact that she didn't want him anymore.

She must be some sort of evil sorceress who cast a spell on him, causing him to become so obsessed with her that he'd uproot himself and follow her to another city just to stalk her. Yeah, I know your type, you twisted son of a bitch. The one and only difference between you and a convicted felon is that you got away with your crime.

"But I'm watching you, preacher," Paulo said, lowering his voice to a silky, dangerous caress. "I know where you live, where you work, where you pray. I'm watching you, and the first wrong move you make, I'm coming down on your ass like fire and brimstone."

Jackson's face reddened with anger and humiliation. "You won't get away with harassing me like this, Sanchez. You're a dirty cop."

"No dirtier than you, Deacon." Paulo reached out, patted his cheek. "Don't let me keep you any longer from your meeting. I've strayed a bit from my Catholic roots, but I still understand and appreciate the importance of doing the Lord's work."

As he turned and sauntered toward his cruiser, Jackson jeered, "How does it feel to have sloppy seconds?"

Paulo chuckled, shaking his head. "Come on, man, you can do better than that. No man in his right mind would think of Tommie Purnell as sloppy seconds."

"Sloppy thirds, then. Or sloppy fourths or fifths." Jackson sneered at him over the roof of the police cruiser. "She's been around quite a bit, Detective."

"So have I." A narrow grin cut across Paulo's face. "So I guess that makes us soul mates."

Jackson's face hardened with hatred. "If you think she's gonna stay with you, think again. She's the love 'em and leave 'em type. I was never good enough for her. No way in hell is she settling down with some wetback cop. You don't stand a chance with her, *mi amigo.*"

"Maybe not, but I'll take my chances over yours any day of the week."

"Good luck then, 'cause you're gonna need it." A malicious gleam filled Jackson's eyes. "Oh, and if you ever find yourself looking for ways to spice up your love life, here's a little suggestion. Invite one of your friends over. She's really into that."

Paulo went very still. "What did you just say?"

Jackson smiled, knowing he'd finally scored a point. "Our girl is into threesomes. Oh, she might protest a little at first. She might even pretend like she's not enjoying it. But it's all just an act, believe me. If you know anything about Tommie—"

Paulo didn't remember moving.

One moment he was standing beside the cruiser, his hand on the door handle. A moment later he was charging Jackson, fueled with lethal rage as he slammed his fist into the man's face. Jackson staggered backward, swung blindly, and caught a vicious blow to the stomach and a hard uppercut that snapped his head back. Blood gushed from his nose and mouth as he went down like a felled tree, howling in agony.

As Paulo stood over him, contemplating whether to finish him off, he didn't notice that another vehicle had pulled into the parking lot. He didn't hear the car door slam, didn't hear the brisk approach of footsteps. Didn't hear anything until a woman's familiar voice said, "Oh, Lord. Not again."

Only then did Paulo lift his head.

As the scarlet haze slowly dissipated from his brain, he realized that the newcomer was Tommie's pianist, Hazel Calhoun. She was frowning and shaking her head at him, hands planted on her hips in a manner that reminded him of the times his grandmother Maria had scolded him for sneaking into her kitchen and swiping churros that were reserved for the church fund-raiser.

Then, as now, he had the grace to look sheepish. "Afternoon, Mrs. Calhoun," he murmured.

"Paulo Sanchez, what on earth are you doing here?" she demanded.

"I came to have a talk with Deacon Jackson."

"Hmmph. Looks like you did a lot more than *talk*," she said, glancing pointedly at the semiconscious man curled into the fetal position on the ground.

Jackson groaned. "Sister Calhoun, call the police," he mumbled weakly. "This officer . . . assaulted me. I . . . want to . . . press charges."

"Oh dear." Hazel looked at Paulo, concern etching lines into her forehead. "Did she tell you what happened?"

Paulo nodded, his jaw clenched.

"Terrible thing he did to her. Just shameful." Her dark eyes misted and her nostrils flared. "I can't believe she's been keeping it bottled up all this time. She tries to be so tough and nonchalant, but deep down inside she's just a hurt, frightened little girl."

"I know," Paulo murmured. "But she's strong, too. Stronger than she realizes."

Hazel's gaze softened on his face. "And she needs a strong man by her side. Someone she can trust. Someone who can take care of her, help heal those wounds." She laid a gentle hand against his cheek. "I think you can be that man, Paulo Sanchez. I saw it in your eyes the first time I met you. The two of you can be so good for each other."

Jackson groaned again.

"Oh dear." Hazel shot a worried glance at Paulo. "You'd better get out of here before the other deacons show up for the meeting. Thank God they're always late, or they would have been here by now." Before Paulo could protest, she began ushering him toward his cruiser as if he were a late congregant being escorted to a pew in church. "Don't worry about Deacon Jackson. I'll deal with him. Just between you and me, I've been wanting to knock him out myself ever since I found out what he did to Tomasina. Lord forgive me, something just never seemed right about him. It's the eyes. The eyes are the window to the soul, and his are just empty. Oh, let me give you something."

She opened the back door of her car, which she'd parked beside the cruiser, and pulled out a covered cake dish. "Tomasina told me how much you enjoyed my peach cobbler," she said almost shyly. "I thought you might like to try my sour cream carrot cake."

Touched by her generosity, Paulo asked, "Didn't you bring it for today's meeting?"

She waved a dismissive hand. "It was Deacon Jackson's turn to bring something, but of course he asked me to do it for him. Hmmph. Showing up empty-handed to a meeting is the *least* of his problems right now."

As Paulo accepted the cake she frowned at his bleeding knuckles, then tsk-tsked after examining them for a moment. "You shouldn't need any stitches, but you'd better soak your hand in some ice and have Tomasina kiss it when you get back to the loft."

Paulo arched an amused brow. "How'd you know I was going there?"

Hazel gave him a soft, intuitive smile. "After you showed up on Monday, I knew you wouldn't be able to stay away."

Chapter 22

"I'm so nervous," Tommie muttered, crossing and uncrossing her legs as she stared out the passenger window of Paulo's Dodge Durango. "I can't believe I let you talk me into this."

Paulo chuckled. "Relax. It's just dinner."

"It's not *just dinner*," she corrected, turning to face him. "It's dinner with your family."

"Okay, then. It's just my family."

"Easy for you to say. It's *your* family!"

Paulo laughed, torn between exasperation and amusement. "*Ay Dios!* What are you so nervous about, woman?"

"Well, gee, let me think. The man I've been dating less than a week is taking me to meet his family, who all happen to be wealthy, successful lawyers with degrees from Ivy League universities and powerful connections that reach to the White House." She shrugged. "You're right. Nothing to be nervous about."

Amused, Paulo shook his head at her. "Not that it matters," he said dryly, "but you're not exactly the girl from the wrong side of the tracks. Your father is a renowned archaeologist, your mother was the CEO of a major pharmaceutical company before she retired, and they live in a million-dollar Victorian. So tell me again why you're so nervous about meeting my cousins?"

Tommie groaned, leaning back against the headrest and closing her eyes. "They're going to hate me. I just know it."

"No, they're not."

"Yes, they are."

"No, they're not," Paulo insisted. "They're going to love you."

"How do you know?"

"Because they're smart, down-to-earth people who know a good thing when they see it. And you, Miss Purnell, are definitely a good thing."

Turning her head, Tommie smiled gratefully at him. "You're so sweet. I know I'm driving you crazy with all my hand wringing."

"Goodness, no," he said, widening his eyes as if the thought had never occurred to him.

"Ha, ha. Very funny." Grinning, she reached over and threaded her fingers through his thick, freshly trimmed hair. "Thank you for not getting too much cut off when you went to the barbershop this afternoon. I've gotten used to your wild, unruly hair. I've grown to love it." *And the rest of you, too*, she added silently.

Paulo slanted her a soft look. "Why do you think I only asked for a trim?"

Tommie stared at him. "You did that . . . for me?"

"Of course." His mouth curved in a wicked grin. "What else are you going to pull when you're having one of those head-banging orgasms?"

Tommie laughed, blushing sheepishly. "Good point."

As Paulo returned his attention to the road, she admired his darkly handsome appearance. Even with the neatly trimmed hair and a fresh shave, he still managed to look rakish and primitively male in an open-necked black shirt, a well-cut black blazer, and black trousers. When her gaze strayed to his bandaged hand on the steering wheel, her smile faded.

She hadn't known what to think when he returned to the loft yesterday afternoon, a cake dish tucked under one arm and his right hand wrapped in gauze. When she asked him what had happened, he told her he'd cut his hand on a sharp object while he was at his apartment packing some clothes. Tommie hadn't believed him. Remembering that he'd intended to speak to Roland while he was out, she'd asked him outright whether he'd gotten into a fight with her ex-boyfriend. He'd flatly denied it, saying that Roland wasn't at the church when he arrived, which was where he'd run into Mrs. Calhoun. Still skeptical, Tommie had called her pianist to thank her for the carrot cake. She, too, had claimed ignorance of any altercation between Paulo and Roland. Deciding that Mrs. Calhoun wouldn't lie to her, Tommie had let the matter go, though doubt lingered in the back of her mind.

She'd gotten sidetracked when Paulo informed her that his cousin Naomi had called to invite him and Tommie to dinner on Sunday evening. Tommie didn't know what shocked her more: the fact that his family thought she was important enough to warrant an introduction, or the fact that Paulo obviously agreed. She didn't know what to make of his willingness to introduce her to his cousins. She was afraid to read too much into it, but it was hard not to. Guys like Paulo Sanchez didn't take women home to meet their families—unless they believed the woman in question had a future in their lives.

It scared Tommie to realize just how much she wanted a future with Paulo.

Still, the thought of meeting his family struck sheer terror in her heart. Although Paulo was unquestionably his own man, she knew how important his cousins were to him, knew what an influence they'd had in shaping his life. It would be naive of Tommie to think their opinion of her, good or bad, would make absolutely no difference to Paulo. She knew better.

So she'd been a nervous wreck since yesterday afternoon, fretting over what to wear, how to style her hair, and how much makeup to apply. After much deliberation—and a desperate phone call to her sister, who'd squealed with excitement upon hearing about her evening plans—Tommie had settled on a simple yet elegant black silk sheath and a pair of Christian Louboutin stiletto pumps she'd splurged on back in New York and had been saving for a special occasion. Because she wore her hair scraped back into a tight bun or ponytail five days a week when she was teaching, she decided to leave it down that evening, loose and caressing her bare shoulders. When she finally emerged from the bedroom and saw the stunned look on Paulo's face, she knew all the hours of agonizing had been more than worth it.

She smiled at him now. "I really enjoyed meeting Cesar yesterday. And you say *I* have interesting friends."

Paulo chuckled. Not taking any chances with her safety, he'd arranged for one of his longtime friends to stay at the loft with her while he ran his errands. Cesar Ortegon was a former bodyguard who now moonlighted as a nightclub bouncer while attending college full-time. Tall, burly, with a shaved head and tattoos covering his thick arms, he could easily have portrayed an inmate in a prison movie—which made his ability to quote Aristotle and Shakespeare at the drop of a dime all the more disarming. While Tommie caught up on her bookkeeping, Cesar had stayed out of her way, working quietly on his midterm paper until she, needing a mental break, had drawn him into a friendly poker game. When Paulo returned to the loft, he'd found them laughing and talking trash to each other like they'd been buddies for years.

Tommie's case of nerves returned as she and Paulo reached his family's palatial Mediterranean-style villa in River Oaks.

"Relax," Paulo murmured when he came around to open the door for her. He kissed her gently, taking care not to smudge her lipstick. "They're going to love you."

The family was waiting for them, crowded expectantly around the front door. Ignacio and Naomi Santiago, a handsome couple who'd graced many magazine covers as Houston's most influential power duo. And their daughters Angela, Rebecca, and Daniela, three gorgeous, confident women who bore just enough of a resemblance to one another to leave no doubt that they were related. The two elder sisters were accompanied by their spouses and children, five offspring between them.

Paulo and Tommie were greeted with huge, welcoming smiles, enveloped in warm hugs, and ushered into the sweeping grandeur of the house. Paulo plucked his youngest cousin off the floor, hoisted the little girl into the air, and spun her around while her delighted squeals bounded up to the vaulted ceiling. Observing the tender expression on Tommie's face as she watched the touching display, Naomi slipped her arm companionably through hers and said, "I'm so glad you could make it."

Tommie turned and smiled at the regally beautiful, dark-skinned woman. "Thank you for inviting me. You have a lovely home and a wonderful family."

Naomi's dark eyes twinkled with mischief. "You know we're always looking for additions."

Before Tommie could respond—assuming she could have formulated a response—Daniela latched on to her other arm, leaned close, and whispered, "Fabulous shoes!"

By the time dinner was under way in the formal dining room, Tommie realized her fears about Paulo's family had been unfounded. While there was no disputing their wealth and status, the Santiagos were completely devoid of pretension. Although they dined on expensive china and the gleaming mahogany table was draped in fine linen, the laughter and conversation that filled the room was anything but refined. It was loud, animated, blissfully chaotic. While Ignacio Santiago was indisputably the captain of the ship, his wife and daughters were equally strong-willed, outspoken, and fiercely devoted to their family. They adored Paulo, alternately doting on him, teasing him, and admonishing him whenever he said or did something outrageous. There was a unity among them all that flowed from one end of the table to the other. A simple, strong, steady flow of love that touched a chord in Tommie and filled her with a sense of belonging.

She was perfectly at ease answering questions about herself, never feeling like she was being interrogated by a team of lawyers—which, in essence, she was. She told them about working for Crandall Thorne, whom they knew personally, and about her dancing. She and the Santiago women reminisced about their various travels abroad, the food and music, the art and culture. When Tommie and Daniela wandered into a conversation about fashion, the men rolled their eyes at one another. Trading conspiratorial grins, the two women agreed to continue their discussion later, when they wouldn't be rudely interrupted.

Through it all, Tommie was aware of Paulo watching her from across the table. She knew that he'd been watching her almost from the moment they'd sat down to dinner.

She could feel his gaze on her, a tactile touch that heated her skin and left her nerve endings tingling. More than once she'd deliberately turned her head to catch him staring at her. He'd winked, the edges of his mouth curving in a secret smile that made her heart lurch crazily.

One such private exchange was caught by Naomi, who gave them a knowing smile before saying conversationally, "So, Tommie, I understand that you and Paulo met at your sister's wedding four years ago."

"That's right." Tommie looked at Paulo, her lips quirking and her eyes glimmering with a veiled threat to tell his family all about his scandalous behavior with the brunette. "It was a beautiful wedding, wasn't it?"

"Absolutely." His own eyes glittered with wicked challenge, daring her.

Naomi sighed. "I suppose the two of you owe a debt of gratitude to Frankie and Sebastien for introducing you to each other. If they hadn't gotten married, you may never have met."

Their gazes softened on each other. "That's true," they murmured in unison.

Conversations around the table died down as eleven other pairs of eyes turned to watch them.

Naomi took another languid sip of wine. "So, do you have any other weddings you're planning to attend in the near future?"

As Tommie started to shake her head, Paulo, wiping his mouth with a linen napkin and rising from the table, said, "Now that you mention it, Naomi. We do."

Tommie froze, staring at him as he rounded the table and came toward her.

The hushed silence that fell over the room was deafening. Silverware stilled, glasses stopped tinkling, no one breathed.

Holding Tommie's gaze, Paulo pulled out her chair, knelt in front of her, and took her trembling hands in his. He raised them to his lips, tenderly kissed her fingertips.

"I love you," he said in an achingly husky voice. "I want to spend the rest of my life with you."

Tears welled in Tommie's eyes, blurring her vision. If she hadn't been sitting down, shock would have sent her swooning to the floor. "What are you saying?" she whispered, heart lodged in her throat.

"I'm saying I want you to be my wife, Tommie. Will you do that? Will you marry me?"

"Oh my God . . . Paulo . . . oh, baby . . ."

He smiled. "Is that a yes or a no?"

"Yes! Yes, I'll marry you!"

As Paulo crushed his mouth to hers, loud cheers and applause erupted around the room. Forks tapped against glasses. Two of the older kids drummed excitedly on the table. Naomi, Angela, Rebecca, and Daniela dabbed at their eyes and exchanged teary, triumphant smiles.

Oblivious of the commotion around them, Paulo and Tommie kissed deeply and passionately. When they at last drew apart, the dining room was empty. Everyone had quietly cleared out, giving them privacy.

Tommie smiled into Paulo's eyes, her arms looped around his neck as he lifted her from the chair, then sat down and pulled her onto his lap. "I can't believe you just did that," she whispered. "I can't believe you proposed."

"Neither can I," he admitted, stroking a hand down her hair and touching her face. "It wasn't planned. But the moment the words left my mouth, I knew it was right. Nothing in my life has ever felt more right."

Tommie's heart swelled with emotion. "I love you," she said fiercely. "I want to have your baby."

Paulo's eyes glinted with tender mirth. "Even if it means you'd have to eat hospital food?"

She let out a whispery laugh. "Even if. Although I seem to recall telling a certain someone that I expect my loving, doting husband to bring me food from outside the hospital."

Paulo groaned. "Damn. I forgot about that."

She grinned. "Too late. You've already proposed. No going back."

"No," he murmured, gazing into her eyes as he gently slanted his mouth over hers. "There's no going back."

The stranger was infuriated. Trembling with a rage as black as the night.

Hidden in the shadows outside the small, brick building, he watched as Paulo Sanchez helped Tommie out of a dark Dodge Durango. The cop was smiling, looking like a fool in love. And she, too, was smiling, her face aglow with happiness as she gazed at him. He folded her into his arms, then lowered his head and kissed her. She responded eagerly, wrapping her arms around his neck, sliding her fingers into his hair. As the kiss deepened, Sanchez pinned her against the truck and gently wedged his thigh between hers.

The stranger gritted his back teeth so hard his jaw ached. His blood pounded, throbbed through his brain, left him feeling weak and nauseated. He felt betrayal of the worst kind, watching Tommie locked in a passionate embrace with another man. Oh, he was no fool. He'd always known there would be others. But it was one thing to imagine her stripping off her clothes and spreading her legs for another man. Being forced to watch the lewd act was another matter altogether. But that was what he'd done.

He'd forced himself to watch via the hidden cameras he'd placed throughout the converted warehouse. He'd watched their naked, sweaty bodies writhing against each other, heard their guttural, animal sounds of lust. They'd defiled every corner of the building. The stairwell, the bedroom, the bathroom, even the studio where he'd installed a camera so he could enjoy the simple pleasure of watching her dance, a pleasure now forever tainted.

But even as fury and revulsion had consumed him, he'd been aroused by their savage lovemaking. He'd stroked himself, masturbating as he imagined that it was he, not Sanchez, having his way with her. As he came violently, tears burned his eyes and a familiar shame engulfed him.

Even now, the memory of it sickened him. *She* had done this to him.

And he would make her pay.

After an agonizing eternity, the two lovers reluctantly pulled apart. Tommie made a teasing comment and pointed at her left hand. Sanchez laughed.

The stranger's eyes narrowed, speculating. What had she said to him? he wondered uneasily. It almost looked like she'd told him to put a ring on her finger. But, no, that couldn't be. Surely she didn't want to marry someone like Paulo Sanchez? It wasn't even possible.

Yet *something* had changed between the couple. There was a certain closeness, a new level of intimacy between them.

His muscles tightened. He clenched his jaw as an awful suspicion took form in his conscience. He refused to identify it, refused to give voice to it. Because if he did, it would send him over the edge, and he'd come too far to lose control now. Not when he was so close to achieving his goal. If anyone knew the lengths to which he had gone, the sacrifices he'd made in order to claim her, they would think he was insane. But he knew he wasn't. He and Tommie Purnell were meant for each other. There were no coincidences. Everything had happened according to plan.

And she had seen him. She'd sensed his presence when he was hiding in her closet. She'd known he was near.

He'd vowed to himself that when she saw him, *really* saw him, he would know it was time.

The time had arrived.

But first he would make Sanchez suffer. The filthy, arrogant bastard would learn the hard way not to take what didn't belong to him.

Just then, the sound of her sultry laughter floated over to him, snaking around him like sinuous curls of smoke. As he watched, Sanchez swept her off the ground, lifted her into his arms as if she were weightless, and strode toward the building.

The stranger's hands curled into fists at his sides. He knew what was to follow, knew that Sanchez would spend the rest of the night making love to her, kissing her, stroking her. Defiling her.

If only he could have put a stop to it now, the stranger fumed. If only he could have charged across the street, wrenched her out of the cop's arms, and slashed his knife across Sanchez's throat, severing his jugular. Ending his miserable life.

But, no, he couldn't act on the violent urge, no matter how strong or tempting it was. He had to maintain control. He had to be patient.

Sanchez had reached the front door when suddenly he paused and glanced over his shoulder.

The stranger shrank against the tree, his heart thudding.

Sanchez's eyes swept the darkness. For a moment his black brows furrowed, as if he sensed another presence nearby, hiding in the shadows. Watching. Waiting.

The stranger held his breath until his lungs screamed for air.

Finally Sanchez turned and carried Tommie inside the building, closing the door behind them. Locking out the unseen threat.

But not for very long, the stranger thought, an icy, feral smile spreading across his face. *I'll be back soon. And no one will ever see me coming.*

Chapter 23

On Monday morning, Paulo was in his office poring through Ashton Dupree's case file when his phone rang. He snatched up the receiver on the first ring. "Sanchez."

"Detective Sanchez, this is Norah O'Connor."

"You must have read my mind," Paulo told her. "I was just about to call and badger you. Got something for me?"

"I do," O'Connor said grimly, "but I'm not sure you want to hear it."

Paulo frowned, his nerves tightening. "What do you mean?"

"I put a rush on the trace results from the Dupree crime scene. The spare key used by the killer to get inside the house had been wiped clean, but not clean enough. We were able to lift a partial print, and we found a match in our database. But *not* where we expected to find one."

Cold unease slithered down Paulo's spine. Every muscle in his body was stretched taut. "Who did the print belong to?"

There was a heavy pause. "You."

Paulo's heart slammed against his larynx. "That's impossible. I never touched that key."

"The results suggest otherwise."

"The results are wrong," he snapped, dread twisting in his gut. "By the time I arrived on the scene, the key had already been bagged for evidence. I never laid a finger on it."

"Unless you handled it beforehand."

Paulo went very still. "What are you saying, O'Connor?" he said softly, tightly.

"Did you sleep with her? Were you having an affair with Ashton Dupree?"

"No!"

"You told us you knew her. If you were sleeping with her, and you used the key to get into the house at some point, I need to know."

"I wasn't sleeping with her," Paulo said, his jaw clenched so tight the words were barely more than a growl.

O'Connor sighed harshly. "Damn it, Sanchez. I can't help you unless you're honest with me. I'm trying like hell to keep this development under wraps. You and I both know what's going to happen if it leaks out to the press."

"Then I suggest you contain the leaks in your department," Paulo bit off tersely.

Bristling, O'Connor shot back, "You have a reputation, Sanchez. Everyone knows you chase anything in a skirt. Ashton Dupree was a beautiful woman, one you just happened to know. When word gets out that your print was found on that key—a key piece of evidence—you're gonna have a helluva time convincing anyone you weren't screwing her. And if you were screwing her, that means you could have killed her."

"I wasn't screwing her, goddamn it, and I didn't kill her!" Paulo exploded.

An officer walking past his open doorway eyed him warily.

Shit!

Lowering his voice, Paulo snarled into the phone, "Someone's trying to set me up. Someone planted my fingerprint on that key."

"Like who?" O'Connor sounded skeptical.

"I don't know, but I intend to find out." Paulo slammed down the phone, his hand trembling violently. Acid churned in his stomach, and his head throbbed as he struggled to process what he'd just learned. Someone with access to his fingerprints was trying to frame him for murder. Someone who knew that he'd once befriended Ashton Dupree, someone who was trying to cover his own tracks.

Almost immediately his mind went to Ted Colston. Colston, who'd been lying and evading questions from the very beginning. Colston, who owned a strip club where his foster sister had worked until a week ago. Colston, who might have had any number of motives for killing her. Colston, who'd conveniently been out of town over the weekend, even after Paulo had specifically warned him not to go anywhere without clearing it with him first.

Suddenly Donovan burst into the office, staring at Paulo in wide-eyed disbelief. "I just came from the captain's office. I've never seen him so pissed! Did you assault a church *deacon* on Saturday?"

"Fuck," Paulo whispered hoarsely, ramming stiff fingers through his hair. His day was going to hell in a handbasket.

Taking the epithet as confirmation, Donovan shook his head at him, appalled. "What the hell were you thinking, man? Assaulting a deacon in a church parking lot? That's just crazy—even for you! I'm a preacher's kid, so you know I don't play that. I mean, did you actually think you'd get away with it? The man just got off the phone with Boulware. He gave him an earful about police brutality and demanded your badge!"

"I don't have time for this right now," Paulo muttered impatiently, his mind racing with questions that had nothing to do with Roland Jackson. How had Colston obtained his fingerprints? When had—

And then it struck him. He'd given Colston his business card!

"You'd better *make* time," Donovan advised, interrupting his thoughts. "The captain wants to see you. When I left his office, he was just taking a phone call from the DA. There's a serious shit storm brewing, Sanchez, and it's got your name written all over it."

Paulo stared at his partner, gripped by a chilling sense of foreboding. Had word already got out about his fingerprint being found on the spare key at Ashton's house? Had someone in the crime lab already leaked the information?

"What have you heard?" Paulo demanded sharply.

"As I was leaving Boulware's office, I heard him say something about calling a press conference to address any rumors or speculation before they got out of hand. He told the DA that you have a good service record, said he was sure you had a perfectly good explanation for it— whatever *it* is." Donovan regarded him suspiciously. "What the hell's going on, Sanchez? If you're up to your ears in some nonsense, I have a right to know as your damned partner."

Paulo didn't answer. The foreboding had tightened like a noose around his throat, strangling him. If the district attorney already knew about the evidence found at the crime scene, that meant the media was all over the story, too. Which meant—

Shit!

Tommie!

Donovan frowned at Paulo as he shot up from the desk, grabbed his jacket off the back of the chair, and strode determinedly from the room.

"Where are you going?" Donovan called after him. "I told you Boulware wants to see—"

But Paulo was already gone.

"I understand congratulations are in order."

Those were the first words out of Richard Houghton's mouth when Tommie answered her office phone shortly before noon. Her surprise at hearing his smooth, cultured voice quickly turned into annoyance.

"Zhane told you about my engagement?" *Damn that Zhane*, she silently fumed. *I don't care how happy he is for me! I'm giving him a piece of my mind when I see him later!*

As if reading her mind, Richard chuckled softly. "Please don't be mad at Zhane. I couldn't help overhearing him on the phone with you when he was in the studio warming up this morning. He squealed so loud I think everyone in the building must have heard him. As you could obviously tell, he was quite thrilled by the news of your engagement. He told me he was heading over to your place this evening to pop open a bottle of champagne and help you start planning the wedding."

"That's the plan," Tommie murmured. "We have a lot to celebrate."

"Of course. He told me the doctors expect his nephew to make a full recovery, and the police caught the man responsible for shooting him. That's wonderful news."

"Yes, it is. And don't worry," Tommie said sourly, "Zhane's coming over *after* rehearsal tonight."

Detecting the note of resentment in her voice, Richard

said, "You know, Tommie, just because I didn't let Zhane perform on Friday evening doesn't mean I'm insensitive or that I don't value him as one of my dancers. Nothing could be further from the truth."

"You don't owe me an explanation," she said coolly. "That's between you and Zhane."

"If that's true," Richard countered, a fine thread of anger tightening his voice, "then why did you boycott Friday night's performance? Renee was there. Why weren't you?"

Tommie bristled at his accusatory tone. "I don't have to answer to you, Richard. In fact, I was in the middle of something important when you called, so—"

"If you're going to boycott our productions simply because your best friend isn't performing, at least have the courage to say it to my face."

Tommie's temper flared. "How dare you! I don't owe you a damn thing! But since you insist on having this conversation, then yes, I *did* have a problem with your decision not to let Zhane perform. I thought it was tacky, punitive, insensitive, and it showed an appalling lack of compassion on your part! But as Zhane pointed out to me, it was your call to make as artistic director, so what difference does it make what I think?"

A low, mirthless chuckle filled the phone line. "I think you already know the answer to that question, Tommie, so I can't even imagine why you'd choose to pretend otherwise. It's no secret that I'm attracted to you, that I've been interested in you for the past several months. The only reason I haven't asked you out on a date is that every time I come anywhere near you, you look at me as if I've got sharp fangs and horns coming out of my head."

"I do not," Tommie grumbled, even as she felt a pang of guilt, because she knew he was right. Heaving a resigned breath, she decided to level with him. "In all honesty, Richard, I'm not comfortable with the way you look at me sometimes. It's unnerving."

"I see." There was a hint of amusement in his voice. "I wasn't aware that I made you uncomfortable. Please accept my apologies."

Tommie hesitated. "Apology accepted."

"Good. Zhane is an important member of my dance company, and obviously a very important person to you. I would hate for him to be caught in the middle of our, shall we say, feud."

"Neither would I," Tommie agreed, glancing at her watch. It was 11:47. She had another hour before the locksmith arrived to change her locks. In the meantime, the main door was locked and bolted, the security company was on standby, and the pistol Paulo had given her that morning was burning a hole through the top desk drawer.

"You know, Tommie," Richard said mildly, "I really wish you would have given me more of a chance. I think you would have discovered that I'm not such a terrible person. After all, I never told anyone what happened to you in New York."

Tommie's muscles tensed. A clammy chill ran across her skin. "You knew?"

"Of course," he said smoothly. "I know a lot of people in New York. It's a small world—dancers talk. You know that."

Tommie swallowed. Indeed, she did know. But the artistic director had assured her that he wouldn't breathe a word about the videotape to anyone. Obviously he'd done a lot of breathing.

"But I kept your dirty little secret," Richard continued in the same calm, placid tone, "because I sympathized with your dilemma. I understood that you'd moved here to start over, and the last thing you needed was an embarrassing scandal from your past following you here. It couldn't be good for business, not to mention your reputation."

Tommie wondered if she was only imagining the veiled threat in his voice.

"I have nothing but the utmost admiration and respect for the Blane Bailey Dance Company, but I thought they were wrong for letting you go. I think they should have stood by your side, weathered the bad publicity. You were worth it, Tommie. You belong on the stage, not in a classroom. That's why I was hoping you would come dance for me. But, to my everlasting disappointment, you refused." He chuckled softly. "I suppose if I ever get desperate enough, I could just blackmail you."

Tommie wasn't amused. "That's not funny, Richard."

"I know, but I couldn't resist. You've already accused me of being tacky, punitive, and insensitive. I figured I'd go for the gusto and add sleazy to the list." He sighed. "Anyway, I don't want to hold you up much longer. I just wanted to call and offer my congratulations on your pending nuptials. I hope you and Detective Sanchez will be very happy together."

"Thanks, I—" She broke off, stiffening in surprise. "Zhane told you his name?"

"Well, yes, of course. Naturally I was curious, so I asked. As it turns out, I'm acquainted with Paulo Sanchez. He may not remember, but we met at a function hosted by his family's law firm two years ago. My parents' multinational energy corporation is one of the firm's biggest clients. In case you've ever heard of the Houghtons of Houston, that's my family."

"What a small world," Tommie murmured.

"Isn't it?" Richard sounded distinctly pleased. "At any rate, I'm sure my parents will receive an invitation to your wedding. Perhaps I'll accompany them. Have you

and Paulo decided whether the ceremony will be held
here or in San Antonio?"

"We haven't gotten that far yet," Tommie muttered,
unnerved by his presumptuousness. Unnerved by the
entire conversation. "I really have to go, Richard."

"Of course. Please convey my congratulations to your
lucky fiancé."

"I will." Tommie hung up, then shuddered. Now that
she was engaged, with any luck she'd finally heard the
last of Richard Houghton.

Shoving the thought aside, she returned to the paperwork she'd been reviewing before Richard called. She'd
dismissed her last class of the day an hour ago, and had
vowed to get as much work done as possible before Paulo
came home.

She smiled at the thought, marveling at how right it
sounded. As natural as falling asleep in his arms last
night, and waking up with him buried deep inside her.
She flushed with pleasure as her mind conjured an
image of their entwined bodies, the sinewy cords of his
muscles straining as he thrust into her, the way his black
hair fell over his eyes as he called her name and clutched
her as if he'd never let go. Even before he'd proposed
she had been fantasizing about what it would be like to
spend the rest of her life with Paulo, to live together as
man and wife. She had no illusions about his job; she
knew the long hours and dangerous nature of his cases
would take some getting used to. But the nights, oh, the
nights, would be nothing short of spectacular.

They'd stayed at his cousins' house until well after midnight, drinking wine and basking in the family's joy
and excitement. By the time they left, Tommie swore
she'd spoken on the phone to every living member of the
Santiago family. Paulo's parents and siblings were shocked

but pleased that he was taking another chance on love. Tommie, who'd decided to tell her own parents over Thanksgiving dinner, had sworn Frankie and Sebastien to secrecy, because of course she couldn't keep such a big announcement from her sister. Her ears were still ringing from Frankie's—as well as Zhane's—ecstatic squealing.

Tommie was so preoccupied with her happy musings that she forgot she'd turned on the office television set for background noise. The midday news broadcast had just come on the air.

"In our top story this afternoon, the police may have a break in the case of two local women who were found brutally murdered in their homes this week, but it's *not* the break they could possibly have anticipated."

Tommie's head snapped up, her nerves instinctively tightening.

The newscaster continued. "In a stunning development in the case, we've just learned that investigators have positively identified a partial fingerprint found on a spare key that was used by the perpetrator to enter the second victim's home. Unnamed police sources have confirmed that the fingerprint belongs to the lead homicide investigator, Detective Paulo Sanchez."

Tommie gasped, shooting to her feet even as the blood drained from her head.

"We're taking you live to police headquarters downtown, where we're awaiting a press conference from police captain Shane Boulware. Mika, what can you tell us about this shocking new development in the case?"

The camera went to an attractive, dark-haired reporter standing outside the bustling police station. "Thanks, Gina. *Shock* is the right word to describe the mood around here. Detective Paulo Sanchez is a seventeen-year veteran of the police force with an impressive service record. Two years ago, after taking a short-term sabbatical to deal with some undisclosed personal issues, he transferred to the Houston Police Department from his hometown of San Antonio. Colleagues describe him as a sharp, aggressive investigator whose methodical investigative work has provided leads in numerous cold-case murders. It is not known at this point whether homicide investigators believe Sanchez, one of their very own, could have committed these heinous murders, but just to put things in perspective for our viewers, we're now learning about the details surrounding the murder of a San Antonio woman six years ago."

No, Tommie thought desperately, wrapping her arms around her stomach and choking down the bile rising in her throat. *No, no, no. It's not possible. God can't be this cruel!*

"Hailey Morrisette was brutally raped and murdered, her body found buried in the woods two days after she'd been reported missing. Then, as now, Detective Sanchez was the lead investigator in the case. But what he failed to disclose at the time was that he'd been having an extramarital affair with Morrisette."

A hoarse scream of denial erupted from Tommie's lips as a photo of a beautiful blond woman flashed on the screen. She stared at the picture in horrified disbelief, shaken by the uncanny resemblance between Hailey Morrisette and Ashton Dupree.

"Morrisette's killer was never caught," the reporter continued, driving the dagger into Tommie's heart with each devastating word. "But three years after her murder, in a dramatic turn of events, Morrisette's younger sister went on a killing spree, murdering five prominent businessmen she claimed were responsible for her sister's death. She pled not guilty by reason of insanity and was committed to a state mental hospital. But to this day, prosecutors believe that Hailey Morrisette's real killer is still at large."

Tommie was trembling violently and shaking her head in virulent denial, unable to believe what she was hearing. In just the blink of an eye, she'd been wrenched from her rapturous utopia and thrust into a nightmare reality. She should have known. Experience had taught her that the higher she soared, the harder her fall back to earth.

"As you might imagine," the reporter was saying, blissfully oblivious of the torment she was causing Tommie, "the Morrisette case has fueled speculation about Detective Sanchez's possible involvement in the recent murders of Maribel Cruz and Ashton Dupree, both of whom he knew. According to an anonymous police source, Dupree, a stripper at a local nightclub, was arrested for soliciting an undercover cop four months ago. When she was brought to the police station for booking, she and Sanchez had what one eyewitness described as a 'passionate reunion.' Sanchez later intervened on Dupree's behalf, getting the charges against her reduced to a fine. Shortly afterward, Sanchez and Dupree were overheard having a heated argument, after which Dupree stormed out of his office." The reporter paused, glancing over her shoulder before turning around and adding, "At the time of our reporting, Detective Sanchez could not be reached for comment. We're staying on top of this unfolding situation and will bring you live coverage of the press conference once it gets under way. Back to you in the studio, Gina."

No sooner had the news report ended than Tommie heard the bell above the main door tinkle softly. Her heart lurched to her throat. She bolted from the office, knowing Paulo had let himself in with his key even before she saw him striding swiftly toward her with a look of fierce desperation.

"Tommie—"

"How could you!" she choked out, her voice trembling with anguished fury. "How could you keep those things from me? *How?*"

"You have to let me explain," Paulo said urgently.

"*Now* you want to explain?" she demanded in outraged disbelief. "*Now?* After you've made love to me, made me believe I could trust you, made me fall in love with you? *Now* you want to explain?"

"Tommie," he tried again, reaching for her shoulders.

"Don't touch me!" she cried, jerking out of his grasp and backing away from him, her hands thrown up to ward him off.

He stared at her, chest heaving, black eyes glittering with feverish intensity. "I know how shocked and hurt you must be feeling right now, but you have to listen to me, Tommie. I didn't kill anyone."

She glared at him, her heart hammering so hard she thought it would burst through her chest. "I confided in you, poured my heart out to you. I shared a painful, humiliating secret with you that I'd never told anyone else! Why didn't you trust me enough to do the same?"

"I don't know," he mumbled, jaw clenched.

"You don't know," Tommie mocked bitterly. "So it never occurred to you that I might want to know that the man I was falling in love with had cheated on his first wife with a woman who wound up brutally murdered? And when you were telling me about Ashton Dupree's murder, you didn't think it was worth mentioning that you and she were lovers?"

"No," he growled, "because we weren't lovers. We were childhood friends, nothing more!"

"That's not what some of your colleagues seem to think," she flung at him.

"I don't give a damn what they think!" Paulo roared, his face hardening with fury as he advanced on her. "All I care about is what *you* think, and if you stand there and tell me you actually believe I'm capable of murder, I'm walking out that door right now."

"Damn you!" Tommie hissed furiously. "You're in no position to be making threats. *You* lied to *me*!"

"I didn't lie to you," he bit out.

"Right," she said, sneering. "You just committed the sin of omission. No big deal."

"Damn it, Tommie, I didn't kill anyone!"

"Why did you cover up your affair with that woman in San Antonio?"

"Because I was ashamed!" he exploded, his face inches from hers. "Getting involved with Hailey Morrisette was a huge mistake, one that I'll regret for the rest of my damned life. Whatever else you might think of me and my track record with women, believe me when I tell you that cheating on my wife was the absolute *last* thing I'd ever planned."

"It just happened, right?" Tommie couldn't keep the bitter mockery from her voice.

Paulo lifted his head and took a step backward, a muscle working in his jaw, a dangerous glint in his eyes that warned her not to push her luck. When he spoke, his voice was raw with emotion. "I met Hailey when I was at the lowest point in my marriage. She was smart, funny, and the way she looked reminded me of Ashton, a woman I'd known since we were kids in summer camp. One day Hailey invited me out for coffee, then it was lunch, and things just spun out of control after that. Jaci and I were miserable with each other, two strangers living under the same roof. But that's no excuse for what I did. I not only broke my marriage vows, I ruined

Hailey's life. She made the mistake of falling in love with me. She wanted me to leave my wife, and the more I refused, the unhappier she became. Damn it, I'm not proud of the way I handled things. If I had a chance to do it over again, I swear I'd do things a helluva lot differently. But I don't have that option."

He blew out a ragged breath and jammed a trembling hand through his hair. "After Hailey was killed, I felt even guiltier. She didn't deserve to die like that. Hell, *no one* deserves to die like that. I started having nightmares, horrifying nightmares of what had been done to her. To cope with the guilt I was feeling I started smoking again, and my drinking got even worse. By the time Jaci asked for a divorce I was a complete disaster, a train wreck waiting to happen. She's lucky she got out when she did. As for me, it would be another four years before I could climb my way out of a bottle. How I managed to still do my job during that time is a miracle in and of itself." He shuddered, shaking his head and closing his eyes as if to shut out the painful memories.

Tommie stared at his haggard, handsome face, her heart constricting with compassion, aching with love. She wanted to comfort him, soothe him, heal all his wounds. She wanted to take him in her arms and tell him everything was going to be okay. But she couldn't. She was too afraid. Afraid to trust, afraid to be hurt again.

And when he opened his eyes and saw the fear reflected in hers, his face darkened. "You still don't believe me," he whispered in wounded disbelief. "My God, you believe everything you just heard on the news, don't you? You think I killed those women!"

Tommie shook her head vehemently. "No! I don't—"

"Damn it, don't lie to me."

"I don't know what to think!" she burst out, frustrated.

"You're telling me you didn't sleep with Ashton Dupree, but you were overheard arguing with her, and your fingerprint was found at her damned house. What the hell am I supposed to think?"

His mouth twisted cynically. "You're supposed to think that someone's setting me up," he snarled, his voice vibrating with controlled fury. "You're supposed to remember the conversation we just had about being in this together. You're supposed to trust me, believe in me. You're supposed to act like someone who claims to love me. You're *not* supposed to put me in the same category as the sorry bastard who betrayed you."

Tommie flinched at his harsh words, hurt flaring in her chest, tears springing to her eyes. She took a step backward. "I think you should go," she whispered.

Pain flashed in his eyes. His nostrils flared. "Damn it, Tommie—"

"Just go."

"Tommie—"

"Go!" she screamed.

He held her gaze another tense moment, then turned and stormed out of the building, slamming the door shut on her, on them. She stood there for a long time, the deafening silence pounding in her ears, their angry words echoing in her mind, the taste of heartbreak bitter in her mouth.

Chapter 24

"Are you sure you're going to be all right?" Frankie Durand asked, her voice full of gentle concern.

Tommie sniffled into the phone, feeling physically and emotionally depleted after spending the past several hours bawling her eyes out. Her cell phone had been ringing nonstop, and after avoiding calls most of the afternoon—because the only person she wanted to hear from wouldn't be calling—she'd finally mustered the strength to drag herself out of bed and lumber down the hallway to the living room, where she'd left the phone on the ottoman.

"Tommie?" Frankie prodded.

"I'll be fine," Tommie mumbled, though in her heart she knew she'd be anything but.

"You shouldn't be alone," her sister insisted. "Why don't you let Zhane come over and keep you company?"

Tommie shook her head weakly. "I don't want him to worry about me. He's had enough on his mind with his nephew in the hospital. He needs a break from taking care of others. Besides, he hasn't even heard what happened, and I don't feel up to rehashing it."

"What do you mean he hasn't heard? It's been all over the news, even here in San Antonio."

Tommie grimaced, and couldn't help feeling a twinge of relief that she hadn't told her parents about her engagement to Paulo. They'd always accused her of having horrible taste in men. Hearing that the man she intended to marry was a suspected murderer would only validate their criticisms of her, even though *she* knew Paulo was innocent.

"Zhane hasn't heard the news because he's been running back and forth between the hospital and the dance studio," Tommie said wearily. "I don't think he's been anywhere near a television all day. The last voice mail I received from him, he was still talking about coming over tonight to celebrate my—" She broke off, unable to finish.

"Oh, sweetie," Frankie murmured sympathetically. "You're going to have to tell Zhane when he gets there."

"He's not coming," Tommie said miserably. "I called him back and left a message, told him Paulo and I had special plans this evening and asked him for a rain check on our champagne toast."

"Oh, Tommie," Frankie gently chided. "He's your best friend. If he knew how much pain you're in right now, he'd want to be there for you."

Tommie sighed heavily. "I know. If he hasn't heard by tomorrow morning, I'll tell him. I just need to be alone tonight." She hesitated, then confessed in a small, tremulous voice, "I called Paulo right after he left. I wanted him to come back so we could discuss what, if anything, I could do to help him. But he hasn't returned my call. Have Rafe or Sebastien heard anything?"

"No, and they're both worried. We all are. Paulo's not answering his phone, and everyone has been calling him. The entire family's in an uproar. Ignacio and Naomi have already gone to see the district attorney and the police chief, and they're threatening to slap everyone from the police department to the media with defamation lawsuits. I just got off the phone with Korrine, and she said Rafe is on his way to Houston as we speak. Sebastien had to work late tonight, or he would have gone with him."

Tommie squeezed her eyes tightly shut, racked with pain and guilt. "God, Paulo must hate me," she whispered tearfully. "I turned my back on him at a time when he needed me the most."

"He doesn't hate you. This is the same man who just asked you to marry him. And you didn't turn your back on him. You'd just received a terrible shock. No one can fault you for the way you reacted."

But Tommie was inconsolable. "I never should have doubted him, not even for a second."

"Well, after this is over, you can spend the rest of your life making it up to him. Not that he'd expect you to."

"Assuming he still wants to be with me," Tommie mumbled gloomily.

"Oh, hush. That man loves you, and you know it."

Tommie didn't bother denying it. Because even as hurt and angry as Paulo had been when he'd stormed out on her that afternoon, he'd still been concerned for her safety. Concerned enough that he'd left the pistol with her, and had asked his friend Cesar to periodically drive by the building to make sure nothing was amiss.

"I think I should go over there, just to make sure he's all right," Tommie said suddenly.

"You can try," Frankie said dubiously, "but everyone's already been to his apartment, and he's not home."

"Maybe he's just—" Tommie broke off at the loud rapping on the main door downstairs.

Jumping up from the sofa, she rushed to the window and peered out into the night. Her pulse leaped at the sight of a dark Crown Victoria parked beside her car, and for one heart-stopping moment she thought it was Paulo. Until she remembered that she'd left a message for his partner, Julius Donovan, asking him to call her with an update on Paulo.

"I have to go, Frankie," Tommie told her sister. "Detective Donovan's here."

"Okay, but call me the second he leaves. I want to know what the hell's going on."

"Okay. I will." Tommie disconnected, tossed the cell phone onto the sofa, and raced out of the loft. She flew down the stairs and hurriedly opened the door.

When Julius Donovan's dark eyes widened in surprise, she realized that she must look a sight with tangled hair, swollen, bloodshot eyes, and a reddened nose.

"Thanks for coming over," she murmured, gesturing him inside. "I know you're very busy."

"It's no problem." As he stepped past her, his concerned gaze swept across her face. "Are you okay?"

"I've been better," Tommie said ruefully, closing the door and passing a hand over her disheveled hair. "It's been a rough day."

"I know." Shoving his hands into the pockets of his dark trousers, Donovan pushed out a long, deep breath and shook his head at her. "If it's any consolation to you, *he* doesn't look too good, either."

"You've seen him?" Tommie asked hopefully.

Donovan nodded. "About an hour ago. I met him somewhere to give him an update on a few leads he'd asked me to follow up on." He grimaced. "He's been removed from the case and placed on leave pending an internal investigation."

"Oh no," Tommie whispered, stricken.

"I know," Donovan said, scowling. "It's not fair. Sanchez is a damned good cop, the best I've ever worked with. He deserves to be given the benefit of the doubt. I don't care *what* some deacon says about him being corrupt."

Tommie frowned, staring up at him. "What deacon?"

Donovan looked sheepish as he scratched the back of his bald head. "I guess you haven't heard about that."

"No, I haven't. What happened?"

"Seems that Sanchez assaulted a deacon outside a church on Saturday afternoon, damn near knocked him out cold. The man had to be taken to the ER."

Tommie felt light-headed. "Oh God."

Donovan let out a mirthless chuckle. "I'm sure that's who the deacon was praying to all the way to the hospital."

Tommie shook her head, rubbed her pounding temple. Something else Paulo had lied to her about, damn him.

"How much trouble is he in, Detective Donovan?" she asked, dreading the answer.

Donovan sighed. "It doesn't look good," he admitted. "Having his fingerprint found at a crime scene was damaging enough. That stuff surfacing from his past certainly didn't help. Right now, the assault charges against him are the *least* of his problems."

Tommie's heart sank as a fresh sheen of tears blurred her vision. She kept hoping that this was all just a bad dream, that at any moment she would awaken in Paulo's arms, blissfully content and looking forward to the future.

Belatedly remembering her manners, she said, "I'm sorry. Would you like something to drink, Detective Donovan?"

"Sure. And remember I told you to call me Julius."

Tommie managed a wan smile. "All right."

As they started toward the stairwell, his cell phone rang. He dug it out of his coat pocket, frowned at the caller ID, then muttered apologetically, "I have to take this call in private. Do you mind?"

"Not at all. Use the studio. I'll wait out here for you."

As he disappeared down the hallway, a fist suddenly hammered against the front door. Thinking it was Paulo—hoping it was Paulo—Tommie hastily unlocked the door and threw it open.

Too late, she realized her mistake.

Roland barged inside, looking so grotesque that for a stunned moment she didn't recognize him. His left eye was swollen shut, the skin around it blackened and badly bruised. A line of stitches marched down one side of his cheek and crawled over his discolored lower lip.

Tommie didn't know what alarmed her more—his hideous appearance or the look of wild, lethal rage on his face.

"Roland—"

"You fucking bitch!" he roared, spittle flying from his mouth as he charged her. "You think you can get away with siccing that crazy motherfucker on me?"

"You need to calm down," Tommie said, backing away from him.

"Don't tell me to calm down! Did you tell *him* to calm down?"

She cried out as he viciously grabbed her arms and shook her like a rag doll, shouting in her face, "I should have killed you a long time ago! You've been nothing but a thorn in my side since I met you!"

Tommie struggled to wrench herself free, but he had a maniacal grip on her. Shaking with fear, but fortified with anger, she looked him in the eye and spat in his face. "Go to hell."

With an outraged scream, Roland reared back his arm to strike her. Tommie closed her eyes, instinctively bracing herself for the blow.

The sudden blast of a gunshot made her cry out.

Roland jerked against her, his eye bulging in shock as he staggered forward. Tommie gasped at the sight of bright crimson blood blooming across his chest. He looked at her, his face contorted with pain and confusion. A moment later he pitched to the floor with a dull thud.

Tommie lifted her head and stared, openmouthed, as Julius Donovan calmly holstered his gun and strode across the foyer. He knelt beside Roland's body and pressed a finger to his carotid artery, checking for a pulse. Slowly he shook his head.

"You killed him," Tommie whispered shakily.

"I couldn't let him kill you," the detective murmured.

Tommie swallowed, her heart thumping. "It's going to be okay. I—I'll tell them it was self-defense. Y-you were just protecting me."

"No, you don't understand." Donovan raised his head and looked straight at her. The hatred in his eyes seemed to glow red in his dark face. "I couldn't let him kill you because *I'm* going to."

Chapter 25

Tommie quaked with fear as she faced Julius Donovan, the horrifying ramifications of what he'd just told her sinking in. "You . . . you killed those women?" she whispered faintly. "You're behind all of this?"

Slowly, deliberately, he rose to his feet. Tall, dressed entirely in black, he loomed over her like a demon shadow.

Ice congealed in her veins. She shook her head, staring into his cruel dark eyes. "H-how can you do this? You're a cop."

A slow, predatory smile lifted the corners of his mouth. "Ah, but I only became one because of you."

Her pulse thudded. "I don't understand."

"Oh, you will." Stepping over Roland's body, he came toward her. "Before the night is over, Tommie, you will understand everything I did. All for you."

Panic gripped her.

Propelled into motion, she spun around and ran for the stairs. She heard him behind her, lightning-fast footsteps that quickly closed in on her. She screamed, pain ricocheting through her body as he seized a handful of her hair and yanked her backward. She struggled desperately, kicking and flailing against him until she saw something flash in his hand. Instantly she went still, realizing with horror that it was a knife, the long, deadly blade glinting in the light as he brought it to her throat.

"*No*," she whimpered pleadingly, tears spurting from her eyes and spilling down her cheeks. "Please don't—" she cried out as he tightened his brutal grip on her hair, wrenching her head back.

"You have no idea how long I've waited for this," he whispered, making her skin crawl as he brushed his lips across her neck. "I've wanted you for so long, Tommie. Can't you tell?"

She shuddered with revulsion, feeling his erection against her backside. Her heart pounded against her sternum as he traced the cool tip of the blade across her throat, down to the hollow where her pulse beat frantically.

"They both screamed and begged for their lives," he murmured in her ear. "Will you do the same, Tommie? Will you scream and beg the way you do when you're fucking Sanchez like a bitch in heat?"

Tommie swallowed, afraid to speak, afraid to breathe as she watched the knife trail lower, coming to rest at a spot between her breasts. She suppressed a shudder as he let go of her hair and reached around to fondle a breast.

"You think I didn't see you?" he taunted softly, his voice razoring along her jagged nerve endings. "You think I didn't watch you spreading your legs for him, riding him, sucking his filthy dick? You think I didn't watch you whoring yourself for him? Right before you moved into this building, I broke in and installed hidden cameras all over the place. I saw *everything*."

Tommie closed her eyes, a roiling nausea crawling up her throat at the extent of his depravity, at the terrible sense of violation she felt. He'd been spying on her for months.

"You're the only one I've ever wanted," he told her, nuzzling her nape. "The others were merely a means to an end, a way to get your attention. A dress rehearsal, if you will."

Icy foreboding settled over her heart, chilled her blood. "Why are you doing this? What have I ever done to you?"

He chuckled softly. "Words can't begin to describe what you've done to me, Tommie. And before I kill you tonight, there's one more thing I must ask of you."

She swallowed, quivering with fear and dread. "Wh-what do you want?"

She felt him smile against her neck.

"A private performance."

Seated in the shadowy interior of his Dodge Durango, Paulo lit a cigarette and drew hard on it, as if he could burn the bitter taste of bile from his mouth. He'd been camped out in his truck for the better part of the day, avoiding his apartment like a fugitive of the law. Not only were reporters crawling all over the place, but his family, frantic with worry, had stopped by several times looking for him. His cell phone had been ringing off the hook, and Rafe and Daniela had sent him several angry text messages, demanding to know his whereabouts.

He wasn't ready to deal with them, wasn't ready to field questions he didn't have the answers to.

After the devastating confrontation with Tommie, he'd returned to the police station to face the wrath of his supervisor. As expected, Captain Boulware had read him the riot act about Roland Jackson and demanded an explanation about the evidence found at Ashton Dupree's crime scene. Unsatisfied with Paulo's terse responses, the captain had pronounced judgment, placing him on

leave effective immediately. Paulo had surrendered his service weapon and badge, then stormed out of the station
and called Ted Colston's secretary, pretending to be one
of his clients. After learning that Colston had taken the day
off, Paulo had driven straight to the attorney's sprawling
home in Sugarland. But it had been a fool's errand. When
he arrived he was met by two uniformed officers who'd
apologetically informed him that Colston had filed a re-
straining order against him. Paulo wasn't to go anywhere
near the man.

But it didn't matter.

Because even though he'd gone there fully intending
to confront Colston, Paulo no longer believed the attorney was behind the killings.

After speaking to Norah O'Connor that morning, Paulo
had tried to convince himself that the trail, the logic, led
back to Colston. He'd wanted the lawyer to be guilty because he hadn't wanted to face another possibility.

An unthinkable possibility.

He'd scoured the crime scene reports, studied the
grisly photos until the images blurred in his mind. The
killer had been painstakingly meticulous, careful to leave
no trace behind. That pointed to someone with experience. Someone who was perfectly aware of what the cops
would need to apprehend him.

Because he himself was a cop.

Any number of people in the police department could
have had access to Paulo's fingerprints. Any of them could
have witnessed the reunion between him and Ashton
Dupree, and anyone walking by his office could have overheard the final argument they'd had. But only one person
knew about Paulo's connection to *both* victims. Only one
person knew that Paulo was related to the Santiago family,

that two years ago he'd attended a dinner function where he'd met Maribel Cruz.

And if Tommie was in the killer's crosshairs, as Paulo feared, only one person could have known of his previous association with her.

Only one person knew the whole picture.

His partner of the past two years.

Julius Donovan.

As soon as Paulo allowed his mind to go there, he'd felt a tingling sense of awareness, a prickle of knowledge. The quick burst of adrenaline that accompanied cracking a troublesome puzzle.

He'd called Donovan, asked him to meet him somewhere under the guise of pumping him for information about the case. He knew the younger detective wouldn't refuse to see him. If he really was betraying Paulo, he was cunning enough not to tip his hand.

So Donovan had shown up, and they'd talked, and Paulo had watched his eyes like a poker player, searching for something intangible that would give him away. But if Donovan was wearing a mask, it had remained firmly in place.

He'd left Paulo shortly afterward, responding to an emergency call from dispatch. A double shooting on Westheimer, near the Galleria.

So here Paulo was, parked down the street from his partner's silent house, about to break the law and risk losing everything he'd built over the past seventeen years.

Because of a gut instinct.

Someone had drawn him into a deadly game. Someone with a vendetta against him, someone with a sinister agenda.

If he were to have any chance of clearing his name, he had to get evidence.

He had to find the truth.

But it wasn't just about seeking personal justice.

It was about stopping a cold-blooded killer in his tracks.

As Paulo climbed out of his truck, crushed out the cigarette, and started up the darkened street, he told himself that he was already in enough hot water. Might as well add breaking and entering to his list of crimes.

Tommie's hands trembled violently as she undid the top button of her shirt.

"Slowly," Donovan dictated, watching her from a chair tucked into a corner of the bedroom, his eyes gleaming with malicious satisfaction. "I want to savor every moment of this."

Nausea and revulsion churned in Tommie's stomach.

The detective had forced her upstairs to the loft with the lethal blade of the knife pressed to her throat, letting her know that one false move on her part would ensure her swift, violent death. Once inside the bedroom, he'd ordered her to get undressed and put on the costume he'd brought for her. When her gaze landed on the red corset and flowing chiffon skirt, her blood ran cold. Because she'd recognized it as the costume she'd worn in *Black Orpheus*, during the hauntingly climactic scene in which Eurydice had been lured to her death.

Seeing the look of stunned recognition on her face, Donovan had smiled, slow and sinister. "That's right, Tommie. You're going to perform the death scene for me. Only this time, there'll be no rescuing you from the abyss."

Terror sliced through her. "H-how did you get the costume?"

He'd chuckled softly. "Oh, it's not the original, unfortunately. I couldn't risk raising any suspicions by trying to purchase the actual costume from your dance company. But it's a good enough replica, don't you think?"

Tommie stared at him as comprehension dawned. "You were there . . . at the performance in February?"

"Of course. And it wasn't the first time." His face hardened. "Get undressed."

And now as Tommie unfastened the last button on her shirt, she drew a deep, shuddering breath. *Pretend you're performing onstage,* she told herself. *Don't think about the audience. Don't think about who's watching you. Just do what you have to do!*

As a stripper, she'd perfected the technique of blanking out, of becoming detached from herself. When her music came up, she'd pushed all thoughts but her routine out of her mind. When she'd deigned to make eye contact with the customers, it was only to identify the men who seemed most likely to part with their money. And even as their hands had eagerly skimmed over her hips as they'd tucked bills into her G-string, she'd always been the one in control.

It was hard to convince herself she was in control now, with a sadistic monster holding her at knifepoint, calmly dictating her every move.

As she slowly slid the shirt off her shoulders, he leaned forward intently, his long, lean fingers stroking the edge of the knife, caressing it in hungry anticipation. "Now take off the bra."

When Tommie hesitated, he snapped, "Do it, Tommie! Now!"

Trembling and choking back a sob, she unhooked her bra and let it fall to the floor.

"God, you're beautiful," he whispered almost reverently, staring at her naked breasts. "A fucking goddess. No wonder Sanchez can't keep his damned hands off you."

Tommie swallowed the bile that burned the back of her throat.

"Don't pretend you're not enjoying this," Donovan jeered. "I was there four years ago. I saw the way you strutted across that stage with your batting eyelashes and cocktease smile. I saw the way you had those men salivating, eating out of the palm of your hand. I *saw* you."

Chilled to the bone, Tommie stared at him. And as she did, she realized why he'd struck her as familiar when she met him at Paulo's apartment on Thursday morning. He'd been a customer at the Sirens and Spurs Gentlemen's Club. So Paulo had been right about her coming to the killer's attention through her dancing— just not through her ballet dancing.

Donovan smiled, enjoying her stunned reaction. "I was in San Antonio four years ago. I was there on business, attending a weeklong conference. One of my colleagues, who was from the area, talked me into going to a strip club with him one night. He said the Sirens and Spurs had the best-looking dancers, so we had to go there. I was skeptical at first, and I'd never been much into the strip club scene, being a preacher's kid. But you made a believer out of me, Tommie. From the moment you stepped out onto that stage, I was a convert. A goner. I came back alone the next night. And the next. I couldn't help myself. I had to see you. I was obsessed." He sneered at her. "Just like poor Roland. But I won't end up like him. I'm smarter than that. *You* won't destroy *me*."

Tommie could barely breathe. Her heart thundered in her ears as she forced herself to continue undressing, trying to tamp down the fear, the panic clawing at her insides. She knew it was only a matter of time before this psychopath would kill her. Unless she did something, took action.

Covertly she glanced around her bedroom. She had no weapon, and even if she somehow managed to get her hands on a blunt object, he would be on her in an instant. And she couldn't forget that he was armed with more than a knife. The gun he'd used to kill Roland was holstered at his waist, a deadly reminder of just what he was capable of.

"I was in town when the Spider Tattoo Killer struck," Donovan explained, still caressing the knife in a way that made her skin crawl. "I was there the night the homicide detective came to speak to you about the other dancer's murder. I went to the bathroom, and while no one was looking, I crept down the hallway and hid around a corner so that I could eavesdrop on the conversation between you, your sister, and the detective." He shook his head at her, clucking his tongue in disapproval. "It was obvious that your sister had a thing for him, but that didn't stop you from flirting with him, trying to seduce him. You wanted him, badly. And for some reason, that stayed in my mind."

Tommie stared at him, speechless. Her shame over the way she'd behaved with Sebastien was eclipsed by Donovan's implausible revelation. How could he have been there that night, hiding in the corridor, and no one saw him?

The same way he snuck into his victims' houses and brutally murdered them, then left without a trace.

"I read all about the Spider Tattoo case," he continued. "I was fascinated, awed by the killer's cunning and ingenuity. Even after I returned home to Houston, I couldn't stop thinking about it. Or you. You were hot for that detective, so much so that you were willing to hurt your sister over him. I began to fantasize about what it would be like to be

Sebastien Durand, to be on the receiving end of your desire. And that's when I decided to become a detective.

"Oh, I know it sounds far-fetched," he drawled at the incredulous look Tommie gave him, "but the truth of the matter was, I wasn't all that happy working as a securities analyst. Sure, the pay was good, but the work was unrewarding. Of course, my parents weren't too pleased when I told them about my decision to become a cop. But then," he added, his lips twisting bitterly, "my self-righteous father has never been pleased with anything I've done. He wanted me to become a pro basketball player, even named me after Julius Erving. But I proved to be a total disappointment to him. Once he realized that I had no athletic skills whatsoever, he pretty much wrote me off."

Tommie swallowed, and told herself she was crazy for feeling a twinge of sympathy for him, a sense of kinship. How many times had she felt like a failure for not living up to her brilliant father's expectations? How many times had she yearned to see his eyes glow with pride the way they did over her sister's accomplishments?

Did Julius Donovan's father unwittingly create the monster he had become? Had his father's rejection battered at his psyche enough to drive him over the edge?

Don't give him a pass! You're not exactly the apple of your father's eye, either, and you didn't turn into a homicidal maniac!

Donovan wasn't finished with his story. "I seriously considered moving to San Antonio and joining the police force, just to be near you. But when I returned to the Sirens and Spurs two months later, I was told that you no longer worked there. One of the other strippers told me she'd heard that you'd moved to New York to pursue a professional dancing career. I was crushed. I didn't think I'd ever see you again. I went back home, and still decided to go through with joining the police force. But I never forgot you, Tommie. So you can imagine how thrilled I was when, several months later, I found out that you'd joined a dance company that was making a tour stop in Houston. That was the first time I attended one of your performances, but it definitely wasn't the last.

"I scheduled my vacation around your debut appearance in *Black Orpheus*. I flew to New York, and was blown away by your rendition of Eurydice. I wanted to meet you afterward, get your autograph, and tell you how much I'd enjoyed your performance." His expression hardened. "But you weren't available. The other dancers were, but you couldn't be bothered to meet your fans."

"That's not true," Tommie said quickly, alarmed by the lethal fury in his eyes. "I was having dinner afterward with an old employer and his wife. They were flying back home that night, so we had to leave right after the performance to make our dinner reservation."

He looked at her as if he didn't believe her. "I wrote you a letter, and you never responded."

She stared at him, struck by a horrifying realization. "You . . . you sent me the letter about the dream you had? About being Orpheus?"

"So you remember." His tone was bitterly accusing. "And you didn't see fit to respond."

"I—I was busy. We were on the road and—"

"Like I said before," he cut her off, "your fans obviously weren't important to you. I mailed the letter before I left New York, and even though I was too embarrassed to use my real name and address, I provided an e-mail address that I'd set up just for you, hoping you'd respond. But you never did."

"I'm sorry," Tommie said lamely.

"So am I." He raked his dark eyes over her furiously, suddenly realizing that she'd stopped undressing and was standing there in her panties with her arms locked across her chest, covering her breasts. "Keep going!"

His voice lashed her like the crack of a whip, and she jumped.

"You don't have to do this," she tried to appeal to him, hoping to get through to him. He was a police officer, sworn to serve and protect. Surely there had to be an ounce of humanity left in him. "It's not too late, Julius. You can let me go."

His face contorted with rage. "Take off the underwear!" he bellowed.

Tommie complied at once, heart thudding.

A slow, satisfied smile crawled across his face as he took in her nudity. Leaning back in the chair, he reached down and began stroking his erection.

Tommie swallowed her disgust, anger tightening in her chest. *Disgusting pervert*, she thought, fighting the urge to attack, to fly across the room and pummel him with her fists and claw at his face with her long nails. But her fists and nails were no match for a long-bladed knife, much less a gun.

"After you ignored my letter," he said, watching as she reached for the red corset and skirt, "I was tempted to write to you again, to give you the benefit of the doubt. But I was a cop. I couldn't risk coming off as a stalker. But I couldn't get you out of my system, no matter how hard I tried. When I was off duty, I started going to some local strip clubs, half hoping to find another you. But of course that was a lost cause. The more I searched, the more desperate and angry I became, until one night I snapped. The stripper I'd taken home wasn't cooperating. She wasn't satisfying me the way she was supposed to."

He paused, a sinister gleam filling his eyes. "One minute I was wrestling with her. The next minute I had my hands around her throat, choking her. After she was dead, I buried her body in the woods. She was reported missing, but after a while the cops stopped looking for her. She was just a stripper, some junkie whore no one would ever miss."

Tommie stared at him, her face twisted with horrified revulsion. "You're demented," she whispered, feeling sick inside. "You need help."

He smiled slightly, shaking his head as if they were merely disagreeing about the weather. "I'm not a serial killer, Tommie. I'm not controlled by homicidal impulses. If that were true, I would have continued killing after that. But I didn't."

"You just killed two innocent women last week!"

"Only because of you."

"No," she said sharply, angrily. "Don't blame *me* for the heinous crimes you committed!"

"Oh, but I do. You shouldn't have come here, Tommie. You should have stayed in New York. It was too much for me to believe that fate hadn't intervened, bringing you to Houston, of all places. It was too much of an irresistible coincidence."

"So you killed Maribel Cruz and Ashton Dupree to get my attention? To somehow get back at *me*?"

His face hardened with loathing. "They were both lying whores. One was fucking two married men. The other was fucking every man who would pay her, including her own foster brother. It was so easy for me to get to both of them. Maribel simply forgot to lock her front door after seeing her lover off that morning, and all I had to do was flash a wad of dough in Ashton's face in order to set up an appointment. A liar and a whore. Just like you."

Tommie swallowed hard. "Okay, you hate my guts. I get it. But why would you try to frame your own partner? What did Paulo ever do to you?"

Donovan sneered. "Other than the fact that he always treats me like a rookie, like some smart-aleck kid who's still wet behind the ears, he's done nothing." A mocking gleam lit his eyes. "Oh, and he also made the mistake of telling me he'd once met you at a wedding, and had been trying to get you out of his mind ever since.

"Don't look so shocked, Tommie," he drawled, amused by her surprised expression. "You have that effect on men. Haven't we already established that? Anyway, I knew it was only a matter of time before Sanchez would find his way to you. He held out seven whole months—much longer than I expected. But being Sanchez, he had to cave in to his urges eventually. Three weeks ago, I overheard him on the phone with your brother-in-law, casually asking where you lived."

Tommie shook her head. "So that's when you decided to punish him. To punish both of us."

A small, sadistic smile curled his lips. "I can't think of two more deserving people."

The bottom dropped out of her stomach. "How do you expect to get away with this?"

"Oh, that's easy. In every instance, the trail leads right to Sanchez. He's connected to all three of the victims, including you. He had a sexual relationship with each of you, and when things went sour, he resorted to murder. Just like he did with poor Hailey Morrisette. The pending assault charges against him were an unexpected gift I couldn't have planned better myself. I'd 'borrowed' Roland Jackson's Nissan Altima late one night and tailgated Sanchez on the freeway, hoping to plant a seed of suspicion in his mind about your old boyfriend. After what he did to Roland's face, no one will have a hard time believing that Sanchez didn't kill him in a jealous fit of rage when the deacon showed up here tonight."

He smiled narrowly. "Like I said, the trail of bodies leads right back to Detective Sanchez."

Tommie stared at him, chilled by the level of premeditation, the ruthless cunning. She didn't want to imagine the horrors that awaited her. Somehow she had to make it downstairs to her office and get her hands on the pistol Paulo had given her. It was her only hope for survival.

Donovan gave her a slow, appreciative once-over. "You look as magnificent as I remember, Eurydice." He rose, came toward her with the knife in his hand. "It's curtain time."

Terror exploded in her veins.

She waited until he was nearly upon her.

And then she attacked like a ferocious wildcat, stunning him.

Fueled by panic, rage, and a desperate instinct for survival, she kicked, punched at his throat, stabbed at his eyes. He cried out, the knife clattering to the floor. Cursing profanely he launched himself at her, knocking the air from her lungs. They landed hard on the floor, Tommie taking the brunt of the fall beneath his heavy weight. The back of her head bounced off the floor. Pain exploded inside her. But she forced herself to ignore it, kicking and fighting frantically to buck his weight off her before he could go for his gun. She rammed the heel of her hand into his chin, snapping his head back.

"Fucking bitch!" He drew back his fist and punched her across the face. Her vision blurred, her ear rang like a bell, and razor-sharp pain shot across her cheek and down her jaw.

And still she kept fighting for her life, knowing the moment she gave up, he would kill her.

As he reached for his gun she snapped her head up,

banged forehead to forehead with all her might. Lights burst behind her eyes. Her head throbbed.

"Crazy bitch!" he roared in outraged fury.

His big hands seized her throat. She fought wildly, thrashing and clawing at him. But his fingers were too strong, cutting off her airway. She felt her vision dim, felt her brain begin to swell from the lack of oxygen.

God, please don't let me die like this! Please!

Donovan's feral, demented eyes locked with hers. "I've waited too long for this to let you win."

Summoning one last surge of adrenaline, Tommie drew her knee up and rammed it into his testicles, as hard as she could.

He howled in agony and doubled over, clutching himself, giving her just enough of an opportunity to roll free.

Wheezing, gasping for air, she scrambled to her feet with a speed and agility honed from years of dancing and bolted from the room. As she raced toward the front door that seemed miles away, she thought about what she would do if she made it downstairs. She could run outside, but she hadn't had time to grab her car keys. And Donovan was faster, stronger. She'd never outrun him on foot.

If she could just make it to her office, to Paulo's gun—

She screamed as a gunshot blasted behind her, spitting into the wall.

"That was a warning shot," Donovan growled, low and lethal. "Next time you won't be so lucky."

Tommie flung open the front door and ran headlong into the dim stairwell. The lights flickered eerily, heightening her terror. In the back of her mind she heard Paulo's concerned voice, warning her to get the bulbs replaced soon. And she thought of Arthur Lambert, who'd called earlier to tell her that an electrician was coming tomorrow.

Too little, too late.

No sooner had the ominous thought crossed her mind than the lights blinked off, plunging her into blackness.

She swallowed a scream, her heart lurching to her throat.

Donovan's laughter floated through the darkness to taunt her, soft and eerie. Pursuit might not have been part of his plan, but it had become part of the deadly game.

"I must say, Tommie. None of my other victims fought the way you did. I'm going to enjoy killing you even more than I thought I would."

Her blood ran like ice through her veins. She crept carefully down the stairwell, her pulse pounding. No moonlight shone through the opening in the roof. It was so dark she couldn't see her hand in front of her face.

"Setting up Sanchez was brilliant." Her tormentor's voice was growing nearer. "After what Roland did to you, I knew you'd have a hard time believing Sanchez was innocent. If you hadn't had your little lovers' quarrel, he'd be here right now, protecting you. Too bad."

She tried to go faster, and lost her footing on a step. As she tripped she grabbed for the handrail she couldn't see, breaking a nail, skinning her knuckles on the brick wall.

"Be careful," Donovan warned, amused. "Me, I'm used to creeping through shadows and darkness, so I don't need to take my time. But you? Not so lucky."

Like hell, Tommie thought defiantly. *I'm getting out of here!*

But she miscalculated the distance to the next step. As her ankle twisted painfully, she plummeted forward, tumbling down the rest of the stairs.

She landed on something soft lying near the bottom of the stairwell. As her fingers encountered sticky warmth and the scent of blood filled her nostrils, she realized that it was Roland's body.

This time she couldn't stifle the reflexive scream that tore from her throat.

Paulo erupted from Julius Donovan's home, adrenaline firing his blood and fear clutching his heart.

He'd found a shrine to Tommie in a small locked room inside his partner's house. Evidence that confirmed his worst suspicions about the man he'd worked alongside every day for the past two years. There had been pictures of Tommie plastered on the walls, along with programs, brochures, playbills, and other dance memorabilia. He'd found a bookcase filled with videos and DVDs of her past performances, as well as a small wooden chest that contained scrunchies, hair clips, an old tube of lipstick, earrings, and lingerie belonging to Tommie.

As Paulo surveyed the collection of stolen items in horrified disbelief, he'd felt as if he had been punched in the gut. Violently blindsided.

How could he not have known?

How could he not have detected the depravity that lurked beneath the surface of Julius Donovan's boyish charm?

It was inconceivable.

As he charged from the house and strode to his truck, his cell phone rang. This time he didn't ignore it, snatching it up halfway through the first ring.

"Sanchez, this is Cesar. Hey, man, I thought you were placed on leave today."

"I am," Paulo growled, in no mood to discuss the matter.

"So, did they let you keep the cruiser?"

"No. I turned in my keys. What the hell are you talking about?"

Cesar sounded apprehensive. "I meant to call you an

hour ago, but I got sidetracked with this damned paper. When I drove past Tommie's loft a while ago, I saw your cruiser parked outside. I just automatically assumed—"

Paulo's blood froze. "That's not my cruiser."

"Oh, shit. Look, I'm on the other side of town. I'll meet you—"

But Paulo had already hung up the phone. As he broke into a dead run, heart in his throat, he vowed that he would kill Donovan with his bare hands if he did anything to Tommie.

Tommie's ankle was throbbing unmercifully. She'd sprained it when she fell down the stairs, destroying any hope she'd had of reaching her office before Julius Donovan caught her. She could feel him behind her, could sense his menacing presence closing in on her as she lay sprawled across Roland's corpse. She knew her own death was imminent.

Trembling hard, she tried to hold it together. *You can't give up now! You swore you'd never be a victim to any man again! Save yourself!*

Thinking fast, Tommie reached down hurriedly and began checking Roland's pockets.

Tears of relief sprang to her eyes when her searching hands found the pistol she knew he'd always carried, that he'd probably brought with him that night to kill her. Quickly and quietly drawing the gun out of his jacket pocket, she scuttled backward like a crab, taking cover under the stairwell.

Her heart hammered as she held her breath, listening for Donovan's footsteps.

He was deliberately taking his time. Prolonging her torture.

After what seemed an eternity he reached the landing and stopped.

"I know you haven't gone very far, Eurydice," he whispered. "I can still hear you breathing."

Tommie squeezed her eyes tightly shut, wondering whether she should fire blindly into the darkness or remain hidden. If she missed, he'd know exactly where she was.

And she had no doubt that *he* wouldn't miss his shot.

Without warning the stairwell lights blinked back on.

Oh, shit.

Donovan turned unerringly to face her. As if he'd known where she was hiding all along.

Tommie nearly recoiled from the evil malice gleaming in his eyes.

Slowly, deliberately, he licked the blade of the knife. "At first I was only going to make you dance before I killed you," he taunted, stalking her. "Now I think I'll fuck you first."

Tommie looked him straight in the eye. "No, Detective." His eyes widened as she raised the gun in her hand and took deadly aim. "Fuck *you.*"

The bullet blasted through his chest, driving him backward. A moment later he crumpled to the floor, sprawling ignominiously beside Roland.

Tommie slumped weakly against the wall. The gun slid from her limp grasp and clattered to the floor. Her head was pounding, her ankle was throbbing, and she felt like she'd gone through twelve rounds with a heavyweight champion. But she was alive. *Thank God* she was alive.

Suddenly the front door banged open. Paulo stood in the doorway, his weapon drawn.

His frantic gaze swept the foyer, taking in the two bodies strewn across the floor. He rushed inside.

"Tommie!" he shouted hoarsely.

"Over here," she croaked.

When he saw her huddled under the stairwell, a look of anguished relief swept across his face. In a heartbeat he was beside her, pulling her into his arms, kissing her hair, cradling her protectively. "I thought I'd lost you," he said raggedly, holding her as if he'd never let go. "I thought . . . Oh God!"

Tears flooded Tommie's eyes. She broke down and clung tightly to him. "I love you, Paulo. Don't ever leave me."

He cupped her face in his hands, crushed his mouth to hers, and whispered fiercely, "Just try to get rid of me."

Chapter 26

Six months later,
San Antonio, Texas

"You know," Tommie murmured, rousing herself from a state of pleasant exhaustion, "we probably just broke a major rule of etiquette here, leaving our guests in the middle of our reception and sneaking off to have a quickie."

There was a faint rustling of ivory silk before Paulo's face emerged from the folds of her gown, eyes glinting with mischief, a wolfish grin on his face. "You're talking to the wrong guy, sweetheart. I've never given a damn about etiquette."

Tommie sighed, her lips curving. "This is true. So why should you start on your wedding day?"

"Damn straight." He leaned down and kissed her, tasting the champagne and the sweet, buttery cake Mrs. Calhoun had made for their wedding, a lavish, towering confection that had dazzled their guests.

Lifting his head, Paulo smiled into her eyes. "Besides, you can't blame me for whisking you away. I was just keeping a promise."

"Oh, really? And what promise was that?"

His grin widened. "That morning at the Breakfast Klub, I told you that the next wedding we attended together, I'd let *you* molest me during the reception."

Tommie laughed. "Of course! How could I forget?"

He gazed down at her, his expression softening. "God, you're beautiful. The most beautiful woman I've ever seen in my life. Watching you walk down the aisle . . . You took my breath away."

Tears misted her eyes. Amazing, considering how much she'd already wept that day. Trying to stave off another wave of emotion, Tommie teased, "You have to say that. You just pledged your life to me in front of four hundred witnesses."

"*Dios mio.* Is that how many people we're feeding?"

She grinned. "It's all those Santiagos and Sanchezes. And your police friends. My God, Paulo, I think every cop in San Antonio and Houston is here!"

Chuckling, he nipped her bare shoulder and stretched out beside her on the oversize chaise longue in the plush bridal suite. Tommie nestled against him, basking in his wonderful warmth, feeling a heady combination of euphoria and contentment.

Another sigh escaped. "It was a beautiful wedding, wasn't it, Paulo?"

"Hands down the best I've ever been to," he murmured.

The ceremony had been held at the historic San Fernando Cathedral in downtown San Antonio, their concession to Paulo's Catholic parents. Everything had been perfect, from the sun slanting through the stained-glass windows to the lovely bouquets of white roses decorating the domed sanctuary. For the reception afterward, they'd traveled to a private resort nestled deep in the

Hill Country, where dozens of linen-covered tables, ice sculptures, and a five-string quartet were set against a stunning backdrop of blue skies and vast, rugged mountains.

At one point, Paulo had been conversing with his groomsmen when he'd looked across the courtyard and seen Tommie kneeling beside their flower girls and her nephew, Marcos, the ring bearer. She'd been talking animatedly, laughing as the small children vied for her attention. Almost intuitively, she'd glanced up and caught the simmering heat of Paulo's stare.

Before she knew it he was striding toward her, snagging her hand, and leading her back inside the hilltop mansion amidst a shower of catcalls and whistles from their guests—Rafe, Sebastien, Zhane, and Myles being the loudest.

Lying in her husband's arms that afternoon, Tommie couldn't help whispering a silent prayer of gratitude. If Julius Donovan had had his way, she wouldn't have lived to see this day.

News of the detective's shocking, sadistic plot to murder three women and frame his partner for the crimes had hit the local and national airwaves as Tommie lay in the hospital recuperating from the minor injuries she'd sustained in the violent confrontation. The chilling level of Donovan's premeditation, fueled by his maniacal obsession with Tommie, was chronicled in lurid detail, leaving the police department reeling from the scandal and scrambling for answers. Paulo had been fully reinstated and a public apology was issued by the chief of police and mayor.

In the aftermath, Ted Colston had been fired for violating the law firm's employee code of conduct when his affair with Maribel Cruz came to light. He'd confessed to giving a false statement to the police about his whereabouts on the morning of Maribel's murder; the unidentified black car seen arriving at her house had been Ted's rental car. This, compounded by the revelation that he'd also been sleeping with his foster sister and had been dabbling in shady business dealings, had devastated his wife. She'd thrown him out of the house and filed for divorce.

"Come back to me, *querida*," Paulo murmured, quietly watching the play of emotions across Tommie's face. "No thinking about that night. Especially not today."

She smiled, laying her hand against his chest and feeling his strong, steady heartbeat. "I was just counting my blessings."

Paulo drew her closer, running one hand tenderly along her cheek. "I've been doing that since the night you agreed to marry me." His gaze softened. "Your father was so proud of you. I've never seen a man's chest more puffed out with pride as he walked his daughter down the aisle."

Tommie's throat tightened. For as long as she lived, she would never, ever forget the expression on Gordon Purnell's face when he'd beheld Tommie for the first time in her wedding gown. With tears glistening in his eyes, he'd smiled tenderly, tucked his arm through hers, and said gently, "I wish your grandmother had lived to see this day. She would have been as proud of you as I am. I hope that young man out there knows what an extraordinary gift he's receiving today."

Blinking back tears, Tommie had hugged her father tightly and thought, *Maybe, just maybe, there's hope for us yet.*

Smiling at the memory, she turned her head into Paulo's palm and kissed it. "I really like your parents. I was almost afraid they wouldn't accept me. You know, because of that story you told me about the way the Sanchez family rejected Ignacio's mother because she was black."

Paulo shook his head. "My parents aren't like that. They

just want me to be happy. Nothing else matters. And they happen to think you're amazing." He chuckled softly. "They were pretty impressed with your dancing earlier."

Tommie grinned as she thought of their first dance, a sensual, salsa-flavored dance that was traditional for newlyweds at Mexican weddings. His grandmother Maria had stood nearby directing Tommie's movements while their guests clapped to the music and cheered. The way Paulo ground his hips rhythmically into Tommie's had driven her crazy. If he hadn't come along and dragged her off to the bridal suite, she might have beat him to it.

"You still owe me a date for salsa dancing," she reminded him. "You've got some serious moves, Mr. Sanchez."

His eyes glinted wickedly as he began reaching under her dress. "If you're ready, Mrs. Sanchez, I can show you some more."

"Later," Tommie said, swatting at his hand. "You've already messed up my hair and got me all sweaty. And I wasn't planning on sweating in this dress—it's Vera Wang."

"Vera who?"

"Never mind." She sighed. "Thank God for Zhane and Daniela. Trying to talk fashion with you and Frankie is an exercise in futility. Not that you don't clean up nice though," she added, admiring how powerfully handsome he looked in his black tuxedo. "*Very* nice."

"Glad you approve." His gaze sobered. "You sure you won't regret moving back to San Antonio?"

"No," she said quietly. "I think it was time to come home. Both of us."

"I think so, too."

Paulo had sold the house he and his first wife had shared, a symbol of his readiness to finally free himself from the ghosts of the past and start a new chapter in his life. He and Tommie had bought a big, beautiful house that they fully intended to fill with the rollicking laughter and running feet of children.

Paulo had been welcomed back to the San Antonio Police Department with a promotion to sergeant. He and Sebastien now worked out of the same station and saw each other every day. After selling her converted warehouse for top dollar to an eccentric local film producer who'd been morbidly fascinated with the harrowing events that took place there, Tommie had found a new location for her dance studio, a studio used by Korrine Santiago, who enjoyed dancing ballet in her spare time. Tommie would be interviewing dance instructors when she and Paulo returned from their honeymoon in two weeks.

She and Zhane were seriously contemplating launching their own dance company in the near future. He'd been telling her for some time that he needed a change of scenery, a break from his family's nonstop drama. Tommie thought it might do him good.

A change of scenery had definitely done wonders for her and Paulo.

She smiled at the thought, gently weaving her fingers through Paulo's hair, a little sad that Naomi had insisted on the groom getting a haircut.

As if reading her thoughts, Paulo chuckled. "Don't worry. It'll grow back soon."

"I'm not worried." Her mouth curved in a naughty grin. "I still have plenty to grab on to."

"Mmmm. And speaking of . . ."

Deliberately ignoring the wicked intent in his eyes, Tommie sighed. "We've come full circle, Paulo. We first met at a wedding, and now here we are, nearly five years later, at our own wedding."

"Amazing how that worked out." His hand slipped

beneath her dress, slid into her warmth. He groaned huskily. "You're wet, sweetheart."

Tommie nodded, feeling a delicious stab of heat as his talented fingers moved deeper. "I've been wet since the day I met you."

It was either the right—or the wrong—thing to say. Paulo's gaze glittered with swift hunger as he moved his body over hers, raised her gown, and settled himself between her legs.

"We should really get back to our guests," Tommie protested weakly as he ran an appreciative hand over her white lace garter. "What if someone comes looking for us?"

"Cesar's guarding the door. No one's getting past him."

She gasped. "He's doing *what?*"

Paulo flashed a devilish grin. "Why do you think I invited him to the wedding? You didn't think it was because we've been friends forever, did you?"

Tommie's laughter dissolved into a throaty moan as he sank into her.

As she wrapped her arms around his neck and caught his slow, relentless rhythm, she marveled at the beauty of second chances. She and Paulo had made their share of mistakes in the past, but they'd weathered the storm together and had found in each other something they'd both sought for a lifetime. A gift that was almost as priceless as their love: the gift of redemption.

Their honeymoon destination awaited them, a charming bed-and-breakfast tucked away somewhere in Spain.

And their future awaited them.

Bright, glorious, full of passion and promise.